REVOLUTION #9

A THRILLER BY
PETER ABRAHAMS

THE MYSTERIOUS PRESS
New York · Tokyo · Sweden
Published by Warner Books

 A Time Warner Company

Mysterious Press books are published by
Warner Books, Inc., 1271 Avenue of the Americas, New York, NY
10020

A Time Warner Company

The Mysterious Press name and logo are trademarks of Warner
Books, Inc.
Printed in the United States of America

First printing: August 1992
10 9 8 7 6 5 4 3 2 1

Library of Congress Cataloging in Publication Data
Abrahams, Peter, 1947-
    Revolution #9 / Peter Abrahams.
        p.   cm.
    ISBN 0-89296-481-2
    I. Title. II. Title: Revolution number nine.
PS3551.B64R48   1992
813'.54—dc20   91-50847
                                                                CIP

For Seth, Ben, Lily, and Rosie

Golden lads and girls all must,
as chimney-sweepers, come to dust.
—*Cymbeline*

PART I

1

The boy was named Ronnie. The only surviving photograph shows him in his batting stance. What can we tell from it? That he hit from the left side. That he wore his hair long, in the style of the time. That he had a solid-looking body, and a reliable-looking face. That there was nothing particularly cute about him—Norman Rockwell would never have put him in the front of a picture. But Ronnie might have appeared in the background, diving into the old fishing hole. And he might have grown up to be quite handsome. Going beyond that would be pure speculation. How much character can be read in the face of an eleven-year-old boy?

• • •

Ronnie awoke before dawn at the end of a warm May night. He checked the bedside clock. The time must have been between four-thirty and five. The bus for the all-star tournament left at six. Ronnie was too keyed up to sleep any longer. He switched on the light and donned his uniform: white pants that stopped high up the calf for the look he liked, sanitaries, navy blue stirrups, worn cleats, and the navy blue shirt that buttoned down the front and had "All-Stars" written on the front and his surname, "Pleasance," and number, "9," on the back. He put on his cap, picked up his bat, which was leaning against the wall, and took a few practice swings in front of the mirror. Boom. Kapow. *That ball is going, going, it is . . . out of here, ladies and gentlemen! Ronnie Pleasance has done it again!*

Then he realized he didn't have his mitt.

Ronnie's mitt was a Rawlings trapper with Willie "Stretch" McCovey's autograph on the inside. Ronnie had rubbed it with neatsfoot oil and smacked balls into the pocket so many times that it felt like part of him, a fly-paper extension that stuck to every baseball that came near. He hunted for it in the pile of yesterday's clothes on the floor, in the closet, under the bed. Then he walked softly down the hall, past his parents' bedroom and downstairs, where he searched the rest of the house. No glove. Ronnie was getting a little nervous now, but he didn't panic. He was a methodical boy, not flashy, but determined: a born catcher, if he hadn't been left-handed. He tried to remember the last time he'd seen his mitt. Certainly he'd had it at practice the afternoon before. And after practice, what had he done? He'd walked to his father's office on campus. Sometimes they threw the ball around after work, but yesterday his father had been in a meeting. Ta-da. Ronnie suddenly pictured the mitt lying on the visitor's chair opposite his father's desk.

Ronnie, in his all-star uniform, left the house, closing the door quietly behind him, and walked into the predawn darkness. The town was quiet, the air mild. The darkness didn't bother Ronnie. He knew the neighborhood like an Indian scout. Besides, it was only a few hundred feet down the lane to the campus and onto the crushed-brick path. Perhaps because it was night and he was still a boy, he whistled. Ronnie went by the labs, the silent dorms, the chapel, and into the old wood building that housed his father's office.

The office was on the second floor. Ronnie climbed the stairs and opened the door. He switched on the light. There was his mitt, just as he'd thought. He put it on, smacked his fist into it a few times. Perhaps he glanced at the picture of his parents,

4

walking under an archway of crossed swords on their wedding day. Then he turned, shut off the light, closed the door, and started down the stairs. The chapel bell began to strike five o'clock. The fourth ring was the last sound Ronnie heard.

• • •

That is a logical assumption, because the vibration dislodged the clapper from the bell in the stone campanile of the late-eighteenth-century chapel, preventing the fifth ring from sounding. Not long after, Ronnie was found at the foot of what remained of the stairs. Perhaps it was just an accidental result of the way he fell, but the Willie "Stretch" McCovey model first baseman's trapper was clutched to his chest. That's what gave them the idea to bury him with it.

2

The door opened and Svenson looked in. "They're coming back," he said.

So soon? thought Goodnow; and knew the verdict at once. He rose from the state-issue swivel chair of whatever midlevel bureaucrat whose office he had borrowed for the trial—rose slowly, but not slowly enough to keep the pain from reawakening. Lately, like a colicky baby, his pain rarely slept, and when it did, jerked awake at the slightest disturbance. This was physical pain, not metaphorical or spiritual, although some had advised him to fight it with spirits and metaphors—imaging, specifically. For a few weeks Goodnow had attended an imaging clinic, but all he'd been able to imagine was mutant cells, beaky, hairy, rampant, devouring his insides.

"You all right, Mr. Goodnow?" Svenson was watching him, perhaps with concern, perhaps not. It was impossible to tell with Svenson: those eyes, pale as a frozen lake, set deep in the harsh white landscape of his face.

Goodnow released his grip on the chair back. "Just fine," he replied, and tightened the knot on his tie. He could never seem to get it tight anymore, and the collars of his Brooks

6

Brothers shirts grew bigger and bigger. "You've lost weight," said acquaintances he saw infrequently; who never added, "You look great." Goodnow followed the big man out of the office, down the corridor, into the courtroom.

Goodnow and Svenson sat at the back. The court buzzed, like a theater before the curtain. Except for the jury, everyone was in place: the judge, a mediocrity whose appointment had been a bargaining chip in a budget negotiation during the Carter administration; the two prosecutors, who hadn't made a mistake that Goodnow saw, not after jury selection; the defendants, the Santa Clara Five, as they called themselves, whose lives would not be changed one way or the other; their supporters, stern as Puritans, ready to be outraged. All these were without interest to Goodnow. His eyes were on the defense table, where the lead counsel sat, head turned slightly toward a female assistant who whispered in his ear. It was a head that Rodin would have loved to sculpt: big, elongated, with prominent features and long silver hair swept back in two wings. Victor Hugo Klein looked like a hero of the Romantic Age, and a hero was what he had been to a lot of people for almost forty years, fighting the hegemonic brute that others called the good ol' U.S.A. Hugo Klein fought for the little guy—the little union guy, the little McCarthy victim guy, the little sixties radical guy, the little truculent feminist guy, the little tree-spiking eco-lover guy. The details of the cant changed, thought Goodnow, but Klein endured. That his biggest cases almost always seemed to end in long prison sentences diminished his reputation not at all. Everyone knew the system was rigged. Klein rose higher and higher on a stack of fist-clenching martyrs.

Klein smiled at something his assistant had said and turned to look around the courtroom. His glance swept over Goodnow, showing no recognition. Naturally not; Klein had been editor of the *Law Review* during Goodnow's first year. Goodnow, despite his hard work, had not made *Law Review*, graduating in the middle of his class. And after, he had not practiced but had disappeared into the shadows of his chosen field. It was not surprising that their paths had never crossed, that Klein did not know him. But Goodnow knew Klein, probably knew more about him than anyone on earth. Whole megabytes on the VAX were devoted to Hugo Klein.

The jury filed in, their faces without expression. "What's your guess?" Svenson murmured.

"I don't guess," Goodnow replied. "Besides, it's obvious."

"But they drilled that sucker."

Goodnow didn't argue. He was deciding not to recommend Svenson for further promotion when all at once he felt hot and his head began to pound. He rubbed his temples. Hair came away in clumps.

The judge put on his glasses. "Have you reached a verdict?"

The forewoman rose in the jury box. She was small boned and intense, with short, well-cut gray hair, and had once been an art professor at Stanford. Goodnow couldn't understand how the prosecution had allowed her to serve. In a quiet but clear voice, with the slightest underthrob of self-righteous defiance, she spoke the words Goodnow expected.

"Not guilty, Your Honor."

The spectators cheered, except for the friends and relatives of the dead trooper. The Santa Clara Five raised their fists. The judge pounded his gavel. Hugh Klein folded his hands as though in prayer, closed his eyes, sighed deeply; then rose and accepted congratulations like some maestro who had just transported everyone to perfect realms of beauty. Goodnow wanted to kill him.

The court cleared. The Santa Clara Five were taken away first, back to their various prisons. They were all serving life sentences for armed robbery and other crimes, but murder would not be one of them. They had shot the trooper, yes, but the art teacher had bought the argument that it was self-defense. Klein donned a black FDR-style cape and swept out.

Goodnow and Svenson sat alone. Goodnow had a vision of Klein carrying on for years after he himself was gone, of Klein rising over and over to accept congratulations, of his hair growing longer and more silvery, of his great head growing more distinguished. Klein's obituary would be long and fascinating; his own, brief and cryptic.

"I don't suppose it matters much," Svenson said.

Goodnow turned to him.

Svenson faltered a little under his gaze. "With them already in jail and whatnot."

At one time, even a few months ago, Goodnow would have said something cutting. But now he was silent. His energy had to be rigorously husbanded. He couldn't waste his cutting tools on Svenson. His time was limited—although the doctors were coy about its precise quantification.

"Months or years, Doctor?"

"Oh, I hate to say."

Svenson looked at his watch. "So," he said, probably thinking of his girlfriend, "catch the two-thirty flight?"

Slowly, very slowly, Goodnow rose. But not slowly enough. *You hate to say, Doctor? I hate even to think about it.*

They caught the two-thirty flight. It left at a quarter to four, flew toward the coming night, met it east of the Mississippi, and landed in full darkness.

"Need help with your bags, Mr. Goodnow?" Svenson asked.

"I can manage."

"See you tomorrow, then." Svenson hurried away.

Goodnow got into a taxi, gave the driver his address, and then, halfway there, had him turn around and go to the office instead. Soon he was sitting at his desk, terminal switched on, scrolling back through the life of Hugo Klein. The Klein file was his, had been his almost from his first day at the agency. He had asked for it. Not out of animus: it was just that he remembered Klein from his big-man-on-campus days. Surely not from animus. This had nothing to do with personalities. Klein was a danger to the national security, brilliant and mischievous, and protecting the national security was Goodnow's job. In the case of Klein, he had failed.

Goodnow stopped scrolling when he reached the time of the invasion of Cambodia. Goodnow had no interest in the invasion of Cambodia; it was a tiny echo of all that bombing that he cared about, an echo that had sounded in the life of Hugo Klein. A tiny echo to begin with, and now much fainter with the passage of time, but Goodnow had always believed that it carried the sound of complicity and guilt: the sole indication of Klein's vulnerability in a file spanning almost forty years. No one was completely invulnerable. How could you be? If you had a child, like Klein, you were vulnerable. If you had cells in your body, you were vulnerable.

Goodnow leaned close to the screen, studied the green paragraphs, sifted, collated, reinterpreted. Time passed. The metastasizing clock inside him ticked away, then rang its pain alarm. Goodnow swallowed a pill, and soon another. He lay his head on the desk, just for a moment, bowed down before the terminal.

Bunting, first to arrive in the morning, found Goodnow asleep at his desk. Bunting, younger than Goodnow, though not as young as Svenson, was Goodnow's boss. He leaned over Goodnow, looked at the screen. Then he stepped back and cleared his throat.

Goodnow, reading in his dreams—how often he seemed to do that now; this time it had been *Treasure Island*—awoke with a start. He took in Bunting's pink, freshly shaven face, smelled manly cologne, felt nauseated. Bunting's eyes, behind his Harold Lloyd–style glasses, were watching him closely. Goodnow's lips were cracked and dry. He licked them and said: "Just checking one of my files."

Bunting nodded toward the screen. "An old one," he said.

What was the implication of that little comment? That Bunting already considered him a figure from the past? The alternative was that Bunting no longer cared about Klein. An impossibility. Goodnow touched a key. The screen went black.

"I meant what I told you last week," Bunting said.

"Which was?"

"That you're welcome to all the time off you want. With full pay. You've earned it." He held up a pink hand. "Not that we don't need you. Of course we do."

"I don't want time off."

Bunting bit his lip. "Please think about it. At a time like this . . ." He stopped himself.

"At a time like this, what?"

"You should take care of yourself. That's all."

"I am," Goodnow said. Bunting went away.

Now Goodnow wanted to go home, loosen his belt, lie down on his side. But he remained seated at his desk, eyes fixed sightlessly on the blank screen. He knew he would be unable to get up slowly enough to keep the pain from stirring. He took a breath, not too deep, and tried imaging: hairy, beaky, rampant. He reached for the pills.

•   •   •

Hugo Klein relaxed in his study, a wood-trimmed, book-lined room in the stern of his cruiser, the *Liberté*. Klein lived on the *Liberté*—with the smell of the sea, the rhythm of the waves, and a view of the Golden Gate for his constant pleasure— had lived there since his last divorce. It was a lot cheaper than a waterfront house and a lot more fun.

One of his assistants arrived with a bottle of champagne. They drank it. She couldn't stop talking about the verdict, which was fine with him. "God," she said, "what a rush."

And later: "You must be exhausted, Hugo. Do you want a massage?"

In truth, he wasn't tired at all. He had the constitution of a barge worker on the Rhine. That was a factor his opponents often failed to consider. They were so busy trying to counter his knowledge and his imagination that they forgot about his endurance. He thought of the champions of the bare-knuckle days, with no round limitations, no decisions, and the victor distinguished by the fact that he was the one still on his feet.

Still, a massage sounded nice. "That sounds nice," said Hugo Klein.

Much later she left, and he was alone on the boat. He went to the bookshelves and began leafing through his law school yearbooks. He soon found the face he had seen in court, and the name that went with it.

Klein picked up the phone and called an old classmate, an active alumnus who raised money and went to reunions. Klein asked how the latest fund-raising was going, promised his usual contribution, and said: "By the way, I bumped into a fellow I think we were at school with the other day."

"Who was that?"

Klein told him.

"You were in Washington?"

"Here. Why would I be in Washington?"

"That's where Goody works." His fellow alumnus chuckled. "Kind of the opposite side of the street from you."

"I don't understand," said Klein.

"Sorry," said the alumnus. "That came out wrong. He has some kind of classified job, that's all I meant. No offense."

"No offense," said Klein.

Later he looked at the picture in the yearbook. His memory really was prodigious, he thought, to have remembered a face after all those years. Goody. He reached for the champagne bottle, but found it empty.

3

Nuncio looked across his secondhand desk at the client, sitting in the secondhand chair where clients sat. Only Nuncio's chair had been bought new, but so long ago that it now fitted in unobtrusively with the rest of the decor.

"Brucie, Brucie, Brucie," Nuncio said, shaking his head.

"Yeah?" replied Brucie Wine. Brucie wasn't the kind of client adept at reading subtexts. Or any texts at all. Brucie had been Nuncio's client for many years. He seemed to have put on a little weight since their last conference, and he hadn't shaved in a week or so. Not a promising-looking client, but a longtime one. A relationship had been formed.

"First," said Nuncio, "this consultation will cost you one hundred dollars, no matter where we go from here. In cash."

Brucie dug his roll out of the pocket of his jeans, peeled off a C-note, and handed it over. Nuncio took it between his beringed fingers and gave it a crisp snap. The sound proved nothing.

"This the genuine article?" he asked.

"Huh?" said Brucie.

"I'm asking if this is Uncle Sam's product, or something homemade."

"Mr. Nuncio! What do you take me for?"

That was a good one. Brucie Wine had grown up south of Market somewhere, Nuncio didn't know precisely and didn't care. His father had been an honest, hardworking printer who ran a little engraving business on the side. Brucie had learned the trade at his old man's knee. When the old man had a stroke, leaving everything to his only son, Brucie had redirected the business along lines his father hadn't considered: into counterfeiting and forgery, to be exact. Mostly counterfeiting in the beginning, but forgery was big now, what with all the illegal aliens around, needing documents—visas, social security cards, driver's licenses, passports. Brucie was good. He could fake perfect passports, which were the hardest, although recently he had expanded beyond even that and could now sometimes get real ones. That's how they'd beaten his last rap—Brucie had fingered his connection at the passport office. In return, Nuncio had persuaded the D.A. to drop the charges. The bill was fifteen grand. Brucie paid cash.

That was Nuncio's M.O. when it came to mounting legal defenses for Brucie Wine. On the previous counterfeiting charge, Nuncio had suggested to the D.A. that Brucie had printed the phony money under an arrangement with some midlevel mob figure. The D.A., up for reelection, had decided he'd get better press for taking down a mobster, even a minor one, than a working-class nobody like Brucie Wine.

Twenty grand. Cash.

And there had been two or three other busts over the years, with similar play-outs. Brucie did excellent work. His twenties, fifties, hundreds, his passports, his social security cards—works of art. That wasn't the problem. The problem was he did stupid things and got caught.

"Brucie, Brucie, Brucie," Nuncio said, again shaking his head.

"Yeah?"

Brucie was tapping his foot on the threadbare carpet. He couldn't understand what was taking so long. He just didn't get it. How to spell it out for him? There was no one left to finger.

"Brucie?"

"Yeah?"

"There's no one left to finger."

"Huh?"

Nuncio lit a cigar. It was a cheap cigar, the kind that came in a box of five for a buck and a quarter, but he took his time with it, as though it were the finest Monte Cristo, and he, Winston Churchill. He didn't offer one to Brucie. Brucie shook a bent cigarette out of a pack of Camels and lit up. Soon there was a lot of smoke in Nuncio's office, but they were no further ahead.

"Mind telling me something, Brucie?"

"Depends," said Brucie, demonstrating one of his rare and always inappropriately timed outbreaks of low cunning.

"Why," asked Nuncio, "were you doing eighty-five on the Golden Gate Bridge on a night when you had two hundred grand in counterfeit paper in your glove compartment?"

"'Cause of Laverne," said Brucie. "I was late. For picking her up for our date, see? That pisses her off like you wouldn't believe. You know what I'm saying?"

Nuncio didn't know. He didn't want to know anything about Laverne.

"Besides," added Brucie with some pride, "I got the fuzzbuster."

"The fuzzbuster."

"For picking up cop radar."

"If they got their radar turned on," Nuncio said.

"Huh? Oh. Right, sure."

"So I guess it was when you zipped by that squad car on the inside that they musta got suspicious."

"Suspicious?" asked Brucie.

"That you might be exceeding the speed limit."

"Oh. Yeah. They hit the siren right away, Mr. Nuncio. But what right did they have to search the car? Tell me that." Brucie was sticking out his soft recessive chin in an aggressive manner. Whatever happened, he had to be kept off the stand.

"It was the open bottle of Bud on your dash, Brucie. That gives them the right."

"Yeah?"

"Probable cause," Nuncio said. Brucie looked blank. "Brucie, I want you to think very carefully about something I'm going to ask you. Take your time with the answer."

"Shoot."

"Could anybody have had access to your car?"

"Access?"

"Could somebody have gotten into your car without your knowledge?"

"Are you shitting me, Mr. Nuncio? That's a brand-new Trans-Am. Loaded. Don't even have a thousand miles on the odometer, and it's been hooked up the whole time. That baby's locked in the garage under the house every night. And I lock up the car too, and set the burglar alarm. I'm talking about the car alarm and the garage alarm. Plus there's Flipper."

"Flipper?"

"My pit bull, chained up outside. You should see him, Mr. Nuncio."

Nuncio didn't want to see Flipper. Except for the fact that he was often in trouble and always paid up, Brucie was a poor client. You couldn't counsel a client to lie exactly, to make up a false story. That would be unethical. Worse, it could lead to criminal charges, probably disbarment. On the other hand, there was no law against gently guiding a client toward an interpretation of the facts of the case that might raise reasonable doubt as to guilt. That was what the practice of criminal law was all about. Raising reasonable doubts. Raising reasonable doubts meant coming up with one measly crackpot theory and planting it in the mind of one measly crackpot juror. Finding the right juror during the impaneling was Nuncio's job. No problem. He'd done it hundreds of times. Where he needed Brucie's cooperation was in coming up with the crackpot theory. But Brucie was tapping his foot again, and knocking ash on the carpet.

"Brucie?"

Brucie looked like he was about to— Yes, he yawned. "Yeah?"

"Think again."

"What about?"

"About the possibility, however remote, of someone getting into the glove compartment of your car before you drove to Laverne's." Maybe he hadn't been clear enough. Maybe he should have said "getting into the glove compartment and planting that counterfeit money." Dangerously close to the ethical line, though. Besides, wasn't it perfectly obvious what he was fishing for? What kind of a human being could now fail to say: "My God, Mr. Nuncio! Someone must have planted that stuff in my glove compartment!" Then they could rise on wings of creativity, spinning tales of enemies, setups, dark deeds.

Brucie Wine said: "But how could they, Mr. Nuncio? I already told you. I lock the car. I lock the garage. I even lock the goddamn glove compartment. And then there's the alarms."

"You left out Flipper."

"Right. Flipper."

The two men fouled the air with smoke. Nuncio glanced at the clock. He had a nice round belly under his purple vest, and it liked to be fed promptly at noon.

"Brucie?"

"Yeah?"

"This time you're going down, son."

"What?"

"To jail, Brucie."

"Jail?" Brucie was appalled. He was not the kind to do well in jail—or even survive.

"They've got you by the balls, Brucie, and you've got nothing left to give them. No one to finger." Had it been Churchill who had said something about giving me the tools and I'll do the job? Nuncio took a drag on his twenty-five–cent cigar. "You've got to give me some tools, Brucie."

Brucie frowned. "Tools? You mean like the press and stuff?"

God. "A body. Some crook to cough up to the D.A."

Brucie's little eyes lit up. "I did driver's licenses for some spics last month."

"Christ. What does the D.A. want with more spics? He'd probably tack on an extra year for aggravation if I even raised the idea. Think, Brucie. Think." For a moment, Nuncio consid-

17

ered hiring a hypnotist, at Brucie's expense. "Think way back into the past. Is there anybody you've worked with or done work for that the cops might be interested in?"

Brucie scrunched up his face like a five-year-old asked to spell *dog*. It was a revolting sight. Brucie thought and thought. Nuncio's stomach rumbled. Twelve o'clock. He started to get up. Then Brucie surprised him. He opened his eyes and said, "I got an idea."

"Yeah?" said Nuncio, sitting back down.

4

Blurting the answer to twenty-six across in the Sunday
New York Times crossword was the first big mistake Charlie
Ochs had made in twenty years. Playing Ben Webster was the
second.

There had been other mistakes along the way, but small
ones—once when a dog made off with a baseball, for example,
and Charlie, passing by the field, had taken it from the animal's
mouth and unthinkingly zinged it to the catcher, over three
hundred feet away, on the fly. That had been stupid, but
without consequences. The ballplayers were kids and had soon
forgotten. Charlie didn't forget—and never touched a baseball
again, although he sometimes recalled the feeling of that
particular one, worn and slightly damp, in his hand.

The crossword puzzle mistake did have consequences. It
would never have happened at all if he had stayed in bed, or if
a monster hadn't crawled into one of his traps.

But.

Charlie had a little shingle house on Cosset Pond, bought at
a time when you didn't need a city job to afford one. Kitchen
and sitting room on the first floor, bed and bath upstairs. He

19

had a tumbledown garage where he kept his car, a yellow Volkswagen Beetle with almost three hundred thousand miles on it and an engine he had rebuilt twice. He had a patch of land, big enough to stack his pots, and a floating dock with *Straight Arrow* tethered at the end. He had no wife, no kids, no close friends. He had a silver saxophone he played at night.

On the day of twenty-six across and Ben Webster, Charlie awoke at first light, as he always did. He rolled over and raised his head to look out the window. There was frost on the glass. Charlie scraped it away with his fingernails. He saw *Straight Arrow* straining its lines at the dock. White caps stormed over Cosset Pond, and heavy seas roiled outside, beyond the Cosset Pond cut. The flag on the roof of the Oceanographic Studies Center across the pond was flying straight out, and overhead, charcoal clouds sped by, fraying at the edges.

Meanwhile, the bed was warm with the heat of his body. It would have been easy just to lie down, pull the quilt over his head, and listen to the weather, as though it were a New Age recording entitled *Nor'easter*. But he hadn't checked his pots in three days, and if he didn't do it, someone else, someone who didn't shrink from a little weather when there was a dishonest dollar to be made, would. Charlie threw back the covers with more force than necessary and got up.

A few minutes later, carrying a thermos of yesterday's reheated coffee, wearing long johns, wool pants, flannel shirt, sweater, oilskins, and rubber boots, Charlie walked down the path from his back door and onto the dock. The wind was blowing harder than he had thought, whipping sound from the bare trees, the wires, the rigging of the boats on the pond, like the conductor of a rough-and-ready orchestra. It was a cold wind, and stung his face. Charlie, boarding *Straight Arrow*, whistled into it; a tune of his own devising, inspired by bebop, and far from New Age.

Straight Arrow was a beamy twenty-six–foot Corea with a hundred and sixty-five–horse Palmer diesel. Charlie had bought it at a DEA auction of seized smuggling assets. He had scraped off its red paint, repainted it white, changed its name from *Shake Dat Ting* and added a small deckhouse for days like this.

He switched on the engine, felt it rumble under his feet, and cast off.

Charlie took *Straight Arrow* across the pond at half throttle. A plume of light snowflakes hooked down from the clouds, and then another. Not enough to affect visibility, he thought, steering through the cut, under the bridge, out to sea. Almost immediately, a wave broke over the bow, smacking hard against the Plexiglas screen of the pilothouse. Suddenly the air was white with driving snow and Charlie felt as cold as though he were wearing nothing at all. He was considering turning back when another wave came smashing in, looped over the screen and caught him in the face. Icy water ran down his neck, seeped through the wool sweater, the flannel shirt, the long johns. Charlie laughed, laughed at the futility of his preparation, preparation in general.

And all at once he was fully awake, shocked into an acute state of consciousness, where he heard every change in the pitch of the wind, saw the individual patterns of the snowflakes that flew by his eyes, felt the currents of cold, some wet, some dry, that came from all directions. Fully awake for the first time in how long? And fully aware of the power of the sea to do with him as it pleased. Well, you either slipped through the cracks or you didn't. Charlie laughed again, loud and free with no one to hear him, and swung *Straight Arrow* west, into the weather.

Charlie's floats were red with three white stripes. They were lined up with landmarks—the lighthouse, the water tower, the radio station antenna—but Charlie couldn't see any landmarks, only the violent circle of seascape immediately around him, bounded by the pointillist walls of a white cocoon. He kept going, although he knew that he would have to run right over one of his floats in order to see it.

After a few minutes, he did. A wave tossed up a flash of red and white off the starboard side; Charlie slowed, circled, and grabbed the float on his first pass. *My lucky day,* he thought.

With *Straight Arrow* in neutral, rising and falling on moving hills of water, Charlie uncoupled the line from the float, hooked it to the winch in the stern, and hit the switch. Nothing happened. He glanced at the motor. The casing was covered by a sheet of ice. He kicked it, not hard, and tried the switch a few more times. Nothing—and not the moment for taking motors apart. He began pulling by hand.

Charlie had five pots on the line, spread along the bottom at a depth of about fifty feet. They were old, waterlogged, heavy. Charlie pulled. His body wasn't the kind Milanese couturiers cut suits for; but useful for what he was doing now.

The first pot came up covered in seaweed, and empty inside. The second was empty too. And the third and the fourth. Despite the cold, Charlie was sweating by the time the last pot broke the surface. It seemed much heavier than the others—he was barely able to haul it over the stern. For a moment he thought he must be getting old. Then he looked between the slats. In the fifth pot was the biggest bug he had ever seen. It seemed to be looking back at him. After twenty or thirty seconds of that, it jabbed an enormous claw in his direction. The claw encountered the wooden cage, twisted sideways, opened, closed. With a crunch, the slat snapped in two. The claw jabbed through the opening. "Jesus," Charlie said, backing away.

Carefully, he took the fifth pot off the line and lowered the others over the side. There was no point in continuing with a broken winch. Charlie checked the compass and turned for home. All the way, he heard scary sounds from the pot on the deck behind him.

Charlie tied up at the dock behind De Mello's Wholesale Fish. No one was there but De Mello, sitting in his cold office, with fish scales on the floor and Amalia Rodrigues on the tape player. He stuck a bottle in the drawer as Charlie walked in.

"You went out in this shit?" De Mello said.

"Got something to show you."

De Mello followed Charlie down to the dock. He looked in the pot and made no comment. Charlie had always known De Mello was hard to impress. Now he knew the man couldn't be impressed. It was a character defect.

They weighed it on De Mello's scale, the one all the fishermen suspected was a little light. It weighed forty pounds, one ounce.

"Is that a record?" Charlie said.

"Not even close," De Mello told him. "I'll give you one twenty."

"Thanks. And how much for the lobster?"

"That's today's price. Two ninety a pound, times forty, and rounded off in your favor. It was two seventy-five last week."

"Yeah," said Charlie, "but that's for lobster. This isn't a lobster—it's a tourist attraction. No one's going to eat it, De Mello. It'll spend the rest of its life in the display tank at Jimmy's on the Wharf or someplace like that. And Jimmy's going to pay you five hundred." He looked closely at De Mello to see if it was a good guess. De Mello's face was expressionless. "At least five," Charlie said. "So I'll take three now."

They settled on two fifty. De Mello took the roll out of his pocket, the roll that had a fishy smell, and counted out the bills with care. He had to be careful counting money, even if it wasn't sticky—thirty years on a trawler had cost him three fingers and a thumb.

Charlie went home, had a hot shower, came out with his skin tingling and his senses still wide awake. Lunchtime, and a bowl of egg salad waited in the fridge. He saw himself sitting at the kitchen table, eating sandwiches and drinking coffee, alone. He put on a jacket and went out.

Snow was falling thickly now, covering the ground. A woman in black tights clicked toward him on cross-country skis, her eyelashes fluffy white. She didn't appear to see him as she passed. Charlie went the other way, following the road that led around the pond to the Oceanographic Studies Center and the Bluefin Café next to the bridge over the cut. Charlie opened the door and felt a warm smoky breath on his face. It smelled of pine, garlic, oranges. He went inside.

Sunday afternoon at the Bluefin Café. A fire made popping noises in the stone hearth, and Dinah Washington was singing "Unforgettable" on the sound system. The seven or eight little tables in the café were all taken. Charlie sat on one of the two vacant stools at the bar.

"Hey, Charlie," said the bartender. "What'll it be?"

"Egg salad on rye."

"Something to drink? I got Guinness on tap."

That sounded perfect, but Charlie said: "Orange juice." He

23

didn't like to drink in public. It was just a habit now, a long
habit; but habits, in the case of Charlie Ochs, made the man.
Still, on top of the weather, the lobster, the tingling in his skin,
a mug of Guinness would have been perfect.

Charlie was halfway through his sandwich, lost in the sound
of Dinah Washington's voice, when a woman came into the café
and took the only seat left, next to him. With his consciousness
still fully awake, slapped to life by the cold wave over *Straight
Arrow's* bow, Charlie was acutely aware of her presence. The
first thing he noticed was the melting snowflakes on her
eyelashes: she was the skier in the black tights. He glanced out
and saw her skis leaning against the window. Then she took off
her backpack and her jacket and Charlie smelled her smell:
lemon, wool, and the faintest hint of fresh sweat. He breathed
it in, let it linger in his nostrils. He was thinking of doing it
again when the warning went off in his mind. Charlie picked
up the rest of his sandwich.

A minute before he'd been ravenous, on the point of ordering
a second. Now he wasn't hungry at all. He took a bite and
listened to the music. He couldn't get into it.

"I'll have a Guinness and a hamburger," the woman said.
"No, make that an egg salad sandwich."

She had a nice voice, not a work of art like Dinah Washington's, but clear and quiet, with the suggestion of reserves of
power. Or was he imagining that? Charlie wasn't sure. It had
been a long time since he'd known a woman. Not getting close
to women, or anyone, was one of his habits.

Charlie glanced at her profile. A damp lock of sandy hair
curled down from under her tuque around a well-shaped
earlobe, still white from the cold. He guessed she was about
ten years younger than himself, around thirty. *So what?* he
thought, and picked up his sandwich again. *Eat and get out of
here.*

The woman took the *New York Times Magazine* out of her
backpack and turned to the crossword. It was half-done, in ink.
Charlie could see the title: "Tools of the Trade." The woman
took out a ballpoint, quickly filled in seventeen down, nineteen
down, twenty-two across. She tapped her pen on twenty-six
across a few times. Then her beer came. She took a drink—not

a gulp, but a lot more than a sip. It left a golden mustache of froth on her upper lip. Charlie had a mad vision of leaning over and licking it off. He went cold, and at that moment understood as never before how stunted the life of Charlie Ochs had been. At the same time, he had no intention of doing anything about it. *Get out*, he said to himself, and motioned for the bartender. The bartender came over and Charlie opened his mouth to ask for the bill.

"I'll have a Guinness," he said. The words came out, unbidden.

Charlie sat hunched over the remains of his sandwich, staring at the caraway seeds in the rye and knowing that if he didn't get up, his habit-shell, his carapace, might crack at last. But he didn't get up. He listened to the woman's pen *tap-tapp*ing on the page. Then beer came, froth quivering over the frosted rim. Charlie reached for it, picked it up, drank. It was wonderful, the mad, sensual power of the earth, in a glass. Charlie looked over toward the woman, a look, not a glance, saw her tapping the pen, still over the clue to twenty-six across. The answer was one of those long ones that relate to the puzzle title. Charlie read the clue: "Lord Acton's power saw."

He said: "Absolute power corrupts absolutely." Said it right out.

The woman snapped her fingers. "'Saw'—saying," she said, and rapidly filled in the empty spaces. "Of course. God, I'm a dunce." She turned to him with a big smile.

"No, no," said Charlie, or something like that. "I hope you don't mind me—"

"Hell, no," said the woman, looking directly at him, taking him in. Her eyes, the color of the sea on a day just like this, were up to the task—more than up to it, dangerously so. This realization zipped through his mind, almost unnoted. "Two heads, after all," she added.

"Yeah," said Charlie. "Two heads."

She took a drink. "Are you at the center?"

"Nope," said Charlie. "I'm a lobsterman."

He waited for her to say "You're well educated for a lobsterman" or more probably, "I guess that leaves you time for reading," or at least to see some version of that thought flicker in her eyes.

But the woman said: "Bugs? They're my favorite thing in the world."

"To eat?"

"To watch. I spent three summers in a bug lab. Tanks from floor to ceiling. I got to like them. They're so crafty, in a clumsy kind of way, and so futile. It was like watching the Cold War on multiscreen TV."

This was a cue Charlie tried to ignore but couldn't. It was like asking a comedian to keep the punch line to himself. "Maybe you'd like to meet Dick Nixon."

"Dick Nixon?"

"Of the crustacean world." He knew he was being incautious but couldn't stop. Maybe she would say no.

She said yes.

They went outside, into wind and flying snow. Charlie waited for her to flinch, cringe, shiver. She did none of those things.

He took her over to De Mello's and showed her the monster. De Mello had it in a tank of its own. "God in heaven," the woman said.

Her name was Emily Rice. She'd arrived after Christmas to do postdoctoral work for six months at the center. Her specialty was the physics of beach erosion. She was living with the chairman of the ocean geology department and his family, looking for a temporary place of her own.

"You want to stop beach erosion?" Charlie said.

"Can't be done. Not in the long run. But at least I'd like to find ways of not making it worse."

They watched Dick Nixon. Dick Nixon watched them. After a while De Mello shooed them out.

The wind had died down, but snow was still falling. They walked back to the café through a quiet white world. "Is it like this all the time?" Emily said.

"Never."

Emily gathered up her skis and poles. Charlie thought of offering to help her carry them but wasn't sure how she would take it, and said nothing. The chairman of the ocean geology department lived up a wooded hill a few blocks behind Charlie's house. They walked around the pond together. Emily carried her burden easily; Charlie sensed long muscles working smoothly under the black tights.

"What else do you know about Lord Acton?" Emily asked.

"Is there anything else?"

Emily laughed; a lovely sound. "He must have spent his whole life waiting for a chance to stick it in a conversation," she said.

Charlie laughed too. He realized he didn't laugh often, and realizing it, stopped.

"Guzzling port in red leather chairs," Emily said.

"That's the ticket," said Charlie, and heard her laugh again. They came to his house. "This is my place," he said.

Emily studied Charlie's house. A real estate agent couldn't have picked a better moment to sell it. Snow covered the roof, the pots in the yard; icicles hung from this and that. Charlie's house looked like a postcard exemplar of rustic comfort. Charlie knew it began and ended at rustic.

"It's a dream," Emily said. "Have you lived here a long time?"

"Yeah."

"You're from here?"

"No."

Charlie waited for her to ask where he was from, formulating an answer. But that wasn't what she asked. She said: "What's it like inside?"

Charlie's heart beat a little faster. All he had to say was "Want to have a look?" and she'd come in. But that moment Charlie remembered where he'd first heard Lord Acton's aphorism, more specifically whom he'd first heard it from, and everything changed. Maybe her question about where he was from had something to do with it too. "Messy," he said.

Emily turned to him and smiled. "Well, thanks for showing me Mr. Nixon. We'll probably run into each other."

"Yeah," said Charlie. And: "You're welcome," to her back as she walked away. Then he was alone in his house, every drab detail suddenly obvious, the whole small and stifling. "Christ," Charlie said. He sat down, and thoughts of Rebecca drifted into his mind. To make them go away he picked up his sax and started blowing.

It began as "My Romance" but soon changed key and sped up and was probably nothing at all, certainly nothing good, but Charlie got involved in it and forgot about Rebecca, about the drab and the stifling, about everything except the keys at his fingers and the reed at his mouth, didn't notice the fading light outside or hear the knock at the door. At first. Then he did hear something, and stopped playing abruptly. The music died on a vulgar note. Charlie listened, heard the knock.

He was halfway to the door when he had a thought, probably inspired by memories of Rebecca, was suddenly afraid of who might be waiting outside. He made himself answer the door.

It was Emily. She had the *New York Times Magazine* in her hand. "Was that you playing?"

"If you want to call it playing."

"Oh, it was great," she said. She looked up at him. "I thought you might know 'Marilyn Monroe's screwdriver.' Twelve letters. I didn't mean to—"

"No, no," Charlie said. "That's all right. Come in."

Emily stepped over the threshold. "You call this messy?" she said; a little loudly, as though to mask some embarrassment.

There was a silence. "'Marilyn Monroe's screwdriver,'" Charlie said, to break it. The answer didn't come to mind. "Can I get you something while we think?"

Emily took off her jacket. She was wearing an oversized sweatshirt with a purple *W* on it, and the black tights. There wasn't much space in the hall, and as Charlie reached for the jacket, he accidently touched her breast. She reddened.

"Coffee, maybe?" he said.

"No thanks," she replied. "I'd never sleep tonight."

The last phrase took different shapes in Charlie's mind. "There's Scotch," he said. "And red wine."

"Wine sounds nice."

Charlie went into the kitchen, returned with two glasses of wine. They sat on the old corduroy couch in Charlie's sitting room.

"Marilyn Monroe."

"Her screwdriver."

"Do you think it has something to do with Joe DiMaggio?"

"Joltin' Joe?"

Silence. They thought. Charlie remembered the picture of Marilyn Monroe standing over the subway grate, dress blown high. He said: "Do you like jazz?"

"I don't know much about it. But I like music."

"Such as?"

"Barry Manilow." Silence. "Especially early Manilow," Emily added.

"Right," said Charlie. "Before he went experimental." She laughed, and he walked over to the record player. "Maybe you'll like this." That's when he put on Ben Webster. The huge sound, dark and potent, filled the house.

"God," Emily said after a cut or two, "it's so . . . intimate."

The word hung in the air, hung there with other words like *screwdriver* and *tonight*, floated on the gorgeous sound. It was a small couch. Charlie could easily reach out and put his hand on Emily's shoulder. He did. Then they were in each other's arms.

And later they were upstairs in Charlie's bed. Once begun, Charlie had to struggle to hold himself back. It had been so long, and Emily's warmth and heat were almost too much for him. He rose into a little tunnel-shaped world where the climate was tropical and there was only her and him and the air smelled like red wine and moaned in their ears. Then came a tremor that passed from her to him, and slowly Charlie slipped back down to the big world.

"You're so strong," Emily said. "I've never been with such a . . . not that I—"

"It's just steroids," Charlie said, rescuing her.

The second time was slower, more connecting, more . . . intimate, like Ben Webster. Downstairs, where the automatic repeat button had been accidently pressed, the dead man kept playing, prodding them to fall in love, or at least keep jazzing, in the true meaning of the word.

•   •   •

Charlie awoke, not at first light as he always did, like an alert creature on the savannah, but somewhat later. Emily lay sleeping on her side, face slack, mouth a little open, unglamorous, beautiful. He could smell her breath: red wine and sex. He sniffed it in deeply.

Charlie got up and went to the bathroom. He glimpsed his face in the mirror and saw a difference. What? It was the same face, broad and weathered; but there was something positive, even eager, in the eyes.

Charlie scraped the frost off the window. Snow lay thick on the ground and the sun was shining. A boy walking toward the school bus stop threw a chunk of ice at a tree and hit it smack on. He was wearing a jacket that said "Little League All-Stars—South Shore Champions."

Charlie watched the boy till he was out of sight. And he wished he hadn't done it—hadn't babbled the fucking power saw, hadn't taken her to see the monster, hadn't played Ben Webster. What had he been thinking? Wishing to undo something was a physical sensation—it twisted inside him.

"Charlie?" she called.

It was too late.

Charlie went into the bedroom. Emily was sitting in his bed, quilt drawn up to her chin, smiling at him. "Charlie," she said. "I like that name."

"It's just a name," Charlie said.

5

Six weeks later Cosset Pond froze over almost to the cut, ending Charlie's lobster season. On a clear cold day, he and Emily went skating, swooping around the motionless boats like dolphins. Sky and ice were blue, sun gold, blades silver. The whole pond was theirs. Charlie skated faster and faster, could barely keep himself from whooping aloud. *I'm like a goddamned kid,* he thought, and went into a long glide, out past the last boat, its white hull marked by hockey pucks, and almost to the line where the ice turned black and thin. There he dug his edges into a quick, sure hockey stop and looked back in time to see Emily spin, lose her balance, wave her arms at him comically, fall. He skated back and helped her up. She tucked her face into his shoulder.

"I'm pregnant," she said. A vapor cloud rose from her mouth into the blue.

"But I thought—" Charlie began.

"No method is perfect, Charlie," she said, her face still against him: he could feel the vibration of her words in his skin but couldn't read whatever expression was in her eyes. He waited for her to raise the subject of abortion, but she didn't, and he didn't see how he could be the one to do it. Charlie wasn't a goddamned kid; he was old enough to know what her silence meant. She wanted the baby. Did she want it whether he was in the picture or not? Charlie, watching their breath rise like cartoonist's balloons empty of dialogue, was afraid to ask the question.

"That's great," he said.

Then Emily looked up, studying his face in the same probing way she had studied his house. "Do you mean it, Charlie?"

●　●　●

But she had seen the house on its best day; Charlie didn't mean it, not at first. He pretended. Then, after a week or two, the baby crossed some frontier in his mind that separated concept from reality. He didn't know anything about babies, had never even held one, yet suddenly he knew just how a baby's hair—his baby's hair—would feel. At that moment he knew he wanted to be in the picture too. This was wrong, but he had lost the will to do anything about it. A long-stuck brake had been released. Charlie, at last, was on the move.

And picking up speed. First, Emily got a two-year grant from the center to study relationships between water temperature and sand particle movement. Next, she was hired as a consultant by a Wall Street arbitrageur who wanted to save the beach in front of his summer house. After that she began interviewing high school girls who wanted baby-sitting jobs. She also sketched some plans on sheets of graph paper, and Charlie soon found himself building an addition to the house— and knowing the mental state of nesting birds in the spring: happy confusion. He was happy, happier than he'd been in twenty-two years, happy as the safest citizen in the land.

Emily came out one day while he was framing the roof. "Hit your thumb yet?"

"Not hard," Charlie said. Looking down at the top of her head, and thought: *I'm going to make sure you're happy too. That's a promise.* He was so busy making this vow that he almost missed her next question.

"Do you care if it's a boy or a girl, Charlie?"

"Nope."

"Neither do I," Emily said. "So when we have the amnio, let's not find out the sex."

"Okay."

Emily smiled and went back inside.

Charlie smiled too, but he wanted a girl.

•   •   •

The wedding was scheduled for a Saturday in May. They invited a few of the lobstermen and their families, De Mello, some of Emily's colleagues, and her parents, who arrived from the Midwest on Friday. Charlie had no parents—dead in a car crash was the story—or any other relatives. "But that's going to change now," he said to Emily, and for the second time felt the twisting sensation inside. *Don't push it, asshole,* he told himself.

Friday night they had a party on Cosset Pond. The lobstermen lashed some rafts together and everyone rowed out in dinghies. The night was soft and warm. They lit candles and lanterns and fired up barbecues, creating a golden glow in the middle of the pond. A fat white moon was easing its way above the treetops.

"Quite the locale," said Mr. Rice, sitting in a deck chair with a drink in his hands.

Charlie, on his third beer—and last, he told himself—said, "Thanks, Mr. Rice."

"Hey, I told you—Doug."

"Doug."

The raft rose on a slight swell, then sank back down. Someone had brought a tape player. A lobsterman's wife popped Tammy Wynette into it: "D-I-V-O-R-C-E."

"For Christ's sake, Kathy," someone said. Laughter. Charlie heard it, but he was gazing up at a sky full of stars, like sequins spilled on black silk. Sometime later he grew aware that Mr. Rice was looking at him.

"After all," said Mr. Rice, "I can't be much more than ten years older'n you now, can I?"

"Guess not." Charlie noticed how small the drink in Mr. Rice's hands appeared, noticed how broadly built the man was, in fact how much of a physical type the two of them were. He was beginning to deal with the observation when Mr. Rice asked:

"Ever in the service, Charlie?"

"No," said Charlie, taking a drink. "You?"

"Marine Corps," said Mr. Rice. "'Sixty-five to 'sixty-nine. Two hitches." He sipped his drink. "In 'Nam," he added.

Charlie said nothing.

Mr. Rice swirled the whiskey in his glass. He looked up and smiled at Charlie. "How old were you back then?"

"Back when?"

"Back during 'Nam."

"Dougie," called Mrs. Rice from the next raft, "please not the war stories."

"No war stories, hon," said Mr. Rice, with another smile, much briefer than the first. He lowered his voice: "I don't think Charlie here's much interested in war stories, are you, Charlie?"

Charlie put down his beer. "I don't get you, exactly."

Mr. Rice finished his drink. "Nothing to get. You must've grown up in the sixties, that's all. And in my experience sixties people don't care for war stories."

Mrs. Rice approached, a little unsteady on high heels. "I knew it," she said. "You *are* making him listen to your war stories."

"Not true, hon," he said, pulling her over and patting her rump.

"Dougie," she said, but did nothing to stop him. Mrs. Rice was tall like her daughter, with a strong, lean body like her daughter; but born too soon, she didn't carry it with the same confidence. She smiled brightly at Charlie. "What a lovely party," she said. "So . . . different—but lovely. And Emily seems to love it here so, even if it is a little far away." Her smile dimmed. "She seems so happy, doesn't she, Doug?"

"Sure. She's always been a happy kid. Mind freshening my drink, hon?"

"Here, I'll do it," said Charlie.

"Oh, that's all right," said Mrs. Rice, taking the glass. "He likes it just so." She moved toward the portable bar.

Mr. Rice's big hands, with nothing to do, smacked each other lightly. "How's the lobster business?" he asked.

"So-so." Charlie replied. He thought: *Want to go over my bank statements?*

"So-so?"

"The price hasn't been going up, even though the supply is going down. Demand isn't what you'd think. If it wasn't for the Japanese we'd be in trouble."

"The Japs?"

Charlie nodded.

"The Japs," said Mr. Rice. His hands smacked each other a little harder. He folded them in his lap. "How long you been doing it?"

"Eighteen, nineteen years now."

"And before that?"

"I kicked around some."

"College?"

"No."

"No? So you were lucky."

"Lucky?"

"To avoid the draft," said Mr. Rice.

"I never got called."

Mr. Rice nodded and opened another front. "We could have won that war," he said.

Keep your mouth shut, Charlie told himself. But he said: "You think so?"

Mr. Rice leaned toward him. Charlie smelled his whiskey breath, looked into his angry eyes. "You know why we didn't?"

"Because we were fighting in someone else's backyard?"

Mr. Rice put his hand on Charlie's knee and squeezed hard. "No, son. Because this country got its balls cut off by a lot of dopehead hippie liberals."

Charlie laid his hand on Mr. Rice's arm and pushed it away. He knew that in moments he could be in a physical fight with his future father-in-law, rolling across the rafts, falling in the water. "That's an interesting theory, Mr. Rice. What became of these conquering hippies?"

"Oh, God," said Mrs. Rice, appearing with a full glass. "Don't get him started on hippies. Here you go, dear."

"Thought you'd fallen overboard," said Mr. Rice, taking the

glass and drinking deep. He sat back in his chair, giving Charlie a sidelong look.

"Sorry, Dougie. I got to talking to the nicest man, in the fish business, I think. He said Charlie's the hardest-working lobsterman on the coast."

She flashed her bright smile at her husband, then at Charlie, as though trying to warm some cold current running between them. Mr. Rice took another drink, shorter this time. "That's nice," he said. "You from around here, Charlie?"

"I told you, dear," said his wife. "He's from Pennsylvania, isn't that right, Charlie?"

"Right."

"Oh?" said Mr. Rice. "Whereabouts?"

"Pittsburgh," Charlie said.

"Yeah? I've got a buddy in Pittsburgh."

For a moment Charlie thought he was going to be asked if he knew him. Then Willie Nelson started into "Georgia on My Mind," and Mr. Rice stood up abruptly. "Let's dance, hon," he said.

Charlie rose too. Mr. Rice held out his hand. Charlie shook it. Mr. Rice squeezed hard again. "She's a mighty fine girl, that's all," he said. "Mighty fine."

"He knows that, Dougie," said Mrs. Rice, stroking her husband's back. "That's why he's marrying her."

Exactly, you son of a bitch, Charlie thought. The Rices danced slowly away.

Charlie picked up his beer and stepped onto the next raft. Emily was popping a shrimp into her mouth. "You and Daddy had a nice tête-à-tête."

"I look forward to many more."

She touched his hand. "He's a sweet old bear."

Charlie put his arms around her, felt the swelling in her womb. Sweet old bear or son of a bitch, it didn't matter—he wasn't marrying Dougie. He kissed her ear, stuck the tip of his tongue inside. She made a low sound in her throat.

"I want you, Charlie."

"I want you too."

"I mean now, physically."

"It's a small town, Em."

She laughed. Over her shoulder Charlie saw a pickup park under the light on the town dock. A figure got out and busied itself with something in the back.

"Hey! Here's to the happy couple." Everyone was gathered round them, glasses raised. It was getting late. "Come on, Charlie—speech."

Charlie knew the lobstermen and their wives didn't really want a speech. They had known him for years, but not well. They were just doing what they always did at wedding parties. Charlie shook his head.

"Speech, speech."

Charlie looked at their faces. It occurred to him that because he was taking this step, they for the first time considered him part of the community. What, then, had they considered him up to now?

He tried to think of something to say. "I'm a lucky guy," he began. The figure on the dock was lowering something into the water. A kayak, Charlie thought. The figure climbed in. A paddle flashed. Was there something odd about the figure? The kayak slid out of the circle of light and into darkness before Charlie could get a better look.

"You call that a speech?"

"That's the sound bite," Charlie said. Everyone laughed except Mr. Rice, who may have thought that solemnity was called for, and Mrs., whose laughter died quickly when she saw the look on her husband's face. "The speech is even less original," Charlie added. "You don't want to hear it."

"We do."

Charlie was standing in a circle of party guests with Emily beside him, thinking of what to say, when the kayak came cutting out of the darkness into the golden glow and slipped sideways toward the lashed rafts, smoothly docking. The kayaker, dressed in a gorilla suit, looped a line through a ring and climbed up.

The gorilla man was big. He walked across the rafts, through the circle of guests, right to Charlie. He was taller than Charlie, inches taller, though not as broad. He handed Charlie a floral-painted magnum bottle of champagne with a black ribbon around the neck, then turned without a word, got into the kayak and paddled into the night.

Someone laughed, a little drunkenly. Charlie realized he was a little drunk too.

"Who's it from?" Emily asked.

There was an envelope clipped to the ribbon. Charlie opened it and took out the card. It read: TO BLAKE WRIGHTMAN, WITH MY CONGRATULATIONS, UNCLE SAM.

Charlie felt dizzy, a stick figure with its head high in the sky, perched on feeble legs. The bottle started to slip from his grasp. He clutched it hard; the dizziness subsided.

Everyone was looking at him. "Well, who?" said Emily.

Charlie stuck the card in his pocket. "Just an old pal," he said. Nothing else came to mind.

6

Perrier-Jouët," said Emily. "This is the real thing, Charlie. Crack 'er open."

They were back in the kitchen of Charlie's house, their house. Two o'clock in the morning. In hours they would be man and wife—whatever that meant, Charlie thought. Was it the same thing as woman and husband? Big questions; they no longer mattered at all.

"Come on, Charlie."

She wanted champagne. "Now?"

"Why not?"

"The baby," said Charlie. "Alcohol."

"A glass or two couldn't hurt," Emily said. "You're not marrying Jane Brody."

Charlie held the bottle up to the light. There was nothing inside but translucent liquid.

"Charlie, you're acting very strange."

"Am I?"

"Like you've never seen champagne before."

He popped the cork. There was an explosion all right, but it was just the usual fun-promising sound that was part of the champagne makers' hard-won mystique. Foam poured through the opening. Charlie filled two glasses.

Emily clinked her glass against his, looked him in the eye. It was late; she'd been up late the night before; she was pregnant; but slightly flushed and smiling, she looked better than ever. "Us," she said.

"Us," said Charlie, and again felt the twisting sensation inside.

Emily tasted the wine. "Heaven," she said. "Tell me about this mysterious friend."

"It's a long story."

Emily waited for him to tell it. When he said nothing, she stretched up to him and kissed him on the lips. "I look forward to hearing it," she said. "Let's have a little music."

They went into the living room. "Like what?" Charlie asked.

"Like you," Emily said. "Play 'My Romance.'"

"Shouldn't we get some sleep?"

"There'll be lots of time for sleep," Emily said, "but only one night like this. I'm an old-fashioned girl, Charlie."

The saxophone case lay on the floor by the window. Opening it, Charlie couldn't stop himself from looking out. The street was dark, quiet, still. Charlie drew the curtains. For the first time since he had met Emily, he felt the stifling feeling again. He took out the sax and tried to play the feeling away, tried to play something for an old-fashioned girl. He understood what she was telling him: this marriage was for life. Charlie tried to play for her, but he wasn't a pro who could fake it, and what he produced was a short, stifled, angry version of "My Romance," played for Uncle Sam.

Emily was watching him as the last flatted note died away. "That certainly was artistic," she said. "It just needs a different title."

Charlie laughed, couldn't stop himself. This woman was good for him. He put down the sax and held her tight. He wanted never to let go. Some men might have cried at that moment, but Charlie wasn't like that. Just the same, he felt a sudden strange need, a need to confess. "Supposing . . ." he began.

"Supposing what?"

But who was this confession for, he thought, her or him?

"Nothing," he said. "It didn't make sense."

Charlie turned off the lights. They went upstairs, got in bed. Charlie hoped that Emily would just fall asleep, but she reached for him instead. His mind was on other things; his body responded anyway—and once responding, responded with urgency.

"Oh God, Emily."

"Gentle, Charlie, gentle."

He tried to be gentle. He tried to be calm. He tried to make love to her like a loving husband. He owed her that. He owed her a taste of what it would be to have a loving husband. He held her tight and made time go as slowly as he could. Emily relaxed, opened, sighed, moaned, came. "Come, Charlie."

But Charlie, up again in the little tunnel world, didn't want to come. He wanted to fuck and fuck and never stop.

"Not again, Charlie."

Then he came too. They lay together, hot and damp, felt the blood coursing in their bodies. "A whole lifetime of this," Emily said. "I don't know if I can stand it."

Charlie buried his head in her shoulder then, something he had never done. *Don't*, he told himself, but couldn't pull away. He lay like that in the darkness of his house until Emily's breathing slowed and fell into a deep, even rhythm. Charlie heard her heart beating in his ear, strong and steady. He lay still for a long time, eyes open in the darkness, wishing he could crawl up inside her and disappear. Then he slid his arm out from under her, rolled carefully away, and slipped out of bed. He gathered up his clothes, stopped to straighten the covers on Emily, and silently left the room.

Leaving the lights off, Charlie went down to the kitchen. He peered out the window, saw his street, dark, quiet, still. He took a carton of orange juice from the fridge, a loaf of bread from the counter, the keys to *Straight Arrow* from the hook on the wall. Then he opened the back door and stepped outside.

It was the same night, soft and warm. The moon hung higher in the sky now, not so fat but even whiter than before. Charlie didn't move for a minute or two. He heard an animal run across his roof and a fish splash in the pond, but that was all. He walked through the soft grass, down to the dock.

Straight Arrow was tethered to the end, as always. Charlie climbed on, freed the lines, cast off. He took a paddle from the forward compartment and started paddling toward the cut. Nothing happened on shore—no sirens, no lights, no shouts. Charlie leaned over the starboard side and paddled hard. There was no sound but water sound: the tumbling of little waves pushed by the hull, the occasional sucking at the paddle. Charlie paddled all the way to the cut, under the bridge, beyond.

Outside a breeze was blowing, stirring up a light chop. Charlie put the paddle away and switched on the engine. He left the running lights off, idling for a few moments when he should have been on the move. He was trying to make himself not look back. The moon gleamed in endless striations on the water, lighting a silver path that ran from south to north. Charlie swung *Straight Arrow* onto the path. North was Canada, a long way north, and that would mean landing to refuel; but it was better than traveling by road in a yellow Volkswagen Beetle, and that was his only other idea. Brutally, he banged the throttle all the way down, and *Straight Arrow* surged forward.

Then Charlie did look back, once. He couldn't help himself. He saw a faint glow at the opening of the cut, and nothing but darkness beyond.

He turned away, pushed down on the already fully opened throttle, trying for speed that wasn't there. At that moment a dazzling light flashed on, bathing Charlie in brilliant white, like a patient in an operating room. He responded instantly, jerking the wheel to the right, running for open sea. That brought a series of staccato barking sounds. The windscreen shattered in Charlie's face; Plexiglas particles streamed through his hair. He pulled back on the throttle.

Now he heard another motor. He looked around, into the glare. A voice called out: "Hands in the up configuration."

Charlie thought of hitting the throttle. He thought of jumping over the side. Then he raised his hands over his head.

A sleek cigarette boat slid alongside *Straight Arrow*. The gorilla man stood in the bow. He had a line in one hand and an automatic rifle, pointed casually at Charlie, in the other. He looped the line around *Straight Arrow*'s bow cleat. The gorilla head turned to Charlie. The mouth was open wide, revealing fierce plastic teeth. The gorilla man said: "*Finis*, Blakey. Shut 'er down and climb aboard."

Charlie turned the key and stepped onto the cigarette. The bright light went off. Charlie, momentarily blind, felt big padded hands patting him down. "Clean," said the gorilla man.

Charlie's eyes adjusted to the darkness. He soon made out the gorilla man, now leaning against the front of the console, rifle dangling toward the deck. Standing at the wheel was a man in a seersucker suit and bow tie, his gaunt face colored green by the lights of the instrument panel. He switched off the cigarette's engines. Then it was quiet, peaceful almost, out at sea on a calm night. The boats bobbed together on the water. In the distance a buoy bell rang. Little waves slapped the hulls. The extinguished searchlight crackled once or twice, went silent. The bow-tie man said, "You can remove that ridiculous costume."

The gorilla man laid the rifle on the console and fiddled with a zipper on his back. Charlie's gaze was drawn to the rifle. "Don't even consider it," the gorilla man said. He stripped off the hairy bodysuit. Underneath he wore gray sweats with a blue "Yale" on the chest. "The head too?" he asked.

"Is it part of the costume?" said the bow-tie man.

The gorilla man began tugging at his head. It came off with a rubbery snap. "Ow," he said. He didn't look like the kind of man who would react much to pain. He was in his late twenties, big, just as big as he had appeared in the suit, with a bony white face and hair so light it appeared silver in the darkness.

"That was fun," he said, although there was no sign of amusement on his face. "Like Halloween. Do you think I can keep it?"

"It goes back on Monday," said the bow-tie man.

"You're the boss," said the gorilla man. He sat on the gunwale, rifle in his lap.

The bow-tie man turned to Charlie. "Do you need something to stop the blood?"

Charlie touched his cheek. It was wet and sticky, cut by flying Plexiglas. He made no reply.

"A stoic," said the bow-tie man.

"That's rich," said the gorilla man.

"Is it not." The bow-tie man moved to the stern, gingerly, as though he had pulled a muscle in his abdomen, and sat on the padded bench that ran from one side to the other. "Come sit down, Mr. Wrightman."

"That's not my name," Charlie said. He stayed where he was.

The bow-tie man pinched the bridge of his nose, like a man with a splitting headache. Charlie noticed how scrawny his neck was, much too small for the collar of his button-down shirt. "Are you going to begin on that level?" the bow-tie man asked. "I expected better."

"Why?" asked the gorilla man.

The bow-tie man ignored him. "I'm willing, Mr. Wrightman, to imagine that with the passage of time there may be moments when you actually think you are Charlie Ochs. But the fact is that Charlie Ochs does not exist. He's a fantasy, backed up with a phony history and a few quaint props. But unreal. A nonperson, if you will."

"Which raises an interesting question," said the gorilla man.

"It came up a few hours ago, while you were having that heartwarming party," the bow-tie man said. "Svenson here brought it up. I shouldn't be surprised of course. He majored in philosophy."

"Minored, Mr. G," said Svenson. "Art history was my major."

Again Mr. G ignored him. "The question, Mr. Wrightman, is this: is it a crime to kill a nonperson?"

"Shoot him in the head, tie an anchor around his neck, and throw him over," said Svenson. "Or something like that, right Mr. G?"

Mr. G did not respond. He gazed at Charlie. The boat bobbed up and down. A buoy rang far away. Waves slapped the hull. It could have been a peaceful night on a calm sea. Then Mr. G got down on his hands and knees and vomited over the side.

7

Seasick, Mr. G?" said Svenson. He rose quickly, leaving the rifle on the deck.

Mr. G waved him back, then wiped his mouth with seawater. Holding onto the bench for support, he pulled himself to his feet and took a deep breath.

"You going to be okay?" Svenson asked.

"Is that a smart question?" said Mr. G in raspy voice.

"Sorry." Svenson bit his lip like a schoolboy. He watched Mr. G open a bottle of pills and swallow several. Charlie risked another glance at the gun.

"He's still thinking about it, Mr. G," said Svenson, without looking at Charlie, "even though I told him not to." Svenson picked up the gun.

Mr. G sat down heavily and said something too low to hear.

"I didn't quite get that, Mr. G," said Svenson.

Mr. G cleared his throat, making a sound like steel files being rubbed together. "He's still in shock."

"Shock?"

"He hasn't internalized the situation yet. Must I spell everything out?"

"Sorry," Svenson repeated. "Maybe this will help him." He reached into his back pocket. Something crinkled in his hands. He came forward and handed a sheet of paper to Charlie. Charlie held it close to the green console light. The paper was wrinkled with many foldings and brittle with age.

"John Blake Wrightman," it read. "Wanted for Murder."

There was a photograph of the wanted man, and a list of details—his height, 6 feet; his weight, 195; his distinguishing marks, none; and the warning that he was a terrorist, to be considered armed and dangerous.

Svenson came around the console and gazed at it with him. "Look how long his hair was." His eyes shifted to Charlie, then back to the photograph on the poster.

"But he's aged well, hasn't he?" said Mr. G.

"Like Faust," said Svenson, abruptly snatching the poster and putting it away, "or Dorian Gray, I can't remember." He backed away, lounged once more against the gunwale. "He looks more than one ninety-five, though."

"Maybe, but it's not middle-aged spread," said Mr. G. "I'd make a note of that, Svenson."

Svenson snorted.

Mr. G turned to Charlie. "I hope you're not going to waste a lot of time denying who you are. It won't hold up, you know."

Charlie knew that. Did it make him Blake Wrightman? Yes, he had been Blake Wrightman, but that was a long time ago. There was no point saying it, so he said nothing. In the silence that followed came the sound of a splash, not far away, followed by a much bigger one. Hunter and hunted played their parts, down below.

"Should we explain how we found him?" Svenson asked. "I'll bet he's dying to know. If you'll pardon the *double-entendre*." Svenson pronounced the words in the French manner. He had a nice accent.

Mr. G looked at Charlie, but Charlie couldn't read his face in the darkness. "Are you dying to know?" he asked. Charlie did not reply. "Let's just say that a lot of data finds its way to my office," Mr. G said. "It takes time to sift through it, that's all."

"What office?" Charlie said.

There was a pause. "I believe he's trying to establish our bona fides," Mr. G said.

"That's kind of humorous, coming from the likes of him," said Svenson.

Charlie, for a wild moment entertaining the thought that these men might be imposters, said, "Let's see some ID."

Svenson laughed, but Mr. G said, "Show him."

"You're my mentor," Svenson replied with a shrug, and pushed himself off the gunwale. He didn't appear to be moving fast, but he must have been because he drove the rifle butt into the pit of Charlie's stomach before Charlie could even flinch, and Charlie was a quick man. He went down on the deck, rolled over. Svenson kicked him hard in the back. It forced a grunt of pain from Charlie; he couldn't keep it in.

"I don't think we have to worry about that extra bulk after all," Svenson said.

Mr. G got to his feet, stepped toward Charlie, looked down. "Can you hear me, Mr. Wrightman?"

Charlie was silent.

"The point is that if you choose to handle this in a vulgar manner, we can respond in kind," said Mr. G. "That's the meaning of democracy."

Charlie, his ear against the deck, heard the *slap-slap* of the waves. He turned on his side, tried to get up, couldn't. High above he saw their faces in the green console lights, Svenson's harsh and young, like a new world uneroded by the elements, Mr. G's like death.

Svenson turned to Mr. G. "Vulgar?" he said. "I don't think violence is necessarily vulgar. It depends on who's doing it and why."

"You're wrong," said Mr. G. "Violence is always vulgar, if sometimes necessary." He backed out of Charlie's sight and sat down on the padded bench. "I'm talking about physical violence, of course. As violence becomes nonphysical, it ascends the social scale. Like anything else."

Charlie got a grip on the side, lurched to his feet. His stomach lurched with him, and the next moment he was bent over the stern, vomiting, as Mr. G had, into the sea.

"Jesus H.," said Svenson. "You're not on chemo, are you?"

Charlie felt a little better; well enough to do something. He wasn't a trained fighter, but he knew how to move. He spun around and threw a punch at Svenson's head. Maybe not as quickly as he would have liked: Svenson was ready. He drove the rifle butt into Charlie's gut again, striking the same spot. Charlie went down, harder this time, and stayed down. He vomited again too, right where he lay. Then he fought to get a breath inside him.

Mr. G sighed. "Now," he said, "perhaps we might begin. It's late and I'm tired."

"Not me," said Svenson. "I could pull an all-nighter no problem."

Mr. G sighed again, more loudly this time. "Let's start with the girl."

"Woman," Svenson corrected. "Girls are twelve and under."

Mr. G didn't seem to hear him. "Were there other marriages along the way?" he continued. "Or was this going to be the first?"

Charlie, prone on the deck and panting, didn't answer.

"The bride-to-have-been is very pretty," Mr. G said. It sounded like the introduction to further remarks, but none ensued.

Charlie didn't want them talking about Emily. He got control of his breathing, then forced himself up to his knees. His hands squared into fists. Svenson, still lounging, changed the position of his feet.

"Don't worry," Mr. G said. "She's in no danger. Except psychically, of course—and that's your doing. It's a side issue, but did you ever think what in the world she's going to tell the child?"

Charlie got to his feet, swayed. Maybe if he could stop swaying for a few seconds he could kick Svenson's head off. He was still trying to do that when a question arose in his mind: how did they know that Emily was pregnant?

Mr. G seemed to be following his thoughts. "Naturally we've seen the pregnancy test report. And the amnio results. Not so long ago, that kind of information-gathering was a distasteful business—break-ins, burglary paraphernalia, nocturnal excursions, the whole grubby scenario. Now it can all be done

48

during office hours by a clerk in front of a PC. It's a girl, by the way, Mr. Wrightman. I might as well tell you now, since it isn't likely you'll be seeing your daughter for some time."

Charlie dove at Mr. G, got his hands around the scrawny neck. Mr. G fell against the console, Charlie on top of him. Mr. G's skin felt hot. He struggled furiously but not from fear; Charlie saw no fear at all in his eyes. Then something massive collided with the back of Charlie's head, turning everything fleetingly red, subsequently black.

•   •   •

"It's an interesting problem," Mr. G was saying. "How to explain his behavior. Twenty years of quiet, solitary existence, a life structured—realistically—with nothing to lose. Even penitential, or is that going too far? Then suddenly all this... matrimony. What made him think he was safe?"

Charlie opened his eyes. He saw the moon, sliding down the black dome of the sky now; still night. He smelled vomit, saw the white of Svenson's high-top pumps, not far from his head. Svenson squatted down, shone a pencil flash into his eyes.

"There's no statute of limitations for what you did," Svenson said. "No safety."

Charlie squirmed away from the light. He hadn't thought about what he'd done in a long time, not consciously. Now images stirred in his mind, fragments from a day of rage, a night of waiting, a morning that came too soon. Did it all add up to a horrible accident? Charlie had tried to persuade himself of that in the past, never successfully. He didn't try to persuade the men on the cigarette boat.

"Now, all of a sudden, you've got plenty to lose," Mr. G said. Charlie turned to the stern. Mr. G had Charlie's carton of orange juice in his hand. He opened it, tipped it up to his mouth. The tendons in his neck rose like pop-up illustrations in a children's anatomy book. He licked his lips. "Poor timing on your part."

"Is that the home-style?" Svenson asked.

"Home-style?" said Mr. G.

"With the pulp."

Mr. G squinted at the label. "I don't know. What difference does it make?"

"A big one, I hope," said Svenson. "Dad's outfit just bought five percent of Tropicana."

Charlie sat up on the deck. Poor timing, he thought. It was true, now and before. He pictured the wires coiling from the back of Bombo Levine's cheap alarm clock, the one with the plain black hands and the words "Big Ben" on the face. The appearance of that image in his mind was followed by the twisting feeling inside, a sensation that awoke the pain Svenson's rifle butt had caused and then was swallowed up by it. He turned his head and looked back, back through the cut toward Cosset Pond. What had made him dream he could be safe, safe enough for Emily? A cold wave in the face, a monster in his trap, snowflakes on her eyelashes: the stuff of dreams. It was all over. He took a deep breath, blew it out.

"Relieved?" said Mr. G. "It's often like that."

"Fuck you," Charlie said, but there wasn't much force behind his curse. He couldn't deny a sense of rough justice being served. If it had happened before Emily he might not have cared so much.

"Did you hear what he said to you, Mr. G?" said Svenson.

"He's just exercising his First Amendment rights," Mr. G replied.

"So how about me exercising my First Amendment right to kick him in the balls?"

"I don't think that will be necessary, will it, Mr. Wrightman?"

Charlie felt their eyes on him. He put his hands on the rail, got his legs under him, pulled himself erect. The movement awoke a pounding in his head. He took a few steps and sat heavily on the padded bench, not far from Mr. G. "I'd like to talk to her before we go," he said. "That's all."

Svenson and Mr. G looked at each other and some unspoken communication passed between them. Mr. G turned to Charlie. "Go?" he said.

"Wherever you're taking me." His mind screened a quick panning shot of his future: holding cell, courtroom, prison.

There was a silence. Charlie was conscious of the paleness of Mr. G's face, the dryness of his lips, the purple smudges under his eyes. He glanced to the east and saw the faint luminescence of tomorrow on the horizon. "Where you go is up to you," Mr. G told him. "More or less."

"What does that mean?"

"It means we've got a surprise for you, you lucky son of a bitch," Svenson said. "We're going to cut you a deal."

"A deal?"

Mr. G's teeth appeared for a moment. It might have been a smile. "Puzzled, aren't you? A deal means an exchange, and what have you got that we want?"

Svenson said, "The surprise is we don't want you."

"We'll *take* you," Mr. G said.

"But only if we have to," Svenson added.

"After all, you deserve it," said Mr. G, "if you want to think in those terms."

"But we don't think in those terms," Svenson said, "and we don't really want you."

There was a pause. The eastern sky was lightening now, as though something had sliced through the black and photons were pouring in. Dawn reddened the hollows of Mr. G's cheeks and illuminated the shades of purple under his eyes. "We want Rebecca," he said.

"Rebecca?" Charlie said.

"Correct," Mr. G replied. "Give me Rebecca and you go free. I mean scot-free. No one will ever know. You can keep your wife, your daughter, your quaint little house, your quaint little job, your identity. You can live out the life of Charlie Ochs, in toto—lobsterman, husband, father. That's alternative one. Alternative two is spending the rest of your life, or most of it, in a federal penitentiary. It's not very complicated."

"Why Rebecca," Charlie said, "and not me?"

"Orders," Mr. G replied. Svenson turned and gave him an odd look.

"Whose orders?"

Mr. G caught the look in Svenson's eyes. Svenson changed their expression. Mr. G turned to Charlie and said, "They never come from below."

"I have no idea where she is," Charlie said. "I haven't seen her in twenty-two years, not since..."

"The big bang?" Svenson said. Under the brightening sky, he looked fresh and cheerful, overfull of life force. Charlie wanted to empty him of some of it. He was trying to think of a way when Mr. G said, "Have you heard from her?"

"No."

"Or of her?"

"No."

"What about Malik?"

"Nothing."

"Was that the plan?"

"There was no plan," Charlie said. "It just happened."

"Sure," said Svenson.

"There was no plan," Charlie repeated, raising his voice. That made his head hurt more. Svenson shifted the rifle in his lap.

"Then you'll simply have to find her," Mr. G said. "Set a fugitive to catch a fugitive."

"If you're so good at gathering information why can't you find her?"

"I've tried," Mr. G said. "My guess is you'll enjoy a smoother entrée into her circle. The long-lost comrade coming in from the cold. That shouldn't be a difficult role to play."

The answer, the first and instant answer that sounded inside Charlie's core, was no. "You want me to betray Rebecca, is that it?"

"I told you," said Svenson to Mr. G. "These sixties types just never grew up."

"I'm not a sixties type," said Charlie.

"Then what are you?" asked Mr. G.

Charlie, caught in a pincer movement between surrounding generations, didn't answer.

Mr. G leaned toward him. The expression in his eyes was complex—intimate, desperate, beyond Charlie's understanding. He spoke softly. "It's not a question of betrayal. It's a question of who you want to be—Blake Wrightman with all his baggage, or Charlie Ochs with all his future."

"He'll take the past, every time," Svenson said. "They're all living in the past, with their touchie-feelie bullshit and their Beatles records."

"Shut up," said Mr. G.

"Sorry."

"Go away."

Svenson moved up to the bow and stared out to sea.

Charlie said: "What if I can't find her?"

"You lose."

"What if she's dead?"

"Dead?" said Mr. G, as though it was a possibility he hadn't considered. "Dead, and you can prove she's dead?" He thought. "That'll be good enough."

"Meaning?"

"You win."

Svenson turned toward them. "I think we've got a deal," he said with surprise. "At least he's agonizing about it."

"Have we got a deal, Charlie?" said Mr. G.

I hope to God she's dead, Charlie thought. *If not, at least I can play for time. Time might change things*, he told himself, and almost believed it.

"Do we?"

Charlie answered. He didn't say "I've got no choice" or "You've got me in a corner" or "What else can I do?"

He said: "Yes."

• • •

The red curve of the sun came edging over the horizon. The cigarette roared away toward the south. There was plenty of light now, more than enough for Charlie to see that the cigarette was without name or number. He switched on his engine and rode *Straight Arrow* home.

Charlie tied up at his dock, then stripped off his clothes and jumped in the pond. The salt water stung the wound on the back of his head. He scrubbed off the vomit and the blood and went up to the house. It was quiet. Charlie opened the door. He dropped his clothes in the washer and went upstairs.

Emily was still sleeping, her head in the crook of her arm, her hip jutting up under the covers. Charlie gazed down at her for a moment, then went into the bathroom and brushed his teeth. The face in the mirror didn't look nearly as tired, beaten, changed, as it should have. He was about to turn on the shower when she called.

"Charlie?"

He stepped out of the bathroom. Emily lay on her back now, wisps of hair in her eyes, her face a little flushed. She smiled at him. Charlie almost had to look away.

"You're up early," she said. "Thinking of hightailing it? With me standing at the altar?"

Charlie made himself laugh.

Emily stretched out her arms to him. "I had the most wonderful dream," she said. He went closer to her, as if drawn by irresistible gravity. Her arms closed around him. "My big oceangoing man," she said.

"Oceangoing?"

"You smell like the sea," Emily replied. "I love it."

8

Her wedding day: a day, Emily told herself, to savor every moment. Not just because she was old-fashioned: in truth, she wasn't really all that old-fashioned. Marriage would be a rock in her life, a fortress, but it would not be everything. She would never give up her work, her independence, her sense of possibility. Not that Charlie would ever want her to.

Charlie. Just when she had started to fear that the laws of probability governing the random movements of male and female populations were not going to let her course intersect with that of the man for her, along had come Charlie, living right down the street. Charlie was special. Solid and reliable, yes—and she might have settled for that alone in five years or so—nothing was more important to her. But he was smart too, and funny, and strong, and musical. All that, and he smelled like the sea as well. And like the sea, he had things going on down deep that fascinated her. To study the sea, she had her instruments, her computer models, her flair for mathematics. To study the depths of Charlie, she had to catch a look in his eye from time to time, or a strange chorus on that silver saxophone. So it was a day to savor, not just because of the wedding, but because of who he was. She was a lucky girl.

But everything went by too fast, and Emily was left with a memory tape of fragments, like a video shot by a bundle of nerves and edited by someone who didn't know the story. Fragments: the shaving nick on the chin of the nondenominational minister that opened every time he dabbed it with his black sleeve; the baby's flutterings inside her, first when Charlie slipped the gold band on her finger, later when her parents got in the taxi; the tears in her mother's eyes, through the window, as it pulled away.

Then she and Charlie were back in the living room of the little house, their house, packing up their new camping equipment. They were going away for a few days of hiking on Long Trail.

"Charlie, these sleeping bags are supposed to zip together."

"Like that?"

"I don't know. It doesn't seem big enough." Emily climbed into the zipped-together bags. "You'd better come in," she said.

"Now?" Charlie said. One of those strange looks surfaced in his eyes.

"For a test. We don't want to end up like Scott of the Antarctic."

"Were double sleeping bags his problem?" Charlie said. The strange look—what was it? anxiety? sadness?—vanished from his eyes. He wriggled into the bag. "Seems big enough."

"Big enough for this kind of activity?"

"Don't."

"Don't? Are you going to go virginal on me now, Charlie? That would be false advertising." Charlie said nothing. Emily undid his belt, reached inside. "Nope," she said after a few moments, "it's all verifiable."

Charlie laughed, and Emily thought, *It's all true, it really is*. She knew a lot of single women, other scientists and lab workers, who had just about given up on men and paid the same obsessive attention to their jobs that sitcom moms paid to their families in the fifties. Now she wasn't going to be one of them. Ahead lay a life balanced and full. She could almost see it.

There was a knock at the door.

Emily felt her husband's erection soften in her hand. She whispered in his ear, "Let's not answer."

Charlie's face was inches from hers. How alert his eyes were! She loved that about him. He opened his mouth as if to speak, then closed it.

There was another knock, more forceful this time.

"Maybe we'd better," Charlie said.

They crawled out of the zipped-together sleeping bags. Charlie fastened his belt. Emily went to the door and opened it.

Outside were two men with gift-wrapped packages in their hands. The older one was bald with yellowish skin. He wore a bow tie and a seersucker suit that looked a size too big. The younger man stood well over six feet and was almost as broad as Charlie. He wore a blue and white striped rugby shirt and white pants with green whales on them. Both men had big smiles on their faces.

"Would this be Charles Ochs's house?" asked the man in the bow tie.

Emily nodded.

The men's smiles got bigger. "Looks like your nephew's done all right for himself," the one with the green whales on his pants said to the other.

"Buzz," the older man told him, "mind your manners." To Emily he said, "Tell Charlie his Uncle Sam is here."

"His uncle? Charlie never mentioned—"

"It's all right, Em," said Charlie, appearing behind her. He looked out. "Hello, Sam."

"Charlie, Charlie, Charlie," said Uncle Sam, extending his hand. It hovered over the threshold long enough for Emily to see it was trembling before Charlie reached out and took it. Uncle Sam pumped Charlie's hand with enthusiasm and gripped Charlie's elbow, southern-politician style. "I can't believe it's really you," he said.

Charlie said, "It's me."

"Of course it's you," said Uncle Sam. "Haven't changed a bit.

Looking great, just great. This is my associate, Buzz. Buzz, I'd like you to meet my nephew Charlie. And unless I miss my guess, this is the brand-new Mrs. Ochs."

"Emily Rice," said Charlie. "She's keeping her name."

"Quite rightly," said Uncle Sam. "My goodness, Charlie, it's been a while. I'll bet you're itching to know how we found you." Uncle Sam's eyes were bright, his face turned up, like a dog with a trick.

Emily glanced at Charlie. He had never mentioned an uncle. In a flat tone, Charlie said: "How did you find me?" Emily decided that this was the sort of uncle relatives hoped to avoid, and almost smiled at Charlie's discomfiture.

"To make a long story short," Uncle Sam began, and set off on a tale involving a friend of a friend who had once done business with a contractor who had done work for De Mello and had been a classmate of one of the lobsterman's wives, who in turn had talked about the plans for the wedding party at a high school reunion, and by the end of it they were all sitting in the living room with drinks in their hands—coffee for Charlie and her, water for Uncle Sam, beer for Buzz.

"So the champagne last night was from you?" Emily said.

"Why, of course," said Uncle Sam. "Didn't you see the note?"

Charlie, she remembered, had quickly stuck it in his pocket. "There was so much going on, I can't even remember," she said, trying to spare Charlie from embarrassment. "But it was delicious, thank you. And you," she said to Buzz, "must be the gorilla."

Buzz smiled. His eyes traveled down and up her body, fast and furtive, but they did it all the same.

"You've got a live one there, Charlie," said Uncle Sam. He sipped his water, looked around the room. "Going on a camping trip?" he asked.

Charlie didn't answer, so Emily said, "Yes."

"Anywhere particular?" asked Uncle Sam.

"Long Trail," Emily replied.

"Beautiful country," said Uncle Sam. "Although it must be forty years."

"Do they allow ATVs up there?" asked Buzz.

"ATVs?" said Uncle Sam.

"All-terrain vehicles," said Buzz.

"Good Lord, I should hope not," said Uncle Sam, and Emily thought: *He seems like a nice old guy. I wish Charlie wouldn't be so rude to him.*

"Too bad," said Buzz. "Nothing like an ATV for really seeing the outdoors."

"Good Lord," said Uncle Sam. "Good—" And then he started coughing. The coughing shook his body, doubled it over. Red gobbets sprayed from his mouth, landed on the trouser leg of Buzz, sitting beside him on the couch; the white trousers with the green whales on them.

"Shit," said Buzz.

Emily bent over Uncle Sam and patted his back. The coughing subsided.

Uncle Sam sat up, took a silk handkerchief from his pocket, wiped his lips. "Sorry," he said, his voice rough and low. "Terrible allergies."

Allergies? Emily thought. Details—yellow skin, scrawny neck, completely hairless skull—came together in her mind. The prognosis was obvious.

"Shit," said Buzz again. He was gazing with disgust at the red stains on his pants.

"I'm sure Charlie has something that will fit you," Emily said. "Throw those in the wash."

Charlie led Buzz upstairs. Emily took Uncle Sam to the bathroom. Before the door closed she saw him open a bottle of pills.

A few minutes later, they were all back in the living room. Buzz wore a pair of Charlie's jeans that didn't quite reach his ankles; Uncle Sam's skin seemed even yellower than before, and his bow tie was crooked, but he was smiling again. He drank some water, peering over the rim of the glass at Charlie, then at Emily. "What a pair of lovebirds," he said. "You're a lucky man, Charlie. I hate to ask you to postpone that camping trip."

Emily saw Charlie frown. "What do you mean?" she asked.

"I've got some news," Uncle Sam replied. "Good news,

possibly very good news. Certainly the kind of news any couple starting out would love to hear."

"Let's have it," Charlie said, again in a flat tone that struck Emily as rude. Did Uncle Sam raise an eyebrow? She wasn't sure; he smiled and continued.

"It's kind of complicated," he said. "It all goes back to Charlie's grandfather's will. Old Ferdie Ochs—a first-class SOB— you'll pardon the expression, Emily. He left a sloppily prepared will, which he neglected to alter even though one of his children—Charlie's dad—predeceased him. Ferdie died a few years ago, and that's when we got an inkling of the mess he'd made of his affairs." He turned to Charlie. "One of our big difficulties was we had no idea where you were." He shook his head. "You've been a bad boy, Charlie. Avoiding your relatives like this." His smile faded for a moment, came to life again. "But that's all in the past. The point is that Ferdie managed to accumulate some choice hunks of real estate, and since your father died intestate, you became one of the major heirs."

"Choice hunks?" said Emily, and wished at once she hadn't. She liked the phrase, that's all.

"Choice," said Uncle Sam. "But because so much time has passed, we've got some hurdles to jump. Charlie has, specifically. There's a move underway—quite understandable, I suppose, since he hasn't been in communication with the family, presumed lost and all—to cut him out of the will." He held up his hand. It was still shaking. "Not to worry," he went on. "Now that Charlie's turned up everything should be fine. The law is on our side, or at least that's what my legal people say. But we have to move quickly. There are statutory time factors involved and other complications I don't quite understand. The lawyers do. I've scheduled a meeting with them for later today." He leaned across the coffee table, took Emily's hand. His was cold and damp. "So I hope you don't mind if we borrow Charlie for a while, my dear."

"Today?"

"I hate doing this," said Uncle Sam.

Buzz leaned forward in his chair. "But," he prompted.

Uncle Sam sighed. "I don't make the schedule."

Emily said, "Couldn't the meeting be postponed for a few days?"

"Naturally I tried that, with the wedding and all," said Uncle Sam. "They're not in a postponing mood."

Emily turned to Charlie. He was staring out the window, didn't seem to realize she was trying to make eye contact. "I guess our trip could wait for a day," she said.

"It might take a few days, actually," Uncle Sam said.

"A few days?"

"This is a complex matter, as I mentioned. But we're talking about substantial sums."

"Why don't I come along, then? I've blocked off the time anyway." Emily turned to Charlie again. He was still staring out the window. "Charlie?"

He faced her. She waited for him to say "Why don't you?" When he did not, she repeated the suggestion herself.

Was it her imagination, or did Charlie wince, as though with a sudden pain in his gut? Her question was answered by Uncle Sam.

"Ticklish," he said.

"Putting it mildly," said Buzz.

"I don't understand." No one explained. "Do you, Charlie?"

"Not really."

"Charlie's not in a position to," said Uncle Sam. "He doesn't know the *dramatis personae*. They're a suspicious bunch. We told them Charlie was single, not wanting to complicate things with possible heirs."

"*Et cetera,*" said Buzz.

"So now if we turned up with a connubial Charlie, they might think we were trying to pull a fast one."

"Bizarre," said Buzz.

"But that's the way they work," said Uncle Sam.

Emily turned again to Charlie: "You never told me about all this family."

Charlie started to say something, but Uncle Sam interrupted. "He's a bad boy. Now aren't you, Charlie? Admit it."

Charlie looked at him. "Do you really think that, Uncle Sam?" Emily heard the sarcasm in his voice, wondered why he didn't treat his uncle more politely. But she knew nothing of his family, nothing of his relationship with Uncle Sam. She did know Charlie, and knew he must have reasons.

"No, no, no," said Uncle Sam. "I don't really think that. Just getting in the old needle. Wasn't I, Buzz?"

Buzz was draining the last of his beer. "What?" he said.

Uncle Sam sighed. Then he rubbed his hands together, as though trying to generate momentum. "Well," he said, "we'd best be going." He rose. Buzz rose. Charlie rose.

And Emily. "Now?" she said.

Uncle Sam took her hand again. His was hot this time, and dry. "We won't keep him long," he told her. "Promise."

It was happening quickly. The whole day had been like that. Everyone moved toward the door. "Charlie, shouldn't you pack something? He said a few days."

"Not to worry," said Uncle Sam. "If it takes that long, Charlie can pick up new things." He chuckled. "A whole wardrobe, if he wants."

But Charlie didn't care about wardrobes; he wasn't materialistic. That was one of the things she liked about him. Now it occurred to her that maybe she was confusing cause and effect; maybe he lived simply not for philosophical reasons, but because of an inability to make money. And now that money was in the offing, he was off, as if he hadn't been living the life of his choice. But that was speculation, supported by nothing; and it wasn't him.

Buzz opened the door and went out. Uncle Sam followed. A black limo was parked across the street, with a driver at the wheel. Buzz got in the back. Uncle Sam waited on the lawn. In the doorway, Emily turned to Charlie. She looked up into Charlie's eyes. He shied away from her gaze, stepped forward, took her in his arms. He squeezed hard.

"I've thought of a name, Charlie."

"For who?"

"The baby. Who else?"

He made a funny movement, almost a shudder.

"Zachary," she said. "If it's a boy."

Charlie squeezed her a little harder.

"Do you like it?"

"Yeah," he said, a little hoarsely, as though something was caught in his throat. "I do."

She squeezed him back. "Don't be too long, Charlie."

"I won't."

They kissed. She felt his lips, his face, the strength of his arms around her. And then he was gone, across the lawn, across the street, and into the back of the limo with his Uncle Sam. They were invisible behind the blackened windows. The limo pulled away from the curb, purred down the street, turned the corner, and disappeared.

Charlie. Her special, perfect man. And now he was rich too. She'd been off base. He was being responsible, she was being sentimental. Honeymoon: a lovely old word that had lost its meaning, like a glyph in some jungle.

Emily went back inside and closed the door. She separated the sleeping bags and was rolling them up when the washer buzzed, signaling the end of the cycle. She went into the laundry cubicle off the kitchen and began transferring wet clothes into the dryer. There were some of her things, some of Charlie's; and the pants with the green whales on them, left behind by Buzz. As she was putting Buzz's pants in the dryer, she felt something in one of the pockets and took it out.

It was an empty envelope, on Yale Alumni Society stationery. The ink had blurred, but the address was still legible:

Mr. B. W. Svenson
227A Charles St.
Boston, Mass. 02114

Emily dropped it in the trash.

9

Nuncio liked being the bearer of good news and always delivered it to his clients on the phone. Bad news he passed on through the mail, to keep things pleasant. Now, at ten-thirty on a morning in May, with the sun glaring through his dusty windows, Nuncio dialed Brucie Wine's number. It rang many times before Brucie answered it, somewhat reducing Nuncio's enthusiasm.

"Yeah?" said Brucie, his voice thick and sleepy. Then came a horrible sound that Nuncio realized was throat clearing. He held the phone away from his ear, as though germs might be speeding through the wire.

"Good news," Nuncio said.

"Huh?" said Brucie. "Are you tryna sell me somethin'?"

"It's me," said Nuncio. "Mr. Nuncio."

"Oh, hi."

"I've got good news."

"What about?"

"Your case," Nuncio said. "They bought it. You're off the hook."

"Meaning?"

Meaning? How, thought Nuncio, had he been unclear? "Meaning they dropped the charges in return for the tip. You can resume normal life." Nuncio then made the mistake of adding, "Or not, as the case may be."

"Huh?"

Nuncio sighed. "You're in the clear, Brucie. Let's leave it at that."

"Whatever you say." Brucie hung up. No thank-you, no good-bye. Nuncio switched on his Dictaphone. Could a client sue his lawyer on the grounds that he had failed to understand that he was no longer under indictment? Probably. Nuncio dictated a letter to Brucie spelling out the good news.

.   •   •

Brucie's arrest had not been, as Brucie thought, a matter of random bad luck, or even, as Nuncio thought, the inevitable result of Brucie's stupidity. The truth was that Brucie had an enemy he knew nothing about.

Brucie's enemy stood just under five two and weighed 103 pounds. Rodolfo Chang had always wanted to be a cop, but he was far too small and so he settled for a job as a field agent for the INS. He had a master's in criminology from San Francisco State, spoke Spanish, Mandarin, and Cantonese, and worked twelve hours a day, seven days a week. What made him so dedicated was the existence of his many cousins, aunts, and uncles, none of whom he had ever met, in Mexico and China. They were always seeking his help in coming to the United States. Rodolfo Chang steered them impartially toward the proper channels, forwarding all necessary documents at his own expense and advising patience. The thought of these desperate and poor cousins, aunts, and uncles, all waiting their turn, made Chang intolerant of those less-patient types he sometimes turned up in dark, improper channels. Chang had little mercy for corner-cutting would-be Americans, and none at all for the bloodsuckers profiteering from them, profiteering bloodsuckers like Brucie Wine.

Not long after Nuncio woke Brucie with the news, Rodolfo Chang's beeper went off. Chang was sitting in a café near the waterfront, drinking his third coffee. He'd been up all night, waiting for a fishing boat packed with Hondurans that hadn't come. He called the office, was put through to a clerk he knew at the D.A.'s.

"Heard about your pal Brucie Wine?"

"He's not my pal," said Chang.

The clerk snickered. "That's why I called. Thought you'd like to know that Brucie walked."

"What are you talking about? He hasn't even gone to court yet."

"And he's not about to. A deal went down, charges dropped."

"What kind of a deal?"

"Hey, don't get mad, Rudy, I just work here. Gotta run." And he hung up before Chang could say, "Don't call me Rudy." He hated being called Rudy.

Rodolfo Chang spent the next two hours at the office, trying to find out about Brucie Wine's deal. All he learned was that word had come down from a level of the Justice Department that, in terms of his own influence or his boss's or his boss's boss's, might as well have been heaven itself. He stalked outside, got into his car, slammed the door and yelled "Shit" and "Fuck" at the top of his lungs. A woman passing by stopped and stared, then walked quickly on. People weren't used to seeing Chinese faces contorted like that. Rodolfo Chang couldn't help it; he looked Chinese, but he had his mother's temperment, extravagant and Latin, the temperment of a much bigger man. He was trapped in a body of the wrong race and size. Chang turned the key, holding it down longer than necessary, making the starter squeal the way he wanted Brucie to squeal, then sped out into traffic without looking and headed for Brucie's shop.

• • •

Brucie's shop was a three-story Victorian that had been in his family for generations but didn't look as though it would survive Brucie's stewardship. Chang parked across the street from the sagging structure and waited. A man wrapped in a blanket went by, pushing a shopping cart loaded with green plastic garbage bags and talking about moonglow in Spanish. Chang knew at once he was a U.S. citizen, although he couldn't have explained how, and didn't give him a second glance. A few minutes later an old car rolled up the street, burning oil, and stopped in front of Brucie's. It was an American-made car, a Chevy, and bore a California license plate, but Chang knew just as quickly and certainly that its occupants were not U.S. citizens. He copied their plate number in his notebook.

In the front of the Chevy sat a man and a woman with a baby on her lap; in back, three or four kids. The woman counted some bills from her purse and gave them to the man. He got out of the car, walked up to Brucie's shop, spent almost a full minute eyeing the sign that read "Wine Printing and Engraving," and knocked on the door. After a while he knocked again, waited some more. He stuck his nose against the glass and peered in. His wife called to him in Spanish: "Louder, you fool. Don't be so timid." The man banged the door, then looked around furtively in case anyone had heard. He saw Chang. Chang pretended to be searching for something in the glove compartment. When he looked up, the man was getting into his car. The engine made a few explosive noises and blue smoke erupted from the exhaust. The Chevy drove off.

Chang stayed where he was. The old car had barely disappeared from view when a black Trans-Am roared up the street and braked to a hard stop. Chang recognized the car. It was the same one the police had pulled over on the Golden Gate Bridge, acting on Chang's tip that there were stolen passports inside. They'd found no passports but had done even better, from the cops' point of view, seizing 192 grand in counterfeit bills. And now, twenty feet away, there was Brucie Wine, free as the goddamned air.

Brucie, shirtless and holding a can of Bud, got out of his car. He had a skinny chest, a pot belly, a graying rat tail hanging down his back. He glanced around as though looking for someone, checked his watch, glanced around again. Then he tilted the Bud to his lips; his Adam's apple bobbed in the sunshine. He tossed the empty can onto the street and whistled.

An ugly dog sprang out of the car. Chang didn't like the look of that dog at all. He reached into his pocket and touched his nine-millimeter pistol. Brucie closed the door with care, locked it, tried the handle to make sure it was locked, and chained the dog to a No Parking sign within striking distance of the car. Chang took his hand from his pocket. He didn't like dogs of any kind, but especially those bigger and stronger than he was.

Brucie checked his watch one more time, then walked to the front door of the house and let himself in. He was gone for a long time. Chang had nothing to do but wonder what was going on inside. After a while he decided to hazard a peek in one of the windows. He crossed the street and had one foot on the sidewalk when he heard a growl. The dog was facing him, chain pulled taut, muscles popping, eyes narrowed, teeth bared. Chang turned and got back in his car.

Not long after, Brucie came outside. He had another Bud in one hand and a stack of blue cards in the other. Social Security cards. Chang knew what they were immediately, the same way he could identify a U.S. citizen from across the street. He toyed with the idea of drawing his gun and busting Brucie on the spot. But what was the point? They'd had more evidence the last time, and it hadn't stuck. Chang sat quietly. This time he would build a case that no one could deal away.

Brucie unchained his dog. Man and dog got into the Trans-Am. Brucie pulled away from the curb, burning rubber like an adolescent. Chang followed. The beer can soon came floating out of Brucie's window, bounced on the pavement and off the bumper of Chang's car. Chang, perched on the phone book he needed to see over the dash, his tiny feet on the blocks attached to the pedals, spoke aloud. "You're dead meat, asshole," he said. He didn't let Brucie out of sight.

10

Buffalo wings, two double cheeseburgers with fries, a sausage burrito, and a sixty-four–ounce pitcher of Bud. Yvonne laid it all in front of the men at the back table. Their eyes swiveled from the game on the big-screen TV and locked on her: various parts of her, that is. It was a lousy job. Yvonne went back to the kitchen and picked up the tray for table two: a Coors and a shot, three drafts, ribs for four. Paco was shaking the grease off a basket of onion rings. He saw her and got that pouting look on his face. Some kind of male contagion was in the air. She'd seen epidemics like this before. "T-shirt fit okay?" Paco said, with a trace of accent, so *fit* sounded like "feet."

Yvonne shrugged. "I guess so." *You leering bastard,* she added to herself. Last week he'd issued them all new T-shirts, black with "Paco's Sports Bar and Restaurant" written in glitter. They fit tight, hers the tightest. Paco was delighted with the effect. Gave the place a little class, he thought. His kind of class was nipples pressing under black cotton. Yvonne didn't care: Paco's grubby bar was just a stage set, and Paco and his customers, speculatively watching the way her body moved under that T-shirt and her jeans, were without importance,

bit-part actors in a play they didn't even know was in perform-
ance. They didn't count. Only Felipe counted.

It was a Wednesday night. Felipe was off at seven, she was
off at eight, and Delores was working four to midnight at the
nursing home in Santa Whatever-it-was. That gave them four
hours, less twenty minutes or so, which was the difference
between Delores's driving time and theirs.

Felipe walked in at five after seven. He was wearing his
uniform—"Armored Trucking Services, Inc.," read the crest on
his shirt—but he'd checked his gun at the garage, a few blocks
away. He looked for her the moment he came through the door.
He had no cool at all. He saw her, grinned like a boy on
Christmas morning, and sat at table three, one of hers. Yvonne
brought him a draft.

"Hi, Carol," he said. He rolled the r—his accent was a little
stronger than Paco's. Yvonne liked the sound and was glad
she'd chosen a name with an r in it. She was Carol to Felipe
and the gang at Paco's, where she worked off the books, but it
wasn't her real name. Neither was Yvonne, if you wanted to be
a stickler about it.

"Hungry?" she said.

He heard deep meanings in the word and answered with
double underlinings. "You wouldn't believe how hawngry."

Yvonne didn't like too much familiarity in the bar and he
knew it. She snapped out her pad. "What'll it be?"

Felipe looked crestfallen. He ran his finger down the menu
and ordered ribs. Felipe was a carnivore. She could smell it
through his skin when she got close enough. "Your nails are
dirty," she said, then returned to the kitchen and put in the
order. *Hawngry tonight.* She almost laughed out loud.

Felipe left a few minutes before eight. Yvonne balanced her
receipts and went out the back door at ten after. Her car was
parked in the alley. It was a blue Tercel. There were thousands
of them. Yvonne wondered whether Felipe had ever even
looked at the license plate. Almost certainly not, but when the
time came, she would take precautions anyway. She got in,
drove into the street and down the block.

Felipe's car was parked at the corner. It was too dark to see
the velour dice hanging from his rearview mirror. Yvonne

flashed her lights. He pulled out ahead of her and she followed him past an auto salvage yard, a tire retreader, then along a fast-food strip and onto the freeway. Felipe was driving fast. Hawngry tonight. Soon—she hoped it was soon—he'd be hawngry forever. She swung into the passing lane and sped under an overpass. Someone had spray-painted "Amerika" on the concrete abutment. She hadn't seen that in a long time. It cheered her up.

Felipe lived in the sprawl down the 880. Yvonne had never bothered to learn the name of the particular town. How could it be a town, with no border and no center? It was just exit 41B to her. She followed Felipe off the ramp and into a neighborhood of boxy houses, low-rise apartment buildings, and dusty lawns with litter on them.

Felipe and Delores had a one-bedroom apartment on the second floor of a crumbling stucco building. There was a single-leafed palm tree out front and an unstable staircase in back. They climbed the staircase, Yvonne behind, because she didn't feel like having her ass patted. Felipe unlocked the door and they went inside. Yvonne breathed in the smell of the Third World, or what she took to be that smell. She hadn't been out of the country for a long time. Felipe closed the door and switched on the light.

The place was a mess: curlers, Mexican magazines, Felipe's barbells, all scattered on the living room floor; dishes in the sink; leftovers on the counter; dust on everything. Felipe didn't seem to notice. He turned, put his arms around her, stuck his tongue into her mouth and began rooting around. He made a groaning sound. "I been dreaming of this," he said. Yvonne knew it was true. She was the stuff his dreams were made on, an Anglo vision that was realized once a week, their three schedules permitting.

Soon—because time was always a factor in their relationship—they were in the bedroom. It was messy too: clothes all over the floor, opened Coke cans on the bedside table, an ashtray full of butts, beds unmade, and Delores's see-through black baby dolls entangled in the sheets. They got undressed and lay on the bed, leaving the baby dolls where they were. Yvonne felt the cheap synthetic material under her thigh.

Delores's bridal photograph stood among the Coke cans. It showed a young, smiling woman, copper colored, black haired, trim. The problem was she didn't look like that anymore, Felipe had said. Now she was fat. Another problem was that she didn't like giving him blow jobs and never had, skinny or fat. Oh, she would do it, all right, but she didn't like it, and that irritated Felipe. He was *muy sensitivo*, he explained.

The funny thing was that he never asked Yvonne to give him a blow job, never even gave her head a subtle little push, which was the kind of thing she would have expected him to do; and so she never did. He liked to lick her instead. That was mostly what their sex life, which was all they shared, was about. Delores blew Felipe, Felipe licked Yvonne. Some sort of class structure was being replicated, Yvonne knew: the entire U.S. immigration policy could probably be portrayed in one pornographic triptych. She smiled at the thought.

Meanwhile Felipe's mouth was sucking and kissing its way down her body. He had a bristly mustache. She liked that. He liked that she liked it, and made an excited sound, deep in his throat. Displays of female desire got him going. That's what he meant by *muy sensitivo*. But she was being unfair. He was quite good, really, not as good as Annie had been, technically at least, but much more enthusiastic.

He took his time, made her come, moaning to her in Spanish, then kissed his way back up and penetrated her. She didn't mind his body, big and flexible, if a little soft. She smelled his carnivore smell, so different from Annie's, who was a strict vegetarian. He didn't take long; he never did.

Felipe rolled off her, checked his watch.

"What time is it?"

"We got lotsa time."

"But what time is it?"

He looked at the watch again. Could he have forgotten the time that quickly? Yvonne wondered. Felipe wasn't very bright: that was a bonus.

"Ten-fifteen," he said. "Lotsa time." He stroked her arm, brushed her breast with the back of his hand. His eyes were wide and liquid. "I wish you could talk Spanish," he said.

"Why?"

"Because then I could tell you how beautiful you are. I cannot say in English."

"That's sweet, Felipe," Yvonne said. He beamed. It really was sweet, and she wished he hadn't said it. It made her job harder; but changed nothing.

He reached for a Coke can, shook it, drank, offered some to her.

"Not just now."

He drained the rest and tossed the can on the floor. "How is your work?" he asked.

"The same," she said. He wasn't asking about her work. He was asking about Paco. Paco worried him. That was funny. Felipe was under the impression that she was married to a data processor with a nice future and a nice apartment, and that didn't bother him at all. But the thought of Paco as a rival was a continual source of anxiety.

Felipe dropped the subject. He wasn't naturally inquisitive, and that was another bonus. He never asked about her data processing husband, for example. Yvonne had a name all picked out for him, but she didn't have to use it. Felipe didn't know where she lived, let alone where she would have told him she lived had he asked. He knew nothing of her background, her friends, her family. All he knew was that a few months before he'd gone into Paco's after work and noticed a new waitress. Over the next few weeks she'd served him a few times, been reserved at first, then more friendly. After a while he had worked up the nerve to ask her out and she'd surprised him by accepting. Now this.

"Want some weed?" Felipe said.

"Not tonight," Yvonne said. It was a long drive home and she was tired. "Go ahead, if you want."

Felipe shook his head. Declining to get stoned without her was a form of gallantry, she knew. She suspected that Delores no longer saw this side of him, if she ever had.

Their minds might have been running parallel courses, but on different planes, one high, one low, both homing on Delores. "I got a surprise for you," he said. He stuck a tape in the VCR and pressed buttons. The big TV at the end of the bed glowed to life. After a few seconds of noise, a bed appeared on the screen: the bed they were on. "I got a deal on a camcorder," Felipe said. He was whispering, as though they were in a theater full of people. "Fits right in the palm of your hand."

A copper-colored woman appeared in the frame. She wore see-through black baby doll pajamas. It was Delores. She was older than in the wedding picture. She must have been thirty or so, about ten years younger than Yvonne, but she wasn't in the kind of shape Yvonne was. Felipe was right. His wife had put on weight since the photograph. Still, it was ungenerous to call her fat, Yvonne thought. More like plump.

Delores glanced furtively at the camera, looked away. She said something in Spanish. She didn't sound happy. From off-camera came the voice of Felipe, also in Spanish. He sounded encouraging. Delores stuck her hand under her top and rubbed her breast. The picture jiggled on the screen. Felipe's hand appeared. He gave her tequila. She drank from the bottle, glanced at the camera again, had another drink. Now she didn't look so shy.

Felipe gave her some instructions. Soon she was lying on the bed and the baby dolls were off. Marijuana appeared. Delores inhaled it. Her hips squirmed of their own volition. The motion made her flesh jiggle, but not unpleasantly, Yvonne thought. Now when Delores looked at the camera it was brazen. She exposed herself to it. The focus blurred. When it cleared, Delores's eyes were glazed and Felipe was no longer issuing instructions.

In the here and now, Felipe turned Yvonne on her side so they could both see the screen and slid inside her again. *This is quite good*, thought Yvonne. *We're all so simple, really, so corrupt. To each according to his sexual needs, from each according to his sexual abilities. The hormonal manifesto.*

After, Felipe's voice was husky. "I'd love to use that camera on you," he said in her ear.

"Won't that be something to look forward to?" Yvonne replied, sitting up.

"*¿Qué?*"

He didn't get it, neither the text nor the irony. "In the future," she explained.

"Next Wednesday?"

"If you play your cards right. We'll see."

Felipe frowned. She supposed he'd stumbled on the phrase, but it wasn't that. "Wednesday no good," he said.

"Why not?"

"I have overtime. Down at the docks."

"The docks?"

"The bank ships cash to Japan."

"I don't understand."

"Bank of America. We take it to the warehouse. They put it on a boat to Japan."

"U.S. cash?"

"I think."

Yvonne zipped up her jeans, casual, careful not to look at him. "Why would they do that?"

Felipe shrugged. "In the bank in Mexico they have U.S. cash. So why not Japan?"

"Why not, indeed?"

"Huh?" he said. He must have decided she needed help understanding world economic issues. "Japan is a lot richer than Mexico, Carol. Last time it was fifteen, twenty minutes to unload. Many, many bags."

Yvonne laced her sneakers. Her hands didn't shake at all. "I've got a friend who lives near there, Felipe."

"Near where?"

"The docks. She's in the Jack London condos." Yvonne looked up at him then, to make sure he was paying attention. "A friend who'll let me have her place for the night," she went on, breaking the information into little bits. "For when you're through down there. I could pick you up. We could spend the whole night together. You could tell Delores it was for work. That has the advantage of being partly true."

Felipe missed the last bit, but he got the gist. "The whole night?"

"I'll just need to know where you're making this delivery. So I can pick you up."

"Is Nippon-American Import Export," Felipe said, not even pausing to think about it. "But is better we meet at the condo, okay?"

"Okay," Yvonne said. "And Felipe," she added as she finished dressing, "bring that new camera of yours."

"You mean it?"

Yvonne smiled and went out the door without saying another word. She'd laid it on thick enough already.

She got into her car and yawned. She had a long drive ahead of her. As she stuck the keys in the ignition, a car turned onto the block. Yvonne ducked down as its headlights approached. The car parked on the other side of the street. Its motor sputtered a few times and went quiet. A woman in a white nurse's outfit got out, locked the door, and crossed the street, passing right in front of Yvonne's bumper. It was Delores. She walked tiredly across the lawn, past the dying palm tree, around the back to the stairs. Yvonne imagined Felipe brushing his teeth, showering, making the bed. Or maybe he didn't bother. She turned the key and drove away.

•   •   •

It was after two by the time Yvonne got home. Many leaves hung from the palm tree in her yard, all healthy. She had better air than Felipe and Delores and a cleaner street. She also had a two-story house, modest but her own. Not fair, although exchanging domiciles with Felipe and Delores wasn't the answer. Power must be grabbed. Her job was to show them how to grab it, not this particular Felipe and Delores but all the Felipes and Deloreses.

Yvonne went inside. A modest house in her terms, but not inexpensive, and beyond the means of most people, including anyone who had lived the marginal life she had for the past twenty years. Yvonne had occupied the house for much of that time, and that was all it was to her—a building to occupy.

But the gang liked to meet there; it was more pleasant than any of their places. The members of the gang had in common comfortless homes, as well as an inclination to resistance and burning bridges and a disinclination to compromise and going back. Other than that, there was only difference.

The gang—they called themselves the Committee of the American Resistance, but to Yvonne they were the gang—was

76

waiting in the basement. They had a smell tonight, and it had spread through the house, a convincingly proletarian mix of cigarette smoke and melted cheese. The gang:

Eli—the youngest, who'd spent a year at Reed and now worked in a cannery. He had a girlfriend, somewhat older. She was in Leavenworth; jailed for life, like the rest of the Santa Clara Five.

Angel—who came from a rich family in Mexico City but thought that Cuba was the last best hope of mankind. He'd been the lookout during the Santa Clara Five misadventure and had slipped away unnoticed.

Gus—who looked like a retired wrestler and had been on the pro circuit during the fifties. He'd also been an infantryman in Korea, a longshoreman, a union organizer, a volunteer in Nicaragua. He had planned the Santa Clara action.

And Annie.

They were eating pizza and watching a movie on TV; a young Marlon Brando was bleeding heavily. They looked up as Yvonne came down the stairs.

"Bingo," she said.

"Bingo?"

Yvonne told them what they needed to know.

"It's going to involve preparation," Gus said.

"Then prepare."

"Shouldn't we discuss our purpose first?" asked Eli.

"You can if you want," Yvonne said. "I'm going to bed."

• • •

She slept, then woke, lying in the darkness. Someone was in the room, someone who moved lightly on little feet.

"Annie?"

"I didn't feel like driving all the way home," Annie said; she tired easily, like a victim in a Wilkie Collins story. Annie got into the bed, but didn't touch her. "What happened?" she asked.

"I said what happened."

"I mean the rest of it."

"It's not important."

"It is to me."

Yvonne told her about Delores, videotape, baby dolls. She didn't want to be interrogated all night.

"Why someone like him," Annie said, "and not me?"

"It was for a reason. Do you think I enjoyed it?"

"I don't know. Did you?"

Yvonne didn't answer. They fell silent. The silence went on and on. The two women lay where they were, each on her own side of the bed. After a long time there was a little rustle under the covers, and Annie's hand touched Yvonne's thigh.

"Forget it," Yvonne said.

The hand withdrew, and a minute or two later so did Annie, out of bed, out of the bedroom, out of the house. Maybe she was crying, maybe she wasn't; Yvonne couldn't tell, didn't care. That part of their life was long over. What was a condition of Annie's sexual being had been only an experiment for Yvonne, a failed one. The cause lived on, uniting them.

But just before she fell asleep, it came to her for the first time that something bitter might be growing inside Annie, bitter and possibly dangerous. She would think about it in the morning.

PART II

11

Mom drove. Ollie, friend of the family, sat beside her. Blake, leaving home, slept in the back. He missed the frontier between urban and rural, missed the climb into green hills and the gradual transition to wooded tranquillity. He awoke in time to see the valley lying below, with the stone campanile of the college chapel rising from its heart; also in time to catch sight of Ollie's hand between Mom's legs.

In the rearview mirror Mom's eyes shifted, saw her son up and alert. Some silent communication passed from her to Ollie, perhaps through a change in body heat; Ollie's hand slid away, and he said, "Scenery or what?" He twisted around and smiled at Blake. "Four years of this to look forward to. You're a lucky young man." And he was a lucky young man, except that Dad's company was roaming around the jungle west of someplace that had been censored from his last letter, and he wouldn't be home till spring. Ollie shook his head at the wonder of Blake's prospects. He smelled of some cologne with a manly name.

Mom parked the wagon among all the other wagons in front of the freshman dorm, and she and Ollie helped Blake carry his stuff up to his room. Blake and Ollie handled the trunk; Mom took the baseball bag, with his bats, glove, cleats.

"How nice," said Mom, examining everything when they were inside.

It was nice: a bright room with two desks overlooking the quad, and two small bedrooms off the other side. The slightly larger of the two small bedrooms was already occupied by a mom-dad-son combination. The mom was making the bed; the dad was smoking a cigar; the son was saying: "Maybe I should have applied to Harvard, huh?"

"You wouldn't have gotten in," said his dad. A cylinder of cigar ash fell to the floor.

Blake took the other bedroom. "Let's get you unpacked," said Mom.

"That's all right," Blake told her. "I'll do it later." She didn't argue.

"Well," said Ollie, sticking out his hand, "I'll say good-bye. Good-bye and good luck."

Blake forced himself to shake hands. Ollie went out, leaving him alone with his mother. She looked up at him, bit her lip. "Your father . . ." she began.

"Yes?"

There was some more lip biting. Then she said: "He would have loved to be here now."

"Yeah."

Mom's eyes filled, but nothing spilled over. She leaned forward for a kiss. Blake forced himself to do that too. "I love you," she said, her voice breaking.

Like you love Dad? he thought, but didn't say it. Mom left. Blake found himself thinking of *Hamlet*, which he had studied in his last year of high school. Suddenly he understood it a lot better.

Blake went out into the common room, where the other freshman, pale and bony, had taken possession of the desk that was slightly closer to the window. He had opened a new box of pencils and was sharpening them one by one. "Parents," he said. "Gotta love 'em." He looked up, peering through the smudged lenses of his granny glasses. "Stu Levine," he said. "Guess we're roommates."

REVOLUTION #9

The roommates talked. They talked about where they came from, what courses they were taking, what music they liked. Stu Levine didn't mention his SAT scores—760, math; 720, verbal—until at least five and possibly ten minutes had elapsed. Blake's SATs were good but not that good. He kept them to himself.

Not long after, the baseball coach came in and welcomed Blake to the school. He invited him to drop in at the field house anytime.

"You're a jock, huh?" said Stu Levine after the coach left, not looking happy about it. "Far out." He slotted Blake in that category for a week or two, until late one night he heard him playing his saxophone. Then he knocked on the door of Blake's bedroom, said "Far out" again, and offered him half a tab.

"Made it myself," he said, not without pride.

"You made it yourself?"

"In the lab, last spring. It's not hard."

Blake had never dropped acid before, but refusing would have been awkward, like turning down someone's homemade peanut butter cookies. He put the tiny offering on his tongue, swallowed it, and played the saxophone nonstop till noon the next day. Then he laughed for a while, laid down and tried to close his eyes. They wouldn't stay closed. From somewhere in the room, Stu Levine said, "Two weeks and I'm already hopelessly behind in all my courses. Hopelessly hopelessly hopelessly. Fucked fucked fucked. Do you get my meaning?"

"You're not optimistic."

Stu Levine started laughing. It turned to crying. He cried for a long time. Blake felt uncomfortable. "Hey now," he said.

"I hate it here," said Stu Levine. "My father's the biggest asshole you could imagine."

"Mine's a captain in the airborne," Blake said.

Stu Levine stopped crying. "You mean like killing Vietnamese?"

Blake looked at his roommate, sitting on the floor, half-behind the dresser. Light glinted off Stu Levine's glasses, forming silver facets edged in blue; they grew and shrank in crystal shapes. Blake watched the pulsating crystals until they turned red.

Stu Levine cleared his throat. It sounded like a backfiring

truck. "No offense, huh?" he said. "Like about the Vietnamese?" Stu left the room without further conversation. That was the end of their only real bull session. The light show lingered in Stu's absence.

·   ·   ·

"What's the point of this expedition?" said Svenson. "I don't get it."

"The horse knows the way," Mr. G replied.

Svenson sighed. He'd been disputing Charlie's choice of destination for the past forty or fifty miles, ever since the flat tire. Charlie, sitting in the middle of the backseat, glanced at Svenson. His lips were everted in a pout, absurd and girlish, and hard to reconcile with the relish for violence he'd demonstrated on the cigarette boat hours before. Svenson was in a bad mood. Perhaps it was the air-conditioning, Charlie thought, which was producing nothing but noise, or the fact that he'd had to help the driver change the tire and now had grease stains on his rugby shirt and on the borrowed jeans.

"Some limo," Svenson said, confirming Charlie's guess.

"Get used to it," Mr. G told him.

"What's that supposed to mean?"

"This is the limousine of the American future," Mr. G answered.

"Huh?"

Mr. G did not elaborate.

The limo of the American future swayed on its heavy suspension as it climbed into hills that Charlie had not seen in twenty-two years. Had anything changed? Not that Charlie could see—all around lay nature green and undegraded. The difference was one of perspective. Twenty-two years ago these hills had been scenery, the backdrop of college life. Now Charlie was aware of their enduring power, and wondered at the way that he and Rebecca and Malik and so many others had behaved like giants in what they took to be a stage set built just for them.

"Tripping down Memory Lane?" asked Svenson.

Charlie ignored him. The limo topped the last rise and

dipped down toward the valley. The first thing Charlie saw was the stone campanile of the chapel. *Bong, bong, bong, bong.* Four peals of the brass bell, and the fifth that never came. Tripping down Memory Lane was a crude way to put it, but not untrue. Charlie was moving back in space and time, all the way back to the Big Bang. Hadn't the universe begun with an explosion, and hadn't its character been determined by the nature of that explosion? Most people couldn't trace themselves back to a personal Big Bang, but Charlie Ochs could. *Bong, bong, bong, bong*—the sinful start of his own universe. With memory, as with a powerful telescope, you could see all the way back to the beginning, but you couldn't do anything about it.

"I believe he's waxing nostalgic," said Svenson.

Charlie turned to Mr. G. Mr. G's eyes were closed and his face shiny with sweat. "Don't you ever get bored with him?" Charlie asked.

Mr. G opened his eyes, turned them on Charlie and said: "You don't seem sufficiently impressed with Buzz."

"Mad bombers are hard to impress," Charlie said.

Silence. Charlie felt their gazes on him. Then Mr. G decided he'd made a joke, and laughed. It was a harsh, dry laugh that threatened to turn to coughing and blood at any moment. Mr. G cut it off before it could.

"What's so funny?" asked Svenson.

The temperature rose as they descended into the valley. In the backseat Charlie, Mr. G, and Svenson grew clammy together. "How about opening the windows?" Svenson said.

"No breeze," Mr. G answered quickly. The windows stayed closed.

Outside, the town rolled by like a mural: wooden houses, the new ones with decks and hot tubs; the businesses of College Street, Campus Cleaners, 99 Cent Cinema, Catamount Bar and Grille, For the Love of Books; the campus itself, buildings of stone, brick, and wood, none topping the tallest trees, all harmonized by time and clever architects. Again it seemed to Charlie that nothing had changed. This Rip van Winkle effect was reinforced by the absence of people on the streets, a complete absence, making it more like a ghost town than a college town the week after finals. Then a young woman flashed by on a mountain bike, sweat staining her jersey, head tilted up to drink from a water bottle on the fly. She broke the spell, and with it the conceit that nothing had changed. Women like that hadn't been around twenty years ago; they'd still been in the development stage. Charlie thought of Emily, at the top of some evolutionary tree. How had he begun his little speech on the pond? *I'm a lucky guy.*

The limo entered a long leafy drive and stopped at the end. "This all right?" asked Mr. G.

Charlie looked out. He saw a simple white building with the words "Morgan College Admissions Office" on the door. He didn't remember it; hadn't the admissions office been more imposing? "Yeah," said Charlie.

Svenson opened the door and got out. Mr. G turned to Charlie and showed him a card with a phone number on it. "Memorize this," he said. It was an 800 number ending in 1212, easy to remember. "Just call when you're ready," Mr. G said. "Twenty-four hours a day." He handed Charlie an envelope. "Expenses." He put a hand on Charlie's knee. A bony hand, and trembling. He looked into Charlie's eyes. "Be smart," he said. It wasn't a warning or a command; much more like a plea. Charlie drew away, slid across the seat, climbed out of the car. Svenson was gazing at the scenery.

"Hicksville," he said.

Charlie walked toward the admissions office. "She's not going to be dead," Svenson called after him. "It won't be that easy."

Charlie turned. Svenson was leaning back against the car, his big hands splayed on the roof. "Do you know that for a fact?" Charlie said.

Svenson smiled. "It's all a conspiracy, right?" he said. "You guys love conspiracies." Charlie didn't answer. Svenson raised his voice. "I don't know it for a fact, but I do know how your luck's running. She's alive."

Charlie walked away. He heard Svenson slam the door, saw the limo go by, turn, and drive down the lane. He could make out nothing through the blackened windows. Mr. G and Svenson might have been exchanging high fives, they might have had their hands around each other's throats. The limo turned the corner at the end of the lane, flickered through a line of trees, and disappeared.

Charlie walked around the admissions office, through the yard behind it, and onto the crushed-brick path that crossed the campus. The crunching beneath his feet, and especially the crushed-brick smell, awoke long-dormant memories. His mind bubbled with them: the glittering eyes of the freshman dorm janitor; the high, almost female voice of a fat umpire; dry pork chops with watery apple sauce on Tuesdays. He could have named every member of his class.

It was hot, and silent in a muffled way, silent except for the crunching of crushed brick. Charlie walked all the way to the rear edge of the campus, where the field house stood on a rise overlooking the football and soccer practice fields, the baseball diamond, and beyond them the apple groves that stretched all the way to the mountains. He continued down the rise, across the fields to the diamond. It was in good shape, the mound high and roundly sloped, the infield dirt smooth and reddened with the same crushed brick that was spread on the path, the outfield grass thick and even, if a little long now that the season was over. Charlie, walking into deep center field, had a sudden impulse, the kind of impulse he would have never given into before twenty-six across and Ben Webster. But now he thought, *What the hell,* and took off his shoes and socks and stood barefoot in the perfect grass.

• • •

The ball sketched a long white arc across the sky before gravity pulled it down sharply and it fell ten feet short of the fence.

"Top hand, Blake, top hand," said the coach from behind the batting cage, not yelling or even calling. His tone was conversational.

By that time Blake Wrightman had played ball for a lot of coaches. This was one of the better ones. Blake scooped up some dirt, rubbed his palms with it, gripped the bat, took his stance. He was still releasing his right hand too early in the swing, a habit that had passed unnoticed through Little League and high school and probably had something to do with getting a longer look at the ball, but it cost him power and was being noticed now. Blake, eyes on the ball in the batting pitcher's hand as he went into his motion, didn't think, *What the hell's he talking about? I'm still leading the team in batting and RBIs.* He just thought, *Keep that hand on the bat.* The problem was he'd been thinking that for weeks and it wasn't helping. Thinking it and making your hand do it were two different things. All at once it occurred to him to pretend his right hand was the only one he had. *It's up to you, hand,* he thought as the pitcher's hip swung, his shoulder turned, his arm whipped forward and the ball was on its way, starting up high and coming down, seams whistling in the air, down, maybe just out of the strike zone—but Blake stepped into it, maybe a shade late, and caught it square; a low liner that a second baseman might have stabbed, had there been a second baseman, but there wasn't and the ball seemed to gain speed, seemed even to be starting to rise, before banging off the fence in right center. *See, hand?*

Blake sent the next pitch over the fence in dead center, and the next four in a row disappeared in left, the last one landing thirty or forty feet past the fence, somewhere in the rugby practice. That one Blake hadn't felt at all; the equal and opposite reaction had passed unnoticed through his body, like a grounded electrical charge. He'd never hit a ball that far before. He allowed himself to wonder: *How good could I get?*

Somewhere behind him the coach said, "More like it. Laps." Still conversational.

Blake ran three laps around the field, ran on feet so light he felt like pure energy, as though his timing was suddenly in tune with the big forces. They were playing for the division championship the next day. I'm ready, he thought, and trotted down into the dugout, toward the water cooler. It was a moment before he grew aware of the strange quiet. After practice was usually a boisterous time, but the team was silent, silent and all looking at him. Had he really hit that well, so well he'd stunned them into silence? Blake tried to think of something to say. Before he could, he saw the two men in uniform—not baseball, but military—standing at the end of the bench. They looked at him with grave faces. It hit Blake almost at once.

"No," he said, feeling absurdly strong and helpless, hands hanging at his sides. No. But he came from a military family, and he knew from the sight of these men that it was yes. The rest—the quiet words about firefights, heroism, recommendations for this medal or that, the condolences, hackneyed in form although there was real sorrow behind them, however briefly felt—was as nothing beside that awful yes.

"Does my mother know?" Blake asked.

"We haven't been able to reach her yet."

The army found Mrs. Wrightman that night. She'd gone to Freeport for a couple of days with Ollie.

Blake's team played for the division championship the next day. Blake started in center field. It wasn't that he felt like playing, but neither did he not feel like playing. He felt nothing—or so much that it had the same effect as feeling nothing. He pulled on his uniform—red pinstripes, red stirrups, red cap: almost clownish, he thought—and ran out to his position to start the first.

The opposing team had the best pitcher in the state. Big league scouts came to his games and stood behind the cage, motionless except for the chewing of their jaws. The pitcher was a tall right-hander with a good fastball and a great curve, the best Blake had ever seen, hard and tight. It started from behind a right-hand batter's left ear, the way curve balls did, but kept coming, kept coming, until you flinched, or froze, or even bailed out, but at least felt fear, before it snapped down and over the plate. The fastball set up the curve, like the straight man in a comedy team. The curve delivered the punch line. The big righty struck out the side with it through the first four innings, getting Blake looking in the first and swinging in the fourth.

Blake came up again in the seventh. "Sit on the curve," he told himself, "just sit on it." But all he saw were fastballs, the first two for called strikes, then a ball inside, then two fouls, then another ball, and another. Three and two. Blake stepped out, tapped his cleats, dug in. *Top hand, it's up to you.* The pitcher wound up and brought it. Straight at his left ear. Blake

89

waited and waited as it came and came, finally picked up the spin, and just as it started to break he turned on it. This time the force did not pass unnoticed through his body: it vibrated through his bones—up his arms, down the spine, all the way to his feet. He had waited long enough, but barely. The ball shot into the blue sky in left, hooking nastily, and was still hooking as it ducked over the fence and out of sight, fair by three or four feet. Blake circled the bases. The scouts behind the cage watched him all the way. The crowd, not very big, made noise. The score was tied, one all.

It was still one all when Blake batted again with two out and a man on second in the bottom of the ninth. The big righty was throwing as hard as he had in the first, and had given up nothing but an infield single, a walk, and Blake's home run. Blake's team was working on its fourth pitcher and had been in trouble almost every inning. They were running out of chances. "This would be a good time," said the coach, still conversational, as Blake left the dugout.

Blake dug in. He'd been watching the pitcher from the dugout, learned something of how smart he was, baseball smart, as well as physically skilled: too smart to start with the heater this time. The pitcher looked in for the sign, eyes narrow, then went into his stretch, rocked back and kicked. Blake cocked his bat and waited for the hook.

It came, sharply defined and pure white against the background of the green center field fence, came high and hard at his left ear. Blake waited, waited to pick up the telltale spin, waited for that wicked, big-league break. And in that split second he saw, peripherally and far away, the flag, the stars and stripes, flying on the pole in center. And in that split second, when he should have been seeing that the ball had backspin instead of topspin, that it was a heater high and in and not a curve, in that split second when he should have been bailing out, Blake Wrightman thought of his father. Then came a sound that everyone in the park heard but him, and unconsciousness.

12

Shoes and socks back on, Charlie sat in front of a micro-film viewer in the periodical room of the main library. He had the place to himself; nothing moved except the dust motes drifting through the sunbeams and the microfilm blurring across the screen. Charlie scrolled through May 1969 issues of the *Campus Record* until he came to one with a photograph of a falling ballplayer on the front page. The captain read: "Star frosh center fielder Blake Wrightman hit by a pitched ball in yester-day's loss to the Greenmen." In the picture, taken from the first base side, the batter's knees were buckling, and the impact of the ball had turned him halfway around, so his number—nine—was visible. With the severe contrapposto of the figure, the arm flung up, too late, in self-defense, the bat flying out of the top frame, it was a dramatic composition, if not in perfect focus.

The universe started with a Big Bang, but there had been this little bang before it. One triggering the other, Charlie thought suddenly, the way an A-bomb is used to trigger an H-bomb. Had his subconscious self always understood the relationship of the two events? Maybe; and now the knowledge was rising to the surface. In the still, silent room Charlie's vision grew almost intolerably sharp, sharp and clinical. He had no memory of the moment recorded on film, as though it had happened to someone else. He stared at the dots on the newsprint that shaped the face of the someone else, and thought he saw deep inside him.

Three days in the infirmary, head wrapped in bandages: the patient cheerful, relaxed, even funny, the way hospitalized people can be when there is nothing seriously wrong with them and the right painkillers are at hand. The editor of the *Record* sent a writer for a follow-up interview; the photographer who had taken the picture went with him. During the interview the patient was more cheerful, relaxed, funny than ever. Perhaps it was because of the photographer. She had wild black hair, alert brown eyes, flawless skin, even white teeth—a strange, only-in-America combination of both the healthful and the Bohemian ideals.

"Who won?" the patient asked her.

"Won what?" said Rebecca Klein.

The reporter asked a few questions, and the photographer shot a few pictures. They left, the patient slept. He awoke that night, momentarily disoriented, to find the photographer sitting by the bed. She looked down at him. "You saw the picture?" she asked.

"Picture?"

"My picture. Of you."

"Yeah."

Pause. The patient gazed into those dark eyes and saw signs of powerful thoughts and emotions. He was far too young to know what they were.

"Did it . . . ?"

"What?"

"Make you feel used."

"Used?"

"Exploited."

The patient shook his head. That hurt, so he stopped. "It happened, didn't it? It was my own fault."

"It was?" The photographer's eyes narrowed; the intensity of her expression, an expression he would see again and come to think of as her Torquemada face, discouraged him from full explanation.

"I took my eye off the ball," he said.

"Oh," she said, an "oh" that among other things told him she had no interest in baseball. He watched her face relax. She saw him watching and smiled, a wonderful smile that seemed to radiate happiness through the room—a rare smile, he would come to know, seen only when she emerged completely from those thoughts and emotions he had sensed. "I was worried you might be upset about the picture," she said.

"That's why you came here?"

"Partly."

"And the other part?"

She didn't answer.

"You're a ball fan?"

Rebecca laughed.

Overnight, over that night, Blake Wrightman lost interest in baseball. He never played another game, never had another at-bat. Would it have happened without Rebecca Klein? Would it have happened in 1959 or 1989? Or was it all because of the beaning: did Blake Wrightman, secretly knowing he would never be able to stand in at the plate again, take the first life-changing opportunity that came along? These were questions that Blake never asked himself. They were only now rising up into Charlie's conscious mind, stirred by the sight of his long-ago self frozen in a fall.

•   •   •

Blake's bed, Stu Levine's bed, and all the beds Blake had seen on campus, were identical: simple primer-painted steel frames with wire springs and thin mattresses. Rebecca's bed, in her room on the top floor of Cullen House, a neo-Georgian residence for sophomore women, was different: she had brought her childhood bed from home. It was an antique, dating from the reign of some Roman-numbered Louis or other, and had handcarved posts, a headboard with painted putti, a silk canopy, a plump feather mattress. It left room for almost nothing else but the posters on the walls. The posters: Marx, Engels, Che Guevara,

Rosa Luxemburg, La Pasionaria, Mao, Malcolm X, Ho Chi Minh,
General Giap. Late that spring, the spring of his beaning, lying
like a potentate in all that softness for the first time, with
Rebecca's head on his shoulder, Blake asked, "Who's that?"

"You don't know Malcolm X?"

"The guy with him."

Shaking hands with Malcolm X was a smiling white man with
wild graying hair and glasses pushed up on his broad forehead.

"That," said Rebecca, "is Daddy."

"He knows Malcolm X?"

"Daddy knows everybody. Everybody on the left." Blake
examined the poster. He noticed that Malcolm X looked irritated about something, and that while Rebecca's father was
smiling, his smile was directed at someone outside the picture.
He turned to find Rebecca watching him. "You never talk about
your father," she said.

"No?"

The narrow-eyed expression appeared on her face. "No."

"Don't look at me like that."

"Like what?"

"Like you're doing now—trying to see right through me."

"I'm not."

"You are." He rolled on top of her, looked into the dark eyes.
"There," he said, "have a field day."

"That's my plan," she told him, reaching out to switch off the
light. "Bodies like yours aren't found in my circles."

"What circles are those?" Blake asked. But by that time
Rebecca was busy with something else.

•   •   •

Charlie rewound the microfilm and brought it to the desk.
"Is there a list of alumni?" he said.

The librarian looked up from the book she was reading. "The
Alumni Directory, do you mean?" She was young, probably a
student with a summer job in the library, except that Charlie
didn't remember students reading books like *How to Make a
Bear Market Work for You*. He nodded. "This year's won't be
ready till September," she said.

"Last year's will do."

Charlie sat at a desk looking through last year's *Alumni Directory*. The listings, alphabetical, included each alumnus's class, home address, and profession. There were thousands of them, but none for Rebecca Klein or Andrew Malik, as Charlie had expected; otherwise, Mr. G would have no need of him. He had expected an entry between Ricardo Levin, '74, eco-planner from Colorado Springs, and Amy Lewis, '88, analyst at Morgan Stanley, but there was nothing there, either; nothing where Stuart Levine should have been.

Charlie looked up. The librarian was watching him. Why? Had she somehow recognized his face? He had the unlikely thought that he might be the subject of a history paper she'd written on campus unrest, or at least a footnote.

"Need some help?" she asked.

He tapped the directory. "What if someone isn't in here?"

"Then they're on the lost list. Or dead. You'd have to call the Alumni Office to find out which." She picked up a phone and started dialing. "What's the name?"

"Stuart Levine."

The librarian lowered the phone. "Undergraduates aren't in the book either, of course."

"I don't understand."

"They're not alumni, by definition. Like Stu Levine. He's in my class."

Charlie had heard of adults returning to college after long absences, but he couldn't see the Stu Levine he had known in that role. "How old is he?"

"I don't know. Nineteen or twenty. My age."

"Then he's not the one," Charlie said, closing the directory.

The librarian was watching him again. "Stu is a Junior, though, I think." Charlie rose and moved toward the door. "I don't mean a junior, like in freshman, sophomore, although he is one," the librarian continued. She waited for Charlie to respond, but she had lost him. "I mean Junior like in Stuart Levine, Jr.," she said. "Maybe he's the son of the one you want." Charlie stopped and turned to her. "And the thing is you can talk to him if you want. He's got some assignments to finish."

"In the lab?" Charlie said.

"How did you know that?"

The science building was new, and in the context of its red brick and white clapboard neighbors, aggressively so. It might have been designed by architects hoping to land fat contracts when the time came for the colonization of Mars. The lobby had black floors, black walls, a hanging silver globe, and a black leather sign-in book at the unattended modular desk. The last entry, written in an uneven, spiky hand, read "Levine, Rm. 310." Charlie looked for stairs, found none, and rode the elevator to the third floor.

The door to room 310 was closed. Charlie was about to knock when he heard a crashing sound inside, followed by a cry, almost a wail, of "Shit, shit, shit." He opened the door.

There were half a dozen big chemistry desks inside, equipped with sinks, burners, retorts, test tube racks. A skinny young man stood at one of them, staring down at a pool of yellow ooze spreading across the floor. It began to smoke.

"Stuart Levine?" Charlie said.

The young man, a boy really, pale and bony, looked up, squinting at Charlie through the fingerprint-smeared lenses of his glasses. "Geez," he said, "I'm booked in here till three, and it's only . . ." He checked his watch. "Oh, God. I'm hopelessly . . ." For a moment, Charlie, shocked by the resemblance, couldn't say a word. This was Stu Levine, his Stu Levine—Bombo—and twenty-two years hadn't passed and none of it had happened. Except for the Martian building he was standing in, that is, and the pain deep under his sternum where Svenson's rifle butt had struck, he might have almost believed it.

Charlie said, "It's OK. I don't need the lab."

Stuart Levine, Jr., nodded, but might not have absorbed the information. He was distracted by the yellow pool at his feet. It was hissing.

"What is that stuff?" Charlie asked, coming closer.

"This and that," said Stuart Levine, Jr., and Charlie wondered whether there was a gene that programmed helplessness.

"Hadn't we better get it cleaned up?"

"I guess so," said Stuart Levine, Jr. But he didn't move. Perhaps he wouldn't until the liquid dissolved the floor and he fell through.

Charlie opened a closet, found mop, pail, detergent. He filled the pail with water and approached the spill. Remembering rules for dealing with this sort of thing, he said: "Is it acid?"

"Partly," said Stuart Levine, Jr.

Charlie withheld the water, returned to the closet. In the end he scooped the liquid up with steel dustpans and dumped it into a container marked "Toxic Waste." All that remained was a blackened circle on the floor. Stuart Levine, Jr., rubbed at it with the sole of his sneaker but it wouldn't go away.

The top of the desk was a clutter of test tubes filled with different-colored liquids and solids. Two centrifuges spun at the center, and a colorless liquid in a large retort heated over a bunsen burner. "What's this all about?" Charlie asked.

"Oh, ions and stuff," said Stuart Levine, Jr., waving his arm over the desk in a dismissive way. His hand brushed a beaker, which overturned, dumping its contents in the sink. "Christ," he said, quickly placing the plastic cover over the sink. He glanced at Charlie to see if he had noticed this latest accident. Charlie pretended he hadn't. Stuart Levine, Jr., now taking him in for the first time, said, "Uh, thanks for helping with the . . ." He waved his hand in another loose gesture, this time without consequences.

"You're welcome," Charlie said.

"Thanks." Stuart Levine, Jr., out of conversation, at the mercy of events, shifted from foot to foot.

Charlie said: "How's your father?"

Stuart Levine, Jr., squinted up at him through the smudged glasses. "You know my father?"

Charlie thought: *How easy to be a wolf at a place like this, among innocents like Junior.* He said: "I knew him at one time."

"Yeah? When, like?"

"A while back."

"Before SLI?"

"SLI?"

"Stuart Levine Industries," said Junior, looking surprised.

"Right. Before."

"At MIT?"

Charlie couldn't imagine his Stu, Bombo, at MIT. "After," he said. He waited for Junior to ask him when after or who he was or what he was doing here. Instead, the boy stared down at the whirling centrifuges, sighed, and said: "He's going public."

"Stu?"

The son nodded. "Nasdaq," he said. "It's all set. We're going to be rich. Richer." He didn't look happy about it.

"You don't look happy about it."

"I don't?" the boy said, as though it were a revelation. He gazed up at Charlie. His expression changed. *Here come the questions,* Charlie thought, and got ready to trot out the imperfect cover story he'd prepared.

He never had to use it. The next moment there was a tremendous boom, and the plastic sink covers from every desk shot into the air, one or two striking the ceiling, followed by gaudily toned geysers of detritus from the plumbing system.

Junior looked around wildly. He began to shake. It wasn't a figure of speech. "Did I do that?" he said. He was his father's— Bombo's—son; especially if it's true that history is farce the second time around.

• • •

Charlie stood outside Cullen House. It was a rambling structure of brick and stone, sporting columns, a frieze, and other architectural flourishes he didn't know the names of. An industrial-size vacuum cleaner sat on the threshold. The door was open. Charlie went in.

The smell hit him right away, not strong but complex and unique: buffered floor wax and must, ammonia and rot, frying grease and stale beer: the smell of Cullen House when the sun warmed its old wooden bones. The smell hadn't changed at all. Charlie walked past a sign that read "Backhand Clinic—3:30" and started up the broad stairs.

• • •

Rebecca Klein lived at the east end of the hall on the top floor of Cullen House. Strictly speaking, no men were allowed in the women's rooms after eight on weekdays or eleven on weekends, and it was the job of the senior adviser, who lived in a big and strategically placed room at the top of the first floor, to enforce the rules. But by the time Blake met Rebecca there were couples living openly in Cullen House, and the door to the SA's room was always closed, nothing ever emerging but the smell of marijuana.

Blake and Rebecca were one of those couples. Blake ate in the dining room, used the bathroom in the hall, slept in the fairy-tale bed, lay talking for hours in that bed, made love in it. That room, unnumbered, at the east end of the hall on the top floor of Cullen House, with its posters and its bed, was his world during the spring of his freshman year and most of his second, and last, year. There he entered an intimacy he had never known, changing from a boy who kept things to himself to a man who told his secrets, at least to Rebecca. He told her about his mother, about Ollie, and finally about his father in the jungle west of some place with a blacked-out name.

And Rebecca, lying beside him in the bed, with a joint in her hand and Joni Mitchell playing quietly on the stereo, said: "You must be outraged."

"Outraged?"

"About your father."

"Because of Ollie, you mean?"

"No," said Rebecca. "Because he got killed."

"Outraged at who?" Blake asked.

"At the government, of course," she replied, sending some outrage his way. "At Nixon, at Kissinger, at the whole fucking establishment that runs this country. Who do you think killed him?"

From the walls around the fairy-tale bed, Marx, Engels, Che, Rosa, La Pasionaria, Mao, Malcolm, Ho, General Giap, and Rebecca's father all looked on. Everything began to make sense. The political world, a world he had never thought much about, was turning inside out. And as it did, it revealed its ugliness, and he awoke to the idea that there was an enemy to blame for his father's death and all the other deaths, an enemy right here at home, up on top—and to be toppled.

Rebecca was watching him closely. "I want you to meet Andy Malik," she said.

"Who's he?"

"A friend of mine."

"What kind of friend?"

"A very smart one." Rebecca rolled on top of him, rubbing her body against his. Blake lost himself there in her soft bed.

• • •

Charlie knocked on the unnumbered door at the east end of the hall on the top floor of Cullen House. No one answered. He turned the knob and went inside.

The room was vacant. It had a simple, steel-framed bed with a bare mattress on top, a simple wooden dresser, a simple wooden desk. The walls were bare. It was devoid of resonance, atmosphere, magic: nothing, just an empty student bedroom in the summer vacation. But more than all those absences, what impressed Charlie was its size. The room was tiny, insignificant, claustrophobic. He closed the door and went away.

The library was still open, the young librarian still at her desk. This time she gave Charlie a big smile. "Success?" she asked.

It took him a moment to realize what she was talking about, a moment for her smile to begin to fade. "Yes, thanks," he said. *You've got to be quicker,* he told himself, *quicker and smarter.*

A minute later, Charlie had a business directory in his hands. A few seconds after that he was looking at what he wanted:

Stuart Levine Industries
100 Levine Industrial Parkway
Lexington, Mass. 02173

The librarian still had her eyes on him as he walked toward the door. He looked at her, wondering again if she had recognized his face, trying to read her mind. He got ready to run.

She smiled. "I'm off at five," she said. "If you want to go for coffee or something."

13

What I'm saying," said Andrew Malik, "is that power tends to corrupt, and absolute power corrupts absolutely. Not," he added after a pause, "my own. Lord Acton."

The members of the Tom Paine Club, all of whom fit comfortably in Malik's one-bedroom apartment, laughed. Malik, sitting in the only chair, stroked his black Zapata mustache and allowed his eyes to twinkle. He scanned the faces of the members of the Tom Paine Club, gathered on the floor around him, and the twinkling stopped, the way ripples in water flatten when the breeze dies down. "On the other hand," he went on, "life without power is a form of death."

Malik paused again. During that pause, Stu Levine, who came to the meetings with Blake and Rebecca in hope that involvement in the club might lead to getting laid, spoke up: "Is that one Lord Acting's too?

Andrew Malik had a look for moments like that—head tilted back, forehead creased, half squinting—a look he now turned on Stu. "That one," he said, "is mine."

"A form of death," said Stu, nodding and reddening at the same time, the way he did in retreat. "Wow."

It was December of Blake's sophomore year. Outside Malik's apartment—only graduate students were allowed to live off campus—snow fell heavily from the night sky. Blake gazed out the window, not really listening as Malik went on about untruth, injustice, the American way. He didn't need Malik anymore. In the past few months he had torn up his draft card and mailed the pieces to the Selective Service, marched on Washington once, occupied the campus ROTC office twice, and tried to close down the nearby air force base three times. He'd seen Rebecca dragged off by her hair and arrested, and been whacked across the shoulders with a nightstick for trying to stop it. He'd seen murderous hatred in the eyes of cops and bystanders, seen those poisonous emotions that Nixon and Kissinger and the others tried to hide from the cameras, but still seeped from the screen with every broadcast. Blake didn't need Malik anymore. He was radicalized; a true believer.

The meeting ended around midnight. The members of the Tom Paine Club went out into the night and walked back to their residences, silent in the snow. Blake and Rebecca were the last to leave. As they went out, Malik said, "Don't go just yet."

They turned to him. He stood before his bookcase, a sagging floor-to-ceiling structure of bricks and boards. He was tall and thin, with a narrow, fleshless face and a stooped carriage; without the mustache, it would have been easy to imagine him in robe and cowl. He regarded them from across the room, nodded as though he'd come to a decision, then gestured for them to follow. He led them down the short corridor to the bathroom, where he closed the door and turned on the tap in the sink.

"What's going on?" Blake said.

Rebecca was more in tune. "You think you're being bugged?" She seemed excited by the idea.

"Would the government that has no compunction about dropping napalm on innocents balk at planting microphones in my humble abode?" Malik asked.

"But is there any evidence?" Blake said.

"Evidence?"

"Evidence that they're doing it."

Malik gave him the look he'd given Stu. "Evidence, Number Nine?" he said. At times, at this sort of time, he called Blake by his baseball number. "How about strange noises on my phone line? Clicks, echoes, voices. Is that the kind of evidence you mean?" He waited for a reply. Blake said nothing. Even as late as a month or two ago, he might have mentioned hearing similar sounds from time to time on many telephones; now he was finding it easier to believe in conspiracies.

Malik closed the cover on the toilet, sat down. Rebecca and Blake shared the edge of the bathtub. "I'm not satisfied with the club," Malik said.

Rebecca leaned toward him. "What do you mean?"

"It's fine for what it is—a tool for raising consciousness. But useless when it comes to action."

"Why?" Rebecca asked.

"Because it's an officially sanctioned club of the college, with a known membership and a public profile. What we need is a club within the club."

The temperature and humidity were rising, as though the little bathroom had a microclimate of its own. "What for?" Blake asked.

"Action," Malik replied. "Didn't I say that already?" Twisting around, he raised the lid of the toilet's water cabinet and removed an envelope that was taped to the inside. He handed it to Rebecca. She opened it, removed some papers, and held them so Blake could see too.

There were four xeroxed pages in the envelope, covered with densely packed handwriting in German, a language Blake didn't read. But there were diagrams too, and he understood what they were about and why Malik kept the papers where he did.

Malik reached behind him, flushed the toilet. When he spoke, his voice was low; Blake could hardly hear him over the noise of the flushing and the water running in the sink. "I understand your friend Levine is a technical wiz," he said.

"You do?" Blake answered.

Malik ignored him. He lowered his voice a little more. "Do you think the two of you could build something like that?"

"I doubt it," Blake answered. "And I wouldn't even if I could."

Malik nodded and smoothed his mustache. He was in his last year of a master's program in political science, perhaps five years older than Blake, although it seemed like much more than that to Blake, and probably to Malik too. "That's up to you," Malik said. "You're that best judge of the maturity of your commitment." He glanced at Rebecca.

"Maturity?" said Blake.

"I'm talking about political maturity," Malik replied. "Political power, as you know, grows out of the barrel of a gun. That doesn't mean you have to shoot anyone with it. It's enough to show that you've got it and will use it. No one has to get hurt, or anything like that. We just want to make a symbolic statement."

"Who's we?"

Malik looked at Rebecca again. She put her hand on Blake's, gave it a squeeze. "Just listen to him."

"Why?"

"I want you to," Rebecca said, and rubbed the back of his hand.

Blake listened. Malik talked. Rebecca murmured sounds of assent. Water ran in the sink; the toilet was flushed a few more times; the temperature and humidity kept rising.

"I won't do it," Blake said at the end.

Rebecca took her hand away. Malik smiled. "Revolution," he said, "number-nine style."

"What's that supposed to mean?" Blake said.

"Like the Beatles song," Malik explained. "The one that makes a lot of noise and ends up going nowhere." He got off the toilet, shut off the tap, left the room. Rebecca followed him. Blake walked back to Cullen House by himself, got into the fairy-tale bed. He spent the rest of the night alone, and moved back in with Stuart Levine the next morning. Rebecca didn't speak to him again until May.

•　•　•

There was nothing to keep Charlie on campus any longer. He knew the next step. But his feet refused to take it. Instead, when he left the library, he turned not toward town and the bus station, but back across the central quad, past the chapel with its stone campanile, stopping before a white house with black shutters. The sign over the double doors read "Ecostudies Center." The sign hadn't always been there. Neither had the house always been white with black shutters. Once it had been cream with brown shutters and had had a simple single door with a different sign over it. Charlie noticed other changes. There were more windows in the front now, and additions had been built along both sides. He might have been seeing it for the first time, an ordinary building, without resonance, like the bare bedroom in Cullen House. Then the chapel bell began to ring.

Bong, bong, bong, bong, bong. Very loud and very near. Charlie, standing in the heat of the summer sun, went cold. Five o'clock. Of course. *I'm off at five.* That's all it was. Just five o'clock. Charlie realized that right away, but it didn't stop him from vomiting on the well-trimmed lawn. There was no warning, no nausea; just a sudden heaving from deep inside. *If you want to make a symbolic statement,* he thought, twenty-two years too late, *make it on paper.* Hardly aware of his movements, he wheeled around and was on his way, away from that ordinary house, the chapel, the central quad, the campus. He tried to keep himself to a walking pace and almost did.

·   ·   ·

Blake dropped out of the Tom Paine Club, but Stuart Levine did not. With Cassell's *German-English Dictionary* and Berlitz's *German for Travelers* at his elbow, Stu built the bomb during the week before Christmas break. He did it in his room, using speaker wire from his stereo, his Big Ben bedside alarm clock, two D-type batteries, and the contents of a brown bag from the hardware store, the sort of brown bag that would hold a couple of peanut butter sandwiches and an apple.

He opened the back of the clock to show Blake. "You set the alarm for the time you want," he said. "When it rings this little doohickey moves like so, touching the red wire and closing the circuit. Then the current travels up to the charge and—kaboom. Physics one-oh-one."

"Where's the charge?"

"That's not my department, said Willy the Worker."

Stu's fingers toyed with his long, stringy hair. He'd been dropping acid two or three times a week and living on Ritz crackers and cream soda. He had pimples and indigestion, needed mouthwash and a shower, but his eyes were wide open and speedy things were going on inside him.

Blake examined the device on Stu's desk. It didn't look like much—a joke, really, just as dangerous now as it would be if ever connected to explosives. Stu wrapped it in Santa Claus paper and put it under a pile of laundry in the back of his bedroom closet.

A few days later everyone left on Christmas break. Blake took a bus back to Mom and Ollie; Rebecca went with her father to St. Kitts; Andrew Malik went to a meeting in Chicago. Stu went home to Long Island. He stayed there barely twenty-four hours before his parents, disturbed by his appearance and behavior, drove him to a private sanitarium in Connecticut. The chief psychiatrist admitted him at once. Stuart Levine never returned to Morgan College.

The next month, Stu's father wrote Blake a letter asking him to box Stuart's things and send them COD. He enclosed fifty dollars. Blake packed Stuart's books, his stereo, his records, his Erector set, his framed Escher prints. He cushioned anything fragile with the button-downs Stu had arrived with and the tie-dyes he'd acquired, and crammed the laundry from the floor of Stu's closet on top. That's when he found that the Santa Claus package was gone. But what could he do? "Dear Mr. Levine: When you see Bombo could you ask him what happened to the Christmas present?" Maybe he should have; he sent back the fifty dollars instead.

Blake saw Rebecca twice that winter, the first time at Flicks, the only movie house in town, where *Don't Look Back* was paired with *Look Back in Anger*. She was sitting a few rows behind him. He turned more than once to look at her, but she seemed not to see him and was gone long before the end of the first feature. That night Blake decided to transfer to another school. He applied to several the next day.

Blake saw Rebecca again one morning on his way to class. He was crossing the central quad when she came running in his direction. He'd never seen her run before: he was surprised at her speed, and the power and compactness of her stride. In moments she had reached him; she flew by without seeing him. There was no pretense this time: she really hadn't seen him. He turned and watched her run into the parking lot at the foot of the quad. A car door opened and a man got out, holding a bunch of red roses. Rebecca threw her arms around him. The man was facing Blake, saw Blake watching, smiled with pride. Blake recognized him from the poster: Rebecca's father.

On the morning of May 1, the day most of the world learned of the invasion of Cambodia, Blake was sitting at Stuart's old desk, to which he had moved because of its better view, trying to write a paper on the role of apparitions in *Cymbeline* but mostly listening to news reports on the radio. *Incursion* was the word they were using. The word sickened him as much as the act itself; what a giveaway it was, revealing the shame behind all the democratic pieties.

The door opened and Rebecca came in, red eyed. She stood there silently, listening with him. Blake remained in his chair, looking out the window. After a while she crossed the room, leaned over the back of his chair, rested her chin on the top of his head; like faces on a totem pole.

"Help me," she said.

"Help you?" He turned.

Rebecca started to cry. "I never want to be without you again." It was the first and only time he saw her cry. The sight was unbearable. He took her in his arms.

They were in Blake's bed, his steel-framed college-issue bed, a few minutes later. They made love, fell asleep, awoke, made love. Blake forgot about apparitions and *Cymbeline*, forgot about transferring to another school. He couldn't forget about Cambodia: from the other room voices on the radio kept repeating the news. Blake and Rebecca lay in each other's arms and heard. But Blake wasn't really listening. He was feeling that strange, almost masochistic sensation of turmoil and peace that comes when young lovers make up. The bloody news provided background accompaniment.

She said: "Will you help me?"

"What do you mean?"

"There's a problem."

Blake sat up, looked at her, failed to read on her face an expression of the feelings he was feeling. "What kind of problem?"

Rebecca bit her lip, lip so full, teeth so white. "The bomb," she said.

"What bomb?"

But there was only one bomb. Rebecca had taken it from the closet. Malik had supplied dynamite. They had planted it near the ROTC building last night, after the first reports came in from Cambodia. Malik had set it to go off at 4:00 A.M., when no one would be around, but it hadn't gone off at 4:00 A.M., hadn't gone off at all.

"So what do you want me to do?" Blake asked, although he already knew.

"We can't just leave it there. It could be found, or it might..."

"And Malik?"

Her face twisted with contempt. "He's afraid."

Blake got out of bed, reached for his clothes. "Don't," Rebecca said.

"Don't what?"

"Don't be angry."

"Why should I be angry?" Blake tugged on his jeans. "You should have just come right out with it. Then you might not have had to fuck me first."

Rebecca jerked in the bed, as though he'd struck her.

"Don't worry," Blake said. "I'll do it. But not for you."

Rebecca got out of bed, her breasts white and swaying. Her lips quivered, as though she were about to cry again, but she did not. All at once she looked small, even physically weak.

"You're wrong about me," she said. "This has made everything clear."

Blake paused. "Like what?"

"Like you and me." She touched his arm. He held her.

Blake got the bomb that night. Malik had placed it under an

overturned flowerpot in the bushes by the entrance to the ROTC building. Blake picked it up, unhooked the wires at the back of the Big Ben alarm clock, carried back the pieces, and had the pleasure of handing them to Malik. He wasn't afraid. He knew Stu Levine.

•   •   •

Buzz Svenson opened the door of the Ecostudies Center and stepped outside. Charlie was about a hundred yards away, walking across the quad. Svenson moved out onto the grass, glanced down at the pool of vomit, already soaking into the earth, and followed.

14

Four days after the invasion of Cambodia. A rainy afternoon.

Blake lay in the fairy-tale bed on the third floor of Cullen House, propped up against the pillows. *An Introduction to Developmental Economics* lay open at his side, but he wasn't reading it. He was listening to Ben Webster on Rebecca's new headphones, the first headphones he'd ever worn. Blake, who had just discovered Ben Webster, was trying to picture the old man's fingering. Rebecca slept beside him.

The door opened with a bang Blake didn't hear. Malik hurried in and started talking fast, although nothing he said penetrated the sound of Ben Webster. Then Rebecca sat up and began talking too. Blake took off the headphones.

Malik brought news. More bad news, not from faraway Cambodia this time, but from much closer: Kent State. The government, invading Cambodia, had expanded the war all the way into the American homeland.

"We can't just lie down and take this," Malik said, his voice high and rising. "We've got to do something."

"Shut down the campus?" Rebecca said.

Malik's lips turned down, as though he'd tasted a sudden mouthful of bitterness. "That's already happening in other places," he said. "But here at Smug U? Forget it."

"Then what?" Rebecca asked.

"You know what," Malik replied. His eyes shifted toward Blake. Then Rebecca was looking at him too. From the headphones on the blanket came the sound of Ben Webster, now tiny and affectless.

"Please," Rebecca said to him.

Blake turned to her—her wild hair, her lips half-open, her eyes clouded with emotion. His mind was clouded with emotion too; inchoate thoughts about why they wanted his help so badly went uncompleted. "All right," he said. Simple as that.

"You will?" said Malik.

Maybe they saw him as a test case; maybe the conversion of this one real person to violence persuaded them that a real revolution was possible. "I will," Blake said.

Rebecca put her arms around him, her breasts popping up above the covers. Malik smiled, took off his army surplus knapsack, and laid it on the bed. Still smiling, he went out, closing the door after him.

Not long after, Blake, wearing the knapsack—like any student's knapsack that might have held books and pencils and a snack—walked across the rainy campus to his old room, now unoccupied most of the time. He sat down at Stu's old desk and searched through the bottom drawer. Crumpled at the back he found the four xeroxed pages.

Blake smoothed them out. "Red Army Faction Manual," Stu had written at the top. He had squeezed the translation into the margins. Stu had also doodled a series of masked and mustached faces along the bottom, like a gallery of Zorros. Blake read the translation three times, then undid the brass buckles of the knapsack, took out all the parts and the single stick of dynamite, and rebuilt Stu's bomb. He followed the directions precisely, discovering along the way the point where Stu had failed to adhere to his own translation. Blake followed every step; and then added one more. When everything was done, he cut off two inches of electrical tape, trimmed it, and wound the tape all around the red wire, covering it completely.

The alarm bell would still ring at whatever time was set, causing Stu's little doohickey to touch the red wire. But now no electricity would flow. No juice, no boom. Blake closed the back of the Big Ben bedside alarm clock, screwed it shut, taped the stick of dynamite to it, and returned the whole to the khaki knapsack.

He was happy. Ben Webster started playing in his head. The music mixed inseparably with the recalled sensation of Rebecca's body. Blake slung the knapsack over his shoulder and walked back to Cullen House. Night had fallen. The rain had stopped, leaving the the air soft and smelling of flowers. *It's enough to show that you've got it and will use it.*

•   •   •

The bus was crowded and hot, almost as uncomfortable as the limo of the American future. Next to Charlie sat a young woman dressed in black. She was pale, had dark circles under her eyes, wore her hair in a fifties-style crewcut; made him think of Joan of Arc on her way to the stake. After a while, the young woman took out a book: *The Art of Odilon Redon*. She opened it and began reading, highlighting some passages with a yellow marker. Charlie had never heard of Odilon Redon. He glanced at the glossy plates of his paintings, looked more closely. The pictures, obviously full of buried meanings he knew nothing about, were hard to turn away from, yet they called up nameless fears. What was this one? A pink horse hovering over a blue-skinned sleeping woman, possibly pregnant. The young woman highlighted: "The objective correlatives, that is, the pictorial components that the eye perceives, are like the tip of the iceberg in Redon's symbolic structure." She reread the passage several times before adding a yellow question mark and closing the book. Her eyes closed too.

If you want to make a symbolic statement, make it on paper. The thought had not come twenty-two years too late after all. Had he not built a symbolic bomb, a paper tiger: a symbol to be interpreted not by the world, but by the other bombers? All at once, time collapsed and Charlie felt an affinity with Blake, his younger self, felt sympathy for Blake, felt the unexpected presence of Blake inside him; felt whole. The feeling filled him with unease.

The fact is that Charlie Ochs is a fantasy. He doesn't exist. Night fell. Headlight beams shone through the rear windows of the bus. It rolled east on the turnpike.

• • •

Blake walked into Rebecca's room, the knapsack over his shoulder. Rebecca and Malik had their backs to him; Malik was on the phone, Rebecca watching, her face intent, as though it was she who heard the other end of the conversation.

"Tonight," Malik said: "Don't worry—I'll be there." He handed the phone to Rebecca.

"Hi," she said. She listened. "No one will know," she said. "Ever." She listened again, said, "I love you too—bye, Daddy," and hung up. She and Malik turned as one, saw Blake. They looked surprised.

"Back so soon?" Malik said.

"It's done," Blake told him, aware, probably because it was all playacting now, of how melodramatic he sounded.

"Beautiful," Malik said.

And he, Malik carefully set the alarm for 4:30 A.M. "No one's around then," he said. "It'll be safe."

"Safe as houses," said Blake. They stared at him and didn't laugh. On the walls, Marx, Engels, General Giap, and the others looked on.

"The question is," Malik said, "who's going to, like, put it there?"

"Me," said Blake at once, not wanting anyone else to handle it and perhaps peek inside. He felt Rebecca's admiring gaze; knew without having to look the radiance on her face; marveled at its range, from this supernova all the way across the spectrum to Torquemada. "I'll do it."

Blake left Cullen House by the back door just after one. The night was still soft, still smelled of flowers. There had been a moon before, but now it had set and the campus was dark. Blake made his way quickly to the central quad, past the chapel, to the cream-colored building with the brown shutters,

113

black in the night, where the sign on the door read "ROTC." Like neighborhood kids, college students know every inch of their physical territory.

Blake glanced around, saw no one. A few lights shone in some of the residences along the quad, but the chapel and the ROTC building were dark. Blake heard music—something from *The White Album*, but the name of the song escaped him at the moment—and glanced around once more, again seeing no one. Perhaps he might have looked more carefully, but for what? After all, he wasn't a criminal and he wasn't about to perform a criminal act.

He moved closer to the building, a three-story house of the kind that might shelter a comfortable family. Wooden steps led up to what had once been a porch but was now walled in. The flowerpot still lay upside down in the bushes, but Blake rejected that idea immediately. He didn't want anyone to come upon his little package before he could retrieve it.

Blake knelt in the grass, felt the dew on his knees. He examined the steps. Their sides were faced with cheap plywood. There was a hole in the ground beneath the lowest board on one side, as though some animal had been going in and out. Blake stuck his hand in, grasped the bottom of the board, pulled. One end, the end nearer the house, came loose. Holding it out, Blake pushed the knapsack through and crawled into the space under the stairs.

He pulled the board closed behind him and waited for his eyes to adjust to the darkness. Maybe they did, but he still couldn't see anything. He smelled dampness and animal feces. A bug, perhaps a spider, ran quickly across the back of his neck. Blake moved toward the base of the house. He knew he was there when his head bumped something hard.

He stretched out his hand, through cobwebs, and felt around. The house was built on pilings, disguised by a breakaway front. He touched a cement-block support, felt the opening beside it, and above the opening, little more than a foot above, the cement foundation. Dragging the knapsack, he squirmed around the piling and into the space under the ROTC building. It was quiet. Blake heard nothing but his own breathing, and between breaths, the Big Ben bedside clock ticking in the backpack.

REVOLUTION #9

There wasn't room to crawl. Blake made his way under the house on his belly, like a soldier advancing under enemy fire. After ten or twenty feet, his free hand encountered something hard and rough. He explored its surface: it was a cement block. He felt others around it, lying loose, perhaps forgotten there by workers. He patted down a shallow depression in the earth, dry here under the center of the house, and laid the knapsack in it. Then he dragged three cement blocks over it—two on the bottom, one on top, like a pyramid—and backed out, all the way to the space under the steps. He paused there for a moment, listening and hearing nothing, then pushed open the loose end of the plywood board and crawled out. He picked himself up, pushed the board back in place, and walked back to Cullen House. The bell in the campanile rang twice as he went by.

Blake entered the lobby of Cullen House. A girl in a man's button-down shirt was sleeping in a leather club chair, a telephone in her lap, her head tilted sideways, mouth sagged open. Blake went quietly up the stairs.

A bar of light leaked out from under the door of the SA's room on the first floor, and with it the smell of burning cannabis. From somewhere in the house came once more the sound of *The White Album*, as though it were pervasive on campus, a feature of the local climate, like one of those winds that have a name. It was the same song he had heard before, and now he remembered its name: "Cry Baby Cry." The one that came before the long experimental song, the song that Malik had said went nowhere.

Blake reached the third floor, walked to the east end of the hall, opened the unnumbered door. It was dark inside. He switched on the light. No one was there.

Blake saw himself in the mirror. His clothes were dirty, his face unhappy. He got a towel, walked down the hall to the bathroom, showered, and looked in the mirror again. Now he was clean, but the expression on his face hadn't changed. Blake climbed into bed. He lay there for a while, heard the bell ring three, fell asleep. He dreamed of baseball.

Blake slept, but not deeply. When the door opened, he awoke at once. He heard Rebecca whisper, "You're wrong," and Malik answer, "Am I?"

Blake said: "Wrong about what?"

The light went on. Blake sat up, blinking. Rebecca and Malik stood side by side in the doorway; she held a red rose. Their eyes were dark and wide, as though they'd dropped acid, but Blake knew that couldn't be. Drugs were bourgeois and counterrevolutionary. The world had to be seen as it was, in all its ugliness, before there could be any change.

"You're a cool one," Malik said to him.

"Cool?"

"Sleeping like a baby. Did you do it?"

"Yeah," Blake said, trying not to look so cool.

"Where?" Rebecca said.

"Where?"

"This isn't a game," Malik said, coming forward. "Wake up. Where'd you put the goddamned thing?" Blake had never heard him speak like that before. He was often sarcastic, often unpleasant, but never coarse. It angered Blake for some reason.

He got out of bed, naked, and by far the physically strongest person in the room. Malik backed up, half a step, but he backed up. Blake started pulling on clothes. "I planted it on the altar in the chapel," he said, hearing his own voice, now sarcastic and unpleasant too, almost like a stranger's. "Where do you think I put it? By the door of the ROTC, like we planned."

"Where exactly?"

"In the bushes by the stairs." Blake studied them for a moment. "Where've you two been?"

Rebecca and Malik glanced at each other. "We went for a walk," Rebecca answered. "I'm too wired to sleep."

"We discussed the statement," Malik said.

"What statement?"

"The statement I'm calling the press with after the . . . after." Malik took an envelope from his pocket. The back of it was covered in writing; Blake thought of the Gettysburg Address. This was different: "We, the People's Revolutionary Faction, claim responsibility for this brave and necessary act of protest. U.S. out of Cambodia, out of Laos, out of Vietnam. Smash imperialism. Stop the killing. Stop the war. Now."

"I don't like that 'Now,' " Rebecca said. "It doesn't read well."

"It doesn't?" Malik said. He scratched it out.

Then their dark, wired eyes were on him again. "People's Revolutionary Faction?" Blake said.

"We need a name of some—" Rebecca began, but Malik interrupted:

"Can you come up with something better?"

Big Ben's Bombers, Blake thought, and might have said it aloud, but at that moment the bell in the campanile rang four. At the end of the fourth ring there was silence in the room. Blake noticed grass stains on the knees of Rebecca's jeans. And Malik's. "You checked up on me."

They didn't reply.

"That wasn't smart," Blake said. "What if you were seen?"

"We weren't," Malik said.

Silence. Malik and Rebecca checked their watches at the same moment. Then she moved away from him, moving closer to Blake.

"You didn't trust me," he said; he had an irresistible urge to keep playacting.

"He wasn't sure you'd do it," she explained. She turned to Malik and spoke to him in a tone Blake had never heard her use on him before, cold and without deference. "But now he knows he was wrong."

Malik looked at her, looked at Blake, smoothed his mustache. "I owe you an apology," he told Blake.

"Forget it," Blake said, and felt laughter rising inside him, the giddy laughter of someone with a good secret. He swallowed it with difficulty. Surely they noticed this mirth, he thought. But they didn't. They were checking their watches again.

"Christ, it's hot," Malik said. He opened a window, gazed out in the direction of the central quad, hidden by a line of oaks. "I could use a drink."

"I think there's some rum," Rebecca said.

"Rum?"

"I brought it back from St. Kitts."

Malik frowned. Vacations in St. Kitts were bourgeois and counterrevolutionary, and he didn't want to be reminded of hers; but he didn't stop Rebecca from opening a drawer in her desk and fishing out a bottle of Mount Gay, still in its gift package. She unscrewed the cap on the bottle. Malik switched off the light.

They sat on the floor, Blake, Rebecca, Malik. There were no glasses. They drank from the bottle, passing it around in the dark. Blake felt the night coming in through the window, soft and smelling of flowers. He filled his lungs with the sweetness of the night and imagined himself with Rebecca in St. Kitts. He'd never been to St. Kitts, or anywhere really, but he pictured a white beach, a moonlit swim, silver tips on black waves. Eating strange fat tropical fruit, lying in the surf, making love under a whirling fan: heaven.

"Four twenty-eight," Malik whispered.

Blake felt Rebecca's hand on his thigh. She squeezed, with enough force to hurt. Rebecca and Malik were listening so hard he could feel them doing it. He moved his hand, encountered the bottle sitting on the floor by his knee. He picked the bottle up, tipped it to his lips, but it was already empty.

Malik swallowed. Blake couldn't see him, but he could hear the movement in his throat. "Four thirty-three," Malik whispered. Rebecca squeezed Blake's thigh again, harder than before. Blake began to feel sleepy. He stifled a yawn, then another, but the third one escaped.

"You're a fucking natural at this," said Malik, no longer whispering, "aren't you?"

Blake laughed, a short, sharp bark that almost led to a laughing fit.

"Sh," said Rebecca.

Blake was quiet. He wondered how long they would wait before giving up. He felt like Machiavelli's prince.

"Four-forty." There was a doubtful note in this announcement, and Rebecca caught it.

"Did you set it right?"

"Four-thirty. On the dot." Malik's voice rose in annoyance.

"Sh," said Rebecca. "It doesn't matter anyway."

It doesn't matter anyway? Blake might have pursued the thought, but the next minute the sound of whistling came through the window, human whistling, very near. It was tuneful whistling, but high and light, the way a child might whistle. The whistler came close, closer, was right below the window, then receded, farther and farther away, and finally out of range. Blake recognized the tune. It was "Take Me Out to the Ball Game."

"What the fuck was that?" said Malik, trying and failing to keep his voice low; it cracked and wavered in pitch.

"Be quiet," said Rebecca, her voice low and clear, with no wavering or cracking.

She's a natural too, Blake thought. *Especially since she thinks a bomb's going to go off.* He roughed out answers to the interrogation that would come when they made the decision to stop sitting there in wait, answers based on the crudeness of Stu Levine's translation and of the original design.

Malik whispered: "Where's that bottle?"

Blake handed the empty bottle to him in the darkness.

Pause.

"Christ."

"Sh."

The bottle rolled across the floor.

"Sh."

"Christ."

"Shut up."

Blake felt their tension rising and rising. How would they accept the fact that it was a dud like the first one? After all that rising, what would the fall be like? Blake turned his head, noticed that the rectangle of window wasn't quite so black now. Rebecca and Malik emerged from the darkness as silhouettes, no longer invisible. The Malik silhouette moved.

"Four fifty-four," he said.

Blake rose and went to the window. In the east colors were leaking into the black sky in tidy bands—pink, purple, green, and the blue-white of skim milk. Slowly the hills beyond the playing fields came into view, turning dusty rose. It was beautiful. Blake watched until his eyelids grew heavy. He yawned again.

The chapel bell began to ring. *Bong. Bong.* Blake turned his head slightly, could just see the tip of the campanile over the tall oaks. *Bong. Bong.* The break of dawn was beautiful, and the campus was beautiful too, he thought, and he was glad that—

He saw a flash of light. A tremendous flash of light. And then—

Boom. A tremendous boom.

• • •

The young woman with the Odilon Redon book was sleeping when the bus pulled into the station and came to a stop. "Excuse me," Charlie said.

She awoke with a start, eyes wide and afraid, staring at him without comprehension. "We're there," Charlie said.

"Shit," she said. "Was I asleep?"

Charlie nodded.

"Oh, God. I'm not ready."

"Not ready?"

"For the exam, what else?" She got up, stuffed the book angrily into an overfull bag, then sighed. "I guess it doesn't matter anyway."

"No?"

"I'm switching to business in the fall."

She hurried off the bus. Charlie followed more slowly. It must have been a warm night—people around the bus station were lightly dressed—but Charlie felt cold.

It doesn't matter anyway.

A single taxi waited. Charlie approached. Through the open window he heard: "And that one's low and away." The driver looked at him. "Fuckin' Red Sox," he said.

Charlie got in the back. "Stuart Levine Industries," he said, and gave the driver the address. The window slid up, the cab jerked out into traffic.

It doesn't matter anyway, he thought. *It doesn't matter anyway.*

He said: "Mind turning down the air-conditioning?"

The driver said: "It's not on, pal."

The announcer said: "Ball four. That loads 'em up."

The driver said: "Fuckin' Red Sox."

15

"Wow," cried Malik, pounding Blake on the back as though he had just won a big game. "Oh, wow." He put his arms around Blake and hugged him, then clapped his hands and came close to jumping up and down. "We did it, man. We did it."

"Blake did it," Rebecca said, "and keep your voice down."

That was no longer necessary. Somewhere in Cullen House a door banged open; then came running footsteps on the stairs. Rebecca drew closer to Blake and Malik by the window, draped her arms over their shoulders. "We all did it, of course," she said. "But Blake is the one we owe." Softly, she slid the tip of her finger into Blake's ear and gave it a little twist. He jerked away, left the room, almost running, and went down the hall to the bathroom. There was a buzzing in his ears, an enormous weight crushing his chest. What had gone wrong?

He saw himself again in a mirror. He looked the same, the same as always. How could that be? Had he somehow dreamed the whole thing, drunk a bottle of rum and fallen into a nightmare? No: somewhere someone shouted, an alarm begin to ring, then another. It was all real, except for the unresponsive face in the mirror. Blake shaped his mouth in a silent scream, until the face in the mirror resembled the face of someone with a buzzing in his ears and a crushing in his chest, looked as though it might even scream. Blake got ready to scream. The door opened and Rebecca came in.

He turned to her. She didn't say a word. Perhaps his mouth was still not fully closed, had not quite resumed its screamless form. Rebecca grabbed him and drove her tongue into it. She reached down into his pants, roughly, and then his pants were around his ankles and Rebecca was on her knees and sucking his penis, roughly. Furiously. She used her hand, her lips, her tongue, her saliva, her teeth, raking him and raking him back and forth across the borderline of pain and pleasure, at the same time reaching down into her own jeans. The buzzing and crushing inside Blake grew to unbearable levels. He gazed down at the frenzy around his loins, helpless, and came and came. Sirens wailed.

They went out into the hall. Malik was waiting by the door. People were running—barefoot people, half-dressed people, frightened people. They ran with them. Down the stairs, through the lobby, out the door, into a river of running people. They flowed with it, through the line of oaks, into the central quad, past the chapel. Dawn had fully broken now, flooding the physical world with the first, clearest light of day. And Blake, standing in a crowd of superexcited, almost hysterical human beings, saw:

Two firetrucks parked on the grass in front of the ROTC building, engines running, firemen jumping out.

And: A pile of rubble where the front of the building had been. The wooden steps, the door, the wall, the remodeled porch—all gone.

And: The inside of the first floor all the way through the lobby to the staircase, as though it were an architect's cutaway model. Something lay on the charred floor at the foot of the stairs.

And: An ambulance, its door popping open and paramedics jumping out.

And: Little fires burning here and there on the ground floor of the building, hoses uncoiling, an ax smashing through a splintered window frame, smoke rising above all.

And: That something at the foot of the stairs.

"One stick of dynamite?" Blake said. "One stick of dynamite did all that?"

But no one heard him. Noise, cacophonous, incomprehensible human noise, rose from the crowd, the way the smoke was rising from the rubble. A din, a babble, an uproar, but not loud enough to drown the buzzing in Blake's head.

Something was pressing against his back. Someone. Blake half turned. A man pushed by, his face intense, beyond intense, with powerful emotion. A woman in a nightdress and curlers came after him, clutching his shirttail to keep up. The man shoved his way through the crowd, broke free into the space in front of the rubble, the woman in the nightdress and curlers stumbling after him, her face distorted by fear, by terror. A fireman moved to block the man's path. The man pushed him aside and kept going, through the smoke, into what was left of the building. The fireman recovered in time to get his hands on the woman. She beat on his chest, tried to struggle free. Her nightdress tore, exposing one of her breasts: fat, loose, long nippled, maternal.

Then the man emerged from the smoke. His legs appeared first, bare legs: all he wore was his shirt, long enough to cover him to mid thigh. The noise of the crowd died at once, as though this were all being controlled by switches backstage. The man had tears streaming down his face and—

Something in his arms.

Someone. A person. A child. A boy.

A boy in a baseball uniform. A navy shirt, white pants with navy pinstripes, navy stirrup socks, white cleats. The boy's hands were crossed on his chest. In his hands was a baseball glove, a first baseman's trapper, Blake saw, a southpaw's trapper. He could even identify the make and model: Rawlings, Willie "Stretch" McCovey.

The boy's face was tilted toward the crowd. It looked absolutely unmarred, the face of a healthy eleven- or twelve-year-old who happened to be sleeping in the middle of a wild scene. But he wasn't moving at all.

The woman in the nightdress and curlers let out a sound then that Blake had no word to describe. It made the fireman loosen his grip. The woman tore loose, ran into the smoking rubble, looked down into the face of the still boy, fell on her knees, leaning against the bare legs of the tall man. She reached up for the cleated feet, took them in her hands and held them to her breast, started rocking and didn't let go, not for as long as Blake was watching.

•   •   •

It was almost nine-thirty when the taxi left Route 128, went past a field that until recently might have been farmland but was now nothing, and pulled into Stuart Levine Industries. Charlie paid the driver, got out, and only when the taxi was driving away realized that he had come to a place of business long after business hours, and on a Saturday night. He turned to the building. It was long, low, sleek; resembling desktop machinery on a giant scale. The entrance was a huge smoked-glass portal, with the letters SLI imprinted inside the glass in changing shades of blue.

Charlie noticed all that at a glance. He also noticed that lights shone in some of the office windows despite the hour and the day, that the employees' parking lot was one-quarter full, and that two security guards were sitting at a desk in the lobby. He imagined a conversation:

Charlie: I'd like to see Mr. Levine.
Guard: Name, please?
Charlie: Mr. Wrightman.
Guard: (Picks up phone, speaks too softly to be over-
         heard, listens, glances furtively at Charlie.)
         If you'll wait a moment, sir.
Charlie: Thanks. (He waits a moment. The police pull
         up outside.)

Charlie turned away from the fancy glass entrance and moved into the employees' parking lot.

Sodium arc lamps lit the parking lot, casting an other worldly, perhaps futuristic, orange glow on cars from most of the car-making nations—the U. S. A., with one or two exceptions, excepted. The cars increased in sticker price the closer they were to the reserved spaces alongside the building. "Comptroller" drove a Volvo 740; "VP—Finance," a Lexus; "VP—Marketing," a BMW 940i; "VP—R&D," a Porsche. The space closest to the entrance was reserved for "President and Chief Operating Officer." "President and Chief Operating Officer" drove a Rolls-Royce Corniche convertible, green as money. Charlie considered several possibilities. Then he got down on the pavement and slid underneath the Rolls.

Lying there on his back, with plenty of room, Charlie thought of his yellow Volkswagen Beetle with the twice rebuilt engine. It was an amusing thought and made him smile. Cars mean nothing, he told himself, and besides, I've got *Straight Arrow*, transportation that means something. Then he wondered if he could be said at that moment to have *Straight Arrow*, and that led him to thoughts of Emily, and he didn't feel like smiling anymore.

After a while he heard hard shoes walking across the parking lot. A car started and drove off. Then came soft shoes, and another car, farther away, departed. More hard shoes, more soft shoes, more cars departing, many more, including one close by, probably a VP. After that came quiet, with nothing to listen to but the hum of traffic on 128. Then two sets of feet approached, one shod in Nike Airs, the other in black leather wingtips. Charlie heard Nike say, "Guess I'll fire her on Friday."

Wingtips said: "Make it Monday. The bitch is getting on my nerves."

Nike said: "What about her health plan?"

Wingtips said: "Whatever you can get away with."

Car doors slammed, and Nike and Wingtips drove off. Twisting around, Charlie saw that the Rolls was the only car left in the lot.

He heard more voices, coming from the entrance. A man said, "Good night, Dr. Levine."

And a man answered, "'Night, boys. Keep on truckin'."

Laughter, swallowed by the soft impact of the closing door.

Keep on truckin'. The argot hadn't changed in twenty years. But the voice had, deeper, louder, full of confidence and authority. Charlie almost hadn't recognized it.

He watched the final pair of shoes come closer, gleaming leather tassel loafers. They came right to the driver's side of the car, stopped. Nice tassel loafers, and gray pant cuffs that looked like silk. Charlie smelled cigar smoke. Then he heard the jingle of keys. Would all the locks pop open when the front door was unlocked? If so, he could roll out from under the car and jump into the front passenger seat. But the locks might not all pop open in a Rolls, and even if they did, the driver might have time to do something reckless, such as leaning on the horn until the guards came running. Better, Charlie thought, to act before the key slid in the lock. He reached out from under the car and grabbed a silken ankle.

"Bombo," he said in as close to a normal tone as he could manage, "be calm."

Under the silk the calf muscle, thin and gristly, stiffened. A cylinder of cigar ash dropped to the pavement and fell apart. The voice—Stu's voice, but presidential and chief executive officer–like—spoke: "Who are you?"

A good question. Charlie said, "Your father smoked cigars too, didn't he?"

"I know you from somewhere."

"True."

"You called me Bombo." A long pause. "Not Blake?"

Charlie was silent.

The speaker sighed. His calf muscle went soft. "Aw, shit," he said. His voice began to lose its presidential tone.

"Unlock the car," Charlie said. "You can take me for a ride."

The calf muscle hardened. "No need to waste time, Blake. How much do you want?"

For a moment Charlie didn't get it. "Money, you mean?"

"What else?"

"Unlock the car, Stu."

The keys jingled. Charlie heard the locks pop. "Get in," he said.

"With your hand on my ankle?"

Charlie let go. The tassel loafers climbed quickly up, out of

126

sight. Before the door closed Charlie rolled out, sprang up on the other side of the car, the side away from the building's entrance, opened the passenger door and jumped in. Levine, still reaching for the lock button, said, "Shit." And there they were, together in soft leather and polished walnut luxury, bathed in an orange glow.

Stuart Levine, president and CEO: still bony, although flesh sagged under his chin. The boniness now gave him a look that was almost ruthless. The stringy hair was gone. All of it. The baldness made him look smart. Gone too were the granny glasses. Now he wore something in tortoiseshell that might have been designed by Ralph Lauren. They went nicely with the gray silk suit, the white-on-white shirt, the subdued tie. Rich, ruthless, smart, well dressed, Charlie thought. He himself wasn't the only one with a new identity.

Levine was watching him. "Christ, Blake, you look good. Young. A hell of a lot younger than me."

"I stayed away from cigars."

Levine glanced at the fat cigar in his hand. For a moment Charlie thought he was going to toss it outside. Levine stuck it in his mouth instead. His lips closed comfortably around it. When he spoke again, he had recovered some of his presidential tone.

"Reunion," he said. "Class of 'seventy-two."

"Ex–'seventy-two," Charlie said.

"Yeah," said Levine. He blew out a thin stream of smoke, studied it. Charlie waited for him to say "I always thought this might happen" or "How did you find me?" but Levine's mind was on another tack. "It wasn't the right place for me," he said. "For someone like you, maybe, but not for me."

How about for Junior? Charlie thought. He was wondering whether to say it aloud when Levine turned to him and said, "I've got to ask."

"What?"

"If it was the one I made. The . . . device."

"What else?" said Charlie. "Let's go."

Levine sighed and put the key in the ignition. Before turning it, he looked at Charlie again. "I sometimes think maybe I dreamed up the whole thing. A lot of drugs went down in those days, of course. And then there was my . . . episode."

"It wasn't a dream," Charlie said.

"I guess not." Levine turned the key. The car made quiet and powerful sounds. The radio was tuned to classic rock. Levine switched it off. "Still play the sax?" he said, wheeling out of the parking lot like a Rolls-owner from way back.

"A little."

"You were good. Damned good."

"Not that good."

They drove along the road toward 128, past a dark car parked on the shoulder, with someone sitting in the front seat, past the barren field. "Where to?" Levine said.

"Somewhere we can talk."

"My place? It's not far."

Charlie thought for a moment. Levine watched him from the corner of his eye. "Okay," Charlie said.

Levine, driving up the ramp to 128, spoke around his cigar. "When are you going to name the figure, Blake?"

"Figure?"

"How much you want."

"This isn't about money."

"Everything's about money, old friend."

Levine lived in a suburb west of Boston, the kind of suburb newspapers call affluent. His house, which stood well back from the road, with no other houses in sight, was very different in spirit from his place of business. It was all stone, wood, and leaded glass, evoking thoughts of a long-vanished England and Fielding's cream-and-beef–fed squires. Levine, so clearly American, contemporary, unsquirelike, and probably on a low-cholesterol diet, pulled off the circular drive and parked in front of the four-car garage. He noticed Charlie looking at the house and said; "Home, home on the range."

They went in through a side door, made their way down marble halls, across Persian rugs, past displays of displayable art, and into a big room that had a red-tiled floor but was otherwise all white. Charlie knew it was the kitchen from the many built-in appliances; but of the other attributes of kitchens—that they had good smells, made you think of cooking and eating, invited relaxed conversation around the table—it had none. A woman in a short black cocktail dress was standing at the counter, pouring vodka into a crystal glass.

"What are you doing here?" Levine said to her.

The woman turned. "I'm your wife," she said. "I live here, at least for now." The woman had a British accent, not the rock star kind, but not like the queen's, either. She had a body in its forties, a face in its fifties, and a voice somewhat older.

Levine reddened. "I meant what are you doing here now. I thought you'd gone to the symphony."

"The theater, in fact. We left during the interval." Her eyes slid over to Charlie.

"This," said Levine, "is Deirdre. My wife, as she so rightly points out. Deirdre, meet—"

"Charlie," Charlie said, just as Levine was about to come to grips with the problem of what to call him; had they developed some sort of teamwork as roommates, ready to reassert itself even now?

"Charlie," said Deirdre, raising her glass. "One of my very favorite men's names."

"I like it too," Charlie said.

"Well then," said Levine, "if you'll excuse us, sweetheart, Charlie and I have some work to get through."

"Naturally," said Deirdre, and took a big swallow of her drink. She gave Charlie a little wave good-bye.

Levine had a library at the back of the house. It had a claw-footed desk, oak panels, club chairs, a stone hearth, even books. "You want a drink?" Levine said, going to a wall cabinet.

"I sure as hell do."

"Okay," Charlie said.

Levine handed him a heavy snifter. "Armagnac," he said. "Sixty years old."

"What's the occasion?"

Levine ignored him. "It's like cognac, only from another town. One of Deirdre's little men sends it."

"Little men?"

"That's what she calls them. She has little men all over the world, on the lookout for this and that. It's the way they are, the Brit aristocracy."

"Is she a founding member?" Charlie asked, telling himself too late to knock it off.

Levine, in midsip, glared at him over the rim of his snifter. "You're an asshole, you know that? You all are. Fucking assholes. You know absolute bugger-all about real life."

Charlie could see that despite the anger, despite the new air of authority, Levine was afraid. "Who is we all?" he said.

"You. Malik. Rebecca."

Did Levine imagine that the three of them were still together? He tasted the Armagnac. Perhaps it was good, better than good, but he found it sickening and put it down.

Levine took another drink. "Just tell me one thing," he said. "Why did you do it?"

"Do what?"

"Blow up that fucking building, what else?"

"Cambodia," Charlie said.

"Cambodia? What kind of answer is that?"

A lousy one. Charlie had known that right from the beginning.

A computer on the claw-footed desk made a beeping sound. Levine got up, glanced at the screen, tapped a few keys. Charlie realized Levine could probably use it to summon help. He moved quickly to the desk, looking at the screen over Levine's shoulder. He saw nothing but columns of numbers, meaningless to him. Levine turned, gazed up at him.

"What's it going to take?" he asked.

"To do what?"

"To make you go away and stay away." Levine twisted one of his fingers until the knuckle cracked. "All it would take is one anonymous call, right? 'Stu Levine made the bomb that killed the little boy in nineteen seventy. But no one connected him to it because he was in the booby hatch at the time.' That kind of call. Maybe you even have some proof, although I doubt it. You certainly won't be taking the stand yourself. But you've already figured out that none of that will be necessary. With this SDI thing I couldn't afford even that one phone call. The DOD is paranoid and stupid. I'm paranoid and smart—that's why I'm so good at dealing with them. So how much will it take?"

"SDI thing?" said Charlie.

Levine waved a hand in dismissal. "Don't play dumb. It was in all the papers. That's what gave you the idea to put the bite on me, isn't it?"

Charlie, understanding nothing, said nothing.

Levine nodded, satisfied. "That contract's worth a hundred million dollars in the first three years alone. After that, anybody's guess."

"What's it for, exactly?"

"The contract? Software. That's what I do. And Star Wars is all about software. If there are glitches in the software, we've got nothing but a lot of junk floating around up there, maybe exploding at unexpected moments."

They thought their thoughts about that. Charlie said: "What were those SATs?"

There was no hesitation. "Seven sixty, math; seven twenty, verbal," Levine said. "Now what do you want?"

"I'm looking for Rebecca."

Levine blinked. "You mean you're not with her?"

"Why would I be with her?"

"I just thought . . . you two." Levine emptied his glass. His eyes had a faraway look. "Rebecca. If it hadn't been for her nothing would have happened."

That was true, Charlie thought, but how did Levine know? Did it mean he had seen her sometime after the bombing? "When was the last time you saw her?"

"Back then. At school."

"What did you mean nothing would have happened?"

"I never would have built the . . . thing. If she hadn't persuaded me."

"She persuaded you?" Charlie saw what was coming and didn't like it at all, didn't like the way Blake Wrightman's history was being rewritten.

"Hell, yes," Levine said. "I still get hard thinking about it. She was the first woman I ever balled, as we used to say. A nice crunchy granola word for it, made it so natural and pure—unlike the sex I have now, the semiannual time I have it."

Charlie wanted to hit him. That was a surprise: it was so long ago, and he was in love with another woman. He backed away, sat down in the club chair, picked up the snifter, drained it.

Levine, unaware of Charlie's reaction, got up too. He went to the cabinet, came back with the Armagnac, refilled their glasses.

"If that's all you want, information on Rebecca, you could have it," Levine said. "But I haven't seen Rebecca since my fa— ... since I left the school." Charlie looked into Levine's eyes and saw it was true. "Too bad you're not looking for Malik."

"I beg your pardon?"

"Malik is a different story."

16

Blake didn't know what to do. Had he not wound electrical tape around the red wire to stop the flow of electricity? Or had he dreamed that or imagined it or been stoned at the time or simply screwed up? He stood frozen in front of the ROTC building, rum rising sour up his throat. He sensed Rebecca nearby, saw her beside him, eyes dark and wild, as though emerging from a bad sleep; lips moving slightly, as though trying to find speech. She didn't know what to do either.

Malik knew what to do.

Blake felt him tugging at his shirt, saying, "Come on, come on." He was saying it right into Blake's ear. Blake heard, but that didn't help him move.

He said again: "One stick of dynamite did all that?"

No one heard but Malik. Malik slapped him hard across the face. No one saw but Rebecca. "Come on," Malik repeated, fiercely and through gritted teeth.

Now he could move.

They slipped out of the crowd, Malik first, then Rebecca, half stumbling like the woman in curlers, then Blake, face burning. They left the central quad, moved into the line of oaks, paused.

"Money," Malik said. He was breathing heavily; they all were, as though they had just done something strenuous.

"Money," Malik said again.

Rebecca nodded. The word made no sense to Blake.

Malik seemed to understand that. "We're going to need money," he explained. He opened his wallet, a fancy leather one, a businessman's wallet. Blake stared at it, surprised that Malik would have a wallet like that, but still not understanding. "I've got forty-three dollars," Malik said. "Rebecca?"

She shrugged. "Two or three hundred, maybe. But it's in the room." It struck Blake, not for the first time, that Rebecca, who didn't care about money, always had lots.

"Blake?"

"What?"

"How much have you got?"

"Not much. It's in the room too."

They returned to Cullen House, deserted and quiet now, to the room with the fairy-tale bed. Blake had nine dollars. He handed it over. Malik piled all the money on Rebecca's desk and counted it.

"Three hundred and fifteen dollars." He began distributing it in three equal parts.

"What's going on?" Blake asked.

"Preparation," Malik replied, smoothing his mustache. "Preparation is everything."

Blake heard the words but made nothing of them. He began: "We—"

They looked at him.

"We just—" For a moment the rest wouldn't come, and when it did it was incomplete. "We just—and now you're counting little piles of money. What's the matter with you?"

Rebecca and Malik exchanged a glance. "Talk to him, Rebecca," Malik said.

Rebecca touched Blake on the arm. He backed away.

"Blake," she said.

"What?"

"You're upset. Upset's the wrong word—more than upset. So am I. We all are."

"We wouldn't be human otherwise," Malik interrupted.

Rebecca continued: "It was a horrible accident."

Blake opened his mouth to argue.

She cut him off. "Accident. Accident. Accident. We, none of us, not you, not me, not Andrew, none of us ever intended to harm a single person. We took careful plans to make sure nothing like . . . that nothing would happen."

"Besides," said Malik.

"Besides?"

"Yeah. Compare it with what's happening this very minute in Vietnam. They're dying by the thousand, by the tens of thousands—it'll be millions before it's all done."

"What are you talking about?"

"The Vietnamese, of course."

"What've the Vietnamese got to do with anything?" Blake said, his voice rising again.

Malik's voice rose with it. "Don't be so obtuse. I'm talking about the murder of innocents, the slaughter of the oppressed."

"But we just murdered an innocent."

"It was an accident. Totally different from sending armed killers to a foreign land. Can't you see that? Don't you get it?"

Blake started to get it, although not in the way Malik intended. He thought of the oppressed, the innocents; and armed killers in a foreign land, thousands, like his father, to be killed themselves. Somehow he had sided with his father's killers, even done something shameful to his memory. In this moment of realization, Blake threw a punch at Malik's face. Not well-aimed, it caught Malik on the shoulder, but with enough force to knock him back two or three steps before he recovered his balance. Blake regretted it at once: it was just more of the sickening same.

Malik, rubbing his shoulder, spoke, quietly now, almost like a priest at some intimate ceremony. "You see, Rebecca? Violence is communication. The problem is to aim it in the right direction."

There was a silence. Sirens broke it, coming from the town. Blake and Malik were both watching Rebecca, waiting for her response to Malik's latest *pensée*. Rebecca: her face pale after a sleepless night, her eyes reddened but not from tears, her hair a black and wild framework for her crazy beauty. In the end she said nothing, just nodded her assent.

"Now, then," Malik said, "if we can all keep our composure." He moved to the desk, picked up the piles of money, pocketed one, handed the second to Rebecca, held out the third to Blake. "From each according to his abilities," he said. "To each according to his needs."

Blake kept his hands at his sides. "What's it for?"

"The future," Malik said, still offering the money. When Blake still refused to take it, he dropped it on the desk. "You've got to think faster, Blake. We don't have much time."

"Time for what?" Blake said.

"To get out of here, what else? Do you want to spend the rest of your life in jail for something you didn't do?"

"Didn't mean to do," Rebecca corrected.

Blake knew he wasn't thinking quickly, was barely thinking at all. His mind was back there with the woman in curlers at the rubble pile, assailed by images: navy jersey, white cleats, black trapper, Stretch McCovey model. He wasn't ready to accept that life goes on, let alone to plot the manner of its progress.

Rebecca reached out, touched him again. This time he didn't back away. She came closer, till her face was right in front of his, her eyes the only sight in view, a sight familiar, foreign, fascinating. "Please, Blake." She had a way of saying please. "This is . . ."

"Awful," Malik put in.

"Awful," Rebecca continued, "no one's pretending it's not awful. But we can talk about it later."

"If we get to later," Malik said.

Rebecca nodded. "We've got to go," she said.

"Go?" said Blake.

"That's not the question," Malik said. "The question is where."

Blake thought at once of the baseball diamond behind the field house, in the shadow of the hills. That's where he wanted to go, even if it made no sense. Meanwhile, Malik was finding the answer.

"I've given this some thought." He glanced at Blake to make sure he was following. Blake was, but in his own way. He wondered: *When did you do all this thinking, Andy?*

"There's only one viable course," Malik continued. "We're going underground."

Underground. Blake thought he heard enthusiasm in Malik's voice then, the enthusiasm of a fly fisherman, say, on his way for the first time to a famous trout stream, gear all packed.

Malik went on: "Mao talks about an ocean of support out there, an ocean in which the guerrilla swims."

Rebecca's eyes narrowed. "But where?" she said impatiently. "Where are we going?"

"Berkeley," Malik replied.

"Berkeley?" said Rebecca. "Isn't that a little close to home, my home?"

"Berkeley is our biggest, and therefore safest, ocean."

"But—"

"Rebecca!"

Rebecca and Malik eyed each other. She stopped arguing. "Have we got enough money to get there?"

"We're not *flying*, Rebecca," Malik said. He started to laugh. Blake had never heard him laugh before. It was a strange sound, closer to barking than to anything musical. He quickly calmed himself, but a smile lingered on his face. "And we're not writing checks, or using your American Express card. Going underground means there is no more Rebecca Klein, no more Andrew Malik, no more Blake Wrightman. They disappear this moment, leaving no trace."

He paused to let it all sink in. Blake watched Rebecca. She bit her lip and said nothing.

"And disappear singly, by the way," Malik added.

"Singly?" said Blake.

"They'll be looking for three, not one," Malik said. "We'll meet in Berkeley."

"How?" said Rebecca. "Where?"

"Sproul Plaza," Malik said. "When you get to Berkeley, go to the plaza everyday at noon and stay for fifteen minutes. We'll find each other."

"What's Sproul Plaza?" asked Blake.

"The heart of Berkeley, man, where the Free Speech Movement started," Malik replied. His smile faded. "You haven't heard of Sproul Plaza?"

Blake ignored the question. "Then what?" he said. "After this plaza."

"Then," said Malik, his eyes focusing on something far away, "then we help make revolution. This country is going to be turned upside down in the next year or two. Three at most. And we're going to be part of it. An important part." His gaze retracted to the here and now, taking in Blake, Rebecca, the room. He smiled, as though everything were proceeding smoothly to some plan.

Through the window came the sound of voices approaching Cullen House. A woman was crying, and then a man. And more sirens, coming now from several directions.

Malik's smile vanished. "Any questions?"

There were no questions. The one Blake should have asked did not occur to him until months later. *If we don't run, how will they connect us to the bombing?* A logical question, but Blake wasn't being governed by logic at that moment.

"Then let's go," said Malik. "One at a time. Five minutes apart. Blake first."

Blake didn't move.

"For Christ's sake, man," Malik said. "Are you trying to get us all busted?" The sirens closed in.

"Please, Blake."

Blake reached for the money on Rebecca's desk, picked it up, put it in his pocket. Rebecca came to him, wrapped her arms around him, kissed him warm and soft on the mouth.

"See you in Berkeley," she said, her voice close to breaking, or at least he thought so at the time. Blake let her go, turned, walked out of the room with the fairy-tale bed and out of Cullen House.

He fled. Good and bad both flee their crimes: the good run from the new-revealed self.

•　　•　　•

Charlie thought about that punch, aimed at Malik's face but striking his shoulder. A punch: a tiny dose, a child's dose, of violence in the circumstances, like blowing in someone's face during a hurricane. Then Alex Trebek's announcer was saying: "And now a real estate developer from Toronto, Canada—welcome please—Merv Koharski!"

Applause, covering a shot of Merv Koharski striding in from off-camera, followed by a tighter shot of Merv as he took his place behind the middle podium. Stuart Levine, at his claw-footed desk, pressed the Pause button on the remote. The image of Merv Koharski, real estate developer from Toronto, froze on the screen of Levine's Sony Trinitron. The attached VCR was a good one: the freeze-frame was steady and unstreaked.

Merv Koharski: a fat man with jowls, clean-shaven face, fringe of short gray hair, heavy-framed glasses with smoky lenses, greeny-blue checked sports jacket, brown shirt, beige tie. He was smiling in the direction of Alex Trebek, the smile of someone wanting to be liked.

"Him?" asked Charlie.

"I didn't think so either, at first. That's why I taped it when it came on channel nineteen an hour later." Levine fast-forwarded through the first commercial break and paused again. "This is where they interview the contestants."

"You seem to know the format."

"'Jeopardy!'?" said Levine. "I never miss it."

He ran the tape. Alex Trebek talked to the contestant on the right about a funny thing her parakeet did, then moved on to Merv Koharski. "Toronto," said Alex Trebek. "Quite a town."

"It most certainly is, Alex," responded Merv Koharski. And Charlie knew right away. You can shave off your Zapata mustache, you can put on fifty pounds, you can hide your eyes behind smoky gray lenses, you can turn a Jesuit into Friar Tuck, but you can't change your voice.

"Had a chance to visit that wonderful Skydome yet?" asked Alex Trebek.

Merv nodded happily. "I've got season tickets. Awesome. That's the only word for it."

"That's what I hear," said Alex Trebek, getting ready to turn to the defending champion on the left.

"Buildings have an amazing influence on our lives," Merv

Koharski went on. "An architect is more powerful than a general."

"Very well put," said Alex Trebek, his smile looking a little forced. "And now, our defending champion, Sylvia—"

Levine hit the Pause button. "Well?"

There was no question. It wasn't just the sound of the voice, but its type as well: the voice of the guru and speaker of aphorisms, except now the aphorisms were about architects and ballparks instead of revolution and power. "When was this?" Charlie said.

"Last November," Levine replied. He hit Play.

The category was Johns. Sylvia, the defending champion, got Pope John XXIII for one hundred dollars, Johnny Carson for two hundred, but was too slow on the clue "He died with a hammer in his hand," and the parakeet woman—who, it seemed to Charlie, had quick, birdlike movements—pressed her button, said, "Who was John Henry?" winning three hundred and control of the board.

"Johns for four hundred," she said.

The clue: "English poet who wrote 'no man is an island.' "

Parakeet woman paused. Sylvia hit her button and said: "John Suckling."

Alex Trebek said: "Form of a question."

Sylvia said; "Who was John Suckling?" going immediately to minus one hundred. She was having a rough night.

Parakeet woman was still thinking. Merv Koharski pressed his button. "Who was John Donne?" he said, for four hundred and control of the board.

"U.S. politics for one hundred," said Merv. He proceeded to run the category. "Well, Merv," said Alex Trebek when he was done,"for a Canadian you sure know what's happening south of the border."

Merv Koharski smiled as they went to commercial.

Parakeet woman rallied during Double Jeopardy!, running two categories and adding a thousand dollars on an audio daily double ("What is 'Like a Virgin'?"). But Merv Koharski got three of the thousand-dollar answers and all of the eight hundreds and gambled and won five thousand on the other daily double (Category: "Footwear." Answer: "Judge Kenesaw

Mountain Landis banned him from baseball." Question: "Who was Shoeless Joe Jackson?"). Sylvia, losing her composure and eliciting tight-lipped expressions on Alex Trebek's face—he expected a certain standard from defending champions—jumped in from time to time with a guess, sinking deeper and deeper into the negative. By Final Jeopardy! she was out, leaving parakeet woman with $7,600 and Merv Koharski with $12,800. All Merv had to do was bet $2,401 and get the right question, and it wouldn't matter what parakeet woman did.

Levine fast-forwarded through commercials for mufflers and adult diapers. The Final Jeopardy! category was "The Sixties." The players wrote their secret wagers. Parakeet woman's forehead was deeply furrowed now. Merv Koharski leaned on his podium, looking relaxed.

"And now," said Alex Trebek, "the Final Jeopardy! answer: 'The leader of the Free Speech Movement at the University of California at Berkeley.' You have thirty seconds to write your answer. Make sure it's in the form of a question."

As Alex Trebek gave that warning, Charlie noticed that Levine's lips were moving along with those of the TV figure, mouthing the formulaic words, and his eyes were rapt. There was always something insane about Stuart, and it hadn't gone away. Charlie wondered about glitches in the $100 million worth of SDI software.

The "Jeopardy!" theme played as the camera panned the contestants. Without a moment's pause Merv Koharski wrote his answer. Parakeet woman screwed up her face as though she could somehow squeeze the right answer out of her brain. She tried one thing, then another.

"Time's up," said Alex Trebek, calling first for parakeet woman's answer. "Did I detect a little hesitation making up your mind?" he said with a smile that was not entirely pleasant.

"So did twenty million others, asshole," muttered Levine, talking to an electronic image.

Parakeet woman smiled back at Alex Trebek nervously. Her answer appeared on the screen. Amid scratchings-out and false starts could be read "Who was Savio?"

"'Who was Savio?'" said Alex Trebek. Pause to build suspense, within the limitation of having to hit the next commercial break on the second. "Mario Savio, leader of the Free Speech Movement in 1964. That's the right response." Applause. Parakeet woman heaved a sigh.

"Let's see your wager," said Alex Trebek.

Parakeet-woman had bet it all, $7,600, giving her $15,200. Applause.

"Now," said Alex Trebek, "we go to Merv, with $12,800. First, Merv, did you get the correct Final Jeopardy! answer?" Merv looked confident. His answer, in tidy script, came up on the screen: "Who was Mario Savio?"

"Right," said Alex Trebek. "First name too," he added, in possible rebuke to parakeet woman. "Now, let's see your wager. If you bet a minimum of twenty-four-oh-one, you'll be our new 'Jeopardy!' champion."

Merv Koharski's jaw started to drop at that point. His wager came up.

$2,301.

"Two-*three*-oh-one?" said Alex Trebek, looking puzzled. "That leaves you one hundred short." He blinked, but recovered quickly. There was still that commercial to hit, and he was a pro. "So our new 'Jeopardy!' champion is—"

"He blew the math," said Levine; he laughed a crazy laugh.

Parakeet woman reached out to shake the loser's hand. He didn't notice her. Applause. The camera cut to Alex Trebek, waving good-bye and looking out of sorts.

"He likes a well-played game," Levine explained, snapping off the set.

There was silence in Levine's library. The brandy snifters sat empty.

"Why the hell would he go on 'Jeopardy!'?" Charlie said.

"I guess he thought he could win."

•   •   •

Levine led Charlie back toward the front door, through many square feet of marble and plush. There was no sign of Deirdre, but in the hall Charlie did see a small framed photograph of a spectacled boy flying a kite.

"That's Stu," said Levine. "My son."

"Yeah?"

"From Julie. My first wife."

"What happened to her?"

"Nothing. We got divorced."

Levine looked at the picture. "This was taken some time back. I don't see him much these days."

"How come?"

"He lives with Julie. Anyway, he's in college now." Levine shook his head. "He takes after her in every way."

"He does?"

"Why do you say it like that?"

"He looks a little like you, that's all," Charlie said, although it wasn't what he'd meant.

"I don't think so. He's just like her—except you'll never guess the school he picked."

"No."

"Yes. And he doesn't even know about my brief enrollment there. He just glommed onto the idea for some reason."

"Why doesn't he know you went there? Is it a secret?"

"Not really. It's just that MIT was my school, in every sense." He paused. "Anyway, it's not a secret now, is it? Now that you're here."

"No."

"I hope it won't go any—" Levine began. He tried again: "I've cooperated, haven't I?" He paused, perhaps for Charlie to take him off the hook. When Charlie didn't, Levine said, "Do you need, uh, anything else?"

"Nothing," said Charlie, opening the door. The cab they'd called was waiting in the circular drive. Beyond that, just darkness. Levine gave Charlie a long look, as if making sure that he, this visit, were real.

"What rotten luck, huh, Blake?"

"Luck?"

Levine lowered his voice. "What else? I remember thinking, 'This will never work.'"

"What are you talking about?" Charlie said, although he knew.

"That stupid . . . bomb. One lousy stick of dynamite, that silly clock, those stupid instructions. It was all so Mickey Mouse."

143

They didn't shake hands. Charlie turned, walked down the drive, got into the cab. The door to the house closed, and Levine disappeared inside. The cab drove off, with Charlie in the back, considering two related omissions. One: Levine had shown no sign of feeling bad about the boy. Two: he himself hadn't mentioned that Levine's Mickey Mouse bomb was, in fact, a dud.

Headlights went on in a car parked on the street.

• • •

"Mr. Goodnow?"

It was Svenson. "This is not a secure line," Goodnow said, trying to keep the IV tube from tangling with the phone cord.

"*Compris*," said Svenson. "Our boy's looked up Stuart Levine."

"Roommate?"

"Check."

"Not implicated. Not even present."

"Check."

"So?"

"He heads up one of those high-tech places on the one twenty-eight ring. They do DOD work."

Silence.

"Of a sensitive nature," Svenson added.

Silence.

"I await instruction," said Svenson.

"Do nothing."

"Nothing?"

"It is not germane."

• • •

Svenson, at the wheel of his girlfriend's three-year-old Nissan Maxima, for which she would be reimbursed by accounting at the rate of thirty-one cents a mile, punched in another number on the car phone. He had a problem of the most worrying kind, a career-advancement problem. Although it made him nervous, he accepted the possibility that Goodnow had a

144

certain latitude to operate independently, in order to provide deniability for his superiors. That was the lesson of Watergate. He could see that bringing down Hugo Klein was a good thing, even if a few rules had to be misinterpreted. But what if in the course of the operation, they ignored something else, something more important? Like a connection to SDI?

Svenson's call was answered by a sleepy-sounding woman on the third ring.

"Yes?"

"Mr. Bunting, please," said Svenson.

"Who is it?"

"Work."

Muffled sounds. Then: "Bunting," said Mr. Bunting.

"Yes, sir. This is Svenson."

"Do you know what time it is, Svenson?"

Svenson checked the digital clock on the dash. "Yes, sir."

"What do you want?"

"Counsel, sir?"

"About what?"

"The germanity of something."

"That's not a word," said Bunting.

17

$\mathbf{B}$rucie Wine felt like shit.

"I feel like shit," he said.

"You drank a case of Bud last night is why," said Laverne.

"Got nothin' to do with it."

"Not to mention those pills you popped."

"Lay offa me."

Laverne was quiet. Brucie smelled smoke. He opened his eyes. She was sitting up in bed, smoking a Virginia Slim, in a bad mood. Brucie knew how to fix that. He slid a hand under her heavy thigh.

"Forget it, Bozo," said Laverne.

Jeez, Brucie thought. He got out of bed, rubbed his gummy eyes. "I got work to do, anyway," he said. Laverne snorted. Brucie went into the shower.

He let hot water pound down on him until the stall filled with steam. He still felt like shit, but now hot and wet too. *Hot, wet shit,* he thought, looking for the soap. There it was, lying on the drain. He kicked at it with his foot, hoping it would somehow hop up into his hand. When it didn't, he thought, *Fuck it,* lifted his arms to give his armpits a soaking, spread his cheeks to let water in there, then turned off the taps and stepped out. He dried himself with a Budweiser beach towel and looked in the mirror. He probably needed a shave— yeah, definitely. And there was a Bic disposable and a can of Gillette Foamy right on the counter. But he just didn't have the energy. *Fuck it. And so what. I'm not Joe Salesman.*

Brucie returned to the bedroom, pulled on yesterday's jeans, sneaks, a fresh Grateful Dead T-shirt. Laverne was still sitting in bed, smoking, not looking at him. *Watch this,* he thought. *I'm just gonna waltz out of here without saying a word.* He almost did, almost stopped himself from yelling, "Back soon," as he went out the front door, water dripping from his rat tail. He heard Laverne's snort, all the way from there.

Brucie unchained Flipper, let him piss and shit on someone's lawn, then unlocked the Trans-Am and said, "Here, boy." Flipper charged into the car, banging his head on the rearview mirror. Brucie got in, adjusted the mirror, and drove off to Polly's, forgetting to burn rubber until it was too late. He had a headache anyway.

Brucie liked doing business at Polly's. It was dark inside, never crowded. Besides, he was a regular, considered Polly a friend, felt safe. He locked the Trans-Am, chained Flipper to a No Parking sign within striking distance, and strolled inside. No one there but Polly behind the bar, flexing one of her massive forearms, the one with the Iron Cross tattoo, and a little chink sitting in the corner with a newspaper and a cup of coffee. Brucie took the table at the back, where it was darkest. The jukebox was playing "Stairway to Heaven." Led Zep. Loved 'em.

"Somethin'?" Polly called from behind the bar.

"How about a Bud?" Brucie said. Why not? He felt like shit anyway. Hot, wet shit.

Polly came over with a long-neck Bud and no glass, plunked it on the table. "Buck and a half."

Brucie forked it over, raised the bottle. "Hair o' the dog, right, Poll?"

Polly looked pissed. "I tole ya before, Brucie, and I'm not gonna say it again. You bring that fuckin' dog in here and so help me I'll blow both your pointy heads off with that pump gun I got behind the bar."

"Huh?" said Brucie.

"You heard me."

Polly went back to her post. She flexed her forearm, watched the muscles pop. Brucie watched her watching until he was sure she wasn't going to reach down behind the bar for that fucking pump gun. Then he took his first sip and immediately felt much better. *Hair of the dog*, he thought to himself, very quietly.

So. Where were the spics? He glanced at his watch, checked the front door, checked the little chink reading the paper. *The Chronicle*, he saw. Guy must be a yuppie, one of them Chinese yuppies with a briefcase and a BMW. What the fuck was he doing here?

The front door opened. In walked the spics. Poppa, Momma, baby, kids. Four of them. Christ. They bred like . . . like something; Brucie couldn't think what. They were looking around stupidly like bats in a tanning parlor.

"Hey," called Brucie. "Over here."

They came, stood awkwardly around the table. "Siddown, for Christ's sake," said Brucie.

They sat, as many who could fit around the table. "Couldn't find a baby-sitter?" said Brucie.

"*¿Señor?*" said Poppa.

"Nothin'." *Cut the prelims*, thought Brucie. *Get down to business.* "You guys all set?"

"*¿Señor?*"

Christ. He didn't like spics. For starters, they had their own language. "Didja bring the money?" Brucie said. "*Dinero,*" he elaborated, going more than halfway to meet them. That's what it meant to be an American. They could learn from him.

"*¿Dinero?*" said Poppa. "*Sí, señor.*"

"Give," said Brucie, sticking out his hand in the palm-up way that requires no translation.

Momma opened her purse, took out a wad of bills, laid them in Brucie's hand. Slowly. Looking at the bills with big brown eyes. *Don't make me cry, lady*, thought Brucie, counting it out.

"Twenty, forty, fifty, fifty-five, seventy-five, ninety-five, one-oh-five . . ." He counted it twice, but it came to six hundred both times. "What the fuck?"

"*¿Señor?*"

148

REVOLUTION #9

"There's only six hundred here, asshole. I told ya—a C-note per. There's seven of you, right?" He counted them, stabbing his forefinger at each family member. "One two three four five six seven. Seven times a hundred—seven hundred. What're ya tryna pull?"

Poppa and Momma babbled back and forth at each other. Poppa turned to Brucie. "*Pero*—the baby, *señor?*"

"What about the baby? You think the baby's free or something, like I'm running a goddamn hotel? Give."

More babble. Then Poppa said, "She is born *aquí, señor*. In United States."

"What the fuck you talking about?"

"That baby, *señor.*"

"Oh yeah?" Brucie got it. The baby was a U.S. citizen. All they had to do was walk into Social Security and fill out a form for her. Did they know that? Maybe, maybe not. Did they have the balls to walk into Social Security? Probably not. And anyway, why didn't they tell him before? He'd already made one up with her name on it, made one for all of them, with all those Jesus-long names they had.

Taking everything into consideration, Brucie said, "What? You think she's off the hook cause she's a baby? This ain't Mexico, guys. You're in the big time now."

Babble. Momma seemed to be resisting. Brucie was wondering whether to relent, give them the cards—what the hell, six C's was better than zip—when she gave in. Poppa looked at her with loving eyes as she rooted around in her purse, a grim expression on her face. She handed him some bills. He took them but didn't pass them on right away. Instead, he turned those big browns on Brucie and said: "Is the food money, *señor.*"

Brucie wasn't made of stone, wasn't above offering support and encouragement. "Now you can work, get good jobs, lotsa food—tacos and all that shit." He held out his hand. "Give."

Poppa gave. Brucie counted the hundred, stuck the whole wad in his jeans, came out with seven blue cards. All the big brown eyes locked on the cards the instant they appeared.

"Here you go, guys," said Brucie, handing them over. "Welcome to the U.S.A."

"Don't move a fucking muscle," said a voice. Brucie's head

149

jerked up. It was the chink, suddenly crouched there on the other side of the table. He was tiny, a goddamn midget or something. But the .357 Mag he was pointing at Brucie's face was full-size. "Don't even twitch," said the chink. "Unless you want your brains all over the floor."

"You do that," said Polly from the bar, "you mop up."

•   •   •

"Brucie, Brucie, Brucie."
Back in Nuncio's office.
"Yeah?"
"This was a public bar?"
"Sure, Mr. Nuncio. I don't belong to no private clubs or nothin'."
"What I meant was, you were conducting your business in a public place, where you could be observed by almost anybody?"
"Hell, no, Mr. Nuncio. This was Polly's. Polly and me are like this. And how was I sposta know that little chink was INS? He looked like some yuppie bloodsucker from downtown. How fair is that?"
Nuncio coughed. Maybe it was just cigar smoke going down the wrong way. Nuncio gazed at his client. Brucie gazed back.
"So," said Brucie after twenty or thirty seconds of that, "figured it out yet?"
"Figured what out, Brucie?"
"How to get me outta this. Isn't that what we're here for?"
"Brucie."
"Yeah?"
"Clarence Darrow couldn't figure this one out."
"Huh?"
"You're fucked, Brucie."
"Fucked? You mean like jail?"
"Precisely," said Nuncio. "Barring a miracle."
"What kind of a miracle?" asked Brucie Wine.

PART III

18

June 28, 1970. Sproul Plaza. Noon.

America, but was America ever closer in sight, sound, smell to an Oriental bazaar, the medina in Marrakech?

Bongo players. Dope smokers. Tarot readers. Speech makers. Singers. Dancers. Young men in sandals, with quiet voices and underexercised bodies. Young women with unshaved legs and unshaved armpits. Troubadours from Fort Wayne, Kansas City, Staten Island, Fairbanks, Rutland, Austin, St. Paul, Tulsa, Altoona, Spokane, with guitars on their backs and fingerpicks in their pockets. They played "It Ain't Me, Babe," "Early Morning Rain," "Farewell, Angelina," "Sounds of Silence," and songs of their own devising. Everyone moved inside a bubble of common music, the roofs of their mouths dry with the taste of herb.

Blake Wrightman sat on a bench facing Sproul's four Ionic columns, the stage set for a play that seemed to be over, and waited. He wore a shabby T-shirt, faded jeans, dirty sneakers. In a plastic bag beside him were a red and black checked lumberman's jacket and another T-shirt. In his pocket were two one-dollar bills, a quarter, a dime, two pennies, and a clipping from the *Boston Herald Traveler* with his high school graduation picture—short haired and clean-shaven—accompanying a story about a boy named Ronnie Pleasance; Mina, his brokenhearted mother; and Jack, the father who demanded justice. Blake was hungry, and tired of waiting. He'd been waiting for almost a month, waiting to be taken into the world underground, the world of Malik's tomorrow.

At first he'd bought a newspaper every morning, searched its pages, often seen his name, Rebecca's, Malik's. Now, with money running out, he found his papers in trash barrels instead. Their names appeared less and less often, then not at all. No arrests had been made; none were said to be imminent. He waited, in the beginning staying only the fifteen minutes Malik had prescribed, gradually extending the time until now he didn't leave until after nightfall.

A skinny shirtless guy with shoulder-length hair, an Australian bush hat, rose sunglasses, and a guitar case sat at the other end of the bench. He opened the case, took out a guitar decorated with painted rainbows, and started strumming. Blake listened. The guitarist seemed to know three chords, E, A, D minor, but had a lot of trouble going from E to A, leading to many pauses in the flow. The guitarist began to sing, his voice wavering wildly in pitch, reaching aggressively for notes that weren't there. Still, Blake thought he recognized the tune—something from Buffalo Springfield—although the words sounded new.

> *What a cool day for a treat*
> *Lots of chickies really neat*
> *Walkin' round and just hangin' out*
> *Well you know, I'll just have t' shout*
> *You gotta come, hey, when I call*
> *Everybody knows you love to ball.*

The guitarist, sensing he had an audience, tried to end with a little three-note run that involved one finger change on the fretboard, and bungled it. He turned to Blake.

"New song," he said.

Blake nodded.

"Still workin' on it."

Blake nodded.

The guitarist shook his head. "Poetry's a bitch, man."

"Yeah?"

"Yeah," said the guitarist. "Like you get an idea, you know? And then you gotta put it in words."

Blake nodded.

"And *then* you gotta make sure they rhyme."

"Like 'neat' and 'treat'?"

The guitarist smiled, happy as any author to be quoted by a fan. "I worked on that one till three in the morning. That's why I say—poetry's a bitch." He gave the strings one last fierce strum for emphasis, snapping the narrowest one. "Shitty strings," he said, putting the guitar in the case. "Spade in Oakland. Ripped me off."

The guitarist opened the compartment for spare strings and picks and removed a pack of cigarette papers and a baggie one-quarter full of grass. He took a few pinches and rolled a joint, his fingers suddenly adept. He struck a wooden match on his thumbnail, like a tough guy from a spaghetti western. Then he lit up, inhaled extravagantly, held his breath, passed the joint to Blake.

Blake didn't want it. He thought of how hungry he would feel later. On the other hand, he wouldn't feel hungry now. He took it.

"Acapulco gold," the guitarist gasped. "The real shit, man."

"Yeah?" said Blake, stoned almost at once. For a moment he forgot everything and just sat there peacefully, in the carnival, in the sun.

"I got like a pound of it at my pad."

Blake, looking up at the hills rising above the campus and the blue sky above that, a deep blue sky with a hawk drifting up on rising currents of summer air, barely heard.

"A whole fucking pound, man," said the guitarist. "Didn't cost me a cent."

"No?"

"Not a cent. Traded for it, man. With this Mex that needed ID."

"What did you trade?"

"ID, man. Identification. That's what I do."

155

Blake sat up. "You work for the government."

"Huh? What government? I'm a printer." He saw Blake looking at him closely and misinterpreted. "The poetry's just on the side." He held out his hand, as though to arm-wrestle, for a hippie handshake. "Brucie," he announced. "But everybody calls me The Kid."

"I'm Ronnie," said Blake. The words were out before he had a chance to think. "I know some other chords."

"Yeah?"

They shook hands, Ronnie and The Kid.

• • •

He crashed at The Kid's pad. He stopped going to Sproul Plaza and got a job unloading trucks at Safeway. He saved money, enough to pay what The Kid charged for papers in the name of Charles Ochs, a real person, recently deceased. "So it'll all check out, man. You know?" The Kid never asked why he needed them; Blake assumed he thought it had something to do with dodging the draft.

Except that on the very first night at The Kid's pad, while his guest, having gorged on pita burgers and milkshakes, slept deeply, The Kid took a moment or two to go through the pockets of his jeans. He found the clipping from the *Boston Herald Traveler*, read it, and put it back. He never said anything about it. Why should he? The only thing, when it came to negotiating for the new ID, he upped the price a little. That was just good business. You know?

19

How common was the name "Koharski?"

There were three listed in the Toronto phone book: Koharski, Abel; Koharski, J. and D.; Koharski, M. Koharski, M., lived at "192 Howland Ave." Charlie rented a car at the airport and asked the clerk for directions.

"Is maybe map in car," said the clerk.

There was a map, but of Detroit. Charlie found Howland Avenue some time later, not far from downtown. The street was lined with large brick houses that looked as though they had been up and down the social ladder several times before arriving at their present state of gentrification. Charlie found a space in front of 192 and got out. One ninety-two Howland: three stories, sandblasted brick, glassed-in porch, third-floor cedar deck, chocolate brown trim. Charlie, on the sidewalk, moved onto the tiny front lawn to let two women pass. One wore business dress and carried a laptop, the other wore shorts and bounced a basketball. The basketball woman said, "Taxes are killing me."

"You're breaking my heart," said the other.

Charlie checked his watch: 5:36. The sun glowed red on the

bricks, the air was soft and only slightly hazy with pollution: a fine urban afternoon. A fat man on a bicycle rode slowly up the street. He wore a summer suit, Birkenstocks, smoke-gray glasses, and had a briefcase clamped to a carrier over the back fender. He turned with a wobble into the narrow driveway at 192, climbed heavily off the bike, and started wheeling it around the side of the house. Then he noticed Charlie on the front lawn and stopped.

"Looking to buy?" he said. "All yours for five fifty."

Charlie said: "How about twenty-four-oh-one?"

"I'm sorry?"

"Twenty-four-oh-one."

"I'm not sure I understand."

"Final Jeopardy!."

The fat face shaped itself in a tentative smile. "You saw me on TV?"

"I saw a tape," said Charlie.

"Yeah?"

"At Stu Levine's house. You remember Bombo, don't you?"

The fat man went still, the smile lingering foolishly on his face. He stood in his driveway, hands on the grips of his bike, smoke-gray lenses fixed on Charlie. There was a long silence, during which the basketball woman walked by the other way, this time alone and without the ball. When she was out of hearing, the fat man said:

"So."

"So," said Charlie.

The fat man nodded, as though reaching some understanding. "I suppose I should have expected this."

Charlie was silent.

"Who else knows?"

"Alex Trebek," said Charlie.

There was a buzzing sound. It came from inside the briefcase on back of the bike. The fat man leaned the bike against the side of the house, opened the briefcase, took out a portable phone, extended the antenna, and said: "Koharski." He listened. He said: "A ten-year lease or nothing." He retracted the antenna, saw Charlie watching him. "Property—the pivot of civilization," he said. "Not," he added, "one of mine."

"I thought property was theft, Andy."

"Merv. That's just the flip side of the coin. Everyone gets so emotional about property. That's what drives the market." He gestured to the house beside him. "They look at this and try to see whether it expresses their inmost souls. I look at it and see a widget. Office towers, apartments, condos, villas on the Riviera, the Trump Plaza—they're all just widgets to me. That's why I'm so good at this."

"At what?"

"Real estate syndication. I corral some investors, do a deal, take a share for putting it together. One two three."

"Corraling's your thing, isn't it, Andy?" said Charlie.

"Merv." Malik looked around, saw no one. He studied Charlie from behind the smoke-gray lenses. "You haven't aged at all."

"Not true."

"Compared to me."

"Fat's a good disguise," Charlie said. "But going on 'Jeopardy!' —that was hubris."

Malik licked his lips. "How much do you want?"

"That's what Stu said."

"And what did you tell him?"

"Stu's rich."

"He is?" Malik glanced up at his house. "I'm not. Don't be misled by all that real estate talk. Business is terrible."

"Let's discuss it."

"If you insist."

"I do."

Malik walked his bike around the house. Charlie followed. Malik carried the bike up three steps onto a porch, chaining it to the railing. The effort left him breathing hard. He took out a key, opened the back door, and walked inside. Charlie went after, closing the door behind him.

They were in a messy kitchen. Remains of several meals lay on the table and the counters; stacks of dishes waited in the sink, and the dishwasher door hung open, revealing more. Charlie sat at the table. Malik went to the fridge, took out a carton of milk and gulped from it.

"I waited for you," Charlie said.

"Did you?" The milk left a white mustache where the Zapata had been, long ago. Malik wiped it off with the back of his hand.

"In Sproul Plaza."

"Where's that?" said Malik; or rather, the words came out of this Friar Tuck face that now spoke in Malik's voice.

The words, the face, the voice, the detachment: something set Charlie off. The next moment the table was lying overturned on the floor, and he had done it.

Malik backed up against the wall, hands raised in an attitude much closer to supplication than self-defense. "Don't," he said.

"Don't what?" said Charlie, standing in a spill of broken dishes and General Tso's chicken.

"Hurt me," said Malik. "Don't hurt me. I'll pay what I can."

"Why would I want to hurt you?"

"You tracked me down. It must be for a reason. How about twenty grand? U.S."

"You didn't show, Andy."

"Merv."

"And neither did she."

"She?"

"Rebecca."

"Ah."

"Ah? What does that mean?"

Malik was silent.

"Take off those glasses," Charlie told him.

"They're prescription."

"Off."

Malik took off the smoke-gray glasses, held them on his palm like a strange object. There were his eyes: unchanged. Instantly he looked a lot less pathetic, less laughable, less benign.

"That's better," Charlie said.

"Thirty," said Malik. "U.S. I can't really go any higher."

They faced each other across the littered floor. The phone on the wall began to ring.

"Leave it," Charlie said.

Malik opened his mouth and closed it, like a fish passing water through its gills. "Maybe we should go into the living room," he said when it stopped ringing.

"Why?"

"More comfortable."

"I'm comfortable." Charlie was suddenly aware of his own size and strength; he felt powerful, in a way he had not for a long time.

Malik might have been aware of it too. "Just a suggestion," he said.

"Your suggestions never did me any good."

Malik put his hands together, cracked his knuckles. "That was all long ago. I was young."

I was younger, Charlie thought, but he kept it to himself. He said, "Suggestions like running away to Berkeley."

Malik frowned. "There was talk of meeting there or something?"

"It all seems distant to you, doesn't it? Like it happened to someone else. Yeah, there was talk of meeting there. At Sproul Plaza. A definite plan, in fact. The three of us were going to turn the world upside down."

The fat face reddened. Perhaps it was only the sinking sun, shining through the dusty kitchen window. "I lost interest in politics," Malik said. "It was just a phase in my development. They don't have politics up here, anyway, not the way I understand it."

The table was already overturned. Charlie just stood there and felt the anger growing inside him. "You lost interest on the way to Berkeley?"

Malik smiled, as though it was all coming back to him. And for a moment he was like himself again, his younger self. "Berkeley was never on, if I recall."

"What are you talking about? It was your idea."

"Possibly. But Rebecca countermanded it. Or I changed my mind. Or something."

"When?"

"When?"

"The minute I left the room? An hour later? A day later? Two days? When?"

"I don't remember."

"Did you start out for Berkeley?"

"Oh, no. We came right here."

"Here?"

"To Canada. Much safer."

"You went together?"

"Thumbed to Albany, I think it was. Then took a bus."

"Together."

"Why not?"

"Because the plan was to go singly."

"Was it? It's all so long ago. But of course Rebecca and I went together. We had a thing going, after all." Malik saw a look on Charlie's face and added, "You knew that, didn't you?"

Charlie didn't answer. He was thinking of that fairy-tale bed, with Malik in it. The thought didn't make him any angrier, but it caused a sort of mental lurch, as if he'd stepped on ground that wasn't there.

Malik licked his lips again. "You had a little... relationship with her too, was that it? Or something of the kind. I'm trying to remember. Things were different then. Conventions, and all that. But it didn't matter who Rebecca slept with—there was only one man in her life."

"Who?"

"Hugo, of course."

"Hugo?"

"Her father. He was a great man. Still is, I suppose. And he adored her too, of course. She was his own Liberty at the Barricades—doing in real life what he did on paper. He got us some money after we arrived. I don't recall how. We were living in Rochdale at the time. A sort of communal apartment complex. Now it's just an ordinary building. Rent controlled."

"And then?"

"Then?"

"You jumped right into real estate?"

"Far from it," Malik said, without a smile. "There were years of scratching and clawing. Flipping dumps south of Bloor, doing all the renovations myself. I didn't really get rolling till the boom started in 'eighty-two. Later, with all the Hong Kong capital coming in..." He stopped himself; maybe remembering that thirty grand was all he could afford. U.S.

They were going to turn the world upside down. Perhaps they had, by growing up to be real estate syndicators, SDI software writers, users of portable phones, connoisseurs of Armagnac, contestants on "Jeopardy!."

"And Rebecca's money got you started."

"I'm a self-made man," said Malik. "Rebecca had nothing to do with it. She was only here for a month or two. Three at the most."

"Where did she go?"

"Back to the States. Abortions weren't legal here then. Not that they were legal down there, either. But she knew someone." Again Malik saw a look on Charlie's face that made him pause. Perhaps he thought Charlie disapproved of abortion. "How could we have had a baby under those circumstances?" he said.

"What circumstances?"

"On the run like that. Living in . . . fear."

"She didn't come back?"

"From the abortion? No. I never heard from her after she left."

Charlie watched Malik's eyes, searching for signs of truth. He saw only the effects of the sun's low-angled light on vitreous tissue.

"That didn't surprise me," Malik said. "It wasn't like we were in love or anything."

"Where did she go?"

"For the abortion? I don't remember."

"Think harder."

"Why? None of this matters now."

Charlie, barely aware of his movements, crossed the kitchen, crunching glass beneath his feet. He took the front of Malik's summer suit jacket in both hands and backed the big, soft man into the wall. Now there was only the memory of Ronnie Pleasance, the memory of violence past, to stop him from hitting Malik as hard as he could. It was enough. "It matters," Charlie said.

Malik was convinced. "San Francisco," he said in a strangled voice, although Charlie was not strangling him. "I think it was San Francisco."

"Is she still there?"

"How would I know?"

Charlie let go. Malik slumped against the wall, breathing hard again. He loosened his tie, blue with an orange pattern that suggested sunbursts. "Maybe she was really going to see you."

Another one of Malik's suggestions. Charlie ignored it. "What was the name of the doctor?"

"Doctor?"

"Who did abortions."

"You expect me to remember that?"

"I don't expect anything from you, Andy."

"Merv."

Silence.

"Let's see your ID," Charlie said.

Malik's brow wrinkled in puzzlement, but he got out his wallet and handed it over as though Charlie were the law. Charlie looked inside. He found an Ontario driver's license, a Canadian social insurance card, a health insurance card, a gold American Express card, a gold Bank of Montreal MasterCard, all in the name of Mervin H. Koharski.

"What's the *H* for?"

"Herman."

"Mervin Herman Koharski."

Malik nodded.

"When did you do it?"

"What?"

"Become him."

"The papers and stuff? Years ago."

"When Rebecca was still here?"

"After."

"So she was still Rebecca when she left?"

"As far as I know," said Malik. He gazed at Charlie, somewhat myopically. He was still holding his glasses. "Why is it important?"

Charlie returned the gaze until Malik broke it. Then he walked away. He didn't like being close to Malik, and he had to think. He tried to think while eyeing the dishes in the sink, the half-full takeout bag from Yong Lok Gardens on the counter, the calendar with a picture of the CN Tower, still turned to the

164

month before. He flicked through the pages, looking for memos. All the days were blank.

"One little stick of dynamite," he said. It was the only thought in his head.

"What?"

"Did all that."

"You're talking about the . . . explosion?"

"What else?" Charlie said. "Where did you get it?"

"What do you mean?"

"The dynamite," Charlie said.

"For the bomb you built?"

"What other bomb is there?"

Malik, fat, myopic, sweating slightly, laughed. That same old laugh, much closer to barking, but he was too short of breath now to sustain it for long. "*Touché,*" he said.

"Is there something funny about it?"

"It depends on your point of view. Like me being in real estate, from yours. What do you do for a living?"

"Trap lobsters."

Malik smiled. "See?" He opened the fridge, drank more milk, removed a takeout carton. "You like *nhem shross?*"

"Never had it."

"Cambodian."

"Solidarity forever."

"Huh?"

"Nothing. You haven't answered the question."

"What question?"

There was only one question, wasn't there? Where is Rebecca? Charlie knew that Malik didn't know the answer. But other questions kept forming in his mind. "Where did the stick of dynamite come from?"

For a moment Charlie thought Malik was about to smile again, possibly even laugh that barking laugh. Instead, he replied: "A construction site, I think. Somewhere on the pike. Rebecca stole it, if I recall."

"Was there anything special about it?"

"Special?"

"To cause an explosion of that size."

Once more Malik's lips seemed to hover on the edge of a

165

smile. Malik licked them and said, "Not that I know of. You're the one who built it, for Christ's sake."

Some expression on Charlie's face made Malik shrink against the wall. But Charlie didn't come crunching toward him across the floor. It was revulsion, not rage, he was feeling. He didn't want to spend another second in this kitchen, in this house, and he had nothing more to say. He went to the door, opened it, stepped out on the porch, breathed a big lungful of city air.

"What are you doing?" called Malik.

Charlie turned in the doorway. "*Ciao,*" he said.

"You're leaving? Just like that?" Malik stood there with shoulders shrugged and puzzled face. "I don't understand what you want."

At the bottom of the steps, Charlie turned. "You've really got baseball tickets?"

"The Blue Jays are going all the way this year."

"You're a fan now?"

"Live and learn," Malik said, putting on the smoke-gray glasses. Charlie walked away.

•   •   •

Malik closed the door, hurried out of the kitchen. He went quickly through rooms that had they been furnished might have been the dining room and living room, but were bare: what was the point of furniture? He'd be selling the place in a month or two when the market started up, and moving into another one he had a few blocks away. Malik looked out a window facing the street. He saw Charlie get into a car and drive away. Malik had time to memorize the plate number and notice the sticker on the bumper: "Maple Leaf Car Rentals."

He phoned Maple Leaf. "Hi," he said. "I'm calling from Mulligan and Urquhart. We just had a customer of yours—"

"All our operators are busy at this time."

He waited. Through the window he saw another car pull out of the parking space and drive off, with a young blond man at the wheel.

"Can I help you?"

"Mulligan and Urquhart," he began again; telling long,

complex lies was tiring, but he was used to it: it was the *sine quo non* of his business. "We just had a customer of yours in here. It looks like he forgot his coat. My secretary ran after him but he drove off. Have you got an address where we can mail it? She wrote down the plate number."

Thirty seconds later, Malik had Charlie's name and address. "Ochs?" he said. "As in Phil?"

"Pardon?"

"Nothing."

Thirty seconds after that he had Charlie's telephone number. He dialed the number, just for the hell of it.

A woman answered. "Hello?" she said. She had a nice voice—warm, educated, poised. "Hello? . . . Hello? . . . Hello?" She was losing a little of that poise by the last hello. Malik hung up.

He made three more calls. The first was to a law office in Berkeley, California. A mistake perhaps? How much protection would come from that quarter? The truth was he wouldn't feel safe as long as Wrightman/Ochs was around. Doing something about that without involving himself was the problem. He considered it for a while and placed a call that made him feel a little funny: to the ROTC office at Morgan College. That got him the number for the third call, to some backwater in Georgia.

Malik felt safer after that, safe and hungry. Food had become his only pleasure. How about it? Was he in the mood for lobster?

20

Ninety degrees. Ninety percent humidity. Ol' J.P.—he thought of himself as Ol' J.P., especially those nights, afternoons, and occasional mornings when he was half-cut, and he was half-cut now—sat outside on a frayed canvas chair, wearing only his briefs. His body was clammy, his mind, like a perfect miniature of the external world, a haze. Ol' J.P. sat there on the edge of the swamp, just breathing.

The phone in his trailer began to ring. He let it; the only calls he got were from people or machines trying to sell him things he didn't need and often hadn't heard of. He raised the bottle in his hand, a bottle of something cheap, and took a small sip. Very small. Birdlike. Abstemious. Was that the word? Was it a word of any kind? He studied the label. "Genuine Tennessee Whiskey," it read. There was a sketch of a man in a coonskin cap. The tune from "Davy Crockett" began running in J.P.'s mind, faded out in the haze. He stared at the label for a while. The phone stopped ringing.

J.P. heard something rustle down by the water. He had excellent hearing. He saw a fern twitch. He had excellent vision. So excellent that there, at the base of the fern, hidden in all that greenery, he could distinguish the outlines of a bullfrog. A big fat son of a bitch. Camouflaged in nature's grand plan—but not from him.

J.P. set his whiskey bottle down in the grass without making a sound. He had a box of nails under the chair, old rusty ones he'd bent into V shapes. He fished through them, slow and silent, until he found one that felt good on the pads of his fingers. He had a slingshot down there too, made from a coat hanger and a wide rubber band. A crude weapon—a kid's toy, if you wanted the truth.

With the toy in his left hand, J.P. fitted the nail into place at the center of the rubber band and drew back. He didn't sight, didn't take aim, simply drew back and released, letting his hands do all the work. He heard a whizzing sound, very faint: that was the nail, spinning through the air. Then came another sound, a little less faint: *plop*. That was the nail making contact with the big green head. Down by the water the frog performed a funny kind of leap, with only one leg extending, and flopped sideways onto the grass.

A toy weapon, good for killing toy creatures.

J.P. got up and walked to the water. They called it a lake, but it was so full of plant life it was almost as green as the land and not much wetter. J.P. examined the frog. The point of the nail had stuck into its head, about a sixteenth of an inch above the left eye. And it was the right leg that had extended. That was interesting. Left brain, right brain—wasn't that the theory? The fact that the nail had hit point-first was dumb luck of course. The frequency of point-first hits was about one in ten. It made no difference. Head shots killed every time, no matter what part of the nail did the job. J.P. squatted down and plucked out the nail. Then he picked up the frog by the extended leg and tossed it underhanded into the water. It described an arc, as they used to say in gunnery school, and fell with a quiet splash.

A mosquito bit the back of J.P.'s neck. He slapped it, gazed at its squashed form lying in a red smear on his palm, wiped it off on the side of his briefs. Then he walked back to the chair, dropped the nail back in the box, and went inside the trailer, pulling the screen door shut behind him.

J.P. was hungry, but it was too hot to eat. The icebox was by the door. He took out a beer. Whiskey was drink, beer was food. Across from the icebox, on the other side of the trailer, about three feet away, was a Formica-topped table with a phone on it. The phone started ringing again. J.P. ignored it, walked toward the back of the trailer. There were no partitions; he could see his domain entire: sink, toilet, stall shower, double bed, bureau. Nothing on the walls, nothing on the linoleum floor. He sat on the bed and took a sparrowlike sip of beer. It took away his hunger, nourished him, although it didn't clear the haze. The phone stopped ringing.

Framed photographs on the bureau. Family pictures, of that three-member family, now down to one. These he found himself staring at from time to time; times like this.

Picture one: Mina at the beach, late fifties. Bikini, flat stomach, round thighs, big smile. He remembered that beach. A nice beach in a nice little town on the south Jersey shore. They had stayed in a motel—the Wee Willie Winkie. He remembered that too. They'd made love for the first time in the Wee Willie Winkie and been married a few months later, after she got pregnant.

Picture two: Mina and the boy, midsixties. Boy on swing, laughing, head thrown back, Mina pushing, mouth laughing but eyes worried he might fall off.

Picture three: Himself, Mina, boy, 1970. Studio portrait. Mina smiling into the lens with enthusiasm because the whole thing was her idea, boy smiling because he'd been told to, himself posed behind them like the great protector.

Family pix. He made himself look away, drained the beer and tossed the bottle into the trash can by the icebox. Didn't sight, didn't aim, just let his hands do it. His hands were good at stuff like that.

The phone began to ring again. "Jesus Christ," he said, or maybe only thought it. All they wanted to do was sell him, sell him, sell him. A goddamn fever of selling. He didn't need anything and even if he did there was no money to buy. He had his pension and that was it. Didn't their computers know that by now? So what the fuck?

Ring ring.

J.P. got off the bed, went to the Formica table, picked up the phone.

"What is it?" he started to say, but the words clumped together; he hadn't spoken in some time. He cleared his throat and tried again. "What is it?"

"Hello," said a voice on the other end, a man, not a machine. "Captain Pleasance, please."

That threw him, but he recovered after only a second or two, ten at the most. "This is him. Except I'm retired." Been retired for fifteen years, for Christ's sake.

"Captain Jack Pleasance?"

"That's what I told you. You better not be selling something."

The man on the other end of the line laughed, at least that's what J.P. supposed it was—it sounded more like a dog barking. "I'm giving, not selling," he said.

J.P. didn't get it, so he kept his mouth shut.

The caller spoke again: "Does the name Blake Wrightman mean anything to you?"

J.P. had trouble breathing for a moment. He leaned against his pasteboard trailer wall for support. "What if it does?" he said. "Who is this?" It occurred to him that he'd got the questions in the wrong order.

It didn't matter: the caller ignored the second one. "If it does mean anything to you, I could supply his present name and address, especially if you're a self-reliant sort of person."

J.P.'s heartbeat quickened then, quickened a lot, pumping strength into his body, driving away the oppression of the heat and damp, driving the haze from his mind. "Self-reliant?"

"Someone who doesn't get bogged down in official channels. A take-charge guy."

J.P. cleared his throat again. "That name means something to me."

"Got a pencil?"

"Hold on."

J.P. put down the phone, searched for something to write with. On the icebox, on the bureau, in a drawer, under the bed: getting frantic, breathing in quick little breaths. A fucking pencil—come on, come on. He found a leaky ballpoint in the pocket of a shirt that had been lying on the floor for a few days, or maybe weeks. He grabbed the phone.

"You still there?"

"What's going on?" asked the caller, affability gone, suspicious.

"Nothing," said J.P. "I'm ready."

The caller dictated the name and address. J.P. wrote it down on the Formica tabletop and repeated it to the caller, spelling out the name.

"You got it."

"How do you know—" J.P. began.

The caller interrupted. "Good luck." *Click.*

"Good luck"? Meaning what? J.P. stood in his clammy briefs by the table, the phone still in his hand. It began blaring the off-the-hook signal. He hung up, stared at the name and address on the Formica for a minute or two. Then he picked up the phone again and called information. He soon had the phone number that went with them. He wrote it on the table.

Three bits of information. He gazed at them for a long time, long enough for them to become part of his memory. J.P. looked up. He needed a drink bad. The Tennessee whiskey was—where? He looked around, finding it in the grass by the box of bent bullfrog nails. He picked it up and drank what was left. The haze returned, but light, like the mist off the swamp in the evening. He was sweating now, dripping with it like a prizefighter in the twelfth round. From down by the water came a wet sucking sound, followed by a splash.

J.P. went back in the trailer, picked up the phone, dialed the number now firmly in his mind. The call was answered on the first ring.

"Hello?"

A woman. J.P. wasn't prepared for that. He tried out various explanations while the woman said, "Hello? . . . Hello?"

She had a nice voice.

"Who is this?" she was saying. "Who is this?"

A nice voice, at least it sounded nice to him. *Nice, and maybe a little scared,* he thought, hanging up. *Scared of what?*

Ol' J.P. went to the mirror, had a gander at himself. Time to get cleaned up.

21

H ello?" Emily said one more time, but even as she did there was a click at the other end of the line. She put down the phone and got back to work.

Emily was sitting at her desk in the bedroom, overlooking Cosset Pond. On the computer screen columns of numbers attended her next move, like soldiers at inspection. She backed the hurricane ten degrees by typing "37H" on the keyboard and waited to see what it would do to her beach. The desktop computer waited too. The mainframe at MIT was doing all the work.

It wasn't a quick job, not even for the Cray. If she was right, her beach would now not only be protected by the jetty she'd angled off the shore almost three miles away, but would also widen ten to twelve feet, padded with sand swept in from the offshore bar. The prospect excited her, not for practical or mercenary reasons, but because she liked solving puzzles, especially those of her own devising: the hurricane, the beach, the jetty, and the sandbar were all just numbers in one of her erosion models.

The phone rang again. Emily answered. "Hello?"

173

Silence.

"Hello? . . . Hello?"

Silence; perhaps the faint sound of breathing. That made her angry. "Who is this?" she said, her voice rising. "Who is this?"

Click.

Emily hung up. She turned back to the screen, annoyed, uneasy, distracted, found herself staring through the numbers into the blackness beyond. *Get a grip,* she told herself. It was nothing but a wrong number, two wrong numbers; probably the same careless caller. But misdialers usually hung up as soon as they realized their mistake, didn't they? And this one hadn't. This one had listened to her for a while; breathing. She didn't like the breathing. It meant a crank. Or a sicko. Emily's imagination ran with that thought, as she sat at her desk, waiting for MIT to do the numbers.

"Get a grip." This time she said it aloud. She was just jumpy. It was all about Charlie of course, off somewhere with his uncle, dealing with a complicated and difficult family she had known nothing about. Charlie's Uncle Sam had said it might be a few days. "A few" meant three, but that was a possibility Emily hadn't really taken seriously. She'd expected Charlie back the next day; that was today, and there wasn't much of it left. Outside the sun was low in the sky, reddening the surface of Cosset Pond. And if he wasn't coming back today, wouldn't he call to tell her? She would in his place. Then she tried to put herself in his place, and could not: there were too many sudden unknowns. Did they make Charlie a puzzle too? Emily shrank from that idea, but she was still thinking about those unknowns when all the numbers on her screen changed.

Emily looked at the new numbers. They would have been meaningless to all but a few dozen people in the world. Emily understood them right away. Her beach was gone.

22

D_{ay} three.

"It might take a few days, actually," as Uncle Sam had said. *Few* was the way to say *three* without being tied down.

Day one: Bombo. Day two: Malik. A logical progression, even if it had led nowhere. There was nothing logical about day three, and Charlie couldn't have explained what he was doing, not even to himself. It had nothing to do with finding Rebecca, nothing he could see. But late in the afternoon of day three he was back on campus, standing outside Cullen House. *Going backward, Charlie old boy, going backward.*

Day three had begun like days one and two, warm and sunny, but now top-heavy thunderclouds were swelling in the west. A tanned woman came out of Cullen House, saw him looking at the sky, and said, "It'll hold off. Are you signed up for the mixed doubles?"

"No."

"We need one more man for the four point fives. What's your rating?"

"I don't know."

"My God, I thought we sorted that out at orientation." She ducked back inside the building.

Charlie walked away before she could return with racquets and balls and evaluate his game. He followed the crushed-brick path, through the line of oaks, into the central quad, past the chapel. He stood in front of the Ecostudies Center, seeking the skeleton of the old structure. This was difficult; the building and his memory of it had both changed.

Charlie circled the building. At the back a gardener watered flower beds, a cigarette drooping from his lips. The gardener's hose ran from a square hatch at the base of the wall. He squinted through cigarette smoke at Charlie. Charlie moved on, around to the front. The door of the Ecostudies Center opened and a woman, this one pale and nonsporty, emerged, eating trail mix from a paper bag. When had he last eaten? Charlie couldn't remember.

He took the crushed-brick path to the edge of the campus, walked along College Street to the Catamount Bar and Grille. In 1970 it had been a dive with a cat's-head sign and cheap greasy food. Everything had changed but the sign. Charlie took a seat under a small painting of an alienated nude, priced at $250, listened to the list of specials, ordered something with sun-dried tomatoes because he'd never had them, and chose a beer he'd never heard of. A book of Catamount Bar and Grille matches lay in the ashtray. Charlie put them in his pocket.

The beer came first. He tasted it. Not bad, but all at once he didn't want beer, didn't want food, either. He got up and walked to the phone by the men's room. "A few days," Uncle Sam had said. "A few" would mean three to Emily, a firm three. He picked up the phone and dialed his home number.

She answered on the first ring: "Hello?"

The sound of her voice choked up Charlie's throat. He knew immediately, too late, that he couldn't speak to her. He had nothing to say but lies.

"Hello?" she said again.

It wasn't just the lying; there was more to it than that. He was like a character in a time-travel story, who could move

176

through different epochs and observe, but enter none. He had traveled back in time, all the way back to Blake Wrightman.

"Hello? Hello? Who is this? Why do you keep—"

Charlie hung up, leaving his palm print in sweat on the receiver.

He walked back through the restaurant, almost out the front door before remembering he was a customer. He returned to his table, where the food had arrived. He asked for the check.

"Is something wrong?" asked the waitress.

"No, I—" Charlie stopped himself; his speech sounded strangled. To him and to the waitress: she was staring openly at him now. "Not feeling well," Charlie said. A lie. He saw himself at that moment naked and revealed to this stranger. He'd been a liar for twenty-two years, a denizen of the unhealthy world portrayed in the $250 painting above his head. He was sick of it.

"Would you like a doggie bag?" the waitress said.

No. Yes. What difference did it make? Charlie nodded. The waitress removed the plates, returned with doggie bag and bill. She didn't hover but didn't go far, either, until he had paid. "Hope you feel better," she said as he left.

Out on the street Charlie took a deep breath. Then he walked back to the campus, dropping his sun-dried dinner into a trash can at the wrought-iron gate.

Night was falling now, and it was quiet. Charlie could hear soft sounds from far away: a guitar, a laugh, a ball smacking into a glove. But it was too dark for playing catch; that last must have been imagined.

Charlie wandered the campus until it was fully dark. The heavy clouds had covered the sky. There was no moon or stars. A breeze quickened in the west, blew harder. Charlie stopped walking. He stood in the shadows behind the Ecostudies Center.

Charlie waited there, waited for someone to stroll past or shine a light or cough in the darkness. None of this happened. He moved forward, knelt in the grass, felt for the square ground-level hatch, found it. The hatch opened at the side and was fastened by two simple bolts. There was no lock. He drew the bolts and opened the hatch. He listened once more for human sounds, heard none, and squeezed inside. His hands explored the earthen floor, encountered a cement piling. Down here at the foundation, nothing had changed. Charlie pulled the hatch closed, once more in the darkness of the crawl space under the house by the chapel.

Charlie took out the Catamount Bar and Grille matches and lit one. In the unsteady globe of yellow light it made, he saw the gardener's coiled hose, watering cans, a spade, a hoe, and two flats of pink flowers he didn't recognize. Beyond that, darkness. He blew out the match and crawled forward on his belly.

The floor felt damp at first, then dry, as before. After a minute or two, Charlie paused, reached for the matches, lit one. Ahead he saw a small pile of cement blocks. Three of them, to be exact. His heart beat faster; he could feel it against the earth. He blew out the match, crept forward, his right hand extended. It touched the nearest block. Charlie felt again for the matches. At that moment a footstep sounded on the floor, directly above him. Charlie froze.

Something squeaked overhead, a swivel chair perhaps. A second footstep drummed once on the floor. Then footsteps began moving, back and forth, back and forth. Charlie thought he heard a groan. After that came a man's voice, intimately close and distinct: "I've got to think." Something squeaked again. There was a sigh. Then silence.

Charlie lay without moving in the crawl space, his hand on the edge of the cement block. Time passed, whole minutes surely. When he could wait no more, Charlie reached for the matches, monitoring every movement. He lit one. The snick of the match head on the striking surface sounded like the cracking of a whip. Charlie lay still, not breathing, the match burning down between his fingers. Something—a spider?—ran quickly across the back of his neck, paused, bit him. He did nothing about it. It bit him again. Above, there was only silence. Charlie reached behind his neck, pressed hard. He crushed a hard little body and dampness spread across his palm.

He crawled forward a few more inches, examined the blocks.

REVOLUTION #9

A pyramid, two at the base, one on top. The match burned his fingertips. He dropped it. It went out, giving off a last invisible plume of smoke that curled up into his nose.

Charlie twisted sideways, felt for the topmost block, got both hands on it. In that position he could use none of the strength of his legs, back, or even upper arms. With just his wrists and hands, he raised the block off the pile and lowered it to the ground behind his head. *Quiet, Charlie boy, quiet and slow.* But the blocks scraped together just the same. How loudly? As loud as shifting tectonic plates on a fault line, as soft as batting eyelashes? Charlie didn't know. He listened for sounds from above and heard none, no footsteps, no groans, no sighs.

He felt for the two remaining blocks, pushed one a foot or two away, dragged the second in the other direction. He listened again. Silence. Then, with his fingernails, he began scraping at the earth in front of him. Moving bits of earth at a time, he dug a small depression, an inch or two deep, a foot or two in diameter. Nothing more was necessary. The tip of his index finger touched something man-made, knew what it was: a buckle, a brass buckle.

Charlie lit one last match. Lying in the depression, the depression he'd now dug for the second time in twenty-two years, was a knapsack, the kind found in army surplus stores. It was coated in mold, slick and dirt colored. Charlie ran his thumbnail across it and saw it was still khaki underneath. If biodegradable, it was degrading slowly: Malik's backpack.

Charlie stuck the match in the loose earth he'd shifted. With both hands free he drew the pack toward him, feeling the weight inside, and unfastened the buckle.

Charlie looked inside. Down in the shadows of the pack lay coils of insulated wire, a stick not much bigger than a cigar tube, a rusted alarm clock. "Big Ben" was gone, all except the second *B*. He checked the red wire, saw—yes!—how it was wrapped all around the electrical tape. He'd made a symbolic bomb, as he'd thought, a bomb that could never explode, could never hurt a little boy, could never bring his mother to her knees, could never make a father cry. This was nothing but the raw material for a bomb, added, it was true, to the idea of bombing. But someone else's idea.

The match went out. Charlie lay in the crawl space, the bomb in his hands, his heart beating against the earth. His personal Big Bang, the beginning of the universe of Charlie Ochs: he hadn't understood it at all. The first roll of thunder sounded in the distance.

23

I s this part of the plan?" Svenson asked.

"What are you talking about?" Goodnow said. He could no longer cope with the allusive, the roundabout; he was in too much pain for anything but precision and hard fact. Signing out of the hospital wasn't the same as being cured.

"Him flipping out, or whatever this is," said Svenson.

Goodnow had no answer. They stood like medieval sentries on the crenellated platform of the campanile. Lightning flashed overhead, a crooked white stick with spiky branches, illuminating for a moment the rear of the Ecostudies Center and Charlie Ochs crawling out from underneath. He straightened, glanced up, directly at the campanile, although he couldn't possibly have seen them, then vanished with the lightning.

"Did you see the look on his face?" asked Svenson.

Goodnow had: wild and strange. Maybe it was just the lightning. He hoped so: the only other explanation that came to mind involved Charlie blowing up the building again.

"Follow him," he said, and Svenson was gone.

Goodnow descended the stone steps that wound inside the campanile, stopping twice to rest. He checked his watch, hoping it had been four hours since his last pill, so he could have another, or even three and a half, which would be close enough. But it wasn't even three. He took one anyway. The pain in his gut didn't go away, but after a minute or two it changed shape. He felt a sense of well-being. That was just the morphine. It was gone by the time he reached the Ecostudies Center.

Goodnow shone his flashlight on the hatch, opened it and bent over to crawl through. The cancer didn't want to be shoved around like that and let him know right away. He heard a gasp, his own, and found himself leaning against the building, biting the sleeve of his jacket. He took a few breaths, shallow, unobtrusive, inoffensive. The cancer gave tacit approval. Goodnow again approached the open hatch. This time he didn't bend but went to his knees like a supplicant, then leaned forward onto his hands and went through the hatchway. He bumped his head, not hard, but the slight pain that resulted stood on the shoulders of a giant, and he almost screamed aloud. He wished that there was a bomb, and that it would explode now.

But there was no explosion, and after a minute or two Goodnow lowered himself to his belly. That reshaped the pain again, but didn't make it worse. He shone his light, saw gardening supplies, and farther away a few cement blocks. He crawled toward them, digging at the earth with his toes. wriggling his body. He reached the blocks. There were three of them, lying together: just blocks. He pushed one of them with his hands, hard as he could. It didn't budge.

The effort caused a funny feeling in his stomach, not pain, almost a release. He rested, his cheek against the cool earth. Something bit the tip of his nose. He started to cry.

After a while Goodnow twisted around, shone his light around the crawl space. He saw nothing but cement blocks and gardening supplies. No new bomb, no explanation, no meaning. What was Charlie doing? Tripping down Memory Lane, as Svenson had said at first? Flipping out, as he seemed to believe now? Goodnow didn't know. He only knew that Charlie had failed to take the logical first step.

Goodnow backed out of the hatch. He got his hands on the top of the door, pulled himself up. The front of his shirt was wet. He touched it. Wet and sticky. Goodnow unfastened the buttons, shone the light on himself. A yellow, viscous liquid was leaking through the almost-healed holes where the stitches had been. Goodnow buttoned his shirt, closed the hatch, moved on.

•   •   •

Charlie caught the last flight to Toronto. It was almost midnight when he stood at the front door of 192 Howland; the house was dark. Charlie knocked. No one came. He pressed the buzzer, heard it buzz, knocked again. Then he walked around to the back.

The mountain bike was locked to the porch; its handlebars gleamed under the pink night sky of the city. Charlie climbed the stairs and knocked on the door. No answer. Charlie wanted answers. He knocked again, hard: pounding more than knocking. The door swung open.

Charlie walked inside. He stepped on something soft, fleshlike. Running his hand along the wall, he found a switch, turned on the overhead light. He was standing on a shelled lobster tail.

The rest of the creature lay with a cut lemon on the table. The table was set for one: one plate, one shell cracker, one lobster fork, one glass, one bottle of white wine, open but full. Someone had cleaned up the mess that Malik had made and that Charlie had made worse. Everything was tidy, as though the maid had just left, tidy except for the lobster tail on the floor. Charlie touched the wine bottle. It was warm.

He walked into the next room, switched on the light. It might have been the dining room, but there was nothing in it except wall-to-wall carpet and a fax machine. Charlie kept going, through other empty rooms—all carpeted, all with telephones, answering machines, or faxes in various combinations, but otherwise empty. He went up to the second floor and saw more of the same. He climbed the stairs to the third floor.

There was a narrow hall at the top of the stairs. At one end was a study with a desk, a chair, file cabinets. At the other was a bedroom with a double bed, neatly made, a television, a closet full of clothes. In the middle was a bathroom with a shower, a Jacuzzi, and a hanging fern, the only living thing he'd seen in the house. Charlie opened the mirrored cabinet, saw razors, shaving cream, toothpaste, foot powder, tweezers. He returned to the kitchen, shutting off the lights as he went down.

Charlie eyed the dinner on the table, the full bottle of wine, the lobster tail on the floor. Dinner was served, but where was the diner? Perhaps he'd forgotten something, had gone out to the store, would be back any moment. Milk, for example. Malik drank milk, straight from the carton, like a man with an ulcer. And in his absence the cat had jumped up on the table and dragged off the lobster tail. Charlie opened the refrigerator. There were three cartons of milk inside and nothing else. And he saw no sign of a cat—no litter, no dish.

There were two closed doors in the kitchen. Charlie opened one. A closet: brooms, mops, vacuum cleaner. He tried the other door. It opened on a descending staircase. Charlie turned on the light and went down.

He was in a one-room basement: gas furnace, cement floor, brick walls, a wooden tennis racquet, washer, dryer, and a freezer big enough for storing sides of beef. He opened the dryer. Empty. He tried the washer, found clothing, slightly damp and twisted, as though it had been there overnight, still waiting for transfer to the dryer. But what did that mean? Who didn't forget about the clothes in the washing machine sometimes?

Charlie picked up the tennis racquet, tapped the strings against his palm. They were brittle; one broke immediately. Then, because he could think of nothing else, he raised the lid of the freezer.

There was an unclothed male body inside, lying on his back in a pool of red ice. It was Malik. He had two little round holes in his chest. One of his arms was twisted behind him; he was holding something. Charlie reached down for it, but Malik's hand was stuck in the red ice. Charlie tugged at the stiff, cold wrist. The hand came free, with the sound that frozen chicken breasts make when they're torn from the package. Malik was clutching a corkscrew with the cork still attached, a poor choice to counter a gun. Charlie closed the freezer.

The room returned to normal. A normal basement with the

normal appliances. *Think. Shouldn't there be blood, on the floor, the sides of the freezer, perhaps the stairs?* There was none. *Had Malik climbed into the freezer before being shot? And if not?*

Charlie opened the washer again, took out the clothes. He found a pair of men's underwear, a pair of socks, a summer suit, a shirt, a tie with sunbursts. The Birkenstocks were at the bottom. Charlie examined the clothing, saw two little round holes in the suit jacket, two in the shirt, one in the tie. He put everything back in the washer, closed the lid, went upstairs, shut off the lights, left by the back door.

Tidy. No loose ends, except for the lobster tail and the question that he had come to ask and that remained unanswered: what caused the explosion at the ROTC? The answer might make him free—not technically free, the way he would be if he kept his half of the deal with Mr. G, but free in his own mind. The list of people who might know the answer had shrunk to one. Now he wanted Rebecca to be alive, and looking for her had nothing to do with the deal. That put him and Mr. G on the same side. It was an unpleasant thought.

• • •

"Where are you?" Svenson said, sounding peevish and tired.

"Coming," Goodnow said into the portable phone. The taxi driver glanced in the rearview mirror.

"The lights are all off again," Svenson said. "I don't know what the fuck he's— Hold it. He just came out."

Pause. Goodnow heard Svenson breathing. He looked out the window, saw a colossal tower that might have been designed on another planet for an unknown purpose. The driver glanced at him again, followed the direction of his gaze.

"Something else, eh?" he said, his voice full of civic pride.

Goodnow ignored him.

Svenson breathed a few more times. He breathed with his mouth open, Goodnow recalled; a disgusting habit. It suddenly occurred to him that Svenson might have fallen asleep.

"Well?" he said.

"Well what?" said Svenson, awake and unhappy.

Silence. The taxi turned north, away from the tower and into the city. Goodnow checked his watch. Not even two hours since the last pill.

Svenson spoke. "Shit," he said.

"What?"

"He's . . . leaving."

"Then go," Goodnow told him.

"You're my mentor," Svenson said. *Click*.

Ten minutes later Goodnow was standing outside the dark house at 192 Howland. He knew that it was owned by a limited partnership called Annex Investments. He knew that the president of Annex Investments was Mervin H. Koharski, that the house had one resident, Koharski, a Canadian citizen and registered voter, with no arrests and no criminal record, unwanted by any of the police forces included in the Interpol net. What he didn't know was why Charlie had visited the house, twice. He swallowed another pill.

Two minutes later Goodnow was in the house. Five minutes after that he was down in the basement—if there was a basement he always checked it first—studying the tableau in the freezer. The fact of death, the dead body, didn't move him at all. He'd seen lots of dead bodies; he'd soon be dead himself. "It's not going to work," he said aloud, to himself, to the corpse.

It was over. Charlie was out of control. Why was he surprised? The man had killed before. Now he was improvising another violent scheme. Perhaps that was his customary reaction to pressure. It was time to pull the plug, play it by the book, cut his losses, surrender to all the bureaucratic clichés. Goodnow pictured Hugo Klein's smiling face and felt empty inside, empty except for the cancer, growing like a Gerber baby. He slammed the freezer shut.

The Gerber baby didn't like that, wasn't pleased when he acted like his old self. It knocked Goodnow to the floor, bent him into the fetal position, made him rock back and forth. "Please, oh, please," Goodnow said. He fumbled for his pills, got one in his mouth.

After a while, he could stand. He was leaking again through the scar. *Leak*, he told himself, *I don't care*. It was over.

The phone in the kitchen started to ring. Goodnow climbed the stairs. The phone was still ringing when he arrived. He answered it.

It was Svenson. "Mr. G?" he said. He was whispering.

"Whispering is stupid," Goodnow said. "You might as well shout at the top of your lungs."

"Sorry, Mr. G," said Svenson in a normal voice. "You were right."

"Right?"

"About him." Svenson's tone was surprised, respectful. "He just got on a plane to San Francisco. Flying coach."

Goodnow's heart started beating faster, much too fast. Hope was a powerful drug. "Has it taken off?"

"Ten more minutes," Svenson said. "They're backed up."

"Where are you?"

"In the departure lounge. What do you want me to do?"

Have him arrested. That was the proper response. But Goodnow said: "Go first class and don't let him see you." *Because you might get killed.* Goodnow kept the thought to himself.

"Of course not, Mr. G. I've already got a ticket."

"Good, Buzz." Perhaps he would recommend Svenson for promotion after all. "Very good."

There was a pause. "Mr. G?"

"Yes?"

"I wish I'd known this before—that it was going to work, and all."

"Before what, Buzz?"

Another pause. "Last call," Svenson said. "Got to go."

Goodnow hung up. He was hot, trembling, alive: Hugo Klein lived in San Francisco. The missile was on target at last.

Goodnow took a taxi back to the airport. San Francisco, San Francisco, the next flight to San Francisco: the saint's name spun through his mind. But before Goodnow could get to the ticket counter he heard himself paged. He reported to U.S. Customs, wondering how Svenson had messed up. But it wasn't Svenson. Bunting was waiting for him.

Bunting took him aside. Bunting, with his Harold Lloyd

glasses, his pink skin, his perfect health. Bunting—Choate, Amherst, Harvard Law. He didn't expect bluntness from Bunting.

He got it anyway. "You're fired," Bunting said.

Goodnow nodded.

"Where is Svenson?"

"I don't know."

"What is he doing?" Bunting almost raised his voice.

"I don't know."

"Then we'll have to hunt him down, won't we?" said Bunting.

Goodnow exercised his right to remain silent.

Bunting glared at him. It was hard to frighten a man with glares through Harold Lloyd glasses, hard to frighten a man with a Gerber baby growing inside his stomach. Goodnow was beyond fright. It was a nice feeling.

A man from the office appeared, a big man, almost Svenson's size. "Escort Mr. Goodnow home," Bunting said. "He's not well."

24

Air Canada's flight 603, Toronto to San Francisco—filled to capacity, lavatories reeking—pounded through the night, fighting headwinds. Charlie, in coach seat 33A, feeling hungry, even hungrier than he'd been at the Catamount Bar and Grille, chose the chicken teriyaki, but found he still could not eat. He fell into an incomplete sleep, his mind flickering with dreams that didn't quite emerge from the shadows. Svenson, in seat 1B, first class, drank a bottle of champagne, ate filet mignon in sauce béarnaise, and watched a movie about terrorists and oil wells that might have been a comedy; it made him laugh, in any case. Yvonne, also in first class, seat 6D, pulled a blanket over herself and slept the whole way.

•   •   •

Malcolm met her. He took her bag, but didn't give her a kiss. "Hi, Mom," he said. "How was the trip?"

"Tiring," Yvonne answered. "What are you doing here?"

"Conference," Malcolm said. "I told Annie I'd pick you up."

They crossed the parking lot to Malcolm's car, a beat-up

Ford compact of a type no longer made. Inside, a clutter: textbooks on marketing, accounting, management, tapes by bands she hadn't heard of, his rugby cleats, his trumpet, two or three empty beer cans. Yvonne got in, forcing herself to keep silent about the beer cans; but she couldn't help imagining possible chains of cause and effect that might follow his arrest. Malcolm squeezed in behind the wheel; he seemed broader, more muscular than ever.

"How's Wharton?" she asked.

"No complaints." He stopped at the tollbooth and paid. There seemed to be a lot of money in his wallet. He caught her glance. "Did I tell you about my summer job?"

When would that have been? she thought. *You never call.* But she said, "No," and left it at that.

"Sony," he said, and it sounded like a magic word. "They've got me in finance."

"In Philadelphia?"

"No. New York. I've been there all summer. Four of us sharing a one-bedroom off Washington Square. They work us like slaves and then we're up all night. I'm exhausted."

He didn't look exhausted. He looked tanned, fit, happy, energetic. Sony, Wharton, finance: anathema. But he made it all sound . . . fun. Did she envy him? Yvonne recoiled from the thought.

"Your place?" asked Malcolm, turning north on the freeway.

"Yes," she said. He no longer called it home. Was that part of growing up? Yvonne didn't know. Her own history offered no guidance.

They crossed the Bay Bridge, climbed up into the Berkeley Hills, turned onto a middle-class street, verging on upper-middle, green and quiet. Here middle-class verging on upper-middle meant that while some of the lawns might need cutting, everyone recycled. Bundled newspapers waited on the sidewalk in front of Yvonne's house, but the little patch of grass growing around the palm tree was short. She glanced at Malcolm as he parked in the drive, knew at once that he had cut it. Whenever he came home, he repaired, maintained, cleaned: a reproach.

They went inside. Malcolm opened the fridge. "Hungry?"

"Not very," she said, noticing how full the fridge was. He must have stocked it.

Malcolm made himself a sandwich. He toasted rye bread, and while it was in the toaster, opened some canned lobster, chopped onions and tomatoes, mixed them with the meat and a spoonful of canola oil mayonnaise, laid a place at the table, and wiped the counter. The toaster popped; he spread the lobster salad on the toast, poured a glass of milk, sat down to eat.

"Sure you're not hungry?" he said.

"Sure," replied Yvonne, but she was lying. She was hungry; she just didn't feel like a lobster salad sandwich. And the efficient way he had made it somehow reminded her of the new world order, hateful and fascist.

"Sony?" she said. Perhaps it was a magic word; it had popped out of her mouth unbidden.

"It's a start, Mom," Malcolm said with a smile. He still had that big, boyish smile, an American smile on a broad, American face. The first time she saw that smile she should have realized it was hopeless.

Malcolm finished his sandwich, washed the dishes he had used, went down to his old room in the basement. Soon the sound of his trumpet came vibrating up through the floor. He began with something that sounded like "Row, Row, Row Your Boat," but quickly developed a syncopated alter ego, far more sophisticated, filling with potential force, like water boiling under a heavy lid. He was having fun; again the word made her pause. She realized Malcolm had always been good at amusing himself; living with just his mother, he had had to be.

Yvonne went down the hall, through the bedroom, into the bathroom. She took off her clothes, threw them in the wastebasket, had a shower. She washed her hair with aloe shampoo, conditioned it with seaweed conditioner. She soaped her body, scrubbed it with a loofah, dug under her fingernails, soaped again, rinsed under the hottest water she could stand. She turned off the hot, letting icy water drum her body. She stepped out of the shower, covered in goose bumps, feeling clean.

Yvonne wiped the steam off the mirror, saw herself. She didn't look like Lady MacBeth. She looked like a half-Jewish

191

middle-aged woman whose hair was still rich and dark, whose face was still beautiful, whose body was still strong and sexual. The mirror steamed up again, and the image blurred. Yvonne wrapped a towel around herself, carried the wastebasket to the trash bin outside the kitchen door, and dumped the contents in one of the cans.

She went to bed. The music had stopped; the house was quiet. A boat sounded its horn somewhere in the bay, faint and distant. Perhaps fog was piling up over San Francisco. She could picture it: a peaceful image, a sleep-inducing image. The quiet, the romance of the boat, the sleep-inducing image: there was nothing to keep her from sleeping, but she couldn't sleep.

Hours later, Yvonne lay in the dark, still awake. She heard a knock at the front door. Annie. Yvonne let her in.

"You're back," Annie said, watching her closely, perhaps sensing that she hadn't been asleep. Annie knew her well—knew Yvonne, that is—had known her almost since there had been an Yvonne. Loved her too, maybe, and Yvonne, for political reasons, had tried to love her back. But Yvonne had been unable to alter the shape of her sexual urges for political reasons, although she had altered almost everything else in her life for them.

"I'm back," said Yvonne. They sat in the dark living room, side by side at opposite ends of the couch.

"How was it?"

"I just had to get away, that's all."

"What did you do?"

"Walked around. Looked in windows. Slept. Nothing."

A horn sounded again in the bay.

"Is it foggy?" Yvonne asked.

"I didn't notice." Annie: too wound up to notice. Was that unfair?

Silence. A silence with nothing in it but the darkness and Annie's edgy presence.

"We had a meeting tonight," Annie said.

Meetings were important. The gang was all they had, the sole model of a just society. "I had to get away" was not a good excuse, but Yvonne made no apology.

"About what to do with the money," Annie continued.

"We don't have it yet."

"But we will."

Only if I pull it off, Yvonne thought, *so don't bug me about your goddamn meeting.* "Yes," she said, "we will."

Her confidence was contagious. Annie's voice became brisker, more energetic; like a salesman's. "The consensus seems to be to buy a ranch for all of us. Not that we'd have to live there, not full-time. But it would be a kind of haven."

"A ranch?"

"Or something like that. The feeling was we need some security."

"That was the only idea—buy a ranch?"

After a pause, Annie said: "Angel mentioned Cuba."

"Cuba?"

"Going to Cuba. All of us. Using the money to get established there."

"Living there forever, you mean?"

"No one said forever."

"Giving up, in other words."

"You don't have to be so angry. The idea was dropped."

Leaving the ranch. "I thought we were doing this to make a statement," Yvonne said.

"We are. But after the statement we'll have all this money. Don't we have to do something with it?"

"Give it to the poor."

"You know that's not practical. It would be misinterpreted. They'd find ways to make it look condescending—find poor people who'd say they wanted no part of it, all that. Poor but proud. All the Horatio Alger bullshit."

"But we'd be making a statement."

Annie sighed. She didn't argue anymore. Maybe she was tired of talking. Yvonne knew that she herself was. Except for the Santa Clara action, there had been so many years of nothing but talk, so many years of nothing but analysis, so many years lived in camouflage. Those years had led to this: a ranch, with one vote for emigration—call it retirement—to Cuba. It was so fucking . . . American; as though the camouflage had become the skin itself.

Annie said: "Malcolm picked you up?"

"Yes."

"You talked to him?"

"Of course."

"Did he mention what he was doing?"

"If you mean working for Sony, so what?"

Suddenly Annie was laughing. She had a pretty laugh, light and musical. Yvonne wanted to shut it off, anyway she could. "It's funny, isn't it?" Annie said. "You name him after a revolutionary, raise him on radical politics, and he ends up at Sony. He must take after his father."

Yvonne kept her tone even, unperturbed. "I don't think so," she said. Of Malcolm's father, Annie knew no more and no less than Malcolm did: he had been the male half of a stoned half-remembered one-night stand, out of the picture long before Malcolm's birth. One of those stories made more credible by the legend of the sixties. Berkeley was full of them.

"No?" said Annie. "What was he like?"

"Who?"

"Malcolm's father."

"I don't remember."

They sat in the dark. Annie moved her hand across the couch. "I've been thinking about you," she said.

Yvonne was silent.

"Maybe we could lie down for a while. Not to do anything, just lie down."

"No," Yvonne said, and tried to soften the response by adding, "I want to be alone." What a stupid thing to say, and not even original, but breathed by a celluloid character in some old movie. Yvonne tried to think of some other softener, but Annie had already gone, closing the door silently.

And it wasn't even true: Yvonne didn't want to be alone. In the dark she suddenly found herself thinking about Felipe; and the thought was arousing. Felipe. Arousing. God in heaven. What was she coming to?

25

I'm always amused by liberals who profess to be such devotees of the Constitution and the Bill of Rights," said the former attorney general of the United States. A tight shot of the former attorney general appeared on the studio monitor over Charlie's head. All the lines on his face pointed down; he was physiognomically incapable of looking amused. "If they're such strong supporters of these documents, how can they ignore the original intent of the Founding Fathers who wrote them?"

Hugo Klein turned to the former attorney general, exposing his telegenic profile to the small but loyal PBS home audience. "The intent of the Founding Fathers was that there be slavery and no female suffrage, among other things. We can't goosestep back to the eighteenth century, no matter how much certain members of the body politic would love to."

That brought a few cheers from the studio audience. Fred Friendly, the moderator, glared through the TV lights in rebuke; it wasn't that kind of show. He leaned toward the former attorney general. "Well, sir, what do you say to that?"

The former attorney general was a TV pro. He had lots to say, washing away Hugo Klein's rebuttal in a river of verbiage. Time ran out. Fred Friendly promo'ed next week's roundtable— "Should there be codes forbidding hate speech on campus?" —and said good-bye.

The studio audience filed out. The TV lights went off. Technicians unhooked the mikes from the panelists and hooded the cameras. The panelists exchanged a few remarks, shook hands with the moderator, began moving off the set and through an offstage door. Hugo Klein, delayed by a woman who wanted his autograph, was the last to leave. Charlie, seated in the shadows of the last row, rose and walked down the aisle, onto the empty set. He saw that it was as make-believe as a display in a furniture store window, and left by the offstage door.

The door led into a long corridor. Charlie went past a props room, with puppets lying in a heap by the wall, a green room, with a coffee machine and Styrofoam cups, and several closed doors, on each of which was taped the name of a panelist. Charlie knocked on the door that read: "Hugo Klein, Esq."

"Come in."

Charlie went in and closed the door. Hugo Klein was sitting in a barber's chair with his back to Charlie, wiping his face with a round white pad. His eyes went to Charlie's image in the mirror on the wall; they were calm, dark eyes, eyes that had seen everything, perhaps several times, and now had nothing to do but categorize. Charlie saw no reaction at all in those eyes, but why would there be? The two men had never met. All the same, Charlie was aware of a minute stiffening in Klein's posture. He thought he saw the explanation for that in the aggressiveness of his own image in the mirror and tried to moderate it.

"I won't be a minute," Klein said, dabbing at the great planes of his face. "How long do you figure it will take?" The white pad turned the color of a surfer's tan.

"To do what?" asked Charlie.

"Get there. Aren't you the driver?"

"No," said Charlie. He had considered several beginnings. Now that he had seen those eyes up close, none seemed promising. This was not a man he was likely to outwit. He reverted to basics: "I've come for your help."

Klein dropped the pad into a wastebasket, studied his own image, and smoothed the long silvery wings of his hair. "If it's about a case, I can't discuss it now. Call my office in the morning."

"It's not a case," Charlie said. "Not in that sense. I'm looking for Rebecca."

Klein got off the chair. He was taller than Charlie, though not as broad. "You people deserve an A for persistence," he said, "like badgers." He didn't sound angry; his voice was weary, if anything. He held out his hand. "Let's see your badge, badger."

"I don't have a badge."

Klein's eyebrows, magnificent speckled cornices, rose. "Then you will kindly leave."

Charlie stood his ground, not easily. He wasn't afraid, not physically—he was younger and stronger. But the other man had a moral presence that was hard to resist, like the aura of some warrior saint. It was in his voice, his bearing, his face, even the silvery hair he must have had cut just so.

"I was a friend of hers," Charlie said. "At Morgan."

"Friend?" said Klein, cloaking the word in ambiguity. "What's your name?"

"It wouldn't mean anything to you. But my real—" Charlie stopped himself. "But back then my name was Blake Wrightman."

Someone knocked on the door. The words "Blake Wrightman" seemed to fill the silence that followed. There was a second knock.

"What is it?" Klein said, listening, intent. His dark, categorizing eyes didn't leave Charlie's face.

"Ready when you are, Mr. Klein," answered a woman's voice.

"I . . . won't be needing you after all."

"No?"

"No."

"Okay." Footsteps moved down the hall and into inaudibility. Klein took his eyes off Charlie and reached for his suit jacket, hanging over the chair. He put it on, began buttoning the middle button. His fingers seemed unsteady. He fumbled for a moment, gave up. Then, still without looking, he lunged forward awkwardly and threw a punch at Charlie's head.

It was a poor attempt, long and looping, and never landed. Charlie caught Klein's wrist in midair and held it. Their faces were close together.

"I deplore violence," Klein said, his tone accusatory, as though Charlie were to blame for the attack. His body was shaking.

Charlie let him go. "So do I," he said. ⏤

Klein made a sputtering sound. "Is that a joke?" His voice rose out of its baritone register. "Your penchant for violence ruined my daughter's life." He rubbed his wrist.

"What are you talking about?"

Klein lowered his voice. "I'm talking about how you destroyed her future. How you exiled her from her friends, her family, me. She could be dead, for all I know. Do you know how that makes me feel? I'm her father. Are you a father, Mr. Whatever-you-call-yourself?"

"No," Charlie said, but thought at once of Emily and the baby growing inside her. Zachary, was that what she had said? If it was a boy. He felt a moral weight shift, pulling him down, and fought to get back up to the level of the argument. "I don't know how it feels, but why am I responsible?"

"Are you baiting me?" Klein's voice rose again, on a fountain of outrage. "You altered the setting on that . . . that device, to activate it after the agreed time. You perverted the symbolic statement she wanted to make into a killing."

"Where the hell did you hear that?"

Klein opened his mouth, closed it tight, as though he had said too much already. He was not a public man in the mechanical style of the former attorney general; he had emotions and sometimes they showed. Perhaps that was what gave him his presence.

"You'd better go," Klein said.

"I asked you where you got that story."

"And I said you'd better go. I have nothing more to say." Charlie didn't move. Klein tried to button his suit jacket but still could not. He held onto the back of the barber's chair, looked at Charlie. "You are failing to grasp the situation."

"What situation?"

"Yours. At this moment. If, as I assume, you are still a fugitive, it is my duty as a citizen to call the police. Under some interpretations, your very presence in this room would render me liable to criminal charges."

"I'm not going to make a citizen's arrest," Charlie said.

Klein smiled; he had perfect teeth, big and white, matching Charlie's memory of Rebecca's. "But I may do just that," Klein said.

"I don't think so."

"Why not?"

"Word would get out. It might scare away clients."

The smile vanished; Klein's face hardened, and for a moment Charlie was reminded of Rebecca again, specifically her Torquemada look. "You take me for a cynic. It's commonplace to hate me but rather unusual to question my sincerity."

"I withdraw the remark," Charlie said. He had nothing to base it on, except one feeble punch from a deplorer of violence. "But I'd like to know who told you that I rigged the timer, if you haven't seen Rebecca since before the bombing."

Klein said nothing, but he was squeezing the back of the barber's chair, as though his body was fighting to contain enormous pressures. Charlie realized that he had indeed outwitted the other man, almost without trying. "I take it you have seen her, then," Charlie said. "Did she feed you that story about the timer? Or was it Malik?"

"You'd better go," Klein said again, but his words had lost their force.

"The truth is you have seen her."

"No."

"And you know where she is."

"No."

"But who else could have told you that? And you got money to her in Toronto. After the fact. So you'd already made your decision about aiding and abetting, or whatever the legal term would be. Why stop there?"

Klein said nothing.

"Where is she?"

"I have no idea," Klein said. He didn't deny giving her money or ask Charlie how he knew about it. "And nothing you say or do will change that."

The door opened and Fred Friendly stuck his head in. "Nice job, Hugo," he said. "See you next week." He nodded at Charlie and closed the door.

Charlie and Klein watched each other in silence. "Why now?" Klein asked, lowering his voice.

"I don't understand," Charlie said, but he knew what was coming. This was the question on which everything turned, the question Mr. G had prepared him for.

"It's been twenty-two years," said Klein. "Why are you looking for her now?"

Charlie had Mr. G's answer ready, a middle-aged answer based on lost love and a long obsession; an answer he had never liked. He had a much better one now, of his own devising: "I may be able to prove our innocence."

"How?"

"That's what I want to discuss with her."

Klein shook his head. "You seem like an intelligent man. Please try to absorb what I'm saying. I don't know where she is. I haven't seen or heard from her since months before the bombing. February of 1970, to be precise—I visited her for one day. Since then no contact of any kind. I won't say it again." He paused. "But proving innocence is a legal matter. I may be able to advise you, if I had the facts."

"Help me by telling the truth."

"I am."

"What about the phone conversation you had with Rebecca the night of the bombing?" He had walked into the end of it, with the just-assembled bomb in the khaki knapsack. Until then, Rebecca and Malik hadn't known there would be a bomb at all. "Isn't that considered hearing from her?"

"There was no phone conversation," Klein said.

"She called someone 'Daddy,'" Charlie said, trying and failing to recall the rest of it. "Who was it, if not you?"

Klein shook his head again, a regal movement. "Your memory is playing you false. It's been a long time, too long to remember clearly, long enough for the mind to invent consoling memories of its own."

"I remember," Charlie said. It was true. Something in him had refused to forget, refused to lose that night in mental haze. He remembered the rum from St. Kitts, the baseball mitt, the face of the boy's father: sharp-edged memories he had lived with for a long time; that had made him what he was; and now might free him. Was that hoping too much?

Charlie and Klein stared at each other; and all their reflections on the mirrored walls of the dressing room stared too. Klein said: "You spoke of proving innocence. Whose did you mean?"

"I said 'our.'"

"Does that include Andrew Malik?"

It was working, Charlie thought. He said: "No."

Klein's eyes looked a little brighter, as though reflecting some mental realignment. "Proof requires evidence. Have you got evidence?"

Charlie nodded. He had evidence all right, evidence that he had altered the bomb so it would not explode, and evidence that it had not exploded: he had the bomb itself.

"Then why didn't you come forward earlier?"

"Because I didn't have it earlier."

"What prompted you to go looking at this late date?"

A shrewd question. "It wasn't a matter of looking," Charlie said. "It was a matter of thinking things out." He felt Klein's disbelief, and more to deflect it than for any other reason, said, "Where were you that night?"

Klein answered with a question of his own. "Do you know a man named Francis Goodnow?"

"No."

"He may be using another name."

"Why would he do that?"

"Why do you?" said Klein. He described the man Charlie knew as Mr. G.

"I don't know him," Charlie said, but how convincingly? The suggestion of congruence between himself and someone like Mr. G, raised first in his own mind and now by Klein, had thrown him. "I asked where you were that night."

"What night?"

"What other night is there?"

"I don't see how it matters," Klein said. "But I must have been in Chicago."

"Why?"

"That's where I heard what had happened, the next day. I was there for one of the Panther trials."

"How did you find out?"

"Through the media, of course. Like everyone else."

There was a phone on the wall. It rang. Klein answered it, listened. "I'll be right there," he said. "I'll want to see everything on the Tettrazzi case." Pause. "Of course including the appeal." He hung up, turned to Charlie, brisk and forceful, as though contact with work had boosted his strength. "If you have evidence, as you say, why do you need Rebecca?"

"I don't have it all. She has the rest, although she doesn't know it." That was the bait.

Klein considered it for a few moments. Then he said, "You don't convince me." He buttoned his suit jacket in one easy movement, picked up his briefcase, went to the door. "I don't suggest you linger here too long," he said. Then he was gone, leaving Charlie alone with his aggressive image in the mirror.

•   •   •

"What's this all about?" asked the former attorney general of the United States, changing shirts in his dressing room. The TV experience always made him sweat.

Svenson, wearing earphones and adjusting the volume on his recorder, said, "God knows."

The former attorney general finished dressing and lit a cigar. "I hope you nail the son of a bitch," he said on his way out.

That's what they were doing all right, nailing Hugo Klein. In Svenson's earphone Ochs said, "You got money to her in Toronto." There was no denial from Klein. They probably had him right there. It struck Svenson then that Goodnow was indeed the mentor for him: the man was a master. He regretted his call to Bunting. Still, Bunting hadn't seemed concerned. He'd just told him to keep his eyes open. There was no suggestion that he was actually going to do anything.

But where was Goodnow?

It was night back east. Listening in one ear to the conversation in the next dressing room, Svenson phoned Goodnow at home. The answering machine picked up.

"Taping successful," Svenson said, and hung up.

26

Not long after crossing the state line into southern New Jersey, Ol' J.P., peering through the bug-smeared windshield of his ten-year-old pickup and holding an almost empty bottle of Tennessee whiskey between his thighs, realized he wasn't far from the beach with the Wee Willie Winkie Motel. Without really knowing why—but what was an hour or two after all these years? and anyway, he needed to piss—he took the next exit and soon drove into the little beach town where he and Mina had first made love.

J.P. had no memories of the town itself and so couldn't tell whether it had changed or not. All he remembered was the motel. He drove along the main drag, past a pizzeria, a liquor store, a pharmacy, a souvenir shop, a bar, a restaurant, an ice cream place, and parked in the court of the motel at the end.

J.P. sat there. After a while he said, "Shit." Could it have been this crummy back then? The pavement in the court was cracked with weeds sprouting through, the shingles on the walls and roof were blotched by water damage, a faded For Sale sign hung on the office door. No: it had been nice and new. Hadn't it?

But crummy or not, it was the same place: a one-story L with about a dozen rooms, steps from the ocean. J.P., gazing at it from behind the wheel, could recall everything: how he'd wrangled a weekend pass from Fort Dix; how he'd done a hundred pushups just before picking her up at her dorm on Friday night, so he'd look stronger; how she'd jumped into the car he'd borrowed from his sergeant and given him a kiss, just on the cheek, but confident and familiar, as though she'd made up her mind about something. And she had: they'd spent the whole weekend in the Wee Willie Winkie. How could he forget the Wee Willie Winkie, even if it looked like a dump now and they'd changed the name to Sea 'n Sand?

J.P. finished what was left in the bottle and climbed out of the cab. Room 3, right there in the middle: he remembered even that, the goddamn room. It had a sliding door opening right onto the sand. They'd gone skinny-dipping under the light of the moon that first night, running across the beach hand in hand, throwing themselves into the waves, then floating together tight, goose bumps on their skins, with all the body parts that could stick out sticking out. J.P., thinking to take a peek through the sliding glass door of room 3, walked around the end of the motel, toward the water. That was when he got a shock: the beach was gone.

Nothing but bare rock, and the ocean rising and falling beyond. Had he come to the wrong town after all? J.P. studied the back of the motel. No, there were the rooms with their sliding glass doors, most of them, he noticed, crisscrossed with duct tape.

J.P. stared out to sea. Time passed. He lowered his zipper and pissed on the rocks. His urine ran like a miniature yellow river through miniature badlands toward the ocean.

Behind him a voice said: "Lookin' for something, bud?"

J.P. zipped up and turned. A man with lather on his face and a razor in his hand had opened one of the glass doors and come out. "Yeah," J.P. told him, "the goddamn beach."

"Beach? Been no beach here in years. Not since the storm of 'seventy-eight."

J.P. glanced around: at the ocean, the rocks, the taped glass, the man. "No shit," he said. Then he walked around to the front of the Sea 'n Sand Motel and got into his pickup. The office door of the motel opened and the man with lather on his face reappeared, watching him. J.P. backed out and drove down the main drag.

He made two stops. The first was at the liquor store, where he bought another bottle. The second was at the pharmacy. He was hungry. The sea air, right? Makes you hungry. Hungry for solid food. J.P. chose a candy bar and a family-size bag of corn chips. On the way to the cashier he picked up a bottle of mouthwash and a roll of duct tape.

"That be all?" said the clerk, totaling his purchases.

"Got any straight razors?"

"Think we do," said the clerk. "I'll check." He went into a back room, returned with two razors in plasticized packages. "Not a popular item nowadays," said the clerk, holding them out. "We've just got these two left."

"I'll take the big one," said Ol' J.P.

27

Charlie walked up a steep hill and looked down at the bay. He had to think. Instead, he watched boats cutting across the water, leaving wakes of red foam in the rays of the late afternoon sun. They reminded him of *Straight Arrow* and Cosset Pond. The next thing he knew he was in a phone kiosk, calling home.

"Hello?" It was Emily.

Again he found himself unable to speak to her.

"Hello? Hello?"

Charlie got ready to hang up. But then she said: "Charlie? It isn't you, is it?"

And he answered: "Yes." The word came strangled, muted, rough, and perhaps only partly true, but it came.

"Charlie?"

"Yes," he repeated, this time with more control. San Francisco Bay, the boats with their sails cupped to the breeze, the foaming red wakes, the famous hill he stood on: none of it seemed real. Reality was this electronically reproduced voice from three thousand miles away, marred by hisses and hums in the wire.

"Charlie," she said, "are you all right?"

"Yes."

"You don't sound all right. What's going on?"

Charlie had trouble recalling the cover story: Uncle Sam, a grandfather's will, choice hunks of real estate, statutory time factors—was that it?

"Charlie?"

"Everything's all right," said Charlie. "It's just taking longer than they said."

"What's taking longer and who is they?"

"Uncle Sam. The lawyers. This inheritance business." His voice coarsened again, this time from having to force out the lies. He didn't want to lie to her. He wanted to confess, as he should have done at the beginning. Or better, to have not begun at all; to have kept his mouth shut about twenty-six across—Malik's goddamned power saw—and to have kept Ben Webster off the turntable. But now what was he to confess? Was he a criminal, a murderer? What had he done? What was he responsible for? He no longer knew. There were unresolved questions, no longer only of motive but of fact: yes, there were problems with his inheritance, the inheritance Blake Wrightman had left to Charlie Ochs. In that sense it was not a lie.

"Is he with you?" said Emily.

"Who?" said Charlie, aware that he was failing to communicate in the easy shorthand of a good marriage.

"Your uncle," she said.

"No," said Charlie, "not at the moment."

"How is he?"

"Who?"

"Your uncle, for God's sake. He has cancer, doesn't he?"

"I guess he does."

"You guess?"

"He doesn't talk about it."

Silence. He thought he felt her mind, clear, quiet, with its reserves of power, probing from across the continent.

"Where are you?" she said.

An inevitable question, was it not? And had he an answer ready? No.

"Where are you? It sounds far."

"It's not far," he said. "I'll be home soon."

Silence. She was waiting for him to be more specific about where he was, but she wasn't going to ask again. He said nothing, searched his mind desperately for a smooth way out of the conversation.

"What's gone wrong, Charlie?" She sounded impatient, like a teacher with a balky pupil.

"Nothing. I miss you, that's all."

"There's an obvious solution," she said, softening her tone a little.

"Is there?"

"Of course," she answered with surprise, surprise that he wasn't following her. "Come home."

Her mention of an obvious solution had thrown him off the track of their conversation, back into what he was doing. He felt a strong desire for her help; he wanted her to think with him at that moment, to put her mind to work on Klein, Malik, Goodnow, and the rusted and incapacitated bomb still in its place under the old ROTC building. But he couldn't imagine a way to begin and just said, "I'll be home soon."

Silence.

"I'd better go now," he said.

Pause. "Fine."

Charlie was about to tell her he loved her; the phrase pressed inside him to get out, but he held it in, not wanting to abandon it among all the falsehoods he had spoken. So he said, "'Bye."

And she said, "'Bye."

And that was that.

Charlie stepped away from the phone. He was still in red sunshine, as were the bridges and the hilltops of the East Bay, but the water was dark now, the boats fading into invisibility. Charlie, who had walked up the hill not to call Emily but to think, had a thought. Perhaps his contact with Emily's probing mind had inspired it.

He checked the telephone kiosk. No directory; not even a place for one in the kiosk's design. Charlie walked down the hill and went into a café near the bottom. There was a pay phone by the door, and Bay Area directories hanging beside it. Charlie opened the yellow pages, turned to the *P*'s, found the listings for printers. He scanned it down to the *W*'s. There it was: Wine Printing and Engraving. The address hadn't changed.

Charlie took a taxi into the Mission, looking out at the half-remembered streets, as though clarifying a dream. He got out in front of the house: a three-story Victorian that had been in need of repair when last seen by him and was now beyond it. The house was dark. Charlie walked up to the door and knocked.

No response. He peered through the little square window in the door, saw nothing. He knocked again, with no result.

Nine-thirty, too early for bed. The shop was in the basement, the office on the first floor, Mr. Wine had lived on the second with his girlfriend, and Brucie had had one of the two rooms at the top. He himself had lived in the other for three or four months.

Charlie raised his hand to knock again. The door opened. A woman with a cigarette in her mouth looked out. Charlie hadn't heard her approach because her feet were bare. As was most of the rest of her: the woman wore only a towel that stretched inadequately around her abundant body, and headphones. It was hard to tell her age by the light of the street lamp; but probably closer to forty than thirty.

"Oh," she said. "I thought you was someone else."

"Sorry if I disturbed you. I'm looking for Brucie Wine."

"If you're talking I can't hear you," the woman said. She took off her headphones, shook her hair. It was wet. A few warm drops landed on Charlie's face. He smelled chlorine. "You needed me," she said.

He took it as a question and answered, "Very briefly."

The woman gestured with the headphones. "Anne Murray. I was just relaxing in the hot tub with some tunes."

"Then how did you hear me knocking?"

She drew on her cigarette, giving him a long look. "I felt the vibes. This old dump is like a medium for vibes, if you know what I mean."

"I think I do," Charlie said. "Does Brucie Wine still live here?"

The woman flicked on the outside light, studied Charlie's face. "You don't look like a cop."

"Why would I be a cop?"

She ignored him. "But neither did the little son of a bitch that busted him. And that question about hearing the knock was like a cop."

"I'm not a cop."

"What are you, then?"

"A fisherman. And an old acquaintance of Brucie's."

"Let's see your hands."

Charlie held out his hands. She felt them. Hers were warm and plump. "Yeah," she said, the cigarette dangling from her lips, "could be." She let go, her fingernails scratching lightly across his palm. "You know Brucie?"

"I knew him years ago. I'm passing through and thought I'd look him up. Is he in some kind of trouble?"

The woman frowned. Perhaps she was closer to forty-five. "No more than usual," she said. "Or maybe a teeny bit more. But it'll come out all right. Like before. He's making his lawyer rich is all."

"What's the problem?"

"Spics, this time. It never ends." The towel slipped a little, revealing demiglobes of breast. She did nothing about it. "Wanna come in and wait for him?" she asked. "He'll probably be an hour or two." She gave him another look. "At least. Maybe you'd like to relax in the hot tub." He felt her smoky breath on his face.

"I'm not an Anne Murray fan," Charlie said. "And my schedule is tight. Do you know where I can find him now?"

She hitched the towel up to her armpits and flicked the cigarette out into the night. She'd lost interest in him; perhaps it was his lack of musical taste. "He's at a meeting."

"Can you tell me where? I know he'll want to see me."

"At the usual place, I suppose," she said. "Polly's." She gave him the address.

"Thanks," Charlie said.

She switched off the light. "And tell him not to be late," she said from the shadows. "Laverne says not to be late." The door closed.

Polly's was a bar beside a Daihatsu dealer off South Van Ness, a fifteen-minute walk. "Beer," read the sign above the window. "Wine, Liquor, Drinks." He got the idea. Through the window he could see a dark room with a few human figures in it. The door was open, exhaling a complex mixture of rough smells: perfume for an anti-universe. Charlie was about to go in when a dog barked savagely, right behind him.

He wheeled around, saw a pit bull lunging at him, jaws open wide. Charlie jumped back. The animal came jerking to the end of its chain, emitting strangled, murderous sounds. Charlie saw that the chain was fastened to a No Parking sign, and his heart rate returned to normal. "Easy, boy," he said, and to his astonishment the dog lowered its head and sidled back into the shadows. A car went by. Its headlights illuminated the features of a Chinese man sitting in a parked car a few spaces away. His eyes were on the dog and they were murderous too. Charlie entered the bar.

A jukebox glowed silently in one corner. Otherwise Polly's was dim. It took Charlie a few moments to distinguish the customers: two women in jeans and jean jackets at a table near the front, a fat man in a sleeveless T-shirt near the jukebox, two black men at the table next to his, a Latino in an unraveling straw hat at the table in the back. Brucie Wine's face was out-of-focus in his memory, and of course he must have changed, but not into anyone Charlie saw here. He approached the bar.

The bartender, a woman as tall as he was and almost as broad, was reading a paperback romance called *Wild Magnolia*. She wore black leather pants, a black halter top, and had a black and red Iron Cross tattooed on one forearm. "Somethin' to drink?" she said, laying the book on the bar.

"A beer," Charlie said.

"Like what?"

He named one. His eyes grew accustomed to the light. He noticed the decor: unlit Chinese lanterns trailing spider webs, blown-up black-and-whites of circus women, a framed poster that read "Impeach the Fucker."

The bartender set a bottle in front of him, forcefully. "Buck and a half," she said.

Charlie handed it over. "Has Brucie Wine been in?" he asked.

The bartender looked at him. Her eyes were round and blue; beautiful, possibly, but unsympathetic. "I don't like trouble," she said. "But I'm ready for it, believe me." She glanced down at something behind the bar.

"Don't worry," Charlie said. "I'm an old friend."

"The dickhead has a friend?" She pointed her chin at something behind Charlie. "Voilà," she said. He turned and saw a man coming through a swinging door that read, "Hombres," zipping up his pants. Pot-bellied, snub-nosed, splay-footed: Brucie Wine. He had hardly changed, although it couldn't be said that the years had been good to him. He shook his ponytail, walked over to the Latino's table and sat down behind a long-necked Bud. Charlie picked up his drink. "Trouble, you mop up," the bartender called after him.

Charlie moved to the table nearest Brucie's, sat so Brucie could see him. Brucie, ten feet away, took no notice of his arrival.

The other man at Brucie's table, who had his back to Charlie, said something Charlie couldn't hear. Brucie sucked his teeth and said, "*Dinero.*"

The other man talked some more. He seemed to be arguing, but calmly, reasonably, even deferentially. He removed his straw hat and held it in both hands.

Brucie said: "*Dinero,* man, *dinero.* Capeesh?" He took a long slug from his bottle, avoided eye contact with the other man. The other man rose and walked away. He put on the straw hat, pulling it low over his eyes, but not low enough to hide their stricken look. Brucie noticed Charlie then, and shook his head complicitously, in recognition of their shared white man's burden.

"Still writing poetry?" Charlie said.

"Huh?"

"'What a cool day for a treat. Lots of chickies really neat.' Poetry, Brucie."

Brucie's eyes narrowed. Then they widened. He got up,

213

slowly, backed away, carefully, like a hiker encountering a coiled snake. He bumped into the wall. "Don't," he said.

"Don't?"

"Oh Jesus God," Brucie cried, his voice breaking. "He's gonna fuckin' kill me." Then he darted around his table, knocking the long-necked bottle on the floor, and bolted outside through the door. Charlie went after him.

"Hey," yelled the bartender after him: "Mop up."

28

Brucie Wine, car keys in one hand and the pit bull's chain in the other, was fumbling at the door of an acne boy's dream car as Charlie ran outside. Like a desperate figure in a nightmare, Brucie was moving frantically but getting nowhere. He saw Charlie, said, "Oooooooo," hunched over the keyhole, made still more frantic motions and finally flung the door open, banging it hard against the No Parking sign pole. Then he ducked down to get in the car, bumped his head, entangled himself in the dog chain, and fell on the sidewalk.

Charlie came forward. The pit bull puffed up its muscles and growled. Brucie, lying on his back, repeated, "Oooooooo," and aimed a kick in Charlie's direction. At the same moment the dog lunged at Charlie, jaws open wide. They closed on Brucie's upraised calf.

"Flipper!" Brucie screamed. "It's me, it's me!" Flipper wagged his tail, but didn't let go.

"Flipper! Flipper!"

"That's enough," Charlie said. Did Flipper hear something *simpático* in Charlie's tone or had he simply realized his error? The dog released Brucie's leg, trotted back the length of his chain, raised his leg, pissed on the rear wheel. Brucie stopped screaming, looked up at Charlie in terror. "What's wrong with you?" Charlie said. "Don't you remember me?"

"I'm sorry. Really and truly sorry. I can't tell you how sorry. Don't hurt me."

"Why would I hurt you?"

"Please. Don't. I'm already hurt. Flipper hurt me." Brucie moaned and grabbed his leg, letting go the chain. Flipper knew at once that he was free. He scuttled off down the street on his stubby legs, dragging his restraint behind him like a chain-gang felon on the lam. The Chinese man in the parked car rolled up his window as Flipper went by.

Charlie knelt, rolled up Brucie's pant leg. Brucie shrank from his touch. "You're going to live," Charlie said.

"I am?"

"Unless your pet has rabies."

"But what about you?"

"Me?"

"Are you gonna let me live?"

"Brucie."

"Yeah?"

"Have you got me confused with someone else?"

The terror faded slowly from Brucie's eyes, replaced even more slowly by craftiness, undisguised. "Should I?"

"Should you?"

Brucie bit his lip. "Never mind." He bit it some more. "Hey," he said, almost cheerful. "So you're really not mad at me?"

"Why would I be?"

"No matter who I think you are?"

"Who do you think I am, Brucie?"

"A draft dodge—resister, right? I got you ID, din't I? Way back when."

"Right. So why would I want to kill you?"

"Maybe I overcharged you or somethin'. Mistakes happen." He rolled over, reached for his wallet, withdrew money. Blue cards came spilling out, fluttered down through a grating and out of sight. "Shit," said Brucie.

"What was that?"

"The mortgage," said Brucie. "No big deal." He held out some bills.

"Put it away," Charlie said. He took Brucie's hands, pulled him up. The Chinese man was watching from his car. "Let's go for a drive."

Brucie cringed. "What kind of drive?"

"A spin."

"A spin like to where?"

"Somewhere fun."

"But—"

"I'm not going to hurt you. Do you want an affidavit?"

"Hee-hee," Brucie said. "That's a good one. I'll have to remember it."

They got in the car, Brucie behind the wheel, Charlie in the passenger seat. Brucie turned the key, stalled, tried again, steered onto the street. Flipper was half a block down, his snout in an overturned trash can. They got him into the tiny backseat and drove on. A motorcycle growled behind them. "Where to?" said Brucie. "Like some real place, right, with lights and people?"

"Berkeley."

"Across the bridge?" Brucie made it sound like some fraying thing over a jungle gorge.

"Unless there's a better way."

"Well, we could go down to San Jose and then maybe..."

They took the bridge. Looking back, Charlie saw Candlestick Park, lit up like a hot spot on an X ray. Not the usual baseball image, Charlie thought. Baseball was romantic, especially to journalists who had never hit a curve, hit a cutoff man, hit behind a runner. Or been hit with a high rider in the face. It wasn't as romantic at field level.

They parked on Telegraph Avenue, outside a shop selling peasant clothing from South America, and walked to Sproul Plaza. The night was warm and the plaza crowded, but it no longer made Charlie think of an Oriental bazaar. It was just a college campus, U.S.A. Either the magic was gone, or it had become part of ordinary life, and unremarkable.

They sat on a bench. Two men went by. One said, "My white count's borderline." The other didn't know what to say. A

217

woman glided past on rollerblades. Brucie glanced around
briefly.

"Haven't been here in a Jesus-long time," he said. He began
tapping his foot, like a patient in a waiting room. "What do you
wanna do?"

"Talk."

"About what?"

Charlie turned to him and smiled. "What are you up to these
days, Brucie?"

"Same old shit."

"How's your father?"

"Pops? Passed away." He checked Charlie from the corner of
his eye. "What about you?"

"I'm a lobsterman."

"What's that?"

"Someone who traps lobsters."

"Any money in it?"

"Not much."

Brucie grunted. The crafty look returned. "And you haven't
had any more trouble?" he asked.

"Trouble?"

"Whatever the trouble was that I helped you with."

"No."

"So," Brucie said. He tapped his foot for a while. "You been
safe then."

"Safe?"

"Like no visits from the law, or nothin'."

"I've been safe. How about you?"

"Oh, yeah. I changed my, you know, life-style."

"Then it's not really the same old shit, is it?"

Brucie blinked. He opened his mouth, to be ready when his
brain formulated a response. None came.

"I want you to think back to that summer, Brucie."

Brucie's mouth closed.

"The summer that you and I met. And the months that
followed. Do you remember that period?"

"Sure. You lived upstairs. Then you split. Right?"

Charlie nodded. "What else?"

"*Let It Be.* Wasn't that the summer of *Let It Be?* There was the Summer of Love, then the next summer and the next and then *Let It Be.*" He bit his lip. "It all depends on when the Beatles broke up."

The woman on rollerblades glided by again, like a visitor from a world where only grace mattered. "Did you sell ID to anyone else?"

"When?"

"That summer, or later. Into the next spring, say."

"Sure. That's my gig. Was my gig." Brucie jumped a little, as though he'd been startled. "You're not workin' for the cops, or nothin'?"

"Why would you think that?"

Brucie thought. "You're right. And anyhow why would the cops be bugging me now? It's too late."

"Too late for what?"

"For me. Unless there's a miracle, he said."

"Who said?"

Brucie waved a tired arm. "This brainy dude I'm makin' rich. You wouldn't know him." His eyes went to Charlie again, narrowing into the crafty look. This time he made an effort to disguise it. It was as though he had had an idea.

"Sounds like you're the one in trouble," Charlie said.

"Me? Nah. Just the cost of doing business."

"What business?"

"Pop's business. Printing. You know. Engraving."

"Let me ask you something, Brucie."

"Ask away."

"About that summer. Or the period after."

"Right. The period after."

"You said you supplied others with ID."

"Sure, I said it. If you're not a cop." Brucie giggled. "Shit," he said. "Life's a gas."

"I'm wondering whether one of your customers might have been a woman."

"They need ID too. Women's lib and all that shit."

"The woman I'm interested in would have been about twenty then." He described Rebecca, the way he remembered her.

"Don't ring a bell."

"Her name was Rebecca Klein, although she probably wouldn't have used it."

"Don't ring a bell," Brucie said; but his eyes shifted toward Charlie, then rapidly away. He had little control over his body language.

"Are you sure?"

"Sure I'm sure."

"You seemed to react to the name."

"The name. Yeah. Rebecca. I reacted to that, yeah. I knew a Rebecca. But it was in the eighties and she was a whore over in Daly City. That's the only bell it rang. I got the clap. Some bell. Christ."

Charlie considered other approaches. None seemed promising, not with Brucie. Brucie had been a long shot in the first place. He rose. "See you, Brucie."

"Huh?"

"Good-bye."

"You're leaving?"

"Check."

"Where are you going?"

"Away."

Brucie raised a hand, as if to somehow bar his way. Charlie turned, crossed the plaza, passed through the gate and onto Telegraph. He walked for several blocks, paused in front of a comic book store. A blow-up of a blue-faced big-brained being from another galaxy hung in the window. He was saying, "The clue is somewhere in the anti-universe, my dear Xanthanza." Charlie decided to approach Hugo Klein again, this time more obliquely.

He looked around for a cab. The acne-boy car came to a squeaking stop at the curb. The window slid down and Brucie said, "I can take you back across if you want."

Charlie got in the car. Flipper was sleeping in the back. Brucie had worked up a sweat in the short time they'd been apart. Charlie could smell him.

Brucie shifted into first and gunned the car through a yellow light. A motorcycle roared behind them. Brucie patted Charlie's knee. "Hey. Great to see you. You know? Brings back old memories. Those were the days, huh?"

"Were they?"

"Shit, yes. The chicks. Remember? Like willing chicks with no bullshit. A dream come true."

An acne-boy dream.

"And the music. Jesus." Brucie, swerving onto the bridge ramp, reached across and flipped open the glove box. Tapes slid out, fell to the floor. Brucie, his head below the dash, scrabbled through them. "Whaddaya like, whaddaya like?" He found something, jammed it in the tape player, jerked the wheel hard to his left to avoid the bridge railing.

"Stairway to Heaven" at 120 decibels plus.

"Led Zep," Brucie shouted. "Did it ever get any better than that?"

Or something of the kind. Charlie couldn't really hear him.

The bridge was a glowing span over a black abyss. They seemed to soar across on a current of energy—Brucie's sudden excitement, the cranked-up volume of the tape player, the souped-up power of the car: each false in its own way. In the southwest, Candlestick was dark, the ballgame over.

"Good to see you," Brucie shouted. "Shit. I mean it." This time he left Charlie's knee unpatted.

Brucie came down off the bridge, turned north onto the Embarcadero. It wasn't where Charlie wanted to go. He glanced at Brucie, saw sweat shining on his face, and an uncharacteristic purposefulness in his eye. Brucie exited, into the heart of North Beach.

Charlie switched off the music. "You forgot to ask where to drop me," he said.

"Hee-hee." Brucie's smell was stronger. "The thing is, old pal, I think we should drop in on this dude I mentioned."

"What dude?"

"Or maybe I didn't. The brainy one."

"It's about Rebecca, isn't it, Brucie? The name meant something to you."

Brucie depressed his door lock; the lock on Charlie's side clicked too. "The name. Yeah. The name, but not the person. See, the name I heard before. The little old geezer kept asking me about her."

"What little old geezer?" Charlie tried to keep his tone calm, casual.

"Oops," said Brucie.

"Oops?"

"I meant I didn't get his name."

"What did he look like?"

"Hard to say." Brucie stopped in front of a restaurant named Fazool. Across the street lay a park, with an ice cream man standing watch over his wagon, smoking a cigarette; beyond the park a big church, its stone facade illuminated in the night. "An everyday geezer," said Brucie. "Except this guy was on chemo."

Now Charlie began to sweat too. "How do you know that?"

"Experience," said Brucie. "What do you think happened to Pops?"

"I see," said Charlie, and he did. Brucie opened the door, but before he could get out Charlie gripped his right arm, not gently. "Brucie."

"Yeah?"

"You turned me in."

Brucie nodded. "I'm sorry. Really. I got nothin' against you. Let's face it—I'd forgotten all about you. But I couldn't face prison. Did you see that movie, what was it? You know what goes on in those places? I wouldn't last a day." With his left hand Brucie brought a silver-plated revolver into view and pointed it at Charlie. "That's why I'm gonna have to do it again. You're under arrest."

Charlie laughed in his face.

"A citizen's arrest," said Brucie. "I mean it." The gun trembled. Charlie let go of his arm. Brucie got out of the car, came around to Charlie's side, opened the door. "Out," he said.

Charlie got out of the car.

Brucie pointed the gun at a door in the stucco wall beside the restaurant. "Let's go."

"Where?"

"To see the brainy guy. He'll know what to do." Brucie motioned with the gun. Charlie moved toward the door. Brucie stepped behind him, touched the small of his back with the muzzle of the gun. In that one touch, Charlie learned all he needed to know about the future that awaited him if he entered that door.

"I don't think so," he said.

"You don't think what?" asked Brucie, behind him.

Charlie didn't explain. He'd always been able to move. He moved: ducking and whirling in one motion, then driving up at Brucie's midsection. His shoulder struck something soft, his fist something hard. Brucie fell back with a grunt; Charlie grabbed at him, caught only a corner of his shirt, which tore off in his hand. Brucie rolled free on the sidewalk, came up on one elbow, the gun pointed at Charlie's head. His nose was bleeding; the expression on his face primitive. He was stupid enough to be dangerous.

"I'm not taking any more shit," Brucie said, his voice too loud for whining, not loud enough for shrieking. The gun wasn't especially steady, but it wouldn't have to be at this distance. Brucie's nose twitched, as though he'd suddenly developed a tic. Charlie knew with certainty that he was going to pull the trigger and that there was nothing he could do about it.

A motorcycle burst out of the park across the street, just missing the ice cream man, jumped the sidewalk, spun in a circle around Brucie. The driver was huge, and dressed all in white, except for his black visor. Charlie had a crazy, childish notion that Brucie had already shot him, that he was already dead and this was an angel sent to take him away. But then the motorcycle roared like a killing beast, a hellish beast, and Brucie's face went white. The driver gestured at him; something shone in his hand. Brucie fell back on the sidewalk, a round red hole now prominent in the center of his white forehead, like a caste mark.

The driver extended one of his feet, pivoted the howling machine, and skidded to a stop in front of Charlie. He backed off on the throttle, reducing the noise to a rumble, and raised his visor.

"You're not having much luck are you, Charlie boy?" It was Svenson.

Across the street the ice cream man was saying, "Mother of God, Mother of God." A car had stopped next to his wagon. A

Chinese man got out, a tiny man, not much bigger than a child.

"Best be moving on," Svenson said, lowering the visor. "Unless you're ready to call it quits." Charlie looked into the blackness of the visor and said nothing.

Svenson revved the engine, pointed the front wheel toward the road. The Chinese man was on the sidewalk now, gazing down at Brucie. He turned on Svenson.

"What the hell did you do that for? I had him by the balls."

"I'll bet you did," said Svenson, bumping the motorcycle onto the street.

The Chinese man ran after him in fury. "What kind of answer is that? Who the hell are you?" He smacked Svenson on the back of his helmet.

Svenson laughed, then gunned the engine; but as the motorcycle shot into the street, the Chinese man dove at it, caught hold of Svenson's collar, held on. The motorcycle wobbled, then veered across the street, smashed through the ice cream wagon, knocking the Chinese man high into the air and twisting Svenson almost backward in his seat. The bike kept going, into the park, into darkness. Then came a boom, a rending of metal, and silence.

The ice cream man's lips were moving, forming the phrase "Mother of God," although no sound came. He moved off down the sidewalk like a sleepwalker. Charlie ran across the street, past scattered Freeze Pops and Nutty Buddies, past the Chinese man, lying open-eyed on his back, his head at an impossible angle, and into the park.

He found Svenson sprawled at the base of a tree. His head was at an impossible angle too.

Charlie looked back at the trail of bodies: Brucie, the Chinese man, Svenson. Facts on the ground, facts that made happy endings impossible. But hadn't that been the case since the instant after the fourth bong of the chapel bell? All this was just one of the possible unhappy playouts. It never ends, as Laverne had said.

Charlie kept going, through the park, past the church, and onto a busy street—a real place, with lights and people.

REVOLUTION #9

• • •

The door beside Fazool opened. Nuncio came out. He spent a few seconds looking down at Brucie, a few more over the Chinese man. Then he went into the park, found the man in white, searched him. He found a wallet with money, credit cards, driver's license, found a folder with a federal ID inside, found an audiotape that said "VHK" on its sticker. He left everything but the tape.

People started coming out of the shadows. Sirens sounded. Nuncio walked back across the street, through the door, up the stairs to his two-floor apartment over Fazool. He picked up a Nutty Buddy on the way. He hadn't had one in years.

Somewhere nearby a dog whimpered.

29

Nuncio awoke early the next morning in a good mood. He'd been blessed with resilience, the way others are born to run and jump. The death of an old and valued client, the long police questioning in his living room that followed when said relationship became known, the resulting late bedtime: all had been, he admitted to himself, exhilarating. He opened his bedroom window and took a deep lungful of the new day.

A man stood outside, examining the chalk figure that had taken Brucie's place on the sidewalk. He wore Harold Lloyd glasses and a dark suit. Nuncio could hear him talking.

"Boy oh boy," the Harold Lloyd man was saying. He repeated it a few times.

The Harold Lloyd man walked to the front door and pressed the buzzer. Nuncio put on a terrycloth robe with "Hedonism Negril" blazed in scarlet on the back and went downstairs. The buzzer sounded again just as he was opening the door.

The Harold Lloyd man stood on the step. Up close, Nuncio saw that the face behind the glasses was nothing like Harold Lloyd's. It offered no promise of entertainment of any kind.

"Mr. Nuncio?" said the man.

"Uh-huh."

"My name is Bunting. I'm from the federal government."

Bunting paused, as though Nuncio might have something to say at that point. Nuncio did not.

"May I come in?"

Had that moron Brucie implicated him in anything? Nuncio tried to imagine possible dangers, and could not. Still, he was a counselor, and counselors counseled prudence. "If it's about last night, I already told the police what I saw. Which was *nada*."

"Our inquiry has a somewhat different scope."

Nuncio wanted to check his watch, to give himself some stage business when he said, "I've got to be in court in an hour," but all he wore was the Hedonism robe, so he had to let the words stand by themselves.

"I'm sure you're a busy man, Mr. Nuncio," said Bunting. "I'll be respectful of your time."

"Make it quick, then," said Nuncio, and ushered Bunting brusquely up the stairs. If the man was going to carry on so politely and pronounce *inquiry* "inkwery," what the hell else could he do?

They sat in the living room, Nuncio in the white leatherette chair with the footstool, his guest on the matching couch. Nuncio opened a pack of El Productos that was lying on the end table. "Cigar?"

Bunting shook his well-barbered head. Nuncio lit up; he preferred not to smoke until his first cup of coffee, but cigars helped him think. He blew a miniature cumulonimbus cloud into the room. Bunting was looking at a videotape box lying on the floor by the VCR. The title was big and garish, possibly visible from where Bunting sat: *Debbie Does It—Up Close and Personal*. Nuncio made a mental note to fire his cleaning lady, or at least dock her pay.

"What can I do for you, Mr. Butting?"

"Bunting." The man turned to him; his eyes were cold. "Perhaps you can tell me what Mr. Wine was coming to see you about last night."

"Was he coming to see me?" How to deal with this jerk, with

funny glasses, Mr. Manners civility, icy eyes? Nuncio formed another cloud, not as big as the first.

"Isn't that a safe assumption? He was your client, unless I'm misinformed."

"My business is the law, Mr. Bunting. We don't make assumptions, safe or otherwise." Nuncio hadn't lectured anyone on ethics for a long time, if ever. It made him feel good, and he resolved to do it again soon.

"Angelica County College, wasn't it?" Bunting said.

Nuncio raised his eyebrows.

"Where you got your law degree, I believe."

Nuncio nodded.

"I've had a little legal training myself. Stuck with it right through to a doctorate, in fact. Didn't have anything better to do, if you want the truth. This was at Harvard." He took out a handkerchief with the initials RSB embroidered on one corner and blew his nose into it: loudly, violently, disturbingly, like some savage form of punctuation. "Wasted time, really. In my present position the law seems small and far away, if you understand what I mean."

"I don't think I do."

"Let's put it this way. Anyone looking forward to a smooth continuance of his or her career would be inclined to agree with my earlier hypothesis re Mr. Wine's intent last night."

Nuncio sucked on his cigar, found it had gone out. "Is that a threat?" he said, pulling the Hedonism robe tighter around his body.

Bunting looked surprised. "Of course it is, Mr. Nuncio. I took you for a man of some experience—haven't you ever been threatened before, or done some threatening of your own?"

Not like this, pisshead, Nuncio thought. He stubbed out the El Producto; it bent in half.

"After all," Bunting continued, "isn't that what the law's about?"

Yes. Nuncio couldn't couldn't argue with that. Threats, promises, deals, wheedling: that was law, and he knew how to practice it. But because they all played by the same rules, they were all protected—by the law. This little East Coast shit had already made it clear that he was beyond the law in some way. What protection, Nuncio wondered, did he have now?

He shrugged. "So Wine was probably coming to see me. So what?"

"Had he notified you he was coming?"

"No. Like I told the police last night."

"As you told the police," Bunting said. Was he correcting grammar or just thinking aloud? "And what do you think he wanted to see you about?"

"I don't know, since he didn't call me ahead of time and never quite got here. Unless you've got another safe assumption that explains it."

"But I do," Bunting said. "I assume he wanted to discuss the Wrightman case. Or perhaps we should call it the Wrightman-Ochs case."

"Don't know it," Nuncio said.

"No? It concerns a radical group involved in terrorist bombings in the early seventies. Wrightman was a fugitive who redocumented himself as Ochs and lived undetected for over twenty years. Does that refresh your memory?"

"I didn't deny knowing the names. But you asked about the case. I don't know anything about that, except what you just told me."

"Well argued," said Bunting with a smile—that is, his face assumed a smiling arrangement. "First-rate."

Nuncio tugged the robe down over his knees, fat and white.

"How much did you make last year?" asked Bunting.

The question, posed in that Mr. Manners voice, was shocking, almost brutal. "That's between me and the IRS," Nuncio said.

"Naturally. But one hundred and thirteen five would be pretty close, wouldn't it?"

Not really, but it was precisely what he had reported. Nuncio reached for the El Productos.

"With that kind of income, you should spring for a better cigar. I'll send you some."

"No thanks."

"A nice income," Bunting went on, showing no sign of

rejection. "Although your expenses have been high. The mining investment was unfortunate."

That was one way of putting it. Forty grand sunk in Hollow Gulch Mineral Resources and gone, on the strength of a tip from his ex-brother-in-law's son's boss's secretary. Nuncio lit another cigar and tried unsuccessfully to blow the cloud all the way across the room into Bunting's face. "You've made your point," he said.

"I make no point," Bunting replied. "I merely hope for cooperation. My information is that late last year Mr. Wine was arrested on various counterfeiting charges and you negotiated an agreement that resulted in the dropping of those charges."

"Correct."

"With whom was that arrangement made?"

"The D.A., who else?"

"That's the question. Did you meet or speak to a man named Francis Goodnow at that time?"

"Never heard of him."

"An older man. Not in perfect health."

Nuncio shook his head.

Bunting took out a passport-sized photograph, crossed the room, handed it to Nuncio. It showed a gray-haired man in a bow tie who looked healthy enough.

"Don't know him," Nuncio said, giving it back.

Bunting held out a photo of another man: much younger, with blond hair and an angular face. This was the white-suited motorcyclist who'd lain in the park last night, neck broken.

"Never seen him, either."

Bunting sat back down on the white leatherette chair. He fished out his embroidered handkerchief, held it in his lap, eyes fixed on Nuncio.

After a moment or two, Nuncio said, "If you're looking for something dirty in that deal, you won't find it. We make deals like that every day, the D.A. and me."

"We're speaking of the federal D.A."

"That's right. Counterfeiting."

"How much time elasped between your proposal and his acceptance?"

"Don't know. Less than a day. He said he'd have to..."

"Have to what, Mr. Nuncio?"

"Talk to Washington."

"Did he?"

"Yeah, but so what?"

For an answer, Bunting raised the handkerchief again and blew his nose, not quite as loudly as before. "Thanks for your time, Mr. Nuncio," he said, and was out the door in thirty seconds.

Through the living room window, Nuncio saw a long black car draw up and take him away. He kept watching until long after it was gone. Then he took a deep breath of El Producto air and sighed it out.

Time to get ready for work, although in truth he wasn't scheduled in court. His only client that morning was a fat widow who'd been caught selling stolen designer dresses out of her little shop in Sausalito, would probably buy him lunch, and might even want more of his time after. Nuncio's policy was to bill for lunch, but draw the line at that. He decided on the brown suit with subtle green checks. It hid his paunch nicely.

Turning from the window, Nuncio noticed Bunting's balled-up handkerchief lying on the leatherette chair. He thought of the way dogs piss to mark their territory. He picked up the handkerchief, dropped it in the trash under the kitchen sink, washed his hands in hot soapy water.

Nuncio went upstairs and changed from the Hedonism robe into the brown suit with the subtle green checks. While he dressed, he clicked on his cassette player and listened to the tape for the third time.

Listened to Hugo Klein say: "Under some interpretations, your presence in this room would render me liable to criminal charges." Listened to Blake Wrightman say: "But I'd like to know who told you that I rigged that timer, if you haven't seen Rebecca since before the bombing." Listened to Klein say: "Do you know a man named Francis Goodnow?"

This was all very interesting, more so since he had kept an eye on Klein's ascending career over the years. He had even faced him in court, working as an assistant state prosecutor in his first year out of law school. An unpleasant memory. Yes, it was interesting, but some indefinite distance beyond his comprehension. Because of that, and because he didn't want visits from Bunting or any like him, and because he knew his own limits, Nuncio decided to destroy the tape.

But how? How to do it and be completely safe? Nuncio popped it out of the player. Ordinary Maxell high bias tape, identical to millions of cassettes in cars and houses across the land, distinguished only by the handwritten "VHK" on the stick-on label. Perhaps all he had to do was peel off the sticker, burn it, flush away the ashes, wipe the tape. But there were rumors that the feds had machines that could reconstruct the electronic whispers left on a wiped tape. Maybe it would be best to wipe it first, then record over it and stick it in his collection. Or better yet, in someone else's collection. He could just toss it through the open window of any car parked on the street. Not simple, not tidy, not brilliant, but good enough.

Nuncio peeled off the "VHK" sticker, lit it with a match, dropped it in the bathroom sink, and washed it down the drain. Then he went to the spare room, searched through boxes of his departed children's old toys and school supplies, found the big magnet bought for one son during a brief period when he thought he was fascinated by electricity. He passed the magnet over both sides of the cassette, then went into the living room and studied his tape collection. He chose Leon Redbone's Christmas album.

Nuncio switched on his Hitachi double deck recorder, stuck Leon Redbone in deck A and the wiped tape in deck B. He hit High-Speed Dubbing, checked his levels, turned off the speakers. Then he waited in the white leatherette chair, dressed in his brown suit with the subtle green checks, tapping his foot.

The buzzer buzzed. It jolted Nuncio, as though he were wired to it. Nuncio glanced around for a place to hide the tape, saw none that wouldn't be discovered in minutes by a well-trained cop, to say nothing of the kind of people Bunting would employ. Nuncio rose, walking past the pulsing lights of the tape player, spinning dually in silence, and went downstairs.

The man outside wasn't Bunting. He was old, bald, gaunt; he wore a seersucker suit and a blue bow tie. Nuncio was sure he didn't know the man; all the same, there was something familiar about him.

232

The old man licked his lips; they were cracked, the tongue was yellow.

"Yes?" said Nuncio.

The old man licked his lips again. "I'd like a glass of water," he said. His voice cracked; Nuncio had to stop himself from clearing his own throat.

"There's a restaurant," Nuncio said, pointing to Fazool. Then the bow tie caught his eye, calling instantly to mind the picture Bunting had showed him: an older man, not in perfect health. Knowledge was power. "A glass of water, you said? Come in."

"Thank you." The old man moved across the threshold with difficulty, took a long time on the stairs. Nuncio left him in the hall and went into the kitchen. When he returned with a glass of water, the old man wasn't in the hall. Nuncio found him slumped in the white leatherette chair, his head back, his staring eyes fixed on the blinking lights of the tape player.

"Hey," said Nuncio, and was relieved when the old man turned his head, proving he was still alive. "You okay?"

The old man nodded. Nuncio gave him the water, accidentally brushing his fingers as he did so. The old man's skin was hot and dry. Nuncio wiped his hand on his suit pants.

The old man raised the glass to his lips and drank. His Adam's apple bobbed up and down like blips on a heart monitor. He lowered his glass. "What's that?" he asked. His voice seemed stronger.

"What's what?"

"That blinking."

"Oh, that. Just the record player."

"But I don't hear anything."

"Right. I shut off the sound when I heard the buzzer."

The old man nodded in a vague way that indicated uninterest, or possibly incomprehension. He looked around the room, as though seeing it for the first time; his eyes came to rest on Nuncio.

"Mr. Nuncio."

Nuncio nodded.

"My name is . . . it doesn't really matter what my name is. What matters is your client Mr. Wine."

"I've already told the police everything I know."

"I'm sure you did your duty. But sometimes the police lack know-how when it comes to..." The old man winced, reached into his pocket, took out an orange pill, popped it into his mouth, sipped from the glass. His eyes closed for a moment. He opened them and said in a voice that had gotten weaker again: "When it comes to stimulating memory."

"There's nothing wrong with my memory."

"I don't say there is, Mr. Nuncio. But perhaps under stimulus it will operate even better."

"What kind of stimulus?"

"I'm coming to that," said the old man. He drank more water, ran his yellow tongue over his crusted lips. "Let me tell you a story," he began. His voice cracked again. He could have played... what the hell was that guy's name? Rumpelstiltskin.

"I'm already late for court," Nuncio said.

"This may be worth your time," the old man said. "It's all about a conversation. A conversation between two men. They were discussing some events of long ago. One of the men was an eyewitness to those events. The other's role has yet to be determined. I'm a... historian of events like that. It's my job to ensure the accuracy of the historical record." He paused, looked once more around the room. Everything was still, except the flashing lights of the tape deck. "You may wonder how I do that."

"I think you're about to tell me."

The old man's lips twitched, as though his brain had sent instructions to smile, but no smile came. "In this case, I made arrangements to have the conversation recorded."

"Did you?" said Nuncio. He couldn't stop his eyes from shifting to the tape player. The lights were on, but as he watched they stopped flashing. He heard the tiny click as the high-speed dubbing shut down.

"It's standard procedure at my... academy," the old man explained. He waved a bony hand in dismissal of the details of his office routine. "The conversation was duly recorded." He paused.

The pause went on and on. "Yes?" Nuncio said at last.

The old man took a deep breath. "I'm sorry," he said.

"For what?"

"I'm going to need to use your bathroom."

"You are?" Nuncio was appalled.

The old man pushed himself out of the chair. As he did, his seersucker jacket opened, revealing a pink stain on his shirt. He walked stiffly from the room, down the hall, out of sight. Nuncio heard him trying one door and then another, until he came to the bathroom at the end. The door closed, the lock snicked shut.

Nuncio jumped up, hurried across the room to the tape deck. He pressed Rewind in the B deck, watched the Maxell tape spin back to the beginning, hit Play, switched on the speakers, lowered the volume to a whisper. Leon Redbone hit the first note of "White Christmas." Nuncio fast-forwarded, caught snatches of "Frosty the Snowman," "I'll Be Home for Christmas," "Let It Snow."

He was safe.

Nuncio walked quietly down the hall, stood outside the bathroom door. He head a groan. Then the old man spoke, in a low, furious voice. "You fucking Gerber," he said. Nuncio backed away. The toilet flushed and water began running in the sink. Nuncio returned to the living room, sat on the couch, lit an El Producto.

The old man came walking slowly back into the living room. His face was white, pinched, his bow tie crooked. He sat on the arm of the chair. Not looking at Nuncio, not looking at anything, he said: "Please don't smoke."

Nuncio stubbed out his cigar. The ashtrays were filling with unsmoked cigars.

The old man watched the cigar for a few moments as though it were some dangerous reptile shamming death. Then he said, "The problem, Mr. Nuncio, is that the tape in question has gone astray."

"That's too bad."

"Too bad. Yes. All the more so since it was almost in my hands. However."

"However?" Nuncio said when the old man paused again.

"However, Mr. Nuncio, I have reason to believe that the motorcyclist who died in your park last night had it in his possession."

"Then they'll have it downtown," said Nuncio, "with the rest of his effects. And it's a public park."

The old man shook his head. The cords in his neck tightened like guy wires in a storm. "They don't have it downtown. And since they don't, and since I have reason to believe it was in his possession, it follows that someone got to the tape first."

The old man looked right at Nuncio, his eyes unveiled: hot, greedy, desperate. Nuncio kept his mouth shut.

The old man looked away, but waited for a long time before he spoke again. "Do you have notarizing power, Mr. Nuncio?"

"Of course."

"And could you see to the proper composition of a will?"

"Yeah." It occurred to Nuncio, for the first time, and much too late, that the old man might be armed. He shifted toward the far end of the couch.

"Could you do it here and now?"

"What are you getting at, Mr. . . . ?"

"G."

"Gee?"

The old man nodded. "I have a confession to make." His gaze focused on something far away. Nuncio waited. "I'm . . . unwell," the old man said. "I don't have long to live."

There was another pause. A question formed in Nuncio's mind, a question he was unable to keep silent. "How long?"

The old man's lips twitched in a second stillborn smile. "Weeks. Possibly months. But not . . ."

"Years?"

"No. Not years." He drew the word out, full of yearning, making Nuncio think of the endless summers of his boyhood.

"I'm sorry," Nuncio said. It seemed appropriate.

"Don't be. It may be the best thing that ever happened to you."

"How is that?"

"Or to some other lucky fellow. I have no heirs, Mr. Nuncio. I'm not rich, but do own an apartment in Georgetown, purchased a long time ago, with a present market value in excess of four hundred thousand dollars. Unencumbered by mortgage, Mr. Nuncio," he added, anticipating the question already rising in Nuncio's mind. "In addition, I have a small portfolio of stocks and bonds, worth about two hundred thousand, and a cottage in the Adirondack mountains, worth a ridiculous amount, considering that my father paid fifteen hundred dollars for it after the war."

"What's ridiculous?"

The old man shrugged. "One hundred and fifty. Possibly more. There's also a 1985 Mercedes sedan in good condition. I don't recall the model number. The point is, Mr. Nuncio—" The old man winced, started to double over, caught himself. He stuck a knuckle in his mouth, bit on it, slowly straightened. He took a deep breath, then another.

"Yes?" said Nuncio.

"The point is," the old man continued, but now so softly that Nuncio had to strain to hear him, "that I would be pleased to write and execute a will bequeathing all the above-named possessions to the person or persons who could provide me with that tape."

Nuncio's eyes went to the unblinking lights of the tape deck. He was suddenly weak, faint, hot. He licked his lips; they felt cracked, his tongue dry. Seven hundred and fifty fucking grand. Plus a 1985 Mercedes, in good condition. Class. The car gleamed in his mind like an ideal. Then it was shoved aside by the seven hundred and fifty fucking grand. There was no God, not for the Nuncios of this world. He started to shake inside the brown suit with the subtle green checks.

The old man followed Nuncio's gaze. He rose, moved across the room, examined the machine's buttons, pressed one. A banjo plinked a little riff and Leon Redbone began singing "There's No Place Like Home for the Holidays" out of the side of his mouth.

The old man turned to Nuncio, his brow furrowing.

Nuncio raised his hands, palms up. "I haven't got it," he said. Understanding of what he had done hit him in waves, each bigger than the last. He felt like crying. He hadn't cried in years, not since he'd been fired by Little Mo Pagliatto, controller of an entire crooked union in the East Bay. "I wish to God I did, sir. God, I wish to God I did."

The old man's puzzlement turned to anger, then to nothing at all. He didn't look at Nuncio again. He just walked out of the room, into the hall. Nuncio heard him on the stairs, heard the front door open and close.

Then there was nothing to hear but "Christmas Island." Nuncio listened to it. Leon Redbone had a snide, insinuating way with a song. It was the perfect accompaniment to Nuncio's thoughts. Seven five oh. Oh oh oh. Plus the Benz. He'd tried to be clever and ended up being dumb.

Like Brucie Wine, Nuncio realized, all at once. Just exactly precisely like Brucie Wine. The disgusting little asshole.

PART IV

30

Emily dreamed she was in San Francisco. She'd been there once, with her parents, years before. In her dream she went into labor while driving the yellow Volkswagen Beetle across the Golden Gate Bridge. Then all the tires burst and the car stopped. Traffic disappeared. She tried to get out of the car, but her stomach was too big. Uncle Sam arrived to examine her. He told her she wasn't pregnant at all; it was a tumor.

Emily sat up in the darkness. She rested a hand on her stomach, just beginning to swell, like some exotic soft-skinned fruit. She waited for the baby to flutter, to move, to do something. "Zachary," she said softly. "Zachary."

Her womb was still.

3:00 A.M. She got out of bed, threw on her robe, went downstairs. The house was hot and quiet. She turned on the kitchen light, poured a glass of water, leaned against the edge of the table. She found herself staring at the phone on the wall.

"It's not far," Charlie had said. "I'll be home soon."

But another day, the fourth, had passed, and he still wasn't home. His phone call had begun in silence, lapsed into silences, ended in silence. In those silences she had heard traffic, a boat whistle; she had heard hesitation and doubt. And what about those other calls, two or three, that had been nothing but silence? Had Charlie been on the other end of them as well, screwing up the courage to talk, like a shy teenager? That wasn't like him. Were those silences then just part of the everyday electronic world of glitches and misdialings? Or something else?

A breeze off Cosset Pond blew in through the kitchen window, subsided. Emily smelled the sea: Charlie's smell. She remembered Saturday morning—the morning of her wedding day—when she'd woken to find him already up, running water in the bathroom. What had she said? "Thinking of hightailing it? With me standing at the altar?"

Charlie had laughed. A strange laugh. Or was it strange simply in retrospect, in the context of what had happened later that day? Charlie's Uncle Sam had arrived with the man in the green whale pants, then there'd been a lot of information to absorb in too little time, after that Charlie had gone away in a limousine. Ferdie Ochs, first-class SOB, his will, choice hunks of real estate: that was the text. The subtext was the rude tone in which Charlie had addressed his uncle, the smirk on the face of the man with the green whale pants, Uncle Sam coughing blood.

Coughing blood, in fact, on the green whale pants. Emily went into the laundry cubicle off the kitchen. There were the green whale pants, folded now on the dryer. Buzz. Their owner's name came back to her. What was his relationship to Uncle Sam? Had anyone said? She couldn't remember. So that's what she had: fragments from a text, shadows from a subtext, a pair of silly country club trousers. None of it told her where Charlie was, what he was doing, when he was coming back.

Emily ran her finger around the outline of one of the green whales, its tail raised as though to smack the sea. She thought of searching the pockets. Then she realized that she already had, when moving clothes from the washer to the dryer. And hadn't she found something? What? An empty envelope, on

Yale Alumni Society stationery, with Buzz's address on the front, smeared from washing but still legible. She had tossed it in the trash.

Emily hurried back into the kitchen, opened the cupboard under the sink, pulled out the plastic trash barrel. Empty. She went cold, thinking for a moment that someone had been through her trash, that she was caught in some horrible conspiracy. Then she remembered that tomorrow—today—was garbage day, and that she had hauled the containers out to the side of the road before going to bed.

Emily took a flashlight and went outside. As she walked to the road, she heard a hull creak against a wooden dock; and somewhere in the pond a fish jumped. A yellow crescent moon was rising over the trees. It illuminated fuzzy shapes—the house across the street, a few parked cars, the two trash containers at the end of the driveway. Emily picked one up. A shadowy creature leaped out, brushed furrily against her skin, ran into the bushes. Emily dropped the container, adrenaline shooting through her limbs. Only a raccoon, but it took a while for her heart to stop pounding.

The container lay on its side in the driveway, contents spilling out. Emily knelt. The pavement, retaining the heat of the day, felt warm against her knees. She switched on the flashlight. The raccoon had chewed through the top of a Hefty bag and dined on corn cob cores and a banana skin. Emily dumped the rest of the bag, sorted through its contents. Wasn't there a man who spent his life pilfering and cataloguing celebrity trash? What would he make of these remains—tomato paste cans, dead flowers, chicken bones, a pickle jar with a pickled onion floating in it, a coffee filter full of wet coffee grounds, floor sweepings, plastic wrappers, an empty box of Tide, wads of wet paper towel, Chinese food cartons, crumpled papers, a champagne cork, the flowered bottle of Perrier-Jouët? She sniffed at the top of the bottle, smelled a sour smell: Uncle Sam's gift, delivered by Buzz in his gorilla suit. She remembered Charlie on the raft, taking it. She pictured him going still as he read the card. He had told her that it was from an old pal. Why, when it was his uncle? Was there something odd about it, or was it just that he didn't like Uncle Sam? And had he really gone still, or was she imagining things, turning raccoons into monsters?

That's what you're trying to find out, she told herself, and uncrumpled every bit of paper. The Yale Alumni Society envelope was not one of them. She took the next bag out of the container, dumped it, searched. Nothing. Then she turned to the second container, tried the top bag, then the bottom, and last, one. She was on both knees now, her hands soiled, picking through the mess in her driveway in the middle of the night. She poked about in a nest of cantaloupe skins and felt a ball of paper, pulled it free, smoothed it out. The envelope. Emily held it under the light; wrinkled, soggy, stained, but she could still read it:

Mr. B. W. Svenson
227A Charles St.
Boston, Mass. 02114

Emily scooped the trash back into the containers, ran into the house. She called information in Boston. B. W. Svenson was not listed.

Emily sat in the kitchen for a few minutes. Then she went out the back door and walked down to the dock. The crescent moon replicated itself in yellow frowns across the pond. *Thinking of hightailing it?* The question popped up again in her mind. Had Charlie had second thoughts about marrying her? That led to the corollary question: was there another woman? Unworthy thoughts, unworthy of them both, Charlie and her. She saw *Straight Arrow* lying still on the water, her lines bowed slackly. *Straight Arrow:* solid, rugged, seaworthy.

Like Charlie.

But then, what? Where was he? What was he doing? Would Charlie have abandoned their honeymoon in a quest for choice hunks of real estate? Maybe honeymoon was just a pretty word, irrelevant to people like her and Charlie, but she had been looking forward to it anyway—a two- or three-day walk on Long Trail, cooking by a lake, sleeping in the zipped-together sleeping bags—and so had Charlie. Hadn't he?

Yes. He had. If she didn't know that about him, she knew

nothing, and that was impossible. Something was wrong. Realizing that was step one. Step two was finding out what it was.

Emily tightened *Straight Arrow's* bowline and returned to the house. She showered, dressed, packed a shoulder bag. She left a note on the kitchen table. "Charlie—be back soon. Stay put. Love, Em." She almost crossed out "love" because she was angry.

The sky was paling as Emily went out the front door and climbed behind the wheel of the yellow Beetle, paling like the dawn in one of Conrad's steamy countries. It was going to be the first hot day of the year, and hotter in the city. The car jerked as Emily backed out of the garage. Zachary fluttered; perhaps it could even have been called a kick.

"Damn right," she told him. She turned onto the street and drove away. A rusty pickup with Georgia plates went by the other way. The red clay motif made them easy to recognize.

• • •

Two twenty-seven A Charles Street was a brick town house at the foot of Beacon Hill. It had black-trimmed windows, black double doors, and a heavy brass knocker. Emily found a parking space behind a florist's truck. The driver was carrying an armful of yellow glads up the stone steps of the town house. He'd sweated dark patches through his FTD T-shirt and was breathing heavily as he climbed the steps. Emily followed him.

He rang the bell. "I'm gonna die out here today," he said to Emily. The flowers were wilting in his arms. Another florist's van appeared, double-parking beside the first. Its driver got out, opened the back doors, picked up a few bouquets, climbed the stone steps.

The door half opened, and out rolled an invisible wave of cooled air. A woman, her hand still on the doorknob, looked out. She was about Emily's age, but taller, thinner, and better dressed, dressed for the kind of high-paying job where a conservative appearance mattered. She was talking on a cordless phone. She took in Emily and the two florists, opened the door a little wider, motioned to a marble table in the hall, went on talking.

"I just don't know," she was saying. "They haven't told me anything at all."

The florists laid their gaudy burdens on the table and went away. Emily stayed where she was. The woman raised her eyebrows.

"Is Buzz Svenson in?" Emily asked, speaking in a low voice to show she didn't want to interrupt the conversation, but interrupting it anyway.

The woman's reaction was a surprise. Her lower lip trembled, like a baby in precry. "Mother?" she said. "I've got to go." She clicked off the phone, lowered it to her side. She gained control of her face. "Are you a friend of his?" she asked Emily.

"We've met."

"What's your name?"

"Emily Rice."

"I don't believe he ever mentioned you."

"Possibly not. But I'd like to see him if he's in. It's important."

The lower lip trembled again, and this time tears welled in the woman's eyes, not quite spilling over. But the woman's voice didn't change at all. It remained cold and condescending, of a piece with the severity of her dress, the perfection of her hair and makeup. "Buzz died last night."

"Oh, God, I'm sorry."

"Or possibly this morning. The facts are still being manufactured."

"I don't understand."

"D-E-A-D. What could be simpler? You're not from the office, are you?"

"What office?"

"Buzz's. The office. That's what they call it, as though it's the only one that counts."

"I'm not from the office," Emily said. The tear level fell in the woman's eyes, her lip grew still. "What kind of work do they do?"

"Motorcycling work."

"What do you mean?"

"I mean I can't tell you."

"You can't or you won't?"

"Both. Now if you don't mind." She put her hand on the door.

Emily didn't move. "I'm sorry. But my husband left home with Buzz on Saturday and I'm worried about him. Now more than ever. I think you can help me."

"I'm not in a helping mode."

"I understand that. But I didn't choose the time."

The woman took a good look at Emily, perhaps her first. "Did he go to San Francisco with Buzz, this husband of yours?"

"No," said Emily, but then wondered how she could say that with certainty. Because they had gone off in a car, she had assumed they weren't going far: to Providence, maybe, or somewhere in Connecticut. "But they didn't say."

"Who didn't say?"

"Charlie—my husband—Buzz, and Charlie's Uncle Sam. Uncle Sam arrived with Buzz. He did most of the talking."

The woman blinked. A tear spilled out of one eye and ran down her cheek, ignored. "What's his surname?"

"I don't know." It could be Ochs, but something told her it wasn't.

"What did he look like?"

"He's sick, for one thing," Emily began, and described Uncle Sam. She cut it short; recognition had appeared in the woman's eyes the moment she used the word "sick."

"His name's not Sam," the woman said, "and I don't think he has any nephews."

Emily, with the hot sun on her back and the cold breath of the house in her face, wanted to sit down. The woman, with her hand on the doorknob, did not invite her in.

"His name is Francis Goodnow. He's Buzz's boss in Washington."

Emily remembered then how she had stood in the doorway of the house at Cosset Pond—the way this woman was standing now—confused at the arrival of Uncle Sam and Buzz because Charlie had never mentioned an uncle. Charlie had appeared behind her and said: "It's all right, Em." And then: "Hello, Sam." That meant Charlie had recognized him. But the man's name was Francis Goodnow, not Sam, and he was not Charlie's uncle. Didn't that mean that the entire visit was a charade, staged for her benefit, with Charlie's knowing participation? What else could it mean?

Emily was trying to find some alternative when the woman suddenly said, "Why don't you come in?"

"Thank you."

$$\bullet \quad \bullet \quad \bullet$$

They sat in a high-ceilinged room lined with empty built-in bookcases. The books were packed in boxes on the floor, the rug rolled against the wall, the lamps in one corner, hung with mover's tags, the furniture lined up in the middle of the room. Emily and the woman faced each other on floral love seats, the width of a subway car apart.

"This is going to be the library," the woman said. "Or should I put that in the past tense?" She glanced around as though this were her first viewing of the room, and she didn't particularly like it. "Buzz and I were getting married in the fall." She laughed, abruptly and unpleasantly. "Two overbred snots with one attitude," she said. "That was Buzz's line." Tears began to flow freely, over the planes of her perfect face. It was almost like one of those religious miracles that backward European villages live on, the kind where statues bleed.

"Are you pregnant?" Emily asked, the question came too quickly for self-censoring.

The woman laughed again, although the tears kept coming. "It could have been worse, couldn't it? No, I'm not pregnant. That wasn't in our plans. We'd agreed to be our own children. That didn't keep Buzz alive though, did it?"

Emily could think of nothing to say.

"My apologies," the woman said. "Self-pity is nauseating."

That made it easier for Emily to ask her next question. "How did he die?"

"Some kind of motorcycle accident," the woman said. "Supposedly."

"In San Francisco."

"Correct."

"Was anyone else hurt?"

"If so, I wasn't told. But there's no reason I would be. They

248

operate on a need-to-know basis. It makes them dull conversationalists."

"Who is 'they'?"

"The office. I thought I'd mentioned that."

"But where is it? What do they do?"

"The head office is in Washington somewhere. Buzz worked out of Boston, I don't know the address."

"You don't know where his office is?"

"Near Downtown Crossing, I think."

"But you don't know exactly where?"

"I had a number to call."

"What was it?"

"The number?"

"Yes."

The woman hesitated for a few seconds, then told her the number. Emily rose, went to a phone lying on the floor, and dialed it. A man answered on the first ring and repeated the number to her.

Emily said: "Francis Goodnow, please."

"One moment." A moment passed. The man returned to the line. "We have no one here of that name."

"I think he works out of the Washington office," Emily said. "Could you give me their number?"

"We have no one anywhere of that name," the man repeated. *Click.*

Emily looked up, saw the woman was watching her, eyes dry again. The woman hadn't mentioned her name; perhaps she too was a believer in need-to-know doctrine.

"What is it they do at this office?" Emily asked.

"Serve and protect us."

"From what?"

"The enemy within."

Emily's voice rose; she couldn't help it. "What are you talking about?"

The overbred face flinched. "Terrorism. Buzz is . . . Buzz was an agent in a counterterrorism unit."

"What's it called?"

"I don't know. I think it's part of the NSA, but I'm not sure. This husband of yours, what does he do?"

"Traps lobsters."

The woman nodded. "They all have cover jobs. Buzz told everyone he was a financial analyst for the Agriculture Department. He even had business cards to prove it. I like trapping lobsters better. At least it suggests the truth."

Emily wondered: Did it? Had Charlie dealt with her on a need-to-know basis? How could that coexist with Ben Webster, their bedroom life, the baby? On the other hand, she realized with a sliding in her stomach, it coexisted nicely with the strange look that sometimes rose in his eyes.

The phone rang. The woman answered it. "I'll pick you up at the airport," she said. "I suppose we'll have to call the caterers." She was discussing the menu when Emily left the room.

Emily stepped outside, into the heat of a planet that seemed to have increased its gravity. Another sweating florist was toiling up the stairs. She unlocked the Beetle, drove out of town, not noticing the parking ticket under the wiper until she was back on her own street, Cosset Pond flashing like a mirror between the trees. The pickup with the Georgia plates was parked in front of the house.

31

Emily parked the Beetle in the driveway, got out, and closed the door. Another door closed almost at the same moment, like the discharge of a shotgun's second barrel. Emily turned and saw a man standing beside the pickup. He wore faded jeans, a T-shirt, and cowboy boots; had gray, crewcut hair that looked almost white because of the darkness of his tan.

He raised a hand. "Hi," he said, coming closer.

The man smiled, the quick little smile of those with bad teeth. His skin had spent years fighting a bright sun; it was leathery and crinkled tight around the eyes, reducing the openings to the minimum for sight.

"Mrs. Ochs?" he said. Emily smelled mouthwash on his breath.

"Yes?"

"Hi," he repeated. "Is Charlie around?"

Emily paused. She had no idea who he was or what was happening, but she sensed that a shifting of roles was taking place, a changing in the nomenclature of the sides of a triangle. Triangle A: Emily, the questioner; Buzz, the missing man; Buzz's fiancée, the woman alone. Triangle B: this man, the questioner; Charlie, the missing man; Emily, the woman alone. With that in mind, she took a guess. "Do you work with Buzz?"

"Don't know any Buzzes, ma'am. I'm an old pal of your husband. An ol' pal. Pleasance is the name. Jack Pleasance." He paused. "Mean anything to you?"

He was watching her closely. His eyes, so small in their protective walls of flesh, seemed colorless; they shone with the same mirrored light she'd seen on the pond.

"Charlie never mentioned you."

Pleasance laughed. "Isn't that just like the son of a bitch. Y'know something?"

"What?"

He leaned toward her and lowered his voice, as though telling a secret. Emily smelled aftershave, deodorant, and possibly body powder. "I never mention him, either." Pleasance laughed again; the kind of laugh that invited others to join in. But Emily didn't get the joke, and remained silent.

Pleasance laid a hand on her shoulder, a lean, muscular hand. "Don't you worry, ma'am. Charlie and I go back a long way. A long, long way. He'll be real happy to see me."

Emily backed out of his grasp. "How long?"

"Well, now. I guess I first came across Charlie during his college days."

"College days?" Charlie hadn't gone to college. He had told her that early on; she also remembered him saying it Friday night on the pond, when her father was veering into one of his Vietnam harangues. She had always known that Charlie didn't sound like someone who hadn't been to college, but she'd considered it one of his self-made strengths. Perhaps he wasn't as self-made as she'd thought. Did she lack hard data about her own husband? He was reserved about himself and she hadn't probed, sensing some hurt or disappointment in his past that would require time to surface. That left her with an incongruence of two Charlies: hers, and some other one from before. She tried to visualize Charlie's face and could not.

"Way back then," Pleasance was saying. "He took care of my little boy."

"Baby-sat, you mean?" Emily asked, and as she spoke, Zachary moved inside her, more like twisting than fluttering.

"That's a good one," he said. His mouth assumed a snarling shape. He wiped it back to normal with the palm of his hand. "My boy was a ball player. First team all-star."

"Baseball?"

"That's right. Funny thing, your husband was a ball player too."

"They played on the same team?"

Pleasance's eyes narrowed, almost disappearing in his leathery face; they were just two dime-edge gleams. "Now how could that of been?"

"I don't know," Emily said, wondering if the man might be a bit mad. "And I'm afraid Charlie's not here right now."

"Aw, that's too bad," said Pleasance. "When's he coming back?"

"I'm not sure."

"No?" Pleasance looked her up and down. She had barely begun to show, if at all, but he said: "Hey! Got one in the oven. Congratulations." He held out his hand. Emily shook it, felt again its strength and capability. "Your first?" he said.

Emily nodded.

"Well, well," said Pleasance. "Old Charlie must be pretty excited."

"We're both very happy."

"I'll bet you are. Thought of any names yet?"

"One or two."

"Is Ronnie one of them?"

"No."

"It's a fine name, Ronnie."

"I'm sure it is."

Pleasance glanced around, took in the stacked lobster pots, the house, *Straight Arrow* tied to the dock, the pond beyond. "That Charlie's boat?"

"Yes."

"*Straight Arrow*. What a card."

"You can read that from here?"

"Sure." He looked surprised. "Nice boat. Nice layout, in fact. I can't wait to see Charlie."

"Maybe you could call in a day or two."

"In a day or two?" Pleasance glanced at the boat. "Where did you say he was again?"

"On a business trip."

"Whereabouts?"

"I'm not sure of the itinerary."

Pleasance's eyes shifted to *Straight Arrow* again. "What's he do, anyway?"

"He's a lobsterman."

"Yeah? Sounds kind of quiet for him."

"What do you mean?"

Pleasance ignored her question. "Ever run into any of Charlie's old gang?"

"What old gang?"

"From college. Andrew Malik, maybe."

"No."

"Or Rebecca."

"Rebecca?"

"Rebecca Klein."

The incongruence grew in her mind, the two Charlies assuming increasingly different shapes. "What college was this, Mr. Pleasance?"

"Those names don't ring a bell, do they?" said Pleasance. "Don't ring a bell at all." He made a clucking sound. "What about Blake Wrightman?"

Emily shook her head. "Who are these people?"

"Just the old gang. I thought maybe Charlie had kept up with them. They were kinda close at one time."

"In college."

"Right."

Facts slid together in her mind. "Was this Yale?"

"Yale?" said Pleasance. "Did Blake tell you he went to Yale?"

"I told you," Emily said, hearing the annoyance in her tone and knowing that Charlie, not Pleasance, was the cause: "I never met this Blake person, or any of those others."

Pleasance laughed. "You never met him. Geez."

"What's funny?"

"Nothing. Slip of the tongue. My mistake."

He strangled the laugh, muting it down to an embarrassed

titter. Emily noticed he was wearing a snakeskin belt. "What college are you talking about then?"

"Morgan."

"Charlie went to Morgan?"

"It's not a bad school."

"It's a good school. It's just that . . ."

"Ol' Charlie never mentioned it."

Emily nodded.

"He's too modest."

"Were you a student there at the same time?" Emily asked. Pleasance looked too old, didn't he?

"I was on the faculty."

"Teaching what?"

"My specialty was tactics."

"Tactics?"

"I ran the ROTC."

"And Charlie was in the ROTC?"

"You might say that. Briefly."

"And that's where you met him?"

"That's where our paths crossed."

Emily had a thought left over from Triangle A. "Did you ever meet Charlie's uncle?"

"What's his name?"

"Sam."

"Nope."

"Or possibly Francis Goodnow."

Pleasance blinked. "Are you having some fun with me, ma'am?"

"No. I'm sorry. I'm a little confused, that's all." She snatched at a sudden idea. "Are you sure you've got the right Charlie Ochs?"

"Sure I'm sure," said Pleasance; but his brow furrowed and doubt altered his tone. "You wouldn't have a picture of him, would you?"

"I would." Emily turned and went quickly into the house. Pleasance followed her as far as the screen door, stood outside. Emily looked back. "Come in," she said.

"Thank you kindly." Pleasance opened the door and stepped inside.

They went into the living room. A framed photograph hung on the wall above the record player. It was a wintertime shot of Charlie and Emily sitting on the dock, lacing their skates. Pleasance took it off the wall, held it in both hands. His eyes were dime edges again.

"Well?" said Emily.

Pleasance didn't speak right away. Emily waited. At last he said, "Looks good, doesn't he? Real good. Young."

"It's him, then? The Charles Ochs you knew?"

"Oh, it's him all right." Pleasance kept staring at the picture, specifically at Charlie's image in it. Charlie was smiling at her; she had just said something funny. Emily remembered that De Mello had taken the picture, but not what she had said to make Charlie smile. Her condensed breath hanging between them was the only record of her words. All at once she didn't want anyone touching the picture. She reached for it, intending to hang it back on the wall. For an instant Pleasance didn't let go. Then his lean hands relaxed, allowing her to take it.

Emily rehung the picture. When she turned, she found Pleasance staring at her. His artificial smells filled the room. "Well, then," he said.

"Yes?"

"Guess I'll be going. Tell Charlie I dropped by. When you see him." He nodded to her and walked out of the house. Emily heard the pickup's door close, heard it drive away.

She reached for the phone, got the number of Morgan College, dialed it. The receptionist put her through to Alumni Affairs. "I'm trying to locate a former student," she said. She sketched in a brief supporting story involving job openings and résumés.

"Name?" said the woman at the other end.

"Charles Ochs." She spelled the surname.

"One moment." A moment passed, then many more. The woman spoke: "We have no one listed under that name."

"You don't?"

"That's correct."

"Did you use the right spelling? O-c-h-s?"

"Yes. We have no such listing."

"But—" Emily tried to think of words to convey her objection. None came.

"Yes?" said the woman.

"I see," Emily said, not wanting to hang up, not wanting to let go of the phone. "What about . . ." She tried to remember the other names. "Blake Wrightman?" Had that been one of them?

"Blake Wrightman?"

"He's named on the résumé."

There was a pause. "Is he?"

"Yes."

A longer pause. "Is this some kind of joke?"

"Joke?"

"If so, it's a rather sick one."

"I don't understand," Emily said.

"Don't you? Are you saying you're not aware that Blake Wrightman is still a fugitive?"

"A fugitive?"

"From justice," said the woman. "He's wanted by the law."

"What for?"

"Murder. In the 1970 bombing. No one has ever been apprehended." Emily heard the woman whisper to someone, heard a whispering voice respond. "The police should be told about this résumé," the woman said. "Can you tell me your name, please?"

Emily lowered the receiver—"Hello? Hello?" said the woman—and placed it in its cradle. The plastic was damp with her sweat.

Emily hurried to the screen door, looked out. The pickup with the Georgia plates was gone. The street was shady and still in the late afternoon heat. It was her street, she jogged on it every day, but it seemed unfamiliar. So did the house, the town, the sea, and sky. Emily went outside, got on her bike, and cycled around to the Oceanographic Studies Center's library.

The library, which took up most of the space in the center's original brick building across from the town dock, never closed. Emily went upstairs to the periodical room. She had it to herself. She took down the *New York Times Index* for 1970 and began with January 1. Forty-five minutes later she had it.

Morgan College Bombing

Warrants have been issued for the arrest of three suspects in yesterday's bombing of the ROTC office at Morgan College, Morgantown, Mass., that left one person dead. The three, all students at the college and members of the Tom Paine Club, a radical campus society, are: Rebecca Klein, 20, a junior; Andrew Malik, 24; a graduate student; and Blake Wrightman, 19, a sophomore. The bombing victim, Ronald Pleasance, 11, will be buried tomorrow.

Pleasance is the name. Jack Pleasance. Mean anything to you?

Emily bicycled home, went into the kitchen. She paced. She looked at the phone. It didn't ring. She hadn't eaten all day, knew she should. She made a sandwich, but didn't touch it. She sat at the table. When that grew intolerable, she paced some more. Then she vacuumed the house, washed the bathroom floors, sinks, and toilets.

Later she opened Charlie's closet, stared at his clothes. It was like a math problem: she had a feeling for the answer even before she did the calculations, a feeling he wasn't coming back.

I ran the ROTC.

And Charlie was in the ROTC?

You might say that. Briefly.

And that's where you met him?

That's where our paths crossed.

Night fell. Emily drank a glass of wine, and a second. Then she thought of the baby and didn't pour another, although she wanted it. She tried to picture Charlie's face again, and still could not. Perhaps Ben Webster would help. She played "My Romance." It didn't help. Worse, it didn't even sound like music: what had before been beauty of the most moving kind was now disordered sounds, impossible to piece together in her mind. Emily went to bed.

She lay in bed—their bed—for a long time. She learned that peace and quiet were not the same thing. She fell asleep—and down into a dream of San Francisco, this time speeded up, like a synopsis. Going into labor on the Golden Gate Bridge. Tires bursting. Traffic disappearing. Getting stuck in the car. Someone coming toward her. But this time it wasn't Uncle Sam. It was Charlie. He had a big grin on his face and a Molotov cocktail in his hand. Her unconscious worked a calculus of its own.

Emily awoke in a sweat. She got up, went into the bathroom for a glass of water. She drank it looking out the window, the back window, with its view of the pond. The night was still, the pond like black glass. Nothing moved except a light on *Straight Arrow*, bobbing down at the dock.

Charlie.

Emily, in her nightdress, ran downstairs, outside, across the lawn, and onto the dock; her bare feet made no noise on the planks. A cone of yellow light shone on *Straight Arrow*'s console. The casing was open. Emily saw wires, tools, the shadow of a man, and his hands, working in the yellow cone.

"Charlie?" she said. But even as she spoke, she was thinking about those hands, too lean, so capable.

Something metal clattered on *Straight Arrow*'s deck. The light went out. Emily heard a grunt, quick footsteps; and then the light was on again, shining in her eyes. She smelled mouthwash, deodorant, aftershave.

"Hi," said a voice, and she felt again one of those hands on her shoulder. The light declined, down her body, clad in the thin nightdress, down to her bare feet. In its penumbra she could make out Jack Pleasance standing before her, pliers and screwdrivers in his snakeskin belt.

"Mr. Pleasance," she said, jerking out from under his hand. "What do you think you're doing?"

"What needs to be done, ma'am."

Emily's voice rose, rose on the force of her frustration, doubt, worry. "You're on our property, Mr. Pleasance. I want you to leave now."

He smiled: a gleam in the night. His hand disappeared in his pocket, emerged with another gleam. He raised it to his teeth, bit into it, pulled. A straight razor opened in the space between them; the kind of razor that cowboys used. It went with his boots, his belt, his squinting eyes.

"Tell you what," he said. "Let's you and me go inside and discuss it."

Emily considered turning to run; she considered jumping into the pond. But with the baby inside her could she outrun him, or outswim him? She didn't know. All she knew for sure was that he would use that razor on her, that he would have no compunction about using it, that he wanted to use it. The proof was in his smile.

32

By the time Charlie found Hugo Klein's office, it was almost dawn, the morning after the deaths of Brucie, Svenson, and the little Chinese man. Klein's office was in Berkeley, on Shattuck, a few blocks below the university. Charlie went into a coffee shop on the opposite side of the street, had a cup of coffee, then another. He tried to remember when he had last slept. Had it been in Toronto, or before? He ordered a third cup. This seemed to please the counterman, who paused to complain to Charlie about the kind of money ball players were making, and waited for some indication of agreement. But Charlie, thinking of Candlestick the night before, and the way it had glowed like an artifact from a more-advanced planet, said nothing.

The night began to pale. Charlie paid his bill and left the café. He stood across the street from Klein's office. Dawn gave it color and shape: a creamy affair with arched windows and red tiled roof, that could have passed for the palacio of some minor Castilian figure, perhaps one who had been unable to land the architect he wanted.

Hugo Klein appeared at seven in a long low convertible. He

stepped out, wearing a sweat suit and jogging shoes, smoothed his hair, and stretched his arms to the sky, like a triumphant Olympian. A young man in a three-piece suit hurried out of the building, got in the car, and drove it away. Klein didn't go inside; instead, he started loping up the street. Charlie, in street shoes, jeans, and a T-shirt, followed him on the other side, trying to pass for a jogger on his morning routine. In some places he might not have gotten away with it; in Berkeley, no one looked at him twice.

Klein wasn't fast, but he kept a steady rhythm, his silky mane bobbing up and down in syncopation. The sun was still behind the hills, leaving them in a half-light. Klein turned right, ran past the university, and up into the hills, not slowing his pace at all. Charlie, on the other side of the street and about fifty yards behind, broke a sweat. Klein was running easily now, and faster. That suited Charlie, although he really wasn't built for distance running. He didn't know where Klein was going, couldn't have explained why he was following him, but it felt good to sweat, to run—as though he was getting something accomplished. He almost forgot about Brucie and Svenson and the little Chinese man.

Three quarters of the way to the top of the hill, Klein turned again, and jogged north on a pleasant street, green and quiet. The sun rose over the hilltop, pouring saturated color on green herb gardens, a red tricycle on an uncut lawn, bundled yellow newspapers, Klein's silvery bobbing mane. As Klein came to a house with a beat-up Ford compact in the driveway and a blue Toyota Tercel on the street in front, he reached into his sweat suit. Without pausing, or even slowing down, he slipped something through the rear window of the Tercel. Something red, Charlie thought: fiery for one moment in the sun, like a hot coal.

Klein ran on. Charlie crossed the street, jogged past the Tercel, stopping to look inside. A red rose lay on the back seat. He glanced at the house: it had a yard just big enough for a single palm tree; weeds grew out of the eaves troughs; 227 was the number on the doorpost, in tin.

Ahead, Klein rounded a curve and disappeared. Charlie quickened his pace. His feet were hurting now, and he thought about removing his hard shoes. He was still thinking about it when he picked up Klein again, turning at a cross street.

They started downhill, Klein about fifty yards in front, a sweat stain growing in the middle of his back. Ahead, the bay was baby blue in the early light, and fog was stacked up over the city across the water like whipped cream on a wedding cake. Klein ran all the way down to Shattuck, then turned left, completing the rectangle. People were on the streets now; a few of them greeted Klein, looking up at him with smiles on their faces. Charlie couldn't see Klein's expression: he could only observe how he lifted his knees a little higher, pumped his arms a little faster, each time someone said hello, the sweat stain spreading across his back. Klein picked up speed as he neared his office. He was almost sprinting when the young man in the three-piece suit opened the front door and let him through.

Charlie stopped on the other side, breathing hard, hard enough to want to hold his sides. He resisted. The young man looked up and down the street, as though storing mental images of the outdoors for the long office day ahead, and closed the door. The city hummed.

Charlie stayed where he was. His pulse and breathing fell to their normal rates; only his mind kept racing. He watched Klein's office, hoping the door would open, hoping Klein would come back out, hoping for something. But Klein didn't come out, and Charlie began to doubt that he would until the end of the day. Charlie didn't want to wait all day. He took off his shoes and socks and started walking.

He walked along Shattuck, up Bancroft Way, past the university; then up the hill, and left, retracing Klein's run along the green and pleasant street until he came to the house with the palm tree and the tin 227 on the doorpost. The old Ford was still in the driveway, but the blue Tercel with the red rose on the backseat was gone.

Charlie stood before the house, shoes in hand. He heard a trumpet playing, not far away. The song was "Row, Row, Row Your Boat," but the tempo was very fast and the tone was honking, rude, funny. Technically the player wasn't bad, almost good enough to bring it off. Charlie listened as the trumpeter tried one thing, then another, moving farther and farther from a simple tune about streams and dreams. The music died abruptly, leaving various ideas unresolved. It was only then that Charlie realized that the sound had come from inside 227.

Charlie had moved onto the driveway and now stood by the old Ford. His mind was back in the spring of 1970, watching Rebecca. She was running toward him across the central quad, her eyes excited and happy. But she wasn't running toward him at all: past him, unseeing, and into the arms of her father. Hugo Klein, smiling with pride, handed her a bunch of red roses. Hadn't there been another time when he had seen Rebecca with red roses—or perhaps a single one? When?

The night of the bombing.

The door of 227 opened. A young man came out. He had a duffel bag in one hand, a trumpet case in the other. He might have been twenty or twenty-one. He was almost as tall as Charlie, almost as broad; his hair and skin were a little darker. Charlie registered all that, but not consciously. His conscious mind, so recently full of images of Rebecca and red roses, was now absorbing the fact the young man looked just like him; or just as he had looked when he was twenty or twenty-one—say, back in 1970.

The young man, carrying the duffel bag and the trumpet case, walked toward the beat-up Ford. Then he noticed Charlie standing at the edge of the lawn, shoes in hand. He gave Charlie a pointed glance, perhaps expecting he would go away, opened the trunk of the car, then glanced at him again and saw he hadn't.

"Something I can help you with?" asked the young man, laying the bag and the trumpet in the trunk. Charlie saw a rugby ball and pair of cleats beside the spare tire. They didn't look like baseball cleats, but he was too far away to be sure.

"What's your name?" Charlie said. It was the first question to separate from the wriggling nest of questions that had risen in his mind; the words popped out before he could stop them.

The young man straightened. His chest swelled, in the inflationary manner of threatened mammals. "Why do you want to know?"

"I heard you playing. You play well."

"Thanks." The young man closed the trunk with a bang.

Charlie stepped forward, onto the lawn. He felt the grass under his feet, drier and coarser than the outfield grass on the ball field at Morgan, and wished his shoes were on. "I . . ."

"Yes?"

What had Malik said? Rebecca, pregnant with Malik's child, had left Toronto in late summer or early fall of 1970, gone to San Francisco for an abortion. But Malik hadn't known that the child wasn't his, and he hadn't known that the abortion never happened. Wasn't that the only explanation of what he was now seeing with his own eyes? That left the question of how to begin.

"I knew your mother," Charlie said.

"Yeah?" replied the young man. "She's not home."

The next question, had Charlie still been following Mr. G's agenda, was: where is she? It remained unasked. Instead, Charlie heard himself say, "What about your father?"

"My what?"

"Your father."

Charlie, almost without realizing it, had begun to cross the lawn. The young man squinted at him over the top of the car. "Who are you, anyway?"

"Blake Wrightman," Charlie replied.

The young man's face, healthy, unwrinkled, unlined, still partly the face of a boy, didn't change expression. "I think there's some kind of mistake."

"What do you mean?"

"My mother never mentioned you. And I don't have a father."

"Everyone has a father somewhere."

"Mine died in Vietnam."

"Who told you that?" Charlie's voice rose despite himself.

The young man's voice rose too. "What do you mean, who told me?" He looked closely at Charlie, his eyes coming to rest on the shoes in Charlie's hand. "I've got to get going," he said, and opened the car door.

Boy, it was your grandfather who died in Vietnam: that was Charlie's thought. He almost said it out loud. Then the lines of the young man's family tree began to come in focus. Everyone

PETER ABRAHAMS

had two grandfathers. The young man's other grandfather was Hugo Klein. What were the implications of that?

The young man was getting into the car; the conversation was over for him, one of those chance urban encounters with a crank. Charlie walked around the car.

"Wait." Afraid of causing damage, he'd been too oblique.

The young man paused, halfway into the car. "Why don't you get out of the sun for a while? You're a little mixed-up." He sat in the driver's seat and started to close the door. Charlie grabbed the inside of the frame. The young man pulled; Charlie resisted. The young man was strong, Charlie stronger. As soon as Charlie realized that, as soon as he realized what he was doing, he let go of the door. It slammed shut. Too late. The young man was looking up at him through the open window with animosity, his tolerance for street-crazy behavior exhausted.

Charlie stepped back. "It's a mix-up," he said, "but not the kind you think."

"No?" said the young man, sliding the key into the ignition. "Who is it you're looking for exactly?"

"Your mother. Rebecca Klein."

"That's not my mother's name." The young man turned the key and shifted into reverse.

"Look at me," Charlie said. "Look at my face."

The young man looked at him, looked at his face. What was obvious to Charlie was invisible to him. "You'd better get some help," he said. "Try the Med Center." He stepped on the gas. The car squealed out onto the street, swung around, stopped with another squeal, then jerked forward and sped away. In a few moments it rounded a leafy curve and vanished.

Charlie stood on the grass, looking at nothing, smelling exhaust. He sat down and put his shoes on. He was lacing them when he saw a man coming along the sidewalk. The man had long gray hair, a full gray beard; he wore sandals and a blue robe that reminded Charlie of some Saharan tribe. He was reading a book, reading aloud: his muttering grew audible. As the man came closer, Charlie could make out the title. It was *Dune*. The man drew alongside Charlie, raised his hand palm up like a priest of some ancient and orthodox cult. He spoke. "How does your garden grow?"

And then walked on. Just another urban crank.

Charlie rose. The questions raised by the sight of the young man with the trumpet coiled and uncoiled in his mind. He had no answers. All he knew were two things: Hugo Klein had dropped a red rose into the blue Tercel, and the young man looked just like him. But could he really be sure of the second? Maybe it was his imagination, coming up with possible complications on its own. Charlie walked up to the front door and knocked.

No one answered. The house was silent.

Charlie opened the mailbox beside the door. Inside were two envelopes and a Sears catalog, all addressed to "Resident." Charlie replaced them and knocked again. Silence.

He glanced around, saw no one, then pressed his face against the half-moon window in the door. He saw an entrance hall with a dead plant in one corner and a coatrack in the other. A black T-shirt bearing glittery writing hung on the coat rack. He could read "Paco's."

Charlie left the front door, walked around the side of the house. A picket fence enclosed the tiny backyard. The gate hung on one hinge. Charlie pushed through.

There was nothing in the yard: no trees, no flowers, no bicycles, no lawn furniture, no barbecue; just a distant and partial view of the bay. Charlie went to the back door.

He looked in, saw a washer and dryer. A brassiere and panties were spread on a towel. Through a doorway beyond he saw into the kitchen: a refrigerator with nothing tacked on it and a bare table.

Charlie tried the door. It was locked. He leaned his shoulder against it. The door gave slightly, as though the lock were loose or the materials worn and second-rate. He glanced around again. No one was watching. He was free to do a criminal thing. And why not? He was a criminal, and he had enemies— yes, why not call them that?—who were prepared to commit violent crimes. Still, Charlie almost turned and walked away.

But in the end he could not. He lowered his shoulder and drove it into the door. Wood splintered around the lock, making a sound like crashing surf. He fought off the urge to glance behind him and hit the door again. It swung open and he went in.

And once in, he searched the house without compunction. He checked the sizes of the panties and brassiere, not quite dry, on the towel. Medium and 36C, but what did that mean? People change shape in twenty years, and he didn't think Rebecca had ever worn brassieres. That didn't stop him from opening the dryer and examining everything inside: all of it women's clothing, all of good quality. He checked the pockets, found nothing but a dollar bill, wadded in a tight, clean ball.

Charlie moved into the kitchen. Searching the dryer had reminded him of Malik, stuck in red ice. He opened the refrigerator. The only corpse was on the bottom shelf, a plastic-wrapped fowl. The perp was Frank Perdue.

The coffee in the coffee maker was still warm. Charlie took a mug marked with two Chinese characters from the dish rack, poured some and tasted it. Very good. He wondered whether the young man with the trumpet had made it.

In a drawer beneath the wall phone was a phone book. Charlie leafed through it. There were no handwritten numbers inside, no messages, nothing underlined. He went into the dining room and then the living room. There was furniture, but it hardly seemed used; there were books, but they didn't look read; a desk, but no bills, letters, bank statements, address books, or anything with a name on it in the drawers. Charlie went upstairs.

On the second floor were two bedrooms and a bathroom. Charlie went into the bathroom first. There was a wet towel on the floor, and water drops still clung to the inside of the stall shower. A blob of shaving cream lay on the counter by the sink. Charlie opened the mirrored cabinet. Inside he found soaps and cosmetics in fancy packages with European names on them. Charlie closed the cabinet, and saw a tired and troubled face in the mirror.

He went into the first bedroom. It had a single bed, stripped, and nothing in the chest of drawers but a few worn sweatshirts—size, men's X-large. Charlie opened the closet. On the single hanger was a purple satin jacket of the size a big twelve-year-old might wear. On the back was stitched in gold thread: "East

Bay Little League Division One 1982 Champions." On the sleeve: "Malcolm." There was nothing else of note in the room except a black-and-white poster of Wynton Marsalis.

Charlie went into the second bedroom and stopped right away. He knew. It was the bed that did it, a big bed with a painted headboard, carved posts, a canopy like soft pink clouds. For a moment he thought it was the princess bed, but it was not. Charlie remembered fat putti on the headboard of the princess bed; the painting on this headboard showed a Tuscan landscape in the evening. But close enough. He knew.

Charlie checked the walls. There were no posters of Marx, Engels, Rosa Luxemburg, La Pasionaria, Mao, Malcolm X, Ho Chi Minh, General Giap; just restful European landscapes, bathed in soft Mediterranean light.

Malcolm X, Charlie thought. He stood in the doorway for a long time.

After a while he searched the room. He found the predictable: clothing, shoes, bedding. The unpredictable: a black, luridly detailed vibrating device. But nothing with a name on it.

Nothing with a name. The phrase stuck in his mind, blocking other thought. He was tired. When had he last slept? In Toronto, or before? Charlie sat down on the bed, trying to remember. He couldn't. He sat there for a long time. *Should I be sitting on this bed? Why not? It's just a bed, isn't it?* And he felt like sitting.

Shadows slid slowly across the floor. The bed was soft, the Tuscan landscape a sleep-inducing sfumato-land of crumbling statues and dying light. Maybe if he put his head down, just for a second, it would come to him, whatever he was trying to remember.

Charlie put his head down.

33

There was a knock at the door. "Don't even think about it," Pleasance said in a low voice, up off his chair and onto his feet with the speed and silence of a forest creature.

Emily thought about it anyway, but what could she do? She was in the broom closet, bound to a chair with duct tape; there was another strip of it across her mouth. Pleasance shut the closet, and then there was nothing to see but a keyhole-shaped piece of daylight.

Emily didn't hear Pleasance's footsteps, but after a moment or two she heard the front door open. Then came a voice: "Is Emily in?"

A man's voice, and not just any man's, but the first man's voice she had known. Still, it was so unexpected she almost didn't recognize it at once: her father's voice.

"Emily?" said Pleasance.

"Emily Rice," said her father. After a slight pause that was full of meaning, although perhaps meaning undecipherable to anyone but Emily or her mother, he added: "Or she may be calling herself Ochs now."

"Emily," said Pleasance. "You betcha. The thing is she's not here right now."

"What about her husband?"

"He's gone too."

"When will they be back?"

"Hard to say. I'm kind of . . . house-sitting, see? While they're away."

"Where are they?"

"New York."

"They are? Emily hates New York."

"Me too," said Pleasance.

There was another pause, longer this time. "You're a friend of Emily's?"

"My connection's more with Charlie, if truth be known. But she's a fine gal, just fine."

"I'm her father." His voice was cold.

"Jack Pleasance, captain, U.S. Army, retired. Pleased to meet you."

Another pause. Emily had the horrid thought that the two men were shaking hands. "Did I see you at the wedding?" her father asked.

"Couldn't make it, to my great sorrow. Heard it was quite a bash."

"I wouldn't say that."

"No? Well, everybody has their own idea about fun, right? I saw things in Saigon you wouldn't believe."

"You were there?"

" 'Sixty-five to 'sixty-seven. It was the biggest fuck-up there ever was."

"I won't disagree with that."

"You were there too?"

"Twice. With the Marine Corps."

"Well *semper fi*, you ol' son of a gun," said Pleasance, and there was another pause. Perhaps they were shaking hands again.

"Charlie didn't strike me as someone with military friends," her father said. Did his voice seem less cold? It did.

Pleasance laughed. "Those fucking radicals," he said.

"Charlie's a radical?"

271

"Oh, not now. For sure not now. Now he fits right in like you don't even see he's there. But me and Charlie go back some, way, way back."

"To Pittsburgh?"

"Pittsburgh?"

"He came from Pittsburgh, didn't he?"

"Oh, sure. Steel City. Right. But we hooked up a little after that. In college, it was."

"Charlie went to college?"

"Hell, yes. How do you think the fucker ducked the draft?"

Come on, Daddy. Pick up on it—he's no friend.

Her father said: "I knew it."

"Huh?"

"But you're friends."

"Why not?"

"What you said. The draft."

"All that's water under the bridge," Pleasance said. "Spilled milk, if you know what I mean. Violence is as American as . . . what is it again? Anyhoo, you gotta love Charlie. Shit, you must know that. He married into your family, right? Draft dodger or no draft dodger."

"Right," said her father; his voice was grim.

Daddy: look at what's in front of your face. But she knew he wouldn't. Pleasance had found his blind spot.

Pleasance said: "Well, then. Anything else I can he'p you with?"

"I don't think so," her father said. "When did you say they'd be back?"

"Be a few days or so, if I know Charlie. The lobsters have been lying low the past while, to hear him tell it."

Emily thought she heard her father sigh. "Too bad," he said. "I was in Boston for the day on business and we got out early. Took a chance she'd be in. Tell her I stopped by, will you?"

"You betcha," said Pleasance.

Emily tried to lean forward, sideways, backward, in any direction, to somehow start the chair rocking and tip it over, to somehow make a noise her father would hear. But she was too tightly bound; all the parts of her body were one with the chair. All the parts except her head. She jerked it back with force, cracking it against the rear wall of the closet.

Then she listened. She heard Pleasance talking; perhaps his voice has risen a little: to mask her sound? "Be seeing you, then," he was saying. "So long."

Emily pounded her head against the wall. She listened.

Silence.

She pounded it again.

And heard her father say: "What's that?"

"What's what?" said Pleasance.

"I heard a noise. Kind of a thump. Inside."

"I didn't," said Pleasance.

Emily forced herself to do it again, with all her strength.

"That," said her father.

"Oh, that," said Pleasance. "Just the darned screen door out back. Old Charlie's not exactly Mr. Fix-it around the house."

"No? He looked pretty handy to me."

Pleasance laughed. "Hell, I thought you knew him. Are we talking about the same Charlie?"

"I know him well enough," Doug Rice said. There was animosity in his tone. Emily couldn't tell whether it was directed at Pleasance or Charlie. The idea that it might be Charlie made her angry. She banged her head again, angrily.

Silence. Then her father said: "Tell her I'll be in touch."

"You betcha."

The front door closed. A few moments later a car started. The sound of the motor faded and faded and died away. And that was Daddy.

The closet door opened and light came in. The first thing Emily saw was a lean, capable hand, contracted into a fist. Nothing moved in the little closet world except one of Pleasance's eyelids: it began to twitch.

"You'll be first," he told her. "You and little Ronnie, of course. So ol' Charlie can see. It's only fair, right?"

Emily, mouth taped, head full of pain, glared at him. He looked down at her, then away, taking a bottle from his back pocket. He gulped from it, once, twice, until it was empty. Sweat popped out on his forehead.

"Only fair," he repeated. "And then a big surprise for ol' Charlie." He tossed the bottle across the room, not hard, but it shattered on the floor anyway.

The act, the noise, the destruction seemed to liberate him in some way. He tore off his shirt as though it were the yoke of civilization. His torso was bony and scarred. He faced Emily again. This time he had no trouble looking her in the eye. He gave her a long uncivilized gaze and shut the closet door.

34

The Committee of the American Resistance—the gang, to Yvonne—was waiting for her in the Estuary Park. She passed the Jack London condos—where soon, if Felipe's dreams came true, they would be in bed in some well-decorated room of the kind he only saw in the movies, with the possibility of videotaping in the offing—and turned into the park. She stopped the Tercel beside a dented van at the end of the brick-top turnaround, and got out. She didn't lock the car. There was nothing in it but a red rose, wilting in the back.

It wasn't much of a park: small and grassless, with a few stunted palms not much bigger than house plants growing by the waterfront. It wasn't much of a night, either: cool and damp, with marine mist blowing in from the west. The mist thickened to fog as she watched, dimming the lights of Alameda in the distance. Across the estuary, on the south side, three silhouetted forms separated themselves from the darkness: the long wooden pier that stretched into the inner harbor, the warehouse that rose behind it, the oceangoing freighter that was docked to its end. She smelled rotting seaweed, rotting fish, garbage, waste.

The side door of the van opened and Eli climbed out. She could smell him, too, smell his nervous sweat, and in the glow of the van's interior light that spilled out, she could see the stains spreading under the arms of his denim work shirt. He smiled at her and said, "A nice night for it." His smile was too tight, his voice too high; and he himself was too young.

"We'll see," Yvonne said, wondering whether the Santa Clara Five fiasco had also begun with a joke. Eli flinched, probably thinking of his girlfriend in Leavenworth and everything that could go wrong. Yvonne stepped up into the van. The rest of them were inside—Angel behind the wheel, Annie beside him, Gus in back—all dressed like blue-collar workers as seen through their own eyes: Annie in clothes too big, making her look more frail than ever; Angel wearing a black beret, which combined with his wispy mustache and copper skin might have made him think he resembled Che Guevara; Gus in a T-shirt that read "I'm in the NRA and I vote." Yvonne, dressed for Felipe in a black Spandex halter and a short leatherette skirt and carrying a disco purse with sequins, felt strangely alive.

"Any questions?" she said.

"Aren't you cold?" asked Annie. She must have suspected that Yvonne was enjoying her costume, and didn't approve.

"I'm hot," said Yvonne, "Very, very hot."

Gus laughed, a brief laugh but real. Then he reached into a gym bag and handed her a police special. She stuck it in the disco purse with the sequins.

"*¡Buena suerte!*" Angel said.

"Luck has nothing to do with it," Yvonne said. Gus laughed again. His belly jiggled in visual counterpoint. She liked Gus. He was competent. In another life—in this life, if he had chosen differently—he might have been the kind of big shot she hated. Like her, he was a winner who had opted out, instead of—*say it*—a loser like the others. Yvonne climbed down from the van and slid the door closed. The light inside went out.

Yvonne started walking, out of the park, onto street, over the estuary bridge. The fog was cold and getting colder, but the funny thing was she really did feel hot. At first she could hear the traffic on the freeway, but then a train approached on the Embarcadero tracks and overwhelmed all sound with its hooting. For a moment she was caught in the glare of its light. She walked unhurriedly on in her little skirt and top, like a whore on patrol. The train hooted again and passed by, leaving her in darkness.

The warehouse stood behind a chain-link fence on the other side of the estuary. It was windowless, with rusty, corrugated walls and a tin roof: the kind of creation commerce makes necessary. There was an office at one end. A single bulb hung over the door, illuminating a sign that read: "Nippon American Import Export. Authorized Persons Only." Fog swirled through the pool of yellow light.

Yvonne moved into the shadow near the locked gate in the chain-link fence and waited. She was hot, but not the sweating kind of hot. She wasn't nervous, either: she was looking forward to it, as though it were . . . what? A long trip. She smiled to herself.

Headlights appeared, coming from the north, swept their beams in an arc along the fence, steadied on the gate. An armored car drew up and stopped. "Armored Trucking Services, Inc.," it read on the side. The driver's door opened and Felipe, in his uniform, got out. He had a gun on his belt and keys in his hand. He went to the gate and unlocked it. Then he returned to the truck and drove it through. The truck halted just inside. Felipe got out again and walked to the gate, keys in hand. Yvonne stepped out of the shadows and walked through the opening.

Felipe stopped. For one moment he didn't recognize her. For one moment she was a person, a person in the wrong place and therefore a threat. The next moment she was a woman, and not a threat, and he was looking at her womanly parts. Only after that did he look at her face.

"Carol?"

"Felipe. I'm so glad you're here." It was fun to say something like that, fun to sound like someone who needed a big strong man.

"What's wrong?" Felipe said. He glanced back at the truck. "We were sposta meet at the condo, no?"

"Yes. But my damned car broke down." Yvonne gestured into the night. "And it's dark out there."

Felipe blinked. "The problem is...is better if you wait outside." He turned to the truck again, then back to her. "We got all these fuckin' rules, you know?"

Yvonne walked up to him and put her arms around him. "But it's dark out there, Felipe." She kissed him on the mouth. At first he didn't respond. Then he did. Yvonne rubbed against him, felt his gun against her bare stomach. She spoke low in his ear: "Did you bring your video camera?"

He shivered, shivered and started to get hard. She felt that too, and moved her hand down his front, down under his cheap work-issue belt and his cheap uniform pants. He moaned. "Not now, Carol."

She heard a soft footstep behind her, outside the gate, and moaned herself, to cover the sound. Felipe tried to push away. "Not now. Be a good girl."

Yvonne held onto him, held him by his cock. "I am a good girl," she said. "I just want a little appetizer." She was watching the truck. Open the fucking door, idiot.

"Appetizer?"

"Like this," she said, going down on her knees and unzipping his pants—slowly, because she wanted the door of the truck to open. But it didn't open, and there she was on the oil-stained pavement outside the warehouse on the waterfront with unseen eyes watching her and her lips around this poor fool's poor nervous thing, and the odd part was that it aroused her.

"No, Carol," Felipe was saying. "Please. Just wait. Be a good girl."

She started to laugh, almost spat him out. Then the rear door of the armored truck finally opened and a man with a shotgun looked out.

"Hey, Felipe," he called, "what's taking— Christ almighty."

"Fuck," said Felipe with anger, putting his hands on her shoulders and pushing her roughly away. Yvonne let herself be pushed, let herself roll back, out of the way. After that things speeded up.

First came a cracking sound from the darkness beyond the gate, and the man with the shotgun fell back inside the truck.

278

That would be Gus's work; he was a dead shot. Then Yvonne caught a brief tableau of Felipe frozen there, unzipped, moving his lips soundlessly. The next thing she knew he was standing over her, gun in hand. She tried to slow everything down in her mind, but it was beyond her control. Eli came charging out of the darkness waving one of Gus's Uzis in Felipe's direction. Then came the first surprise: Felipe snapped up his gun and shot Eli in the head. He surprised her again by reaching for her hand and pulling her up.

"Quick, Carol. Run."

And then Felipe was running toward the office, and she was running with him, his hand tight and protective around hers. There was another cracking sound and Felipe stumbled and fell. Yvonne fell with him.

Yvonne looked back, saw Annie bent over Eli, and Gus and Angel running toward her and Felipe. They were almost abreast of the armored car when the shotgun boomed inside it, standing Angel up straight, splattering his blood like moths in the night sky, felling him. Gus dropped to one knee, spread an arc of automatic fire through the open door of the truck. The shotgun made no reply.

Felipe struggled to his feet, reaching for her hand again like some stalwart out of the *Chanson de Roland*. "Is a robbery, Carol. Run." But Gus was coming and Yvonne stayed down.

Felipe fired. His eyes were so wide Yvonne could see white all around the irises. Gus fired back. Felipe fell again, on top of Yvonne. His warm wetness spread over her body. His eyes were open, but not quite so wide now, and looking right into hers. "Oh, Carol," he said. "I so sorry." She held him. The expression in his eyes turned to nothing.

Gus loomed over her. Blood was running down his arm. "You all right?" he said.

Yvonne nodded. "You?"

"Yeah. Let's go go go." He shifted the gun to his bleeding arm and extended his free hand to her. He didn't see the dog at all.

It sprang out of the darkness, right over Yvonne, catching Gus in the chest, knocking him down. Yvonne scrambled to the side, saw that the office door was open, saw a watchman coming with a rifle. The dog snarled. Gus cried out, a terrible sound coming from someone like him. Yvonne looked around wildly for the disco purse, found it lying a few yards away, crawled to it. Gus's gun went off. The dog went still and slid off him.

Gus got unsteadily to his feet. Now his face was bloody too, and his lip was torn in a twisted grin.

"Behind you," Yvonne said. She got hold of the purse just as Gus spun around and saw the watchman. The watchman was close now, close enough to see what had happened to the dog.

"Jesus fucking Christ," he said. He put the rifle to his shoulder and shot Gus in the neck.

Gus sank down, the torn twisted grin on his face and a fine red spray coming from his throat. But he still had time to get his finger on the trigger, still had time to squeeze it. He died that way, shooting. One of the bullets found the watchman. He was unlucky, and died too.

Yvonne rose. It was quiet. She heard nothing but the sea sucking at the pilings, and then another train coming from the south. The fog rolled in.

Yvonne walked away, away from Gus, the watchman, the dog, away from Felipe, away from truck with the guard's feet hanging out the back and Angel on the ground, his beret upside down beside him, walked back to Annie. She was still crouching near Eli, rocking back and forth. The sweat stains were still visible on his T-shirt but most of his face was gone.

Annie raised her head, looked up at Yvonne. Tears were rolling down her face, as though she'd sprung a leak that could never be fixed. She rose, took a step forward, as though to embrace. Yvonne took an equivalent step back.

"Oh, God, Yvonne, it's so awful."

"Political power," Yvonne said, "grows out of the barrel of a gun."

Annie flinched. "I don't understand."

Yvonne laughed. "It's just an expression, like 'Have a nice day.'"

Annie shook her head, noticed Eli, and began to sob. "Hold me, Yvonne."

The train came closer. Yvonne heard it, felt it in her feet.

"There's no time," she said, taking the disco purse off her shoulder.

Annie raised her hands and dropped them in a helpless gesture. "Oh, God," she said. "What are we going to do?"

"Don't ask me," Yvonne said. She considered several possibilities, all complex, none liberating. Then she took the police special out of the disco purse and shot Annie in the heart. The train hooted, drowning the sound of the gun completely. Annie fell onto the pavement, with no comprehension in her eyes.

Power, which grows from the barrel of a gun, corrupts. And absolute power corrupts absolutely. Where had she first heard that one? From Andrew? Or Gus? Or her father? Or some other idea man along the way. Men and their ideas.

Yvonne stuck the gun back in the purse and walked to the truck. She shoved the guard out of the way and found four canvas sacks. She opened one and saw U.S. currency inside, neatly bound in fat wads. She removed the sacks and laid them on the ground.

After that things slowed back down. Yvonne was sweating now, although she no longer felt hot. She dragged all the bodies to the truck, including the dog's, and got them inside. It was effortless; she didn't feel their weight at all. She tossed all the weapons inside too, except her own. Then she climbed into the driver's seat and turned the key.

A voice crackled out of the dashboard. "Felipe? Where are you? Come in, Felipe."

Yvonne drove the truck carefully around the warehouse and onto the pier. She followed it about halfway to the end and turned the wheel to the right. The truck rolled toward the side of the pier. Yvonne opened the door, jumped out, landed on the rough planks, stayed on her feet. It was easy.

Inside the moving truck the radio crackled: "Felipe? Is something wrong?" Without Yvonne's foot on the gas, the truck slowed, but it had enough momentum to reach the edge, to teeter over it, to plunge into the estuary. The sound it made was thrilling.

The night was making up for a lot: twenty-two years of what she'd always thought of as preparation, but what had it amounted to? A lot of talk, and raising Malcolm—or more accurately, watching him grow. Except for stealing one of the cars used in the Santa Clara affair, she hadn't *done* anything, other than grow middle-aged in the safety of her middle-class persona. A revolution meant action, irrevocable action, death. The night was making up for a lot.

Yvonne walked to the office and closed the door. Then she returned to the four canvas bags. She'd expected more but it didn't matter: she could only handle three. She left the fourth where it was, a gift to the proletariat. That was instead of spraying "Free the Santa Clara Five—Power to the People" on the side of the warehouse, which had been the original plan. The spraying was Eli's responsibility. The spraycan was probably still in his pocket, leaving her nothing to write with but the blood, lying in pools here and there.

Yvonne carried the three canvas bags through the gate in the chain-link fence. She closed it behind her and fastened the lock. She looked back. From there, everything looked tidy, except for the single canvas bag. It brought to mind the image of a lobster tail on a spotless kitchen floor.

The dented van was parked outside the fence. Yvonne walked past it, back to Estuary Park. The Tercel was waiting in the brick-top turnaround, almost lost in the fog. She dropped the canvas bags in the trunk, got inside, started the car. She kept anticipating sirens, but there were none. Perhaps no one had heard the gunfire, perhaps they had heard and no longer bothered to react.

Yvonne drove out of the park and turned left, heading for Berkeley, observing the speed limit. After a while she grew aware of the sticky dampness all over her thigh. She touched her bare skin, just below the hem of the leatherette skirt, felt pain, and realized only then that she'd been shot. She glanced in the rearview mirror. There was blood all over her face too, but that was Felipe's.

35

Charlie, dreaming, heard a woman's voice. "No, Daddy," she said. "Money won't be a problem. Getting there is the problem." When he awoke he remembered nothing.

He had put his head down, just for a second. Now it was night; but city night, radiating enough light for him to see that he was lying on the princess bed: a disorienting observation, especially in those moments preceding full consciousness, when the mind is still pulling itself together. And in those moments when Charlie's mind was still pulling itself together, when it was a chaos of images—Malik in the freezer, Svenson like a white knight on his motorcycle, Brucie's ponytail, Emily's stomach, a red rose—in those moments, Rebecca walked into the room.

She sat down beside him. The hair on his arms rose. That had never happened to him in his life; he had always thought it was the kind of fictive thing found only in stories featuring a haunted house.

"My partner in crime," she said. Her voice was low, as though she were about to tell a bedtime story.

In the half-light the princess bed could have been the bed in

Cullen House, and Rebecca, in jeans and a sweatshirt, could have been the Rebecca of Cullen House, or even before that, Rebecca, girl-photographer in the infirmary, where he had awakened to find her sitting beside him, just like this, with her wild black hair, alert brown eyes, flawless skin. He felt a tightness in his throat, a fluttering in his stomach: sensations he hadn't know since his teenage years, since her. Youthful sensations: swelling with the promise of limitless possibility.

Charlie sat up, reached for the bedside light, switched it on. His head began to clear; and he saw the gun in her hand. She wasn't pointing it at him, exactly. She was just holding it, loosely and resting on her leg, in a natural sort of way.

The wild hair hadn't changed much; a little shorter, that was all. The brown eyes were still alert perhaps, but now there was much more going on in them, not all of it pleasant. And the skin on her face was drawn, with deep dark semicircles under the eyes. She was an adult now: complex, problematical. Charlie understood that, but it failed to quell his teenage sensations. Some part of himself was back in the spring of 1970, prepared to resume course as though she were the same person. That part of him both recalled that she had slept with Andrew Malik and Stu Levine, and didn't care.

"You haven't changed at all," she said, shifting her weight on the bed. He felt the vitality of her body at once.

"That's not true," he said, and heard the words come out a little strangled, a little high. He cleared his throat. "I've changed."

She smiled. "You look good. That's all I meant." The smile had changed the most; it wasn't her smile at all. Same mouth, same lips, same even white teeth; but new smile. He realized it was the smile of someone who had grown unused to smiling, whose face was turning down. The thought saddened him, even made him want to do something about it. He sat up straighter: he shouldn't be doing anything about it; he should be planning his call to Mr. G. He had found her. Wasn't it all over but the mopping up? No: he didn't fool himself for more than a moment. It wasn't over, not with the feelings her presence stirred up, not with Malcolm.

"You look good too," he said. The words were out, in teenage fashion, before he could stop them.

"Don't I though," she said. She ran her eyes down to his chest, then back up. Her eyes narrowed slightly, and he remembered the Torquemada look. "But the question is: why are you here?"

"I've been looking for you."

"I'm aware of that. I'm asking why."

"Because I want to understand."

"Understand what?"

"What happened. Back then." Without hesitation he abandoned Mr. G's cover story about middle-aged obsession, although the effect she had on him made him wonder whether there might be some truth in it.

"It's not hard to understand," she said. "We were opposing a murderous, evil polity."

"I meant the specifics."

"Specifics?"

"Of the bombing."

She shrugged. "What does it matter now?"

"It will always matter, Rebecca."

That remark brought the smile, the unhappy smile.

"You find it funny?" Charlie tried to think of the number Mr. G had made him memorize, and could not.

She shook her head, still smiling. "'Rebecca,'" she explained. "I haven't heard my name in a long time, that's all."

"What do you call yourself now?"

"Other names."

"And your father? What does he call you?" Charlie heard the anger in his tone, residue from the notion that there could be anything funny about the bombing.

"I haven't seen my father in twenty-two years."

"His office is a twenty-minute walk from here."

"That's what makes it so clever. But I haven't seen him. I wouldn't put him at risk like that, his life, his work."

"But you communicate in some way."

"Do we?"

"You do, if red roses mean anything."

Their faces were close. He caught the frontal force of the

Torquemada look, now fully developed, fully mature. The kernel of truth that had made the reference amusing had grown rampantly, rendering it unfunny. Perhaps she was aware of his reaction. She blinked and the look was gone. There was a long silence. Then she said, in the low bedtime-story voice: "It was baseball, wasn't it?" For a moment he wondered whether she was implying that baseball—specifically that long-ago fastball up and in—had been the destabilizing force in his life, and maybe hers. Then she added, "That you played, I mean."

He nodded.

"Not football."

"No."

"That's what I thought. I learned a little about the game . . . later." Charlie pictured the satin jacket hanging in the bedroom down the hall: their son's satin jacket. "A nice game, if you like games," she said. "Still play?"

"No."

It was the moment for her to tell him about Malcolm. He waited, wondering how she would begin, whether she would mention Malik and Toronto. She seemed to be thinking. After a while she noticed the gun, looked down at it almost in surprise, as though she had forgotten it was there.

"There'll never be a revolution," she said. "Not in this fucking country."

"It's not so bad," Charlie said. The opinion was out before he could examine it. Was it just the smug self-defense of a man with a job and a home, a pretty wife and a baby on the way? Or was it true? He didn't know.

Her mood changed. "This fucking country?" she said, no longer speaking in the bedtime-story voice. "Not so bad? You didn't use to think that, my old partner in crime. You used to be a big believer in Marxist analysis."

"I can't argue with the analysis. People just don't seem to fit in it, that's all. Not without getting hurt."

"To right a wrong," she said, her voice rising a little more, "it is necessary to exceed the proper limits. And the wrong cannot be righted without the proper limits being exceeded." She paused and added: "Mao."

"That has a nice ring to it," Charlie said. "But what did

exceeding the proper limits accomplish, other than killing that kid?"

"If you feel so guilty, why didn't you turn yourself in?"

That was a question he hadn't been able to answer honorably for twenty-two years, not until he had crawled under the Ecostudies Center and found the khaki knapsack and what was in it. He kept the thought to himself.

"I haven't got a guilt button," she said, "so don't even bother trying to press it. It was an accident. We were at war. Accidents happen in war."

"You should have been the Pentagon spokesman."

She winced, and for a moment he thought his words had hurt her, that perhaps she had a guilt button after all. Then he noticed she was squeezing her leg.

"Are you all right?"

She smiled again; that same tight smile. "Never better," she said. Then she laughed, a harsh laugh that reminded him of Andrew Malik. "It's true," she said. "Never better." She laid her hand on his. "Let's not fight."

Her touch triggered thoughts of Emily right away, and Charlie would have withdrawn his own hand at that instant, but he felt Rebecca's hand trembling, and so did not. Then it came to him that all his problems had resulted from that kind of thinking, that image of himself as a strongman who could make everything come out right, even a bombing, and he pulled away. Her heat lingered on the back of his hand, warming his skin.

A deep, well-worn vertical furrow of anger appeared between her eyes. Charlie got off the bed, went to the window, looked out at the peaceful neighborhood. Hadn't Mao also said—and Malik quoted—something about the guerrilla being a fish that hides in a protective ocean? Perhaps that was her only reason for coming to Berkeley; perhaps she really hadn't seen her father. He heard her getting off the bed, walking toward him across the room; she stopped just behind him, almost touching. He didn't turn.

"Why are you here?" she asked.

"I told you. I want to understand what happened. The specifics."

"Nixon invaded Cambodia. We bombed a military target in

protest and in solidarity with our Vietnamese comrades. Those are the specifics."

No, Charlie thought. *The specifics are that the bomb I made wasn't meant to go off and it did not go off.* He almost said it aloud.

He felt her take another half-step toward him, closing the space between them to almost nothing. "Have you been safe?" Her voice was lower now, even lower than the bedtime-story level.

"Safe?"

"All these years."

Safe enough to blurt the answer to twenty-six across, Charlie thought, *to finally start rebuilding a life.* He said: "Yes."

"Any close calls?" Her voice was in his ear; he seemed to feel her words as well as hear them.

"No."

There was a long pause. Then she said, "That's good. You've got a new name, I suppose."

He nodded, and left it unsaid.

"Still in the movement?"

"What movement?"

"Well put. But I've made a career of it anyway."

"I don't understand. What do you do?"

"I'm a waitress in a dive. Up until today." She made a strange sound, almost a giggle; its breeze tickled his ear.

"That's not what I meant."

"You meant have I blown up anything recently? The answer is no. But I'm still a revolutionary in my mind."

She took the last half-step and pressed against him. He felt something hard: the gun, tucked in her belt.

Her lips touched his ear. "Let's go somewhere. You and me."

"Where?"

"Cuba."

"Cuba?"

"We wouldn't be the first. It's safe in Cuba. Safe and comfortable, especially if you've got a little hard currency to spread around."

"I don't."

She made the giggling sound again. "Don't worry about the money."

Cuba. Mao. They added up to very little, compared to the sum of Emily and Cosset Pond. And did all their dreaming, all their planning, all their risking—his, Rebecca's, the Tom Paine Club's, the whole movement's—did it all end in only that? Retirement in Cuba? Just a fun-house mirror image of a Republican retirement in Florida, ninety miles away?

But all at once, Charlie thought of a use for Cuba, a third option, a Cuban option. Option one was delivering Rebecca to Mr. G, but that involved a kind of betrayal he had never been sure he could perform, even before learning about Malcolm, even before feeling the effect she still had on him. Option two was finding proof of her death, but as Svenson had foreseen, his luck hadn't run that way. But suppose he told Mr. G that he had traced Rebecca to Cuba. Wouldn't that be enough? A third option, allowing him to keep everything, to lose nothing.

So he said: "I don't think you can fly from here."

"I wasn't thinking of flying. I was thinking of using your boat."

"My boat?"

"You're a lobsterman, aren't you? Don't lobstermen have boats?"

Had he told Hugo Klein what he did for a living? He couldn't remember. But if he hadn't told Klein, how did she know? Had he told anyone else, anyone who could have told her? He said: "It's not exactly the kind of boat for going to Cuba."

"Where's your sense of adventure?" she said, making him wonder whether Cuba weren't just some metaphor. She moved her hips against him, just barely.

"Why the gun?" he asked.

"I panic when I find my back door broken in and an intruder in my bed." She put her arms around his neck. "We could live a good life in Cuba."

"Doing what?"

"We wouldn't have to do anything."

Still standing behind him, she took his chin in one hand, turned it, pulled his face toward hers, kissed him hard on the mouth. Charlie kissed her back. He couldn't stop himself. He had never felt a kiss like this. It had the power to rejuvenate him; more, to reincarnate him: he was moving fast toward rebirth, rebirth as Blake Wrightman, continued.

She reached down his front, under his pants. He was moving, faster and faster. Then he felt the gun digging into his hip. He stopped moving; stopped moving and had a sudden vision. It was a vision of the future, the very near future, fifteen or twenty minutes away. They would be lying on the princess bed, hot maybe, panting maybe, sticky maybe, but not touching. He would still be Charlie, and she would be whoever she was now, this woman with a gun. Blake was gone, lost in the bombing.

Charlie stopped kissing her. He pulled her arms apart and pushed away.

They faced each other, a body length apart. The anger furrow appeared between her eyes. Charlie could think of nothing to say. Beyond her he noticed a black skirt on the floor, lying near a small black sequinned purse, and beyond that the open door to the bathroom, with a white towel, smeared with pink, hanging on the knob.

"Are you in some kind of trouble?" he said.

"You haven't gotten any smarter, have you? We've both been in some kind of trouble for twenty-two years." She rubbed her forehead, smoothing the anger furrow away. "Aren't you tired of living like this? I'm sick to fucking death of it."

I've come to terms with it, Charlie thought. But it wasn't true. Perhaps it had been almost true, until the night before his wedding, when the gorilla arrived bearing champagne. But it wasn't true now, and it could never be again. "Yes," he said, "I'm sick of it. That's why I want to understand what really happened."

"You're starting to bore me," she said. She stood there with the gun in her belt: Liberty at the Barricades. Malik's image. Malik had also told him not to be jealous of their affair. Hugo Klein was the only man in her life. She and her father were a team, Charlie saw: not exactly good cop/bad cop, but more like a politician and a soldier—Mazzini and Garibaldi, say. Or possibly Ronald Reagan and Oliver North. Was this something that Mr. G knew as well? That thought brought others, crowding into his mind, and with them came Mr. G's 800 number, ending in 1212. It loomed there, like a signpost at a crossroads.

All at once, Rebecca stiffened; listening. Charlie listened and heard it too, a sound too soft to be called knocking. She moved quickly; in an instant the gun was back in her hand, the light was off, and she was out of the room.

Charlie followed her dark shape, down the hall, down the stairs, to the entrance hall. She glanced through the half-moon window in the door. The soft sound came again, fingerpads tapping on wood. She opened the door.

A figure stepped quickly in: a man. She closed the door. Charlie watched the two dark shapes, the man's taller than Rebecca's, motionless in the hall. "Oh, God," the man said. "It's been so, so long." Then the two shapes came together. They were still for a few moments; after that they began to shake as one. Charlie heard crying, male and female. It went on for a long time.

"Rebecca," the man said.

And she answered: "Daddy."

36

If Hugo Klein had not risked seeing his daughter in twenty-two years, why was he doing it now?

"Why now?" Charlie said.

They sat—Charlie, Rebecca, Hugo Klein—at the dining room table, with the blinds down and a single light burning on the buffet. Hugo had made coffee; steam rose from mismatched cups.

"Why now?"

"Because of you," Rebecca answered. The gun was no longer in her belt; Charlie didn't know when or how she had gotten rid of it.

"Me?" he said.

"Your little quest has stirred things up," Klein said. "Perhaps that was not unintentional." The crying was over, and had left no trace on the surface of Klein's calm, dark eyes. But loose skin sagged below his cheekbones, under his chin, and his silvery wings of hair sagged too, yellow at the roots. Charlie had felt that same calm regard when he had first walked into Klein's dressing room, but now he remembered the minute stiffening in Klein's posture that had accompanied it. At the time he had thought his own aggressiveness was the cause; now he wondered whether Klein had suspected who he was, had known he was coming.

"Did Malik call you?" Charlie asked him.

"Andrew Malik?" Klein said, as though remembering a name never familiar, now almost forgotten. "Why would he do that?"

"To tell you about me."

"He most certainly did not," Klein said. But he didn't ask how Malik would be in a position to do that: didn't that mean he already knew that Charlie had seen Malik?

Charlie turned to Rebecca. "Maybe he called you."

"How? Without knowing my name or where I am?"

It was a good question. Charlie caught himself gazing at Rebecca, searching for the answer in her face, and looked away.

Too late. "My God," she said. "I think he's jealous." She laughed—not the Malik laugh, but something closer to the one he remembered. She reached across the table and laid her hand on his; now her touch was cool. "Don't be," she said. "He must have told you about our little . . . dalliance. It was meaningless, especially in context."

"What context?" said Charlie, withdrawing his hand.

"The context of back then."

"I'm tired of back then. And it had some meaning for him. He thought you were leaving to abort his . . . child, fetus, whatever the right word is."

She laughed again. "Politics was always hard for you, wasn't it?"

Charlie ignored her. "But he was wrong, on two counts. The abortion never happened, and he wasn't the father."

Klein turned to his daughter. She stopped laughing.

"I was," Charlie told him.

Klein raised his eyebrows, inviting Rebecca to deny it. She said nothing.

"I saw Malcolm yesterday," Charlie went on. "Just before he left. It would have been nice to know."

"Know what?" asked Rebecca.

"That he existed."

"What would you have done about it?"

"Something."

She glared at him, into his eyes, and saw an expression there that made her stop.

Klein said: "Is it true?"

"Is what true?" Rebecca's voice rose impatiently.

"What he says. About being the father."

"You just have to look at us to know," Charlie said.

Klein said: "I've only seen him at a distance. And then not often. It wasn't worth the—"

And Charlie saw how one long-ago act had twisted a family forever. Perhaps more than one family: he thought of his own, waiting in the house on Cosset Pond, generating. He had an urge to pick up the phone, to call Emily, to tell her everything. But first he needed some answers about that long-ago act.

Klein was watching Rebecca. She was sipping coffee; her eyes had an inward look. "It's true, then," he said.

She put down her cup; coffee slopped over the side. "What difference does it make, whether it's Malik or him?"

"It doesn't make any difference to Malik," Charlie said. "He's dead. Someone shot him and put him in his freezer, very tidily."

Klein pushed himself away from the table abruptly, violently, as though physically repelled by the idea. He walked to the blind, peered through. "Who and why?" he said. His voice slipped its baritone moorings, drifted higher.

"I don't know.," Charlie replied. But it must have been Svenson. He had seen how Svenson dealt with others in position to disrupt Mr. G's plan—Brucie Wine and the little Chinese man. So it must have been Svenson; yet something bothered him about that theory, something he couldn't define.

"But you have suspicions, don't you?" Klein said.

"No."

Rebecca took another sip of coffee. "Does it really matter? All it does is confirm the wisdom of my plan."

"What plan?" said Charlie. *Does it really matter?* When had he heard her say that, or something like it, before?

"I told you the plan," she said. "Cuba."

She had told him; but it was only when Hugo Klein took a

map from his suit jacket pocket and spread it on the table that Charlie knew for sure that she was speaking of the geophysical Cuba, and not some metaphor.

"Where are you, exactly?" Klein said, handing Charlie a pencil.

Charlie leaned across the table. It was a map of the eastern U.S. and Canada, extending south to the Caribbean. Cosset Pond wasn't marked. Charlie made an X where it should have been.

Klein laid a finger on the X. The nail was bitten to the quick. "It could be better," Klein said. "But . . ." The finger flew up into Canada, landed in Montreal, voyaged down the St. Lawrence to the ocean, paused in Halifax, continued south, pausing again about a hundred miles off Cosset Pond, and then skimmed all the way to Havana. "There is a freighter," Klein said. "You don't need to know the name. It left Montreal three days ago, will be in Halifax tomorrow to take on a cargo of used farm machine parts, donated by the Cuba-Canada Friends Committee. It's on a run to Caracas, with stops in Havana, Kingston, and Santo Domingo. The freighter is also delivering a small, fast boat consigned to one of the hotels in Varadero. When the freighter is here," he pointed to a spot off Cosset Pond, much closer than one hundred miles, "this second boat will be offloaded. And then . . ." His finger slid over the blue sea to Cosset Pond, and back, intersecting the freighter's course to the south. He looked up at Charlie. His voice had dropped into its normal register; it was the voice of the experienced campaigner, used to getting his people into battle and safely back out. "Your job is to fly with her to this place of yours and wait until the boat comes for her."

Option three: the no-loss way out, Charlie thought. He said: "Who's going to be driving it?"

"Me," Klein replied. "Who else?"

Charlie looked at the map. It might work. He resisted a temptation to run his finger over the route Klein had traced, all the way to the baby-blue Caribbean, all the way to Cuba.

"Any questions?" Klein asked.

There was only one, a question he'd already asked: why now?

295

He wasn't satisfied with their answer but he didn't ask again. "When do we start?" he said.

"Tonight."

They all glanced at the closed blinds. Light, gray and faint, leaked in around the edges.

•   •   •

They went over everything again. Rebecca walked Klein to the door. They embraced. Charlie heard them whispering. Klein opened the door an inch or two, peered out. He did it stiffly; from his posture alone, Charlie could see he hated sneaking around, hated what it did to his dignity. He had the wrong body for furtive behavior, the wrong face, the wrong haircut. He stepped out, glanced around, went quickly away.

Five minutes later, Rebecca was packed. All she had was one suitcase, small enough to fit under the bar at an airport security belt, and a brown paper bag half-full. "That's it?" Charlie said.

"What else do I need?" she asked. The question had no overtones; she was puzzled. Charlie realized that this was almost easy for her.

Before they left, he went upstairs to the bathroom. The white towel was still there, but no longer on the doorknob. It lay soaked in the tub, bearing no trace of pink. Charlie picked it up and sniffed at it. He smelled nothing but soap.

They went outside. The sky was pale yellow with the promise of heat to come. A man came out of a house across the street tugging at his tie, hurried into his car, sped away. He was too worried to see them. Rebecca tossed her suitcase and the brown bag into the backseat of the Tercel and took the wheel. Charlie sat in the passenger seat. Rebecca started the car and drove off down the leafy street. She didn't look back.

"Who owns the house?" Charlie said.

"I do."

"What's going to happen to it?"

"Who cares?"

But she did care. After a few blocks she stopped at a mailbox, took a letter from her pocket. "The deed," she said, getting out of the car. He had time to read "Wharton" on the envelope, and not much else. Rebecca got out and dropped the letter in the box. In those few moments Charlie twisted around and looked in the paper bag. Inside were the sequinned purse, the black skirt, a black Spandex halter. The skirt and halter were damp and twisted, as though they'd been washed and wrung.

Rebecca drove down out of the hills. San Francisco rose on the other side of the bay, the marine layer spreading through its canyons like tongues of a glacier. "What a pit," Rebecca said.

She turned onto the freeway and headed north, away from the bridge. "Which airport?" Charlie asked.

"No airport."

"We're driving across the country."

"Got it in one."

"Why?"

"Safer. And we've got three days. What else would we do?"

Three days: he thought of Emily. He'd already been gone for six.

Rebecca drove all morning, first north, then east, into the heat. The air conditioner labored, discouraging conversation. There were no tapes in the car. Charlie turned on the radio, found an all-news station.

"It gives me a headache," Rebecca said.

He switched it off.

They picked up sandwiches and coffee at a fast-food stop in Nevada, gassed the car, switched places, kept going. On the way out of the parking lot, Rebecca rolled down her window and tossed the brown paper bag containing the purse, the halter, the skirt, into a trash basket.

"What's that?" Charlie said.

"Garbage."

Charlie drove. The miles went by. The sky was yellow, the earth was brown, the road was black. Charlie remembered how he had come the other way twenty-two years before, by bus and by thumb, looking for Rebecca. He sensed that he was in orbit, a long orbit with a twenty-two–year period; now he was closing the circle, like a comet completing a revolution around the sun. He glanced at Rebecca, saw that she had been watching him.

She smiled. "I'm enjoying this," she said. "I've been so bored. Haven't you?"

"No."

The land wrinkled up in the distance, casting shadows at them, longer and longer. Night fell. They stopped, bought more sandwiches, more coffee, switched places again. Charlie saw she was limping.

"What's wrong?"

"Nothing. Twisted my knee."

"Do you want me to drive?"

"No. I'm fine. Why don't you get some sleep?"

Charlie lay down on the backseat. He watched her silhouette, backlit from time to time by oncoming headlights. He imagined he could see abstract things about her in the way she held her head: her strength, her will, her determination. She could drive nonstop across the country if she had to. Getting to Cuba was not a fantasy to her. It was as good as done.

•   •   •

When Charlie awoke, it was day and he was alone. He sat up. The car was parked beside a diner in flat country. Rebecca's suitcase was on the floor. He opened it. There was little inside, no wallet, no money, no credit cards, no ID; just clothes, toiletries, two pairs of shoes, and the gun: what to pack for a long vacation in Cuba. He closed the suitcase, got out of the car.

Rebecca came out of the diner with a cardboard tray. She saw him and smiled. "How's tuna?" They might have been any contented couple on vacation. Perhaps that's what the policeman thought, glancing at them as he got out of his cruiser. Rebecca walked up to Charlie, gave him a kiss on the mouth that he couldn't back away from, not with the cop watching. "Morning," she said. "I think we're in Nebraska." The cop went into the diner.

Rebecca laughed. Charlie found himself laughing too: partners in crime. Partners in crime who had been on the run for a long time, so long they might have lost their bearings, might no longer know the difference between careful and careless. He stopped laughing. His lips still tingled from her kiss.

"What is it?" she said, no longer laughing either. The expression in her eyes intensified quickly from inquisitive to inquisitorial, in that old familiar way.

"Nothing."

They sat on a bench, ate the sandwiches, drank the coffee. Rebecca wolfed her food, barely stopping to chew, then rubbed her hands together as though anticipating a productive day. She didn't look like someone who had missed a night's sleep, didn't look tired at all.

"Ready to roll?" She got up.

Charlie followed her to the car. She didn't look tired, but the limp was worse.

He drove. She sat beside him. They were the sole voyagers in a little tin probe that sped through a bicolored space, blue above, green below. Adam and Eve, he thought, after the fall. Twenty-two years after. Again, he was aware of her gaze on his profile.

"You're not what I would have thought," she said.

"No?"

"You're much . . . tougher. Much more competent. You remind me a bit of someone."

"Who?"

"Guy named Gus. No one you'd know."

"Who is he?"

"Nobody important." She yawned and stretched. A crow swooped across their path, landed in a cornfield. "My God," she said, "I'm going to be free. Really free." There was a pause. "Aren't you tempted?"

"By Cuba?"

"You make it sound like the ninth circle of hell."

"It's not the place of my dreams, that's all."

"What's the place of your dreams?"

"You'll see."

"This pond place? How romantic." There was another pause. Then: "Are you married?"

He nodded.

She laughed. It began as the barking laugh but grew wilder, almost out of control. "God, how stupid I've been," she said. "That should have been my first question. Of course you'd be married. You're... invested. Invested in all this shit." She gestured at the blue-green space outside. "I suppose you've got children too."

"Just Malcolm," he said, in case she had forgotten her own investment.

Rebecca whirled and struck at his face, much too quickly for him to do anything about it. The car swerved into the next lane. He swung it back, steadied it, and only then felt a sharp pain, from just under his right eye down to the chin. He checked the mirror, saw three red tracks on his cheek where she had raked him.

His right hand came off the wheel, rounding into a fist. But that was silly. He couldn't bring himself to hit a woman, and no amount of living in late twentieth-century America could change that. He didn't say a word. He just drove.

For a minute or two he felt her gaze, and then he did not. After a while he glanced at her, saw she had fallen asleep, sitting up straight. Later her head fell to one side, and not long after that she came sloping his way and settled with her head in his lap. Looking down into the wild darkness of her hair, he saw gray ones, more than a few, scattered here and there.

Charlie drove, across the Mississippi and into the night. She groaned, once or twice.

●　　●　　●

He pulled into a truck stop after midnight. The sky over Chicago glowed pink and orange in the distance. He slid out from behind the wheel, lowering her head to the seat. She didn't wake up.

Charlie went in, sat down, ordered coffee. A tabloid paper was open on the table. While he drank, his eyes scanned an article about an armored car heist: robbery at the Oakland docks, seven dead, $860,000 missing. He looked a little more closely when he saw that some previously unknown radical group was suspected of the crime, more closely still when he saw that one of them was named Gus. There was a picture of Gus. He was fair, with a broad face and intelligent eyes. A waitress from a place called Paco's Sports Bar and Restaurant in Hayward was being sought for questioning. Paco was quoted, expressing bewilderment.

Charlie walked outside. He half expected the car would be gone. But it was still there, and she was still asleep. He went around to the trunk and unlocked it. There were three canvas sacks inside, one bearing a large red-brown stain. He opened one of the others, reached in, and pulled out a wad of bills wrapped in a yellow paper band that read "50 × $100." There were lots of identical bundles in the canvas sack. He replaced them and closed the trunk.

She was still asleep. Charlie pushed her aside, squeezed in, started the car. She stretched out, her head moving toward his lap. He put his hand on her shoulder and kept her where she was. She groaned and went still.

Charlie pulled out of the truck stop and onto the highway, heading east, distancing them from Oakland with every rotation of the wheels. He realized after a little while that he was driving the getaway car. She'd done it to him again. "God damn it," he said aloud. She groaned.

•   •   •

She awoke just after dawn. They were in a paved world under a brown sky. "Where are we?" she said.

"Toledo."

"I'll drive."

"I'm okay."

She rubbed her eyes, stretched. He was conscious of her gaze again. Then she leaned toward him and kissed his cheek. "I'm sorry," she said.

"For what?"

"Last night. Or whenever it was. I've lost track of time."

"What about last night?"

"Clawing you. It doesn't seem to have made much of an impression. Maybe because you spend your time with lobsters." He felt her fingers lightly tracing the marks they'd made. Soft and gentle: but the salt from her skin stung him all the same. An ambulance howled by on their left.

"I don't remember telling you what I did for a living."

Silence. "It must have been Daddy."

I don't remember telling him, either, Charlie thought. He tried to remember whom he had told.

They stopped at a gas station outside Ashtabula. Rebecca opened her door, looked around at the wasted landscape, said: "I feel so alive." But she had trouble getting out of the car and stumbled to the ground after two steps. Charlie helped her up, carried her into the women's room. She seemed light, much lighter than twenty-two years before; the only other possibility was that he had grown stronger.

"I'm fine," she said. "It's just my knee." But she didn't resist.

The women's room had a sink, a toilet, a greasy mirror, grimy walls. As Charlie crossed the threshold with Rebecca in his arms, he glimpsed their reflection: a man and a woman, exhausted and worried, in dirty clothes, like a misanthrope's comment on honeymoons. Charlie sat Rebecca on the sink, then closed the door and locked it.

"Let's see that knee," he said.

"It's nothing." But she let him undo her jeans and pull them down.

It wasn't her knee. The problem was higher up, on the front of her thigh. She'd wrapped it with bandages and taped a wide clear plastic strip over them. The bandages were saturated with red, and the plastic strip bulged with it. Charlie tore away the tape. Blood splashed on the floor, ran down her leg. He unwrapped the bandages, slow and careful. He thought again of her sitting beside his bed in the infirmary, long ago; then he had been wearing the bandages. Charlie examined her leg. There was a small round tear in the flesh; blood seeped out.

"That might have to come out," Charlie said.

"What are you talking about?"

"The bullet that's in there."

There was a knock at the door. "All gassed up, you two," said the attendant, not quite concealing his amusement.

Footsteps moved softly away. Charlie washed his hands, pulled strips of coarse paper towel from the dispenser and dampened them, then pressed them on the wound to stop the bleeding.

She cried out. From outside the door came a snicker.

When Charlie lifted the wad of paper towels, blood still seeped out. "We have to find a doctor."

"No doctors."

Charlie dampened more paper towels, covered the wound, wrapped his belt around the covering. He picked up the bandages and the tape and flushed them down the toilet, washed off the plastic and threw it in the trash, wiped up the blood with paper towels, flushed them away too.

"You're good at this," she said, tilting her head as though to see him from a new perspective. "You're not what I would have thought."

He helped her pull up her jeans.

"I can walk," she said.

They went out together. Rebecca was limping badly, but she walked. Charlie paid the grinning attendant. They got in the car and drove off. Rebecca was silent for a minute or two. "The honeymooners," she said. Then she began to laugh. It went on and on. Tears leaked from the corners of her eyes, ran down her face. It was abandoned, hilarious laughter, but not contagious enough to infect Charlie.

He found a drug store and bought what he thought he needed. He got off the interstate and followed an old highway until he came to a motel. It had a broken sign, dirty windows, no customers.

"Check-in's not till four," said the man behind the desk.

"We're not staying the night," Charlie told him.

This man had been around longer than the gas station attendant. He wasn't amused, or even interested. "Twenty bucks," he said, sticking a fresh toothpick in his mouth and handing Charlie a key. He didn't ask him to sign anything.

The room was at the far end. Charlie parked in front of it. "The locals think we're sex maniacs," he said.

"Is that so bad?" She limped in.

Charlie had expected the room to smell of Lysol, but it smelled of other things instead. There were ants in the sink, mouse turds on the floor, cigarette burns on the bedspread.

"I suppose you're faithful to this wife of yours," Rebecca said.

I haven't been tested, Charlie thought. He said: "Let's see what we can do about your leg."

He spread towels on the bed, had her lie down. He cleaned the area around the wound with sterile pads and hydrogen peroxide, then dripped some hydrogen peroxide into the round tear. She hissed. He rolled one of the pads into a taut cylinder and stuck it inside, gently as he could. She hissed again. He withdrew the pad, now bloody, and for a moment could see deep into the wound, all the way down to a stubby chunk of metal. He took a long pair of tweezers from its package, dipped it in the hydrogen peroxide, and said: "This is going to hurt like hell."

"Do it."

He did. She didn't make a sound.

•　•　•

Charlie drove. Rebecca slept in the backseat. They crossed the state line into New York, got on the Thruway. Night closed around them. Charlie's body was tired, his mind wide awake. He found himself picturing the two round holes in Andrew Malik's chest. Then he began remembering their conversation. He remembered telling Malik what he did for a living. And he remembered Malik's barking laugh after he had said: "What other bomb is there?" And: *It doesn't matter anyway.* She had said that. He began pushing pieces around in his mind, and was still pushing them around when he turned onto the Mass. Pike, and not long after, as he approached the exit that led up into the hills to Morgan College.

"Rebecca?" he said. There was no answer, no need to mention the detour.

He took the exit.

Charlie drove up into the hills and down into the valley, as he had driven with his mother and Ollie; with Svenson and Mr. G. The town was dark, the campus a darker shape inside it. He checked his watch: 4:05.

Charlie parked near the central quad. He rolled down his

window. The air was warm, the night quiet. He heard a few notes of music in the distance; then a breeze rose and swept the music away. Rebecca stirred in the back.

"Blake? Are we there?"

He turned to her. She sat up, looked around. "Where are we?"

He didn't answer. A few moments passed. Then she stiffened.

"I want to show you something," he said.

"We don't have time for nostalgia."

"It won't take long."

"Or is it some kind of therapy?"

"No," he said, but maybe it was.

"Because I told you—I don't have a guilt button."

"There's nothing to feel guilty about. It was an accident, right?"

"Right."

They got out of the car, walked onto the quad. It was lit here and there with dim orange lights. Rebecca was still limping, but not as badly. They crossed the grass, stepped onto the crushed-brick path. The crunching under his feet suddenly opened Charlie's mind, releasing clear memories. He remembered that night: remembered Malik and Rebecca talking to her father on the phone; remembered that when he returned from planting the bomb, they had been out and had come back with grass stains on their knees; and most of all he remembered their tension, rising and rising, even after four-thirty passed, and their refusal to accept that the bomb was a dud.

Rebecca took a deep breath. "It's a pretty place," she said.

"Quiet," Charlie said.

Someone was coming toward them. Rebecca took Charlie's hand, squeezed it hard. The figure came closer, a male figure, talking to himself. "Isotopes, isotopes, isotopes," he was saying. As he went by, Charlie recognized him: Stuart Levine, Jr. He didn't appear to see them at all.

The chapel loomed on their right. Rebecca didn't glance at it. They stopped in front of the Ecostudies Center.

The boy's face was tilted toward the crowd. It looked absolutely unmarred, the face of a healthy eleven- or twelve-year-old who happened to be sleeping in the middle of a wild scene. But he wasn't moving at all.

"Well, well, well," Rebecca said, looking at the ecostudies sign. "Success."

"Success?"

"At least we got rid of the ROTC."

"They've got a new building near the gym. Bigger and better."

He led her around to the back, knelt in front of the hatch, drew the bolts, swung it open. "Inside," he said.

"Why?"

"You'll see."

Rebecca crawled in. Charlie went in after her. He felt in his pocket, found matches, the matches from the Catamount Bar and Grille. He lit one, crawled past her, across the earthen floor, first damp, then dry, past the gardening tools, all the way to the three cement blocks. The match went out. Her hand found his ankle, grasped it, dug in. He lit another match. She let go.

He turned, handed her the burning match. He twisted around, pushed the blocks aside. The match went out.

He lit another, felt for Rebecca's hand, took it, pulled her forward. "Dig," he said.

They lay on their stomachs, side by side, heads almost touching, the match burning in Charlie's fingers. She looked at him, the anger line a deep shadow between her eyes. "Why?" she said.

"Dig."

She dug her hands into the earth. Already dug once, it offered little resistance. Her finger hooked a strap. She pulled out Malik's khaki knapsack.

"Look inside."

She looked. "What is it?"

The match went out.

"The bomb I made," he said. They were in a tiny black universe where his voice was everything. He lit another match, then drew the insulated wires out of the knapsack. "It didn't explode—it couldn't explode—because I'd taped this wire, right here." He held it in front of her eyes.

She barely glanced at it. "So?"

He grabbed her wrist. The match fell, went out. And they were back in the tiny universe with just his voice: "So something else exploded, some other bomb. A bomb you and Malik planted—under the flowerpot probably, because you came back with grass stains on your knees."

Silence.

"I want to know about that bomb."

More silence. At last she said, "You want off the hook, is that it?"

"Where did you get it?"

"Keep your voice down. Someone might hear."

"Where?" He tried to keep his voice down, but it wouldn't obey.

"Christ. Daddy got it for us. I think from the Panthers. Is that what you want to know? You turn out to be a fine upstanding citizen. Congratulations."

It was what he had wanted to know, but he felt no relief. "Why did you do it?"

"Get another bomb? Because we didn't think you could pull it off. Malik didn't think you could. I knew you a little better—I didn't think you would. And I was sure you'd done something tricky—the way you were so calm that night."

"But that didn't stop you from telling your father that it was my fault, that I rigged the timer."

"That wasn't to protect me. It was to protect him. He couldn't have lived with himself if he'd thought someone had actually died because of something he'd done. He's an idealist."

Charlie laughed out loud. "But you're a pragmatist."

"Correct."

"Committing pragmatic little murders when necessary, like down at the Oakland docks."

Rebecca said nothing. Charlie reached for the matches, wanting to see her face, but the package was empty. He felt for the knapsack, took it, began backing away, toward the hatch. "I'll leave the keys in the car," he said.

"Meaning what?"

"Meaning I'm not going to help you. Not this time."

He felt her shift her body. He half expected her to reach for him, to hold on to him. Instead, something hard and cool touched the side of his head. She hadn't been sleeping that whole time in the backseat; she'd had time to push a few pieces around in her own mind, time to silently take the gun out of the suitcase.

"Yes," she said. "This time too."

The chapel bell struck five.

37

It was the kind of freighter Hugo Klein always imagined when he pictured freighters: old and slow, streaked with rust on deck and hull, smelling of oil and grease. This one was Polish: the *Wladyslaw Gomulka*, too decrepit to bother renaming. Simple, heavy meals were served for passengers in the officers' dining room at seven, noon, and six; simple, heavy snacks at ten and three. Klein, following the captain's instructions, stayed in his cabin. At six, ten, noon, three, and six, he would hear a metallic clatter outside his door, open it, and find food, little of which he ate. He napped during the day, slept as he hadn't slept in years at night. No phone calls, no clients, no enemies, no battles: just the throb of the engines deep below, and the constant rocking of the sea. In this rusty cocoon Klein dreamed boyhood dreams of adventure and desert isles, and imagined sailing the *Wladyslaw Gomulka* forever.

But Klein didn't lose track of time, and he was up early, dressed and alert on the morning he had to be. He gazed out the porthole. The ocean was deep blue and smooth, like blueberry jelly. It was going to work. She would be safe in Cuba, and he would be safe too. Safe from her: that was the

implication, and he didn't shrink from it. Whatever had happened
at the pier—and her story was that she had gone along reluctantly
and that the group had been on the point of abandoning the
idea when the guards saw them and started shooting—she
seemed to be the only survivor. That didn't surprise him. She
was strong and brave, and in another time and place might
have become an historic figure, like La Pasionaria. She'd been
willing to...yes: throw her life away for a cause. He remembered
her as a baby, the most beautiful thing he had ever seen—and
those eyes, shining with her brightness. His own eyes dampened.
No, he told himself. How could he think like that, so conven-
tional, so bourgeois? She hadn't thrown her life away. That was
how others lived—in office towers, factories, country clubs,
compromising their identities away. She was pure. And if not
effective, so what? Even Christ had been a failure in his
lifetime.

But she was the only survivor. That bothered him. And if
Andrew Malik had indeed been murdered, that bothered him
too.

There was a knock at the door. It was the captain, a fat little
man in skimpy shorts and a sleeveless undershirt. He beckoned
with a hairy finger.

Klein followed him down the corridor, up stairs, on deck. It
was deserted. A bright red boat hung on a hoist at the stern: an
inboard, about twenty-five feet long, with a dive platform, a
Canadian flag sticker on the windscreen, and no name.

"Pretty pretty," the captain said.

He took a chart from his pocket, unfurled it. Three X's were
marked on it, two offshore, one on land. The coastal X marked
Cosset Pond, the offshore X's their present position and the
rendezvous point. The hairy finger traced the route: the inward
and outward compass bearings were written on the chart. The
offshore X's seemed close to land, not far outside the territorial
waters. The captain was earning his money.

"Hokay?" he said.

"Okay."

He handed Klein the keys. Klein climbed into the red boat.
The captain went to the controls, pressed a button. The hoist

swung the boat out, high over blueberry water. It was going to work.

"Pliss to fair liv yacket," the captain called, and lowered him over the side.

• • •

Spanish voices woke him. Soft Spanish voices in the corner of a dark room, a man's and a woman's. They fell silent. There was a giggle, later a moan, then footsteps, going away.

Goodnow sat up. Something tugged at his arm. He looked down. His arm was a shriveled white thing emerging from the shadows. There was a needle in it, attached to a tube that ran from a plastic bag hanging on a hook. Hospital: but he had no idea what hospital, or how he had entered. He searched his mind for his most recent memory, and found it: fluffy clouds, seen from above.

A lovely image, like fields of snow and childhood Christmases, and he savored it for a while. Some time passed before he made an astonishing discovery: he was without pain. Goodnow was not a religious man, but his first reaction, perhaps stimulated by those thoughts of Christmas—not any Christmas he had known, but the Christmas of Dickens and advertising—his first reaction was that he had died. Was this the afterlife, Spanish lovemaking in the corner, a needle in the arm, no pain?

The tube was taped to his arm. He stripped off the tape, pulled out the needle. Blood bulbed out, trickled over his skin. He raised his forearm to his mouth and sucked it. Why? He didn't know, but it tasted good.

Goodnow swung his legs over the side and stood up. He did it easily, like a young, healthy man, without pain. He felt strong. It had been so long since he had felt any strength at all that he almost couldn't put a name to the feeling.

He went to a closet, found his clothes. He let the pajama bottoms he was wearing fall to the floor and dressed himself. He couldn't find his shoes and socks, but his wallet was there and so were a set of Avis car keys. He walked barefoot out into a hall, entered an elevator, pressed G, was lowered, got off, crossed a lobby, and went outside.

He looked back: "Boston City Hospital," read the sign. He moved away, around a corner, up a side street, not thinking, just going in the direction his feet wanted to move. Cars were parked in the lane. One of them had an Avis sticker on the bumper. The horse knows the way, as he had told Svenson. He stuck the keys in the door. They worked.

Goodnow got into the car and drove. He turned this way and that, and then saw the expressway. It loomed ahead of him, a skeletal structure, black against a band of red that had broken through in the east. He turned onto it and headed south, toward Cosset Pond.

Day broke overhead, a beautiful blue day. He pressed his bare foot on the gas and swung into the passing lane; *driving like a teenager on a big date*, he thought with a smile. Yes, he'd lost Svenson, and that was too bad. And Charlie Ochs had proved unpredictable. But Hugo Klein had talked to Charlie on tape, and if Svenson hadn't had the tape when he died, then it was possible that Charlie did. Even if he didn't, he would remember the conversation. That might be enough. Goodnow pressed a little harder on the gas.

He didn't slow down until he came down off the highway and into Cosset Pond. *A pretty little place*, he thought. His plan was to follow the road over the bridge that spanned the cut, where the Pond emptied into the sea, and continue around to Charlie's house. But just before the bridge, he saw a restaurant, the Bluefin Café, and all at once was hungry. He couldn't remember the last time he had felt a hunger so deep. He was desperate for food. He parked, went in, almost running, and ordered two roast beef sandwiches and a piece of pecan pie to go. The waiter glanced down at his bare feet but said nothing.

Goodnow carried the food back to the car and crossed the bridge. Instead of driving to Charlie's, he turned onto the little track that led to the lookout over the cut and parked at the end.

Goodnow gazed across the water, all the way to the horizon, where sky blue and sea blue met. Lovely. He unpacked a sandwich, took a big bite.

REVOLUTION #9

The pain got him then: pain that made all his previous pain unworthy of the name. The Gerber baby had sprung up to full size during the night and was going to split him apart. Goodnow's new strength vanished at once. His hands, frantic, rooted in his pockets for the pills. They were gone. He thought of the needle, the tube, the drip, knew what had been in it, and started to cry. He had the strength for that. Then the Gerber man inside him flexed his muscles. Goodnow doubled up, his head against the glass.

The line where sky blue met sea blue was a black line. It began to thicken, to thicken and thicken, eating the blue away.

38

W hat does wifey know?" Rebecca said. She sat in the passenger seat of the Tercel, the gun in her lap, her fingers loose around the grip.

"Her name is Emily," Charlie said. "And the answer is nothing."

"What are you going to tell little Emily?"

"She's taller than you are. And she'll probably be at her office. If your father comes soon I won't have to tell her anything."

"And if not?"

"Some story. A favor for a friend, boat rides, bullshit."

Rebecca nodded. "And after?"

"After what?"

"After I'm gone. What are you going to tell her then?"

"As little as possible," he said. The truth was: everything.

He looked at Rebecca out of the corner of his eye, scanning her face for some reaction, some sign of belief or disbelief. There was none. That left him with three facts he didn't like: the fact that she knew that he knew what Hugo Klein had

314

done; the fact that she believed her father was a great man; and the fact of the gun.

The Atlantic came into view, blue sparkles between the tourist traps. "Are we there?" Rebecca said.

"Almost."

They had crossed the country. He remembered how long it had taken to go the other way, by bus and thumb, twenty-two years before. If he was an orbiting body, his path of revolution was eccentric. Otherwise the country had shrunk; perhaps it had, perhaps that explained the past twenty-two years.

The road wound through forests of scrub oak and pine, topped the rise marking the glacial moraine, and dipped down into Cosset Pond. He had driven into Cosset Pond many times, but never with this feeling that stirred in his chest. He knew what it meant: for twenty-two years he had lived here as an imposter; now it was his rightful home. And he'd only been gone for nine days.

"Quaint," Rebecca said, taking it in.

Charlie drove past the Bluefin Café and onto the bridge. He glanced over the water, saw a trawler, sailboats, a water-skier, but no speedboats coming in from the open sea. A lone car was parked on the lookout. Charlie crossed the bridge, followed the road around the pond. Through the trees he caught his first glimpse of *Straight Arrow* tied to the dock, and the house in the background. He had to force himself not to press harder on the gas.

Charlie turned onto his street. The yellow Beetle was in the driveway. He parked in front of the house, behind an old pickup with Georgia plates. They got out of the car. Rebecca had her suitcase in one hand, the gun in the other. It wasn't pointing anywhere, just hanging at her side. "Open the trunk," she said.

Charlie opened it. They looked down at the three canvas bags, one stained red-brown. "Bring them," she said.

They walked to the house. Rebecca hardly limped at all. Charlie set the canvas bags on the stoop, took out his key and unlocked the door. *Be at the office*, he thought. *Be anywhere but here.* He opened the door, pushed the canvas bags inside with his foot, went in. Rebecca followed.

"Emily?" he called. "Em?"

No answer.

Rebecca looked around. "I expected a higher standard of housekeeping," she said.

The house was a mess: papers on the floor, plates of half-eaten food here and there, an empty quart of whiskey on the saxophone case.

"Em? Em?"

No reply.

Rebecca went on into the kitchen. Through the doorway Charlie saw her peering out the window at the pond, the cut, the ocean beyond. He bent down and picked up the bottle: some bourbon he had never heard of; the price sticker read "$6.95." It had left a ring on the saxophone case. He opened the case, half expecting to find a pool of bourbon soaking into the velvet. There was no bourbon inside, just the saxophone: but broken, smashed, flattened, as though someone had jumped on it with both feet.

He went into the kitchen, thinking she might have left a note. But there was no note, just dishes in the sink, garbage overflowing the bin, more empty bottles. Rebecca was still looking through the window. She pointed. "Is that where he'll come from?"

"Yes."

"Have you got binoculars?"

"Upstairs." Charlie went to get them. Rebecca remained at the window.

Up the stairs, along the hall, to the bedroom. The door was closed. Charlie opened it. There was something on the bed.

Something. He couldn't pull all the visual pieces together at first; they were like parts from different puzzles: rounded form, duct tape, straw wastebasket. He just stood there with wild sounds roaring in his ears. The puzzle parts assumed a shape, the shape of a woman, lying on her back, bound to the bed with duct tape that wound over her legs, under the bed and back around, over and over, from her ankles to her shoulders; with the upended wastebasket where the head should be.

Then he was standing over the bed, in a world with nothing in it but those wild sounds and that wastebasket. He raised it.

And underneath was Emily's face. There was duct tape wrapped around it too, covering her mouth and her ears, but her eyes were open and they were alive. They saw him, recognized him, filled with an expression he would never forget. He found the end of the duct tape, over her ear, got his fingernail under it, ready to peel it back. Her eyes shifted, looked over his shoulder; she made a sound in her throat. Charlie understood, and started to turn, but too late. Strong, lean arms grabbed him from behind and a cold blade pressed against his throat, just hard enough to cut.

"Don't make a move, Blakey-boy," said a voice in his ear; he smelled whiskey breath. "First I'm gonna wreck your whole life like you did to me—your wife, your little Ronnie, your everything—zip zip zip. Like you did to me. And then we'll see what we shall see. Get the picture?"

Charlie looked into Emily's eyes. He got the picture: despair, so profound that it loosed him from his fear of death. He didn't think, didn't calculate, in any case knew nothing of the science of fighting. But he knew how to move. He moved with all his strength, straight back, cracking the man behind him into the wall; then up and sideways and out of the lean, strong arms. The man with the blade could move too. It cut him, under his chin, down the right side of his neck, deep into his right shoulder, down his chest. He whirled, spraying a fan-shaped pattern of tiny blood drops.

The man faced him, razor held high and a terrible excitement on his face. "You're dying already," he said. There was something familiar about him, but Charlie didn't know what it was, couldn't think at all, stopped trying. He took one step and launched himself at the man, feet first, to keep that blade away from his face. The man went down, slashing hot stripes across Charlie's legs, but he went down, his back striking the edge of the open door. He cried out, and lost the razor.

Then Charlie was on him, banging, banging, banging with his fists—the left one mostly, since his right arm didn't seem to have much strength in it—until the wild roaring in his ears ceased.

Charlie rose. The man moaned and tried to sit up. Rebecca ran into the room, the gun in her hand. She took it all in very quickly: Emily, the man, the blood. "Who the fuck is this?" she said.

Charlie looked down at the man's face. He had seen that face before, when it was younger and unworn by alcohol, the sun, and other things he couldn't put a name to. Yes, he had seen that face, seen it with tears streaming down it.

"Ronnie Pleasance's father," Charlie said.

"Who's Ronnie Pleasance?"

"The boy, God damn it."

"Oh," said Rebecca. Ronnie Pleasance's father sat up, a little at a time. There was blood on his face, some of it his, some of it Charlie's. He saw Rebecca and recognized her.

"You're all still together," he said. He sounded surprised. "It didn't change your fucking lives at all." He spat out a tooth, saw the razor lying on the floor, reached for it.

"This is getting out of hand," Rebecca said. She raised the gun and shot Ronnie Pleasance's father in the head. Then there was a lot more blood in the room, and Ronnie Pleasance's father was still.

In that moment of stillness, Charlie made a grab for the gun with his left hand. But slow, so slow. Rebecca stepped aside easily, pointed the gun at him. Her eyes focused on a spot in the center of his forehead. He was aware of that spot, felt, it, felt nothing but. Then all at once Rebecca looked past him, out to sea.

"There he is," she said, lowering the gun and going to the window. Charlie turned. He saw a red boat beyond the bridge, slicing a white V across the water. The binoculars were on the desk in the corner. Charlie took them, adjusted to infinity, looked out.

It was Hugo Klein. The wind swept back the long silver wings of his hair, baring his face, making him appear much older and at the same time revealing how much Rebecca resembled him.

As Charlie watched, Klein approached the bridge, slowing the boat. The bow rose in the air, settled back down. Then, just as he was about to pass under the bridge, Klein glanced at the lookout on his left. Something caught his attention. Through the binoculars, Charlie saw Klein's eyes and mouth widen, like three black holes. In the next instant Klein jerked the wheel hard right and gunned the engine. The red boat swung around, banging its stern on a bridge support, and sped back out to sea, slicing a white V the other way.

"Give me those," Rebecca said.

He handed her the binoculars—who cared what happened out there?—and walked away, to Emily. He cared about her. He bent over, kissed her forehead. He tried again to untape her mouth, left-handed this time. His blood dripped down on her, but there wasn't much of it, he thought, not enough to worry about. But she was worrying; he could see that in her eyes. There was so much to explain. He reduced it to one simple hackneyed declarative statement: "I love you." Then he peeled back a corner of the tape and started to pull.

"What's he doing out there?" said Rebecca from the window.

•　•　•

It was going to work, thought Hugo Klein. The sea was calm, the boat fast, the visibility clear. He hadn't seen a Coast Guard boat, hadn't seen any boat at all until he was in sight of land and part of normal traffic, just another recreational boater out for a spin. Now he saw the bridge, almost straight ahead. The compass bearing had been perfect. He made a slight steering adjustment, eased back on the throttle and headed for the bridge.

He was almost there when he glanced at a bluff on his left, overlooking the channel. A car was parked on the edge. There was a man inside, his face pressed against the side window. The man was staring, staring at him. There was a grin on his face. All at once Klein recognized him. The face had thinned, but the features were the same features he had seen in the courtroom at the last Santa Clara Five trial, the same features he had seen in the law school yearbook. Goodnow. Goodnow had gotten to Wrightman. It was a trap.

Klein swung the boat around, pushed the throttles all the way down. His back felt cold. He hunched forward, making himself small. He forced himself not to look back. By the time he did he was almost out of sight of land. That's when he thought: *What about Rebecca?* Goodnow had her now, that was certain. But she wouldn't talk. He knew his daughter. Hugo Klein moved on.

•   •   •

"There," Rebecca said, watching through the binoculars. "He's stopping. Something went wrong. He wants me to go meet him."

Charlie, unwrapping the tape from Emily's face as gently as he could, wasn't listening. He was concentrating on his work. It was going slowly, very slowly perhaps, but he was doing a good job. It was important to get this right. Blood dripped down on the duct tape around her body; that couldn't be helped; besides, there wasn't much of it, like a bad shaving cut, or two, no more than that.

"I'm talking to you," Rebecca said. She was standing beside him. He felt the gun in his side. The touch hurt him for some reason.

"Don't," he said.

"I want that boat."

"What boat?"

"Isn't that your boat at the dock? With the stupid name?"

He nodded.

"I'm taking it." She prodded him again. Again it hurt. He glanced down and saw that his shirt was shredded and bloody. Something was hanging out of one of the holes. A muscle? It embarrassed him. He rearranged his shirt so no one could see. "You'll need the keys," he told Rebecca.

"Give them to me."

"No," Charlie said.

"No?" She jabbed him again, hard. It hurt.

"But I'll trade them," he said.

"Trade them?"

"For the gun."

She laughed, that barking laugh. "Don't try to be smart, boyfriend. It doesn't suit you."

"Then shoot me and try to find them."

Rebecca pointed the gun at Emily. "What if I shoot her, instead?"

"Then you'll never get the keys, no matter what you do."

The anger line deepened between her eyes. She glanced out the window. Hugo Klein's boat seemed far away now, a red period on a blue page. Rebecca broke open the gun, pulled out the shells, dropped them in her pocket, and handed the gun to Charlie.

"They're on the hook in the kitchen," Charlie said. "The ones that say 'boat.'"

The anger line deepened a little more. Rebecca looked down at Emily. She smiled. "Do you find him funny?"

Then she stepped over the body of Ronnie Pleasance's father and was gone.

Charlie leaned over Emily. He took up the end of the duct tape, began pulling on it again. He wound it back around her head, lifting gently, trying not to pull too hard where it stuck to her hair. Red dripped down in interesting patterns. He heard Rebecca moving on the floor below, heard the back door open and close. The last of the tape came free in his hand.

Emily's lips moved. Sound came out, but not speech. He lowered his head to hers. Their foreheads touched. It felt good. He looked right into her eyes. She licked her lips. "Don't," she said.

"Don't?"

"Don't let her go."

"It's all right, Em. It doesn't matter what she does. I'm going to tell you everything."

"No, Charlie."

Charlie. The sound of the name—yes, his name—the way she spoke it transfixed him. He laid a hand on her forehead.

Emily shook her head. "No, Charlie. Stop her."

I couldn't and I wouldn't, Charlie thought, but he rose and walked to the window. Hugo Klein was almost out of sight, smaller than a period, black instead of red. Rebecca was on the dock, tossing her suitcase and the three canvas sacks onto *Straight Arrow's* deck. Then she hopped on, freed the lines, shoved off from the dock with a powerful push of her leg, and stepped up to the console. The keys flashed in the sunlight.

"He was out there, Charlie."

Rebecca stuck the key in the ignition, turned it. The big diesel throbbed to life. She hit the throttle.

"He was out there?" And Charlie saw it all, just before it happened.

There was a boom, not unlike the boom of twenty-two years before. Then came an orange ball, like a small-scale model of the sun. After that there was nothing but bits of this and that, splashing down on the pond.

Charlie looked into the distance, over the pond, over the bridge, all the way to the horizon. Not a speck. Hugo Klein was gone.

He turned away. He picked up the razor, cut through the tape binding Emily to the bed, helped her to her feet. There was a red streak down the inside of her leg. He must have dripped on her.

Charlie put his arms around Emily. She kept hers at her sides.

"Are you all right?" he said.

"Yes."

And what if the blood on her leg wasn't his? That would mean . . .

"But I've lost the baby."

He went on holding her, tighter; and didn't let go. What else could he do?

There were sirens. He took her hand, but she withdrew it, and walked with her out of the bedroom, down the stairs. That took something out of him. Then she had his good arm over her shoulder, and he leaned on her a little. They went on, out the front door, across the lawn. Charlie began to feel light, lighter and lighter, light enough to walk forever. He had walked almost as far as the ambulance before he went down.

39

The night before Charlie left the hospital, he had a visitor. The visitor wore Harold Lloyd glasses, but one look and Charlie knew that nothing madcap was in the offing.

"My name is Bunting," said the visitor. "Mr. Goodnow was an associate of mine."

"Was?"

"He passed away. Or died, if you prefer. Of natural causes, if cancer is natural. It happened the morning of all that ruckus. The only unexpected part was the venue."

Charlie sat up, hoping to think more clearly. Instead, the motion made him light-headed. Or maybe it was just the painkillers. "Venue?" he said.

Bunting didn't answer right away. He was gazing at the stitches. "Yes," he said. "He was found sitting in a car parked on that bluff by your bridge."

Charlie nodded.

"What does that mean?"

"I capeesh."

"I don't," Bunting said. "He should have been in the hospital. Why wasn't he?"

323

Charlie didn't know the answer to that, not the real one, the one that would explain Mr. G.

Bunting pulled up a chair, sat down. "I haven't made up my mind what to do about you."

"I came through on my end of the deal."

"What deal?"

"With Goodnow."

"He's dead, as I told you. And any deal he made was unauthorized."

"That's your problem," Charlie said.

Bunting smiled. "True "

"But it doesn't matter anyway," Charlie went on. "There's nothing you can do to me."

"Oh?"

"There's a knapsack on the floor of the blue Tercel in front of my place. Take a look at it."

"It's already in our possession. What about it?"

Charlie told him.

"I'll send it to the lab."

"And then?"

"Then it depends on whether your story checks out." Bunting glanced at the stitches, furtively this time. "If it does, the question arises: what caused the explosion?"

Charlie shrugged. It hardly hurt at all.

Bunting was silent. Then he sighed. "Perhaps it's best," he said, gazing into some imaginary distance. "Mr. Charles Ochs and his wife were terrorized by two drifters, an alcoholic ex–Vietnam vet and a woman of unknown identity. The cause of the explosion is being investigated. How does that sound?"

"Fine, except for the car."

"Ah," said Bunting. "I see you're a natural at this kind of thing."

"No," said Charlie. "I'm not."

Perhaps he'd raised his voice. "No offense," Bunting said. "The car doesn't appear to raise any difficulties. It may have been stolen. It's registered to a San Francisco woman. Annie something. I don't have all the details. We're trying to trace her."

"And Hugo Klein?"

"Hugo Klein? What's he got to do with this?"

REVOLUTION #9

• • •

Charlie drove himself home in the Beetle. He got out of the car and saw his view had changed. *Straight Arrow* was gone, and so was the dock. The weather had changed too. It was hot, and the pond glowed like lava in a crater.

He went inside, stepping accidently on one of Emily's running shoes by the door. That was good. He'd been afraid she'd moved out and just hadn't told him, not wanting to impede his recovery.

He found her at her computer. The windows were open, but there was no breeze. She turned to him and smiled. Tiny beads of sweat clung to her upper lip.

"Watch this," she said.

There were columns of numbers on the screen. She touched a few keys. "Here comes a category four hurricane, right onto my beach."

He watched the screen for a while. "Nothing happened."

"That's the point. I've found a way to protect it."

"A storm like that went by and did no damage?"

She nodded.

"It's a nice thought," Charlie said.